J0699644

J. A. GOOD

MYSTERIOUS FATHOMS BELOW

VOWS OF VENGEANCE
BOOK 1

This one is for those who were different in a world that didn't understand them. When you read these pages, I hope you see a little of yourself in Rose. You are exactly who you are meant to be and the world is a better place because you exist in it.

Playlist

All of my books have a playlist on Spotify that inspired the words on the pages before you. You can scan the QR code below to access or search me in Spotify under J.A. Good.

Contents

Chapter One
Parties and Ill Tidings

Let it be known, the Mysterious Deep has claimed more human lives than any disease or man-made war underneath the sun.

-An excerpt from The Mysterious Deep: A Comprehensive Understanding

Of all the mysteries the world had to offer, why men loved to hear themselves speak was always the most confounding to me. Even more so than the Glass Sea, where wraiths haunted sunken treasures or the sirens that lurked fathoms below with insatiable hunger. This might have seemed like a dramatic exaggeration, but listening to Brody Wilkes talk of his hunting exploits for the last ten minutes was taking actual years off my life.

"Fifteen feet long. The beast was from the Mediterranean Sea, and I nearly lost half my crew in harpooning it. It dragged our ship for several miles before I silenced it with a strategically placed harpoon... right here." He pointed to his forehead dramatically.

A long sigh left my too-tight chest that he would no doubt interpret as swooning. The brave, rich boy who likely hadn't lifted a single harpoon but would be the first to take the credit. Lord save me from self-important aristocrats.

"I've heard the sea monsters in the Mediterranean are meant to be fifty to a hundred feet. Are you sure it wasn't an adolescent?" I asked in my nicest party voice.

Scarlet claimed his round white cheeks while he sipped amber liquid from his glass in an attempt to recover his pride. As he swallowed, his lips turned down in a pitying smile.

"Ah, Miss Bailey, you mustn't believe everything you read in the London Gazette. Real science and academia are found in journals, but of course, that is not your concern. I would not expect a lady such as you to have the time to set aside for such pursuits."

Bless his heart. It was the old, "such an accomplished lady would never understand written words and be able to decipher them." This was a prime example of why I could not, in fact, begin to understand how men tolerated listening to themselves. The same techniques had to get old at some point.

"Remind me again, you know my head is full of sewing and etiquette lessons, was it the North Star Line you commissioned for your excursion, Mr. Wilkes?" I asked sweetly.

He inclined his bobbing head graciously, tight curls bouncing slightly. "Indeed it was, we would never consider using a privateer line and are most loyal to your father's company. Practically barbarians, those pirates. It is no wonder they lose ships so often, considering they allow women on board."

If he wrinkled his nose in distaste anymore, it was libel to get stuck that way. That could be entertaining potentially. Every now and then, I enjoyed reminding overeager suitors that my wealth was equal to theirs. Lest they think I need them. The fact was that my father was the co-owner of the largest shipping company in all of England.

"Yes, because women are bad omens on ships. Isn't that correct?"

Blink three times and tilt your head up, lips pursed when asking a question so he knows you are interested, but not challenging him. Mama's lectures bounced around in my head.

"Rightly so, Miss Bailey," he said, delighted.

"And which journal researched this phenomenon? Perhaps The Royal Society or The Edinburgh Review?"

"Excuse me, Mr. Wilkes, I must steal my sister for a moment."

A rough tug on my arm had me sliding into my brother's side where he held his arm around me much too tightly.

"Of course," Mr. Wilkes stammered, ever the gentleman. "I hope to speak with you soon, Miss Bailey. It's been a pleasure."

I opened my mouth to speak, but Oliver ushered me away quickly enough that it was a marvel I didn't trip over my own heels.

"Rose," he chastised as he steered me toward the refreshment stand.

"I was showing polite interest without indicating any notion of superior knowledge," I said.

Oliver ran a hand over his short brown sideburns and heaved the most dramatic of sighs.

"When Mother asked me to chaperone you, I tried to plead illness, but she said unless I was in my grave, you were my responsibility tonight. So then, like any reasonable brother, I pleaded with you. One night of not making rich suitors feel inadequate. Was that truly too much to ask? Truly?" he asked.

Reaching behind him, I grabbed a freshly poured glass of champagne and gently handed it to him with a light pat on his shoulder.

"Inadequacy cannot be forced on another, Brother. It is an organic condition immune to human scheming," I explained as gently as I could.

He downed the champagne and set the empty glass on the table before searching the room above my head.

"I need something stronger than champagne," he pouted. "Look, there is Ruby. See how she is speaking with other human beings and soliciting laughter and smiles. Why can't you do that?"

I turned to see my older sister as radiant as ever, with her shiny diadem and perfectly silky hair curled over her shoulders, glittering emerald fabric falling over them and down her thin body. A small gathering had found its way to her, and she was regaling them with an apparently delightful tale.

"Yes, well, Ruby is married, so she is not forced to engage with unpleasant acquaintances," I said, resisting the urge to cross my gloved hands.

"Even before she was married, I recall feeling entirely at peace when chaperoning her," Oliver said.

"Not all of us can hope to aspire to the majesty of Ruby Hardy," I said, eyes rolling.

"Lord, grant me strength. This should not have fallen on me," he whispered dramatically.

"I suppose you have Oscar to thank for that. After all, had he not died, you would not be so put out," I said.

The gathering in the hall was especially stuffy tonight. With the season now open, London was filled to the brim with dashing suitors and swooning ladies eager to make a match. Sometimes, I wondered if it wasn't any different from the way animals preened and danced in hopes of finding a mate. At least for them, it was usually a one-time act, and then they could be free to live in peace. No, civilized people were much worse. One was forced to be stuck with their mate. Until death, at least, which in some cases was much too long.

"Not this again. When are you going to let this go?" Oliver sighed.

"You shouldn't sigh quite so much; it wrinkles your eyes, and they may get stuck like that. '*Wrinkles are most unbecoming in aristocracy. Be sure to smooth out your face and breathe deeply, extenuating your neck with effortless ease.*'"

Oliver shuddered and fiddled at his cravat, loosening it. "Your impression of Mother is uncanny. I find it rather unsettling."

"*Oliver, darling, my firstborn angelic baby,*" I mimicked.

"Oh, heaven above, save me. Please never do that again. Also, she does not call me her baby," he said, a smile curving onto his lips.

My own smile was impossible to suppress as, for the first time this evening, I could breathe and speak freely. If I had known Oliver would whisk me away if I insulted suitors, I would have begun much earlier.

"Also, the answer to your question is never. I intend to take my grudge against Oscar to my grave with gray hair, an abundance of wrinkles, and, ideally, a cat or two. One should not have to live without their twin. It is the gravest of offenses," I said.

"Lord, Rose, Oscar isn't—"

"Darlings?" I groaned at the sound of my mother's voice.

"We've been found," I whispered.

"Should we play dead?" Oliver asked.

"No, she senses weakness. Best to remain upright," I reasoned.

"I can hear the two of you perfectly well," Mama said, disapproval diminished beneath her smile.

I quickly threaded my arm through hers and smiled up at her. "Thank goodness for that. We were concerned, given your old age."

"I was not worried," Oliver said quickly.

"Traitor," I shot at him.

Mama's lips curled up, plumping up her rose-colored cheeks. The truth was, no one could confuse her for an elderly matron. Ruby had gotten every ounce of beauty from our mother. The same golden hair and high cheekbones. The same soft jawline. In fact, all four of my sisters had inherited her timeless beauty. It was only me that got my father's round face and bushy brown eyebrows. How fortunate for me.

"What did she do to be dragged away from Mr. Wilkes?" Mama asked.

"Insulted his intelligence— though I don't think he had quite caught onto it yet," Oliver said.

"I am right here," I said with a long sigh.

"Try not to sigh, my love. It wrinkles your eyes. Try to smooth out your face and breathe deeply, extenuating your neck," Mama said, gently.

I made the mistake of catching Oliver's blue eyes, and the mirth that shone there as his lips quivered was my undoing. A laugh bubbled up from my chest without my consent, bursting forth with determination. Oliver covered his mouth to hide his own laughter.

"I fail to see what is so funny about wrinkles," Mama sulked.

It was almost enough to make me feel guilty. She may harp on etiquette lessons until my head hurt, but she was the best of mothers. Good-natured and far too patient for the likes of Oliver and me. It used to be even worse when Oscar was around. He always made me laugh, even from across the room, as we exchanged a silent conversation meant only for the two of us. It was what he liked to call the only mystery on soil: twin telepathy.

It would be the first mystery ever to be discovered on land. After all, everyone knew only the seas held the mysteries that plagued and fascinated us. This was the reason people like Brody Wilkes risked their lives just for the chance of hunting or seeing a sea monster. Many went again and again. After all, no two sea monsters were alike in color or build, as if they had no genetic code and merely sprung up from the seabed.

All a curious person could hope for was a sturdy ship, a good crew, a capable captain, and that the sea witches or sirens didn't find them first. And if they were bold or stupid enough to enter the Glass Sea? Well, a prayer for their soul would be their best hope. Many had commissioned ship and crew to seek the Glass Seas' innumerable treasures, but very few ever returned with their whole crew, if they returned at all.

"Mama, have I done enough penance in chaperoning her? Can we retreat before she makes a lord's son cry?" Oliver asked, eyes squinting hopefully.

Mama pursed her lips, eyeing us both disapprovingly.

"I've done remarkably well tonight, all things considered. Best to end on a good note." I winked at her.

"Rose," she said in her quintessential Mama lecture voice. "You are six and twenty—"

"Am I?" I said with mock shock.

"I would have said seven based on maturity alone," Oliver added, helpfully.

"You two should leave poor Mama alone." Ruby's silken voice said as she appeared and threaded her arm through their mother's. "What she is trying too gently to say is you are verging on spinsterhood."

Oliver choked back a laugh and covered it with his fist. Traitor.

"A lifelong dream not yet realized," I said wistfully. "I aspire to have three or four cats, all different colors, of course."

"Rosamund," Mama chastised.

With every passing year, these conversations seemed to happen more frequently. As if there was a clock on my chest that only others could see counting down at a rapid pace. My youth and worth dwindling with every second that passed. Yet, for me, every tick of the hand felt like another step closer to freedom. One day, I would wake up, and every suitor would only see my age and not my fortune. Then I would be free.

"Not all of us are so fortunate as to fall in love with Father's foreman and have a small army of babies. It's not my fault Ruby swiped up the only decent man in London, probably England, maybe even the world," I said.

Ruby's pale cheeks grew red, but the way her lips curled up could not hide the pride she radiated. As she should. Her family was beautiful. Most aristocrats would have fainted when their eldest daughter announced she fell in love with a lowly foreman, but the Baileys were... progressive. With money and daughters to spare, they gave their blessing. Ten years and six children later, Ruby's family was always loud and always doting.

George Hardy was a gentle husband and an engaged father. Truly a rare specimen and not likely to be replicated. My brother-in-law was the exception, not the rule. A fact I was painfully aware of. I had been out in society for eight years. In that time, I had learned all I needed to know about the nature of men, and spinsterhood was a welcomed fate.

"I am very grateful for George," Ruby conceded. "But, Rose, you chase away suitors at every opportunity. You never even get a chance to know them."

"All you need to know about a person can be summed up in three minutes of meeting them," I said, eyeing the exit.

It wasn't too far. Yes, she would have to go around the myriad of dancing bodies and gossiping aristocrats, but the archway that bespoke freedom was free for the taking.

"Oh, darling, you still have so much to learn about the world," Mama said, mournfully.

The eye roll came of its own volition, and I could not be held responsible. I had seen enough of the world. If it didn't break you into a thousand pieces, it used you and left you bereft and grieving. I was more than content in my manor house with my family for company. It was a prison I chose. Marriage would not be the same.

"Lady Bailey." A servant with a mop of white hair appeared. "This came for you."

I watched as my mother gently reached out and took the missive. I watched as her skin paled and as her eyes welled with unshed tears.

A rather large rock settled in my stomach.

"We must go," she said, voice raspy and hurried.

"Mama?" Ruby asked.

For all my complaints and disparaging thoughts, my life was a happy one. I was content, fulfilled. The way my mother clutched the small parchment to her chest made my heart clench.

"Lord Allan has died," she whispered. "Your father calls us home urgently."

Lord Richard Allan. Father's business partner. The co-owner of North Star Line Enterprises. A man who had always been kind and lit up the room with every booming laugh. A man who, despite a generous drinking habit and a large gut, should have been healthy as a horse. If he was dead, that meant—

"James Allan has taken his share of the company," Oliver said, watching me carefully.

There were unspoken rules within the Bailey family, and not saying *that* name in my presence was one of them. A chill ran down my back and wrapped around my neck, squeezing, squeezing, ripping precious air from my lungs.

I could feel their eyes on me. Worrying I would make a scene, and god, I wanted to. I wanted to scream and throw my legs like I did every time I heard that name, but more so because this meant that he was now the co-owner of the business my father had built from the ground up alongside Lord Allan. Which meant that he would be returning from Paris, where he had been blissfully away for the last year. It meant I would have to face my ex-fiancé once more.

Chapter Two
Unwelcome Reunions

The wealth within the Mysterious Deep has long been inaccessible to those with any sense of life preservation. However, in 1659, Great Britain launched a revolutionary shipping company known as North Star Line. Not only did it open trade between civilizations, but it also allowed those wealthy enough to afford the pricey ticket an opportunity to see and even hunt the creatures of the Deep. However, the ethics of this are another story.

–An excerpt from The Mysterious Deep: A Comprehensive Understanding

There is a sort of quietness that descends upon a home where death has recently visited. It seeps into the walls and crawls beneath every footstep, which is always a little bit too loud. Though the quiet consumes everything, the silence begins to sound more like a scream. So it was in Bailey Manor the last two days.

Lord Richard Allan had been a good man, and he'd seen my father's potential despite his family's tarnished name. They had gone to university together, and when they finished, Lord Allan made my father an offer that would change his life forever. The world was getting smaller, and men were more curious. The seas were known to be dangerous, but what if there was a way to offer reasonably safe travel across the seas? He knew the wealthy would throw their money at a chance to claim they saw an actual sea monster, let alone hunt one.

Lord Allan had the money and the vision, but lacked the charisma and charm needed to woo investors. My father may have come from a family that had tarnished their name amongst good society with gambling debts, but charm he had by the bucketful. So together they began not only the first of its kind, but also the most successful shipping company in all of Europe. The North Star Line.

Theirs was the perfect partnership and soon my father had crawled out of debt and renewed the Bailey name. More than a partnership, they had a beautiful friendship. My father often said that North Star Line would have never made it off of paper and into the shipping yard had it not been for the trust that the two men shared.

The parlor room of Bailey House was now littered with flowers and notes of well wishes from all of London Society. They made a rather despairing backdrop for my father as he sat by the fire with his head in his hands, gently massaging his temples. Ruby and Mama hovered nearby, watching him and waiting for him to ask them for anything.

"I saw him just that morning. We did a walk-by of the dock. He was in perfect health. Even bragging about how he was less out of breath than I was at the end," he said, more to himself than anyone else.

"I know, my love," Mama said.

"At least the will was changed in time," Papa said.

At least there was that, indeed. It turned out that Lord Allan had changed the will so that the shipping company was bequeathed only to Father. It was a blessing that none of us had seen coming, but one father had quickly explained the night of the ball. A year ago, Lord Allan had fallen out with his only son and heir, James Allan. A falling out that had everything to do with me, even though Lord Allan had never blamed me.

A knock on the door had everyone jumping out of their skin. Every sound was too loud amongst the grief.

"My lord, Lord Allan is here to see you," the servant said.

Confusion laced its way through the room till understanding fell like a sword to the neck. James. It was as if a noose had wrapped around my throat, constricting. I could still feel his palm hot and stinging across my cheek.

"Rose, let's go check on the children." My sister's words rang in my ears.

Slowly, my hand was guided from my face, even as I began to feel nothing and everything at once. Back. He was back.

"Why?" I asked.

"It's possible he doesn't know about the change of will or, more likely, he has come to argue it, but there is nothing to argue, love. Lord Allan was very clear that he had met with his solicitor and had the will changed," Papa said.

"You don't have to see him," Ruby said.

That was true. I could go with her and hide with the children until the storm blew over.

"James!" A loud squeal came from down the hall.

"Oh no, Ramona," Mama groaned.

Oh no, indeed. Ramona was my youngest sister at just six years old. She was spared the reason James went away, and so her fondness remained.

"Mona, look how you've grown," his voice crooned.

Silken sweet and laced with honey. A voice that had once whispered in my ear and brought smiles to my face. A voice that had promised everything only to give nothing.

"Send him in," I said to the servant.

"Rose," Papa said.

"Do it, please," I said, steeling my nerves.

A year apart had done nothing to ease the pain that lanced through my chest as he stepped through the archway with Ramona's hand tight in his. It was like nothing had changed since he broke my heart and left me ruined in a thousand pieces. It was my fault. That's what he'd said, wasn't it? If I had given him more love, if I hadn't been so stubborn, my heart wouldn't feel like it was made of porcelain glued back together.

Looking at him, it was easy to see he was right. There was no man more handsome than James Allan. Dirty blond hair perfectly combed and just the right length. My fingers tilted with the memory of how it felt to tangle them in it. How it felt to be the reason his firm chest worked for breath. My lips burned as I took in his full, heart-shaped lips. Remembered the way they felt over my skin, hot, desperate for more.

"Forgive my intrusion," his elegant voice spoke.

You are the reason I wake up. You are everything. You make me better. You. You. You.

"Rose?" Ruby's voice cut through my intrusive memories.

It was like being shaken from a deep sleep. Like being stuck between the waking world and the dream that won't relinquish its control. Everything was muffled, blurry.

"Yes?" I asked, throaty.

"I was just saying that you look well and that I wanted to give my condolences over my father's passing. I know he was like a second father to you," James said.

Pretty words laced with barbed wire, ready to strike if the bearer was quick enough. Unfortunately, I was quick enough. I heard the insults and the insinuations within the flowery prose. *His* father. His father who had chosen me over him. At least that was how James saw it, would always see it.

"We feel his loss deeply," I managed.

His eyes whispered over my skin as his lips tugged into a thin, imperceptible smile.

"I'm sure you do," he said. "I fear my visit is not one of pleasure."

Pleasure.

My chest ached terribly. The need to take a breath, an urgent whisper at the back of my mind, drowned out by him.

"I do not mean to be rude, James," my father began.

"Lord Allan," James corrected.

A hum of unspoken curses created a mist inside the parlor. Sinking into the furniture and soaking into our skin. It permeated minds and hearts alike.

"Lord Allan," Father said, the words tight as if they had fought to escape. "Your father was my greatest friend, and despite the distance the last year between the two of you, I have received you into my home. As you likely know by now, there is to be no business between us, and as such, I would thank you to conclude your visit."

Pride bloomed over my skin, covering the wounds and festering blisters the man standing before me had placed there. I placed there. I. Me. It was my fault.

"Ah, I am relieved to hear you know of the change to my father's will. Though I had worried there would be reservations on your part, Lord Bailey," he said.

"Reservations?" My father's usually quiet voice boomed.

Whatever Ramona heard had her leaving James's side and running to our mother, who whispered in her ear with flushed cheeks. Ramona's eyes narrowed, but within moments, she withdrew from the room, though I would put good money on her having gone to find her twin, Rebecca, or eavesdropping nearby.

"Yes, I admit I considered you might try to oppose the changes, but I am relieved to hear that it will not be an issue," James said, painfully polite.

My father stood, and if eyes could burn through skin, James would have been afire, though, from his cool countenance, one would not have known it. How many times had I basked in that coolness that made him a skilled debater? He used to wipe the floor with men's arguments before they realized what was happening. *What a mind*, I used to think.

It hurt. My chest, my arms, my very soul ached and groaned against the weight of before. The before I tried to bury away like treasure in long-forgotten sand. I had dug my hole deep, but some things could not be hidden away. Some things demanded to be felt.

The burning in my chest was one of those things.

"*Lord Allan*, I assure you, your father's decision to remove you from North Star Line was a welcome one. You can be confident that your presence is an unwelcome one at Bailey House. His provision means that future meetings may be brief and happenstance in good society, sir, though the decision to hide your transgressions was one your father and I disagreed on. However, I will not fault a man for the love he bears his children no matter how undeserving they are."

My father's words were sharp and calculated. A thousand arrows were launched in my defense. I had never heard him speak as vehemently or honestly before. He was a generally charismatic and generous person. The whole reason North Star Line had risen to the top. That he spoke now, filled my eyes with heat I hadn't asked for. It made me feel too much and that was what I hated more than anything. Feeling.

James tilted his head, and I recognized it. Knew all of his small tells and mannerisms. After all, I had basked in each and every one of them. The tilt to his head, the shine in his eyes, the curve of his lips slightly turned down to mask his delight. He was a predator playing with his prey. Enjoying the trap, he laid so carefully.

Dread coiled within my stomach. Words fought for voice but were trapped within the confines of a coil that squeezed with every breath.

"Remove me?" Lord James Allan spoke with mock confusion though to anyone else it would seem genuine. "I'm afraid there has been a terrible misunderstanding."

A cat with a mouse. All dread and coils sank to the bottom of my stomach, taking my heart and my dreams with it. Like the murky depths finally claiming the sunken ship and everything it might have been. Lost beneath the waves. Forever and for always relegated to a what if.

Noise rang in my ears, but I could only hear him and what he used to be to me. What, if I was being very honest with myself, what he would always be.

"Lord Bailey, I am truly sorry to be the one to tell you this. My father did not remove me from North Star Line. Quite the opposite. He has left it all to me. I regret to say, you are no longer co-owner or in any way associated with North Star Line."

The proverbial hammer stuck once. Fatal and eviscerating everything beneath its metal.

The courtroom was as stuffy and pretentious as I imagined it would be. The walls a dark oak, and everything devoid of color as if it might inspire too much passion. I stared at the back of my father's head as he exchanged quiet words with our lawyer. A shake of the head, a long sigh.

I felt the caress of eyes on me like an ant crawling over my body on the warmest day of summer. Turning my head, I found James' gaze trained on me, a small corner of his lip pulled up. I quickly turned my gaze away and felt Ruby's hand tighten over mine, though I didn't know how that was possible. Both of our hands were entwined and white-knuckled.

"It'll be over soon, and it will all be set to right. You'll see," she said.

God, I wished she believed herself so that I might believe too. Instead, her doubt was an anchor to my own, weighing me down to where the light couldn't touch me.

It had been a week since James Allan stood in my family's parlor and declared my father excommunicated from North Star Line. A company he had built with his bare hands. A company that would not exist if it weren't for him.

In the last week, my father had met with our solicitor and Lord Allan's who determined that the will James' spoke of was legitimate, but we all knew that was a lie. Lord Allan would never have betrayed my father and our family. This was a play, orchestrated carefully by James.

A hush fell over the courtroom, and I was forced to consider that my corset was laced far too tight. Every breath felt like effort as we all stood as the jury room opened and out poured the men who would decide our fate. None of them looked out into the room, filing slowly into their spots to the side of the room, one row and then the other.

The judge came next, a white wig hanging off of him, radiating importance as if we weren't already aware that he could ruin us all in the next few minutes. What he said would decide the fortune of Bailey House and all its occupants.

Hungry reporters and masses waited outside for the verdict that would fall from his lips. All of London was eager to see how the feud between the new Lord Allan and Lord Bailey would end. Bets hedged, and whispers percolating like a tea bag steeped too long.

I reached my hand out and it was quickly retrieved by Oliver, whose strong grasp left me feeling slightly more tethered. It felt strange without my mother, but she had declared that she was just as likely to murder the 'cheating, scheming, monster that was the new Lord Allan' as pass out and cause a scene before the decision could be delivered. So she was sequestered at Bailey House with the rest of our siblings. Ruby's husband had been kind enough to stay with her and their children to keep an eye on Mama.

"Lord Bailey," the judge intoned.

A hush fell over the room much like I imagined death did when it finally claimed its victim. It was a darkness that stole words and breath alike.

My father's solicitor stood and nodded his head once.

"I am to understand that you and Lord Richard Allan had an agreement that you would pay for your portion of the company over time as deducted from your shares."

"That is correct, Your Honor," our solicitor said.

"And this was done via handshake?" the judge asked.

"Yes, Your Honor, Lord Bailey and the former Lord Allan shared a close relationship built on mutual trust and understanding, as can be witnessed by the success of the company."

"A simple answer will suffice, Counsel," the judge said, his white mustache hiding his lips.

"And I am to understand that there are no records of these transactions, which were thousands of pounds?" he asked.

"One hundred thousand pounds, Your Honor, and yes, it was done in good faith though my Lord Bailey was under the impression the former Lord Allan had kept records."

The judge had only one answer for that: a small hmph. In that one little sound, I felt my heart crash against my ribs. He didn't believe us.

"And Lord Allan, I am to understand that no record of any such transaction has been found."

James' solicitor stood and nodded once. "Yes, Your Honor, Lord Allan, in appreciating the relationship his father had with Lord Bailey, has searched Grey Manor for any sign, but we have yet to discover anything like what Lord Bailey has described."

The fake regret was almost laughable.

Silence stretched as the judge sat back in his chair and crossed his arms. All the courtroom, despite being packed full with those eager to see what justice the crown would dole out, was painfully silent. Hanging on a string for whatever words came next.

The judge heaved a great sigh and leaned forward.

"This is a rather distasteful business. Two houses, well respected, creating a scene over a legal dispute. I would rather not have it—" The judge began.

"Your Honor," James' solicitor interrupted. "Lord Allan would like it known that were such papers stating payment was received, he would honor the agreement without hesitation. As it is, he only seeks to honor the wishes of his late father, with whom he shared a close relationship."

"Do not interrupt me, Council," the judge boomed.

A dark sort of satisfaction coursed through me as I watched James' council sit hurriedly. Sniveling dog. He knew what he was doing. Knew he was working for his pretty shilling with lies and fraudulence.

"You would do well to remember that your client's ended engagement was well publicized, and his subsequent retreat out of the country is well noted."

"Your Honor, while Lord Allan regrets the dissolvement of his relationship with Miss Bailey, there is nothing to indicate it affected his relationship with the late Lord Allan."

"As much conjecture as these damned papers," the judge growled. "As far as I can see it and as far as the law is concerned. Without those papers, the court must side with Lord Allan, though it is with a heavy distaste. The will stands as it is, and North Star Line will remain in Lord Allan's name."

It felt like being held beneath the ocean's waves. Like the eruption of chatter and the way Oliver's hand ripped from mine so he could add to the endless voices was happening in slow motion. My ears and chest clogged with seawater.

"Order! Order!" the judge yelled as he banged his gavel.

The world hummed by. They had lost the company. Lost their means of existing.

"Speak council," the judge demanded.

Vaguely, I was aware of my sister crying and Oliver swearing, but none of it seemed to register. I couldn't force tears, and I couldn't feel. Like a wall was placed up or I was in someone else's body, watching through their eyes.

"My client, Lord Allan, recognizes the difficulty this decision will cause Lord Bailey. He has requested that Your Honor postpone an official decision for one year to allow Lord Bailey the time to procure any existing documents. Lord Allan recognizes that one week while all our grieving is an unagreeable situation. In addition, he will agree to Lord Bailey paying the one hundred thousand pounds by the end of the year."

Surprise should have lit my chest, but instead I was numb. A year or a day, we all knew very well no such papers existed any longer. My father had trusted Lord Allan as a brother. It was Lord Allan who insisted on having a record of the payments to protect my father. As it were, neither of them had ever considered that the person who had access to them might hold them hostage.

In addition, that sum had been paid over two decades. Even with the success North Star Line provided, it was an impossible number for one year.

It was a truth I knew in my bones. James Allan had destroyed those papers or was holding them somewhere no court would ever find them. It was all one big game to him. A game of chess, and he was the king, the rest of them pawns to be sacrificed at will.

"This might have been said earlier, Council," the judge said.

"Lord Allan did not want to influence the case in any way; however, if Your Honor is agreeable, he would be happy to provide this sacrifice to Lord Bailey."

"I'd sooner be done with this matter than not, but in lieu of Lord Bailey's influence and dedication to the North Star Line, I will not take away an opportunity for him to claim his side of the company. Very well, in one year, we will reconvene on this day. If no papers have been presented, one hundred thousand pounds not received, or an agreement *in writing* found, the North Star Line will be placed in Lord Allan's name."

A strike of the gavel had the hourglass flipping over. One year.

Through the haze of minds and crowding bodies, James turned and met my eyes. A hunger in them I hardly recognized.

One year.

Chapter Three
Checkmate

With the rise of private shipping lines, privateers rose in numbers. While some resort to hiring privateers, it is generally frowned upon by good society. After all, they are known for their ruthless procurement of shipping vessels and the goods onboard.

–An excerpt from The Mysterious Deep: A Comprehensive Understanding

The Port of London was best viewed at sunset when crews were retreating to enjoy dinners and respite from the labors of shipping. It was when the city was quietest, and the pink skies lit London Bridge just right. I realized this when I was about thirteen years old and had made a habit of sneaking out of Bailey House and coming whenever the world was too loud.

North Star Line owned the largest warehouse and it made for the perfect building to climb and see the Thames. As my legs dangled over the side of the brick building, I watched sailors make their way to The Siren and The Kraken, where they would consume ample amounts of alcohol to forget the images that the sea plagued them with. More often than not, they would stumble out and find themselves at Mermaid Chalice, where they would pay for the touch of another. It was an old dance. One I knew by heart now.

One year, one-hundred thousand pounds. Any hope of buying out our side of the company was gone. Father had paid it over the course of the last twenty-five years and even if we sold Bailey House and all our assets, we had too many mouths to feed. Not to mention the shame that would follow us through London Society. As of now, society saw us as victims and a warning. A reminder of how not to do business.

I couldn't, wouldn't fault my father for trusting Lord Allan. A man he had named his fifth child after. If anyone was to blame, it was me. I had brought this on our family. James' vendetta was for me, and everyone else was just crossfire. All because I hadn't been enough.

"Some things never change."

It was as if just thinking his name had summoned him. Even as my heart skipped a beat, I wouldn't give him the satisfaction of turning back to face him. Wouldn't let him see the warning that my heart beat like a lighthouse signaling sharp rocks ahead.

"Still coming out here like the river might hold the answer you are looking for," he said.

It was the voice he had only ever saved for me. The one without pretense or show. Just James.

I held perfectly still, eyes locked on the sinking sun as he lowered himself next to me, swinging his legs over the side.

"Just like old times," he said with a long sigh.

"You could just push me off and end your revenge scheme," I said, my chest tight.

I could feel his eyes over me, marking everywhere they touched. My face, my neck, down my body. It wasn't lust, it was ownership. That's all he had ever wanted from me. To own me.

"Rose. I think we both know I don't want to hurt you," he said, chiding.

I couldn't stand the sound of my name on his lips. A right he had forfeited a year ago. I snapped my eyes to him and watched as his lips curled up in satisfaction. It was the reaction he wanted from me, and he knew just how to solicit it.

He lifted his hand to brush a strand of ink-black hair from my face, but I was quicker. I slapped his hand away and reveled in the sting I felt reverberating from him.

"Do *not* touch me."

There was no reproach glittering in those amber eyes. No, he knew what he was doing. James Allan was many things, but above all, he was calculating. Every tilt of his head, smile, laugh, and word was carefully crafted to paint a picture of his choosing.

How many times in the last year had I wondered if any of it was real?

"You used to beg for my touch," he said, eyes drinking me in like he was savoring every moment.

"You lost that right when you touched someone else," I snapped.

I refused to look at him any longer. Refused to give him any more of the satisfaction he gathered from the emotion in my voice. I tried to carve him out. I repainted every moment with what I knew about the real him. Every angle reviewed and translated into something new. Despite all of that, a piece of my traitorous heart still beat for him.

He heaved a great sigh as if I were some petulant child in need of reason.

"It is the nature of men to seek out female company. Do you think Oliver doesn't wander over to The Mermaid? How do you think Oscar came upon that information which you hold over my head at every opportunity?"

"It was a betrayal," I snapped, refusing to allow tears to my eyes no matter how much they burned.

Instead, I watched the white sails of the ships of London Harbor billow in the evening breeze. The Thames gently rolled its water below the ships' hulls. Despite myself, I scanned the masts, searching for just one. Like all the times before, she wasn't there. The

Sea Wraith was on the other side of the continent, looting foreign treasuries and searching for god only knew what.

"I didn't come to fight, Rose," James said.

"No, you came to punish me for leaving you by destroying my family. We both know that the payments were there and that Lord Allan didn't leave the company to you."

A seagull cawed overhead before dipping down to the river in search of fresh fish. How quaint and common to wish wings would sprout from my back so I might join it. If only to get off this roof.

James leaned back, propping himself up on his arms. If only he wasn't as attractive. Lithe and sure of himself. More than that, he reminded me of a time when I didn't feel as weighed down. It didn't matter that he ended up being the weight because he was also the memory.

Movement along the harbor caught my eye, and I watched as a sailor left the tavern and stumbled down the street. Watched as he made his way to The Mermaid, just as James had done a year ago. As he likely had numerous times before that.

If anyone other than my twin had been the one to tell me, I would have laughed in their face, but it hadn't been anyone else. It'd been Oscar. Once, when we were younger, my favorite cup was shattered into a thousand pieces. It was a present from my father when he traveled to China for the first time. It had been white with a red dragon wrapping around it and curving down the handle, golden talons stark against the rest.

Oscar blamed it on Roberta, who was only one at the time. Guilt had eaten him up to the point that he came down with a sickness and threw up whenever he tried to eat. Finally, desperate for absolution, he confessed that he had been the one to break it, albeit an accident. From that moment on, we agreed never to lie to each other. Making the gravest of bargains, a pinky promise.

So when Oscar, pale and anxious, told me of what he had seen of my fiancé, I didn't doubt him.

"The truth is, Rose, you are in a predicament. We both know that no force on heaven or earth will make the money or the papers appear. The Bailey's will last a few years on their trusts, but it will run out eventually. Unless your father comes up with a way to earn income, but he was never the brains of the partnership so it seems unlikely. London society might feel sorry for you all now, but as the coffers dwindle, their need for blood will grow. You all will become social pariahs. Oliver will never make a decent match, given they all know he won't have a shilling to his name. Your sisters won't make it to their first season out. I might let Ruby's husband keep his job, but more than likely, he will find himself encouraged to seek employment elsewhere, leaving them and their children without income."

"And all because I left you." My voice shook.

I hated that my voice shook. Hated that I gave him that power, but the picture he painted was all too real. As vivid as London Bridge in the distance, raising herself to allow a ship to pass. As real as the gas lamps that lit the cobbled pavement below. As tangible as the brick holding me up. It was in screaming color, and it burned. It cleaved a hole in me that might never close.

James leaned forward, eyes narrowing. This was it. His big moment. I knew him well enough to see that everything he had done so far had been in preparation for this single moment. Those amber eyes flashed with hunger as he drank me in. Witnessing the fruits of his labors.

"Because you made a fool of me. Rosamund Bailey severing the engagement with her betrothed. It must have been something terrible to let a catch like that go. Maybe he was cruel, maybe he was dull, maybe he was impotent. They all whispered. The shame, the ridicule, I could have endured that. What I couldn't endure was my father staring at me with disappointment and writing me out of his will. What I wouldn't tolerate, Rose, was him choosing you over me."

There was nothing of the man I knew in those words. They were fueled by well-nursed hatred and malice.

"I never asked him to," I said, tight-lipped.

James chuckled, a cruel sound. "You didn't have to, did you? He wrote me last week. Said that he was done waiting for me to accept responsibility. That he didn't approve of my actions. That he was writing me out of his will."

The breeze died down to nothing at all as I stared at him. Even the men laughing below went quiet.

"So what? So now he's dead, and you bribed his solicitor to back the forged will?"

I said it like it was an impossible flight of fancy, but it turned out I hardly knew up from down.

He cocked his head like a bird of prey and smiled. When he stood, my body shook. I needn't have worried he would push me, though, because standing above me was a hunter, and I was the prize.

"Your family *will* be ruined, Rose, unless you find papers that don't exist, one hundred thousand pounds, *or* you agree to marry me," he said.

Trap sprung.

"You would force me to marry you knowing that everything in me will hate you till the day I die?"

Another cruel smile.

"You *will* fix my name. I will have everything I am owed. It's a generous offer and more than you deserve. You could single-handedly save your family from ruin; all you have to do is say yes. Unless you prefer traversing the Glass Sea for sunken treasure?"

"Sea wraiths would be preferable to you," I snapped.

Maybe it was true. I mean, sea wraiths were the things of nightmares told to naughty children to keep them in bed and obedient. Except they were also real. Souls lost in the Glass Sea where the ocean stood perfectly still, reflecting everything that it saw. While eerie quiet reigned above, below perished souls clung to sunken treasure and thirsted for the living. Only pirates of the most vicious nature attempted to loot the cursed water. Yes, there was treasure, but more than that, there was death.

He shook his head, chuckling softly. "Always so goddamn stubborn. You have a year to decide, Rose. One year."

The only satisfaction I could find in the wake of James' devastation was the way London Society treated him. It wasn't hard to pick through the niceties and the false regret that he wore like a second skin. Beneath it all, they knew what he was, and he knew it as well. Unfortunately, issues of morality were weighed less than financial success. With North Star Line practically in his sweaty hands, they all tolerated him far more than they should have.

I missed my brother. For a family with loving parents and eight children, it was terribly lonely. Oscar had been by my side since my first breath. It had never been "just Rose," but always the twins or Rose and Oscar. Without him, well, it was as if a fundamental part of me was missing. A small section of my heart ceased to beat the moment he left.

Without him, there was no one to tell about James' offer. If I told Oliver, he would likely rant about the principle of the matter as he marched to duel James. While seeing James take a bullet was something I had fantasized about, I wasn't willing to risk my brother. Not to mention, Oliver had begun to make a name for himself in Parliament. If we lost everything, that name might not count for much, but for now, it mattered.

Ruby was a nonstarter. She was struggling with what all this meant for her six children and husband. Marrying for love was all good and well until money became an issue. Now, they were scrambling to determine how they would survive the coming storm. Unlike the rest of us, George Hardy had a skill that could potentially create revenue. Being the foreman of the most successful shipping company counted for something. The rest of us were only good at being ostentatious as much as the rest of the aristocracy.

Talking to my younger siblings was just as impossible since Roberta was seventeen and knew everything already. In fact, a regular conversation was insufferable. Richard was fourteen, and though I liked his quiet, contemplative nature, I didn't think asking for advice on whether to get married to a monster or let the family fall into ruin was an ideal plan.

Ramona and Rebecca were six and in the habit of repeating everything they heard. This meant that all I had was my own council, which was highly unfortunate because I was on the side of getting married to a monster. It actually wasn't a choice in the end. Eighteen other people depended on me. I wouldn't be the reason they went hungry.

In fact, I had known the moment he offered the bargain that I would take it. Part of me pretended that someone in my family would be clever enough to come up with a solution. Except day two of talking to the solicitor proved that to be a fool's dream. James had set his trap with every loose thread firmly tied into a knot.

I tried to think of what Oscar would have said. Probably something stupid, and then he would ramble on until a halfway clever plan emerged. That was always Oscar's way. Say enough words, and something decent would eventually come out. In reality, he would have offered a completely insane proposal. Probably suggest traversing the Glass Sea. I would have told him he and James must have the same mind since he also made a jest about facing off sea wraiths for treasure.

Just like that, I sat up in my canopied bed and stared into the darkness lit only by the moon's light outside. I flung my blankets and ran to the double windows, opening them. The river lay several miles away, but the night sky reflected its darkness. I knew this feeling. It was the goosebumps that rose along my arms, the flutter of my heart, but mostly, it was the warmth that spread throughout my chest. Hope.

It was an idea.

With shaking hands, I lit the gas lantern and watched the kerosene turn into a long flame. I pulled out a piece of paper, and I wrote.

When I was through, I held up the letter and smiled.

Chapter Four
Moves and Countermoves

-An excerpt from The Mysterious Deep: A Comprehensive Understanding

A haphazard, thrown-together plan was better seen through without delay lest you have too long to see all the cracks and flaws. However, I battled that particular side effect by thinking as little about it as possible. Which was surprisingly easy given I had several choices of uncomfortable situations and thoughts to keep me company.

The jostle of the carriage over brick and rock shook the nerves right out of me. Goodness knows I had played this conversation a hundred times in my mind. I only wished I had the tact to see it through without suspicion.

"How are things in Parliament?" I asked.

Oliver, who had been staring out the window with his fist scrunching up his cheek, narrowed his eyes at me.

"Why?" he asked.

I did my best offended scoff and grabbed at the pearls around my neck. They would probably be sold soon, so I might as well enjoy them while I could. After all, we had already begun selling and pocketing away money where we could. I saw the light dim in my mother's eyes every time she said goodbye to a painting that was a family heirloom or a piece that held memories like intricate lines on a pattern.

"Can I not take an interest in my brother?" I asked.

"Please don't fight. It's far too early in the night for that," Mama said, lips pursed.

"They can't help it." Ruby shot me a warning look.

I heard her as clear as day. Don't upset Mama. She deserves a nice evening, and I am to be on my best behavior.

While I agreed with her wholeheartedly, Oliver had been tucked away hard at work making his name in Parliament and trying to find loopholes that didn't exist. If I threw away this opportunity, my plan held no merit.

"How would a pirate get a pardon from the crown?" I asked.

Gasps erupted around me, and my father grabbed at his chest, a motion he had begun to do more of late.

"Seas, Rosamund," he scolded.

Little flecks of white peppered his graying hair, and lines I had never noticed before popped up every time I looked at him. My poor, good-natured father. He deserved better than what was happening to him.

"Are you considering pirating as a career option?" Ruby asked, with a sharp glare in my direction.

Yes, I knew I was failing miserably at the proverbial task of making Mama's night pleasant. One day, she might understand.

Oliver, on the other hand, lost all sense of smile. His eyes—so like Oscar's—burned into me. Willing me to be quiet. Willing me to keep my silence.

I was used to failing people.

"Well, it's an interesting subject, so I don't see why everyone has to stare at me like I've suddenly grown horns." I pouted. "I've read several articles about how to combat the plague that is pirating, and pardons often come up. How many ships have you had looted, Father?"

"Rosamund, I am begging you," Mama said, fanning herself with extra fervor.

My father paled, and I knew what I was doing was cruel, but after tonight's Christmas gathering, Oliver would go back to Parliament, and I might lose my last chance.

"More than enough to hurt, though the last year has seen a drastic decrease, though I can't account for the why of it," he said.

Oliver's eyes bore into the side of my face.

"See, a relevant question then, perhaps the cause is more pardons," I said, wondering what it would be like to have any sense of tact.

"Anyone who chooses pirating knows they are risking the gallows. I don't see why they should be able to do whatever they want and receive a piece of paper saying, "Oh, yes, we know you stole and murdered, but all is forgiven," Ruby said with a huff.

"Not you as well," Mama lamented.

At least Ruby had the decency to drop her head and lean over and squeeze Mama's hand in apology.

"Thank god, we are here," Oliver said.

Lit flames illuminated Fairview Manor in all its glory. One of the older homes on the outskirts of London, it was breathtaking. White stone with peaked roofs that sloped and rose with a sense of ownership. Countless windows overlooking the world, like they saw everything and it was just as it should be.

"It's beautiful," I murmured, all sense of purpose forgotten.

Smooth steps lit the path to the great wooden doors carved with intricate patterns.

"It always has been," Mama said. "Though why Lord Smith opened it up once more is a mystery no one can quite answer."

"Maybe he's finally searching for a wife again," Oliver said, kicking me in the shin with raised eyebrows.

I stuck my tongue out at him. "He's a hundred years old and smells like garlic."

"He's three years older than me," Father chastised. "We went to school together."

"And did he smell like garlic then as well?" I asked.

Done with my antics, Father waved me away.

"Remember that Lord Smith has suffered more than we can imagine. The carriage accident that killed his wife and son was very hard on him," Mama said.

It was true enough. Though it happened when I was only ten years old, people still talked of what a tragedy it was to lose a wife and heir at the same moment. While it did sound terrible, sometimes a wicked thought passed my mind that perhaps they had escaped. Lord Smith had an unnerving way about him. He reminded me of a crow, seeing everything and finding it all lacking. Joy leached from him like he repelled any notion of it.

The carriage doors opened, and Oliver removed himself from the carriage with the speed of a gazelle, eager to put distance between him and me. However, it was a fool's errand as he was, once more, my invaluable chaperone.

He paused halfway up the house and held out his arm to me, refusing to make eye contact.

A bit mad then.

"Have you lost your mind? Are you trying to put Father in an early grave?" he whispered furiously.

"I just want to know if it's possible," I said.

The lines on his face softened, and when he peered down at me, his lips turned into a frown.

"Yes, a pardon is possible, but it won't help, Rose. There isn't any going back. It would destroy what's left of our family," he said.

Annoyingly, my eyes stung with emotion I had not requested.

"I wonder what he would say if he knew how easily you gave up on him," I murmured.

"Some choices can't be undone," Oliver said.

I hated the mourning in his voice. The regret. Those emotions had no place where there was any chance of hope.

"What would constitute a pardon?" I asked.

He blew out a frustrated breath.

"I am always thinking about it, Rosamund. I haven't given up on him, but the truth is I could get a pardon. I could get a hundred pardons passed by both houses. There's even talk of a universal pardon to try to turn pirates against one another, but it won't change what is already lost. A reformed pirate may avoid the gallows with a pardon, but places like this," he said, gesturing to the estate in front of us, "They will never be open to them."

"So what you are saying is you will try," I said with a sweet smile.

He stared at me while his mouth worked to hide his humor. When it came to Oliver, I would always be his weakness. It was a strength I had perfected over the years.

"God, won't you just get married already so you can be someone else's problem?" he said, the words light, a truce.

"I promise not to tell Lord Smith he's grumpy and smells of garlic if you promise to keep trying," I said, batting my eyelashes.

Shaking his head, he gave a small chuckle, and I knew I had won the battle.

"If you become the next Lady Smith, promise me you'll change this decor."

I wrinkled my nose at the open-mouthed stone gargoyles carved above the wooden doors. I wondered if maybe they were inspired by sea wraiths, given the way their eyes stared into my soul with hunger. I shivered, trying to shake the feeling of eyes on the back of my neck. The manor itself continued with the theme of ancient and creepy. Black drapes, dark oak furniture, with inlaid crimson carpets overdone with a falcon swooping from the clouds. The crest of the Smith House.

It reminded me more of a mausoleum than a home. A sneeze ripped from me at the unmistakable scent of tobacco with lavender that could only join the aroma instead of defeat it. It all settled wrong in my stomach.

"One of the richest men in England, and this is probably the most horrifying estate I have ever had the misfortune of being in," I said.

"You are going to be insufferable tonight, aren't you?" Oliver asked.

A tight-lipped smile fell onto my lips, and if my time at events like this was on a countdown, I couldn't see the harm in enjoying myself. Torturing suitors would at least bring some joy to my dark days.

The entry gave way to a large arch of dark oak that must have taken months to carve. Such beauty tarnished by poor taste. It was a shame. However, I was unprepared for the ballroom. Where I had expected more outdated carvings and dull colors, everything transformed in a single instant.

Gold tiles dressed with floral paintings and silver wisps danced across the room with their delicate song. The many oval windows were decorated with silver curtains that reminded me of the first snowfall. It all paled in comparison to the ceiling. Dark oak accented by numerous gold and silver chandeliers alighted with flames that lit up the entire room. At the center, a chandelier larger than five carriages combined watched over the hall with dripping diamonds that hung about it like a caress.

"Are you rethinking the garlic smell?" Oliver asked.

I could feel his eyes on me, but there was absolutely no scenario where I could take my eyes away from the beauty encapsulated in a single room.

"Lord Bailey, Lady Bailey, Mister Bailey, Miss Bailey, and Mrs. Hardy," announced someone I hadn't even noticed.

If I squinted just right I could see more of the carvings in the ceiling with the repeated pattern of raven and clouds. Amid the rest were hints of rain and suns that shone through the storms. It was art in every sense of the word.

"It's incredible," I whispered.

Beside me, I barely registered Oliver's hand tightening over mine.

"Definition of a snake," he muttered.

It was a strange enough thing to say that I tore my eyes from what I rightfully could have spent all night admiring. Oliver's eyes were locked across the room to where two men were speaking. My heart sank, and just like that, the air went out of the room, tobacco polluting my lungs.

"You said—" I began.

"I did, and all my sources, Ruby's sources, and Mama's agreed. He claimed he would be out of town tonight," he said.

It was the clever ones who were the most dangerous.

"He realized we were purposefully not attending events he RSVP'd to. So he planted a trap," I said.

"We can't leave. It would spark too much talk," Oliver said, regret making the words heavy.

Of course we couldn't and James Allan knew it. Not so long ago I admired that mind. Loved watching it work and come to conclusions that were three steps ahead. Now it was a weapon used against me.

Eyes were on me from all sides. People who claimed to be our friends and, on our side, had waited two months for this moment. They hoped that they would be there to witness the tension wrought by scandal. Vultures, all of them.

Well then, best not to make them wait. Despite the lack of air in my lungs, I released Oliver's arm and walked with purpose across the room. If I thought too long about it, I would see all the pitfalls and reasons I shouldn't.

Despite the music and dancing in glittering dresses that swayed, the room had gone quieter. Oliver cursed behind me but followed all the same, muttering that he should have seen this coming. James stood out in a pristine black coat and dark green cravat—my favorite. Everything he did was to remind me.

I should have told him I heard his voice in my mind all the time. That he didn't need to remind me what I did every single minute I was awake.

Beside him was a man who stood tall but was dwarfed by the fifteen-foot tree lit and decorated with sparkling gold and silver ornaments. His face was all hard edges. Where my father was covered in soft lines at his eyes and mouth, Lord Smith had none. His thin lips pressed together in a way that made me wonder if he even knew how to do such mundane things as laugh and smile.

James watched me with the side of his mouth quirked up as he whispered something to Lord Smith. His gaze cold over my body, assessing.

"Miss Bailey, you look absolutely stunning tonight. That dark green has always been your color," James said, dipping his head.

"I like to wear it for the Christmas ball, as you might recall," I said.

James raised his eyebrows and raised his glass to me. "I had not, but what a happy coincidence."

Maybe where love had once lived was rich soil eager to grow with whatever came after. Surely, the amount of hatred I felt at that moment was unlike any I had ever known before.

"Lord Smith, your home is lovely. Thank you for the invitation," Oliver said, slightly breathless as he gripped the back of my arm.

I was fairly certain that meant, "What the hell are you doing?" in Oliver etiquette.

Lord Smith raised a single brow like such compliments and gratitude were beneath him.

"Well, I did feel it important to get to know the woman James speaks so highly of, though I think that is a testament to his character. Not many men scorned would act with such grace," he said.

The way he scanned me made me want to pull up the bust of my dress, which had a moderate dip, but suddenly felt too low. My hips were too form-fitting. In fact, I was sure this was among the top five worst ideas I had ever concocted.

"I did not know you were so familiar with each other," Oliver said, his voice too tight.

James smiled that devastating smile, heart-shaped lips disarming anything and anyone within a mile's radius. My knees used to go weak at the sight. Now, my stomach rolled with nausea.

"Smith here has been invaluable to me as I prepare to take over my father's legacy. In fact, without his support, I would be quite lost," James said.

The ancient man, who did indeed smell like garlic, clapped my former fiancé on the back.

"An effort I am more than thrilled to help with. I believe the future is bright with you at its helm. We have been discussing ways to mitigate the pirate scourge effects on honest trade and exploration," Lord Smith said.

Despite his profound elation, there was no hint of it upon his face giving merit to my previous theory.

Oliver's grip tightened on me, and I knew he was thinking exactly what I was.

Did he know?

The game had changed more times than I could count, but this sinking in my stomach was more than money and prestige; it was life and death.

"Yes, I have been in touch with a new and promising Captain in the British Navy, Captain Edmonds. He has had a few run-ins with pirates and agrees that the problem grows by the minute. How my father ever tolerated the issue and allowed the losses he did is quite unimaginable."

"Here, here." Lord Smith raised his glass. "They should all swing."

My blood ran cold, like ice freezing over my calloused heart. One beat more, and it would shatter into my lungs, and my breathing would cease altogether.

He knew.

James met my eyes and smiled, checkmate.

"You always have thoughts on such things, Miss Bailey. What do you think about it all?" he asked.

He was winning. A plot thought out beyond my wildest imagination.

"Excuse me," I murmured.

My heels clipped across the floor, and just like that, the shards of who I was scattered around the ballroom. By the time I made it to cool air and lush bushes, I emptied what was left of my stomach into the foliage.

Chapter Five
Of Sea Monsters and Maidens

Rumors have abounded for centuries that some cultures sacrificed young virgin girls to sea monsters in exchange for safe passage through the Mysterious Deep. No evidence of this barbaric practice exists, and it is based on unscientific postulations.

–An excerpt from The Mysterious Deep: A Comprehensive Understanding

A nother four months went by like sand to the hourglass. Each grain a promise of matrimony. In fact, with every social gathering, more people seemed to lose faith in my father that he would somehow talk his way out of it. It was certainly not for lack of trying. He had solicited other shipping companies, but the general consensus was that although he had built a successful company, he was a ruined man. After all, who paid a massive sum of one hundred thousand pounds without requiring assurance of payment?

So it was that the aristocracy, who only valued money, laughed more at James' jokes and invited him to more and more gatherings. Now, it was impossible to go to any social event without him there, without him watching me. I was under no pretense that my family would escape this fate if left to their own devices.

Luckily, spring had come, and with it, the day I had waited for. As the sky turned its dusky pink that ebbed and waned until the night sky consumed it, I grabbed my brown satchel filled with essentials and snuck out through the garden.

I wished I could have said goodbye to them all, but the notes I left for each of them would have to do. Not one of them would have let me go if they knew where I was headed. All I could hope was that I might see them again and explain. A pretty thought wrapped in a touch of delusion.

Where I was going, most people didn't come back from.

Despite the warm night, I lifted the hood of my cloak and slunk out through the shadows. London was made for nights such as these. No one batted an eye at a cloaked figure lurking beneath gas lamps. It was a usual enough occurrence that they simply kept their distance. A seagull ahead made my heart jump, but it also meant I was close.

This wasn't good London Society; no, this was the bowels of it where gambling and prostitution guided commerce. Shady dealings and imposing figures held the power here. As horse-drawn carriages lessened, the smell of liquor increased.

The docks here were not the clean and respectable ones that North Star Line watched over. Pulling my cloak further over my head, I approached a foul-smelling man who held a bottle of whiskey in hand. Beggars couldn't be choosers.

"I need passage to Corpse Cove," I said.

He raised his eyebrows and looked me up and down as if I were a spectacle akin to the circus. My skin crawled under his gaze, but I held my ground. The only way this worked was if I held myself like I deserved to be here. Men like this didn't respect status or birth; no, they spoke another language.

I pulled out four shillings from my pocket and held it out to him. More than generous.

"Oy, four shillings ain't goin' pay my bail for kidnappin', aye little miss? Whatever ya runnin' from ain't worth goin' to Corpse Cove. They'll ransom ya and have their way with ya before they do it. Ain't nothin' worse out here than on that island," he said.

The smell of rotting teeth blew with each word he spoke. I was well aware there was no moral code among these men.

"Maybe three more shillings can assuage your concern?" I said, pulling them out.

He clicked his tongue before swiping the coins and biting hard on one. Blackened teeth gnawed at it, and it was an absolute wonder they didn't fall out with the effort. When he was satisfied, he stuffed them into his torn shirt pocket and shrugged his shoulders.

"Your funeral, Miss," he said, gesturing for me to enter the dingy.

As soon as I stepped into the swaying coffin, all the reasons this shouldn't be happening came rushing forward. Marriage probably wasn't so terrible. Even if it was to James. He'd probably gloat for a few years and then forget I existed. This was dramatic. What I was doing was dramatic. This was stupid.

I opened my mouth to say so when the beastly man swung his oars, making my entire body rock down into the seat. He flashed a horrifying smile.

"No refunds. Mo' like you are about to find out why they be callin' it Corpse Cove. Dun say I didn't warn ya."

I turned, watching the harbor drift away, the flickering light of lanterns dimming until they were specks like stars. Alone with a heavily breathing and chronically drunk sailor, a swinging lantern, and the sea, I had ample time to think about how much of an idiot I was. It isn't even like it was an impulsive plan. I carefully thought every aspect over for the last six months.

It had all seemed like a decent plan until I was actually doing it.

The water was like midnight around us. It would be so easy for him to kill me and toss me into its depths. Even so, I would not be going down without a fight. I may not have been intelligent enough to bring a weapon, but my nails would do just as well. If he thought to rob me, he would be going overboard with the sharks as well.

"I ain't gonna murder ya," he said, taking another sip from his bottle. "As far as I can see, ya runnin' from someone, and they'll be lookin' for ya."

I cocked my head. "But if I wasn't you would murder me?"

Excellent idea. Start a discussion about murder with the drunk chauffeur.

He shook his head as he went back to rowing.

"Nah, ya wouldn't have anything worth stealing if ya weren't," he said.

"Charming," I said, biting my tongue to keep from saying more.

Dammit, Oscar. At the end of the day, this was his fault. A twin shouldn't be without their twin. It was our solemn promise, and he broke it. Everything would have been different.

The gentle sway of the boat as it pushed through the water was enough that my frustration was quickly on the verge of being forgotten. A swirling in my stomach reminded me why I had only gone on a ship once. I had been ten and had almost died of dehydration due to the amount of vomiting the sea induced in me. My father had said some people weren't made for the sea. It turned out that over a decade later, that hadn't changed.

Excellent. My plan was proving to be ingenious. Why anyone would want to marry me when I was so inept was beyond me.

Distraction. I needed distraction.

"What is Corpse Cove like?" I asked.

His laughs were accompanied by snorts of an alarming nature. At least I was funny.

"Oh, miss, ya about to find out," he said.

Just like that, the boat lurched, and I fell back into the tiny space between the seat and the end of the boat. Legs sticking straight up in the air, I frantically clawed at the sides to try to get myself right side up. I might have been worried about the fiend in the boat with me if it weren't for the sounds of his laugh snorts that ricocheted all around us.

I hauled myself up and found him standing outside of the boat, surrounded by pitch black.

An abandoned island.

I stood and lunged for one of the oars he had left, pointing it at him. My heart a symphony of alarm.

"I thought you said you weren't going to murder me?"

He bent his head shaking it, belly still shaking with laughter. The swaying lantern at the tip of the boat illuminating him.

"Them pirates are gonna have a time with you, Hellcat," he said. "Ya picked a hell of a night to show up. The Sea Wraith docked today, and Captain Flynn is in a shitty mood. Ya best be prayin' to whichever god ya believe in."

My heart fumbled as I stepped onto the midnight sand. Sebastian Flynn, Captain of The Sea Wraith. The deadliest crew known to piracy with a pension for traversing the Glass Sea more than any other ship. I clearly had a death wish.

However, this point was moot if I didn't actually make it to Corpse Cove.

"Why have we stopped here?" I asked, still holding the oar out between us.

God, it was pitch black. With the moon seemingly hidden behind the clouds, there was no light. More likely, the clouds weren't the real issue at all. This was probably a mysterious island. One of the many oddities and unexplained phenomena of the seas. There were tales of carnivorous islands, islands that appeared only at certain intervals—a favorite of pirates trying to hide treasure, and islands that did unimaginable things. It stood to reason this was one of them.

The not knowing was the worst. It was an affliction I had since I was a child. Too curious, they said. Everyone begged me to stop asking questions, but if I didn't know something it was like an itch that began behind my ears and spread the longer the not knowing lasted. Once it reached my feet, I was insufferable.

The drunken man reached next to me and lifted the lantern off its hook, holding out his arm and grinning.

"Ya lookin' at it, Hellcat."

Absolutely not.

Narrowing my eyes, I stared at the darkness.

"I suppose you might be inclined to explain how that is possible?" I said.

He winked, which appeared menacing in the low light, though I was at least partially convinced he didn't mean to kill me. It was a gut feeling, and I took some comfort in that.

"Oh no, Hellcat, I'll be showing you."

He turned, practically radiating delight, and I stumbled forward, trying to keep beneath the lantern's erratic light. When he stopped, I collided with his back and nearly gagged on the smell of unwashed sailor.

"Give me yer hand," he said, holding out his own.

"I'm inclined not to," I mumbled, righting my cloak.

He shrugged his shoulders. "Well enough. I said I'd take you to Corpse Cove, and I have."

Turning to leave, I reached out my hand, holding him in place.

"Fine."

He chuckled, and before I could object, I watched in horror as he lifted a knife and slashed his palm and then mine before bringing them together. It stung in the worst sort of way, and I clenched my jaw to keep from screaming. As he held our palms together, I counted the diseases I likely just inherited.

Realizing that was a poor use of my limited time, I lifted the oar still clutched in my other hand and made to swing it down when he took my hand and dragged it over a rocky surface that I hadn't even known was there.

I could practically feel the blood on my hand being pulled into the rock. An itching filled my palm, and as it grew, I pulled my hand away, desperate to scratch it. Yet there in the light was my hand perfectly untouched.

Before I could wonder at it, a rumbling beneath our feet shook me to my core. Laughter filled my ears, but I was unprepared to die. I lifted the ore and slammed it into his stomach. Somehow, even amidst a grunt of pain, he was still able to laugh. What I needed was distance. A roar overhead had my blood chilling. A sea serpent.

I had heard tales of superstitious seamen who sacrificed young virgins to sea serpents in hopes of staying their wrath.

"Joke's on you. I'm not a virgin, so guess what? You're getting eaten too, prick."

His laughter dying in the serpent's belly would be a decent consolation prize for dying. Except, if I died, my family was doomed. That wasn't an outcome I was willing to face.

Digging my feet into the sand, I felt sand fill my boots, but it didn't matter. I faced the sea and held my oar out to the ocean. With any luck I would see it before it came at me. With better luck, it would eat the crazy laughing man first.

The earth groaned, and the sound of laughing grew, except it wasn't the boatman's laughter. Hundreds of voices gathered around me, and light poured over the area, illuminating a peaceful, gently rolling sea. Stars burned to life above, followed by a moon full and bright, as if it had all been hidden by a cloud.

"Welcome to Corpse Cove, Hellcat," he said.

I turned and an entire island filled before my eyes. Colorful buildings of the most obscene color choices, brightest blue, pink, purple. Any color the aristocracy would have found indecent, littered the landscape. Lamp lights scattered the island, perfectly illuminating everything the moon didn't quite catch.

There was music and raucous laughter. The sea hitting the shore was the backdrop to a symphony of sounds. It was... It was overwhelming.

"You should see yer face. How you be thinking the good police and law don't find this place and round up all the pirates? Did ya think they was just sunnin' themselves on an island where anybody can come lookin'?"

Well, I was forced to concede that it was a decent point. Piracy, after all, was illegal. Any pirate caught would meet the gallows, and the crowds would cheer. Why I hadn't ever considered that Corpse Cove was a mysterious island was beyond me. I had believed some piracy to be a necessary evil. After all, respectable shipping companies like North Star Line rarely ventured to the Glass Sea.

Someone had to do it, and it was not going to be those who already had money.

Recovering, I held out my chin, reaching into my pocket to pull out two more shillings.

"I need to find The Sea Wraith," I said, holding out the coins.

He should have been surprised, but he was not.

"Aye, so you do," he said, waving his hand for me to join him.

Clutching the oar with both hands, I followed behind him and tried to take in everything all at once. Men and women drank and spoke over tables inside and outside each establishment. No one at all seemed concerned that they were wanted for piracy.

Palm trees crowded the island, but as we walked the path I stared as a whole new world opened up. This was not London, this was something else entirely. Two women kissed passionately beneath a gaslamp, one of their hands pulling up the other's skirt. They didn't notice anyone else existed, and no one minded what they were doing at all.

"Oy, Hellcat, it's impolite to stare," he called up ahead.

I closed my mouth and clutched my oar tighter. This truly was a land of debauchery and sin, as the Vicar liked to say on Sunday mornings. However, neither of those women looked as if they cared an iota for the prayers said in pursuit of their eternal soul.

A harbor much like London's came into view, and I fought to keep my feet moving. There, larger than any of the other ships, was the most feared vessel in the known world.

The Sea Wraith.

This had been a terrible idea.

"Don't get cold feet now, on up ya go," he said, gesturing to the ladder that soared high onto the ship's deck.

This wasn't for me. It was for my family. They didn't deserve the fate that awaited them.

I repeated those words in my head as I dropped my oar and climbed. It was regrettable to leave it, but I wasn't under the delusion I had the strength to carry it and myself up. When I made it to the deck, I swung my leg over, but my cloak snagged beneath me, and before I could think any better of it, I was cascading over the side and landing on the wooden deck with an offending thump.

Laughter, as to be expected, greeted me as the man swung himself over the edge like he had done it a thousand times. I glared at him when he offered his hand.

Nope. I pointedly ignored him and plied myself off the deck. That only amused him more.

Shoulders shaking, he walked to below the stairs where yellow light poured from a small window on a door. I glanced around, desperately seeking what chaos I landed myself in, and found the ship... empty. Not a soul in sight except for us.

"What is this?" I asked, staring at the wooden beams stretching to the sky with folded sails.

"A ship, Hellcat, musta hit your head harder than your arse." He practically giggled.

At least he thought he was funny. He didn't even seem mad that I had whacked him with the oar. Maybe there was something wrong with him mentally. Perhaps a head injury.

He placed a firm knock on the door before opening it and holding it open for me.

I sucked in a deep breath. It was now or never. I had come this far.

I stepped into the cabin, and there at a desk with papers neatly stacked was a man who was far too handsome than what should have been fair. When his lips turned up and he tapped his fist once, twice on the wooden desk, it was clear he knew it too. Dark brown hair pulled back into a small bun while the rest of the silky strands lay at the base of his neck. Blue eyes that should have been a crime aside from the piracy. The way his shirt hung from his body, exposing a chest with fine hair and alarming muscle, was disgusting.

"She did just as you said she would, Cap'in. Though you might have warned me she'd be taking an oar to me stomach," the man said.

I swung my head toward him and found him rubbing at his stomach as if I had offended him.

"I bet she did." That deep, midnight voice I still heard in my dreams said, "Hello, Rosamund."

Chapter Six
The Captain and The Lady

The Glass Sea was formally documented in 1657 when Roald Amundsen discovered the fabled Northwest Passage. However, rumors of a sea that was still with dead lurking below existed ten years prior to that when the Queen's Bounty, an English ship, was lost at sea. A sailor, half-mad and delirious with dehydration, washed up on the shores of Brazil and claimed to be the sole survivor of the Bounty. He told a tale of a still sea and undetectable wind, but more concerning was the creatures that smelled of death and salt that swarmed their ship not ten minutes into their time into the strange new world. The creatures claimed all lives on board by consuming them. Shortly after his appearance, the sailor either died or went missing.

–An excerpt from The Mysterious Deep: A Comprehensive Understanding

How unfortunate.

Maybe I could reach for one of the candles, light the stack of papers and books on the desk, and set the whole ship on fire. Honestly, that was more preferable to standing here realizing two minutes into my scheme, and I had already been played. It was demoralizing.

"I have absolutely no regrets about hitting you in the stomach with *me oar*," I said to the actor.

No wonder he had found the whole affair entertaining.

The pirate grinned his rotting tooth smile, reached into his pocket, pulled out the shillings I gave him, and set them on the desk.

"Got eleven shillins out of her. Just waving around money like she was askin' to be robbed," he said.

"Thank you, Billy," the captain said, a small smirk creating a dimple on the left side.

Annoying.

"I'll be on to my next task then," Billy the traitor said.

"Madame Serenades," Captain Flynn said.

"On to trick your next innocent female, then?" I said with a sneer.

Billy gave a booming laugh. "You ain't innocent, Hellcat. Dun forget you screamed yer lack of virginity to the sea."

Captain Flynn, who had been taking a sip of his drink, coughed, roughly patting his chest till he recovered.

Heat bloomed in my cheeks. Mortification filled me from the tips of my toes all the way to the top of my ears. Damn pirates. This was a complete disaster.

Still choking slightly, "Thank you, Billy. If you please."

"Aye, Cap'in," Billy said, eyes narrowing on me. "Be on your guard with this one, though. Practically savage."

"I am well aware," he said it like a purr.

With shoulders shaking, he left me alone with the notorious and deadly Captain Flynn. However, I was more annoyed than scared.

"That man laughs entirely too much," I said, folding my arms across my chest.

"He's a good man," Captain Flynn said.

Slowly, he rose from his seat and walked around the desk before coming to lean against the front of it, twirling a familiar letter in between his fingers.

"He's a pirate so..." I shrugged.

This was not going according to plan in the least, and my body was also not cooperating. Warmth bloomed low in my stomach as the Captain's gaze ran over me, drinking me in like he could see every curve beneath my cloak.

"I've known many pirates to be good men, and I believe you have too," he said.

I snorted. "Absolutely not. They are all cheats and liars."

"I know one particular pirate who would be saddened to hear that," he said.

"That letter in your hands is all the proof I need of the morality of pirates," I snapped.

Captain Flynn unfolded the letter and scanned the page before lifting his ocean eyes to mine.

"You look well for someone who is dying," he said.

"I never said I was dying."

He cleared his throat and read, "*I fear I do not have much time left. My greatest wish is that you make port in London so we may see each other once more.*"

I scratched at my arm and shuffled my feet trying not to let the guilt consume me. I may have chosen colorful words in my deception, but at their core they were still true.

"We were on the other side of the world, Rosamund, which you very well knew," he said.

"Miss Bailey," I corrected.

He snorted. "Standing on formality, are we? Seems a bit late for that, don't you think?"

I was not prepared for the direction this conversation was going, though I probably should have been. I may not have inherited an iota of my father's charisma or charm, but

I had spent enough time with Lord Robert Allan to know how to conduct a business deal.

Carefully, I undid the clasp of my cloak and laid it on a nearby chair with plush red fabric. For a pirate ship, The Sea Wraith certainly was decorated like a London townhome. The foyer held a matching crimson carpet, and the long oak desk was of the finest quality. Endless windows gave views of the harbor. It was both cozy and stately.

I took a seat directly in front of the desk and him. His eyes were locked on me like I was a predator lurking in his home. Maybe I was.

Crossing my legs, I folded my hands on my lap.

"I have a proposal for you," I said.

He arched an eyebrow. "I confess that I have wondered at it for the last six months."

I should have known he would see through my words. He was annoyingly astute. However, when I had sent that letter I had hoped The Sea Wraith would return to London earlier than intended. There had always been the chance that it wouldn't have worked, but desperate times and whatnot.

I opened my mouth to speak, and all at once realized how ridiculous of a plan this had been. There was no conceivable reason this would work. I was a ridiculous human being. The best I could do for myself was to find traitor Billy and traipse back to London to pick out doilies for my impending wedding.

"You have my attention, *Miss Bailey*," Captain Flynn said, sending shivers down my back.

It was almost worse than saying my Christian name. If I made it back to London I might need to stop by the church and take confession. The last time I had felt so compelled was a year ago. An irony I was unprepared to analyze.

"What I am offering, Captain Flynn, is a letter of marque for The Sea Wraith and pardons for you and any who sail beneath your hideous flag," I said.

For a moment, he went utterly still as if I had cast a spell over him. Not even his chest rose and fell. I was reminded that he was the most dangerous pirate of them all.

"Miss Bailey," he said, eyes locked on mine. "My flag is not hideous."

I should have known. I pressed my lips together to keep the mild amusement forcing its way through my chest at bay.

"It is a skeleton next to three clouds dripping blood. Not to mention, the skeleton has its hands neatly folded as if waiting patiently for dinner to be served," I challenged.

"Men have pissed themselves at the sight of that flag," he said, bracing his hands on the desk behind him.

"I think you have missed the point of the proposal," I said.

"What makes you think I want either of those things? Unless you haven't heard, I am rather good at pirating," he said.

In all honesty, I hadn't considered that. I hadn't considered that one would wish to be a criminal.

"I imagine it would be nice not to worry about being hanged," I said.

"Miss Bailey, when I lay down to sleep at night, the thought of hanging never once crosses my mind. Would you like to know what does?"

"Absolutely not," I answered too quickly.

I regretted the loss of my oar deeply.

He huffed out a laugh that was roguish and sent warmth blooming low in my belly. Damn traitorous body.

"Pray tell, what service am I to provide that would earn me this prestigious gift?" he asked.

I took a small breath, reminding myself I had made it this far. Reminding myself what was at stake.

"An attempt at the Spanish galleon treasure, La Maravilla," I said slowly.

He pushed himself off the desk and gave a rough laugh before running a hand over his short beard.

"You are really something, Rose."

"Miss Bailey," I corrected.

He took one step forward and placed his hands on either side of my chair, pinning me in. Warmth seeped from his body, and I was forced to remember things I tried very hard not to. Things that were very hard to forget. Lord save me.

Truth be told, God probably forsook me the moment I fell onto the deck of The Sea Wraith. At least, that's what Father John would have said. Maybe two confessions might do the trick.

"Oh no, *Rose*. You came onto my ship asking me to go after the most notorious treasure trove on the Glass Sea. I can call you whatever I damn well please." His breath crested over my face and chest, smelling of lemon and stolen midnights.

Maybe three confessions, after all.

Was that sweat running down my back? It *was* ungodly hot in here. Would it be wrong to ask to open a window?

"I would think you would be more amenable after what you took from me." I tried for confidence and fell somewhere among stressed and concerned.

His full lips curved up ever so slowly. "I don't remember you complaining about it at the time."

Oh god. "Not *that*."

His smolder softened. Thank the powers that were. Maybe I was not forsaken after all. As he pushed himself off my chair and gave me blessed space, I was inclined to think the good Lord had at least forgiven me a little.

He went back to leaning against the desk which was a vast improvement for my mental well-being.

"And what exactly did I take from you?" he asked, arms crossed.

"You murdered my brother," I snapped, remembering why I hated the man before me.

Despite the grievous accusation, he rolled his eyes to the sky.

"Don't you think that's a bit dramatic, even for you?" he asked, unapologetic.

The door behind me opened, and I felt him before I saw him. I should have known what Traitor Billy was up to. Damnit. I had hoped to get an agreement in place before this happened.

Captain Flynn's notorious left dimple appeared, gloating.

"Oh look, it's your murdered brother back from the grave."

I groaned, turning to see my twin standing in the door frame, looking with wide eyes from the Captain and then back to me.

Fuck.

Chapter Seven
Of
Resurrections
and Souls

I believe that five hundred years from now, we will still only understand a fraction of the Mysterious Deep.

–An excerpt from The Mysterious Deep: A Comprehensive Understanding

"Did I die?" Oscar asked, closing the door behind him.

"Per your sister, I murdered you," Captain Flynn said.

I sank further into my chair, wishing I had not acted so rashly.

"That seems dramatic even for you." My dead brother said before gasping, "God, Rose, have you been telling people I died?"

I covered my eyes with my hands and bit my lip. "Better than a pirate," I moaned.

"I take great offense to that," Oscar said, sounding not offended at all as he took the seat next to me. "Also, you look remarkably well for someone dying. What is your affliction anyway? All my letters went unanswered, and I thought you might already be dead, unlike me."

"So concerned you went to Madame Serenades to ease your worries rather than coming to see me?" I glared at him.

One year and he hadn't changed at all except trading his aristocratic sideburns for a spotty beard, he would have been better off shaving. And, oh god, was that an attempt at a mustache? How the other pirates didn't laugh him off the ship, I did not know.

"We have a firm policy of not going into London proper for the first night of docking. A safety measure, if you would," Captain Flynn said.

I wrinkled my nose. "Safety for who?"

"Anyway, I knew nothing was physically wrong with you. I can tell when you are lying," Oscar reached out and poked my nose. "Twin, remember?"

"I hate you," I said.

He booped my nose once more. "Lyiiiiiing," he sang.

"Touch my nose again, and I'll cut off your finger," I snarled.

"With an oar, Rosie? Billy said you were a right natural with it." He grinned.

"Don't call me that," I snipped.

Oscar's shit-eating grin reminded me why the last year had actually been somewhat peaceful.

He laced his fingers and leaned back in his seat, the picture of comfort.

"So what plot did you hatch that required such deception?" he asked.

"She has offered us a letter of marque and pardons for the ship in exchange for going after the Maravilla," Captain Flynn said, eyes locked on me.

Silence leaked into the cabin with expert precision. I turned to my twin, who was busy looking between his captain and me. Just as I thought I might have to be the one to say something, he burst out into laughter, great big belly laughs complete with snorts.

I groaned once more and covered my eyes with my hand, wishing this had gone closer to the way I had spent months imagining it.

"It isn't a joke, Oscar," I said.

His laughter trickled down until he at least stopped snorting. How anyone could take him seriously as a pirate, I would never understand.

"Of course it is. That's ridiculous. No one would suggest going after the most notorious and wraith-infested treasure in the Glass Sea in seriousness. That's a death wish. And certainly not a rich girl who only has to worry about what color dress she has to wear to the next party."

It was as sharp as a knife to my chest. The barb hit harder coming from him. He who knew me better than anyone. The person I had spent the last year mourning. Of all people, I didn't expect it from him. Maybe a year had changed more than just his facial hair. His black hair was the mirror to mine, but his brown eyes were all his own. When we were little, I used to tease him they looked like chocolate, and he would tell me at least his didn't look like an olive like mine.

"I think you'll find your sister is very serious, but I am curious as to why she has devised this plan," Captain Flynn said, no amusement on his chiseled face.

I sighed. There had been no delusion in my mind where this conversation didn't happen, but I dreaded it all the same.

"Lord Allan has died," I said.

That wiped all the amusement off Oscar's face at least. He reached out and wrapped his hand around mine, resting on the arm of the chair.

"I'm sorry, Rosie. He was a good man," Oscar said. "So the bastard has taken over as the new Lord Allan, is that it? You want to prove something to him by going after gold? You have to know how insane that is?"

How little he knew me now, when once he could read my thoughts as easily as a book. What had happened across the world to paint me in this light in his mind's eye.

"I think it's a bit more complicated than that, Oscar," Captain Flynn said.

I shot him a glare and withdrew my hand from Oscar's, already missing the connection it had provided. I had missed my twin more than there were words, but at the same time, I couldn't forgive him for leaving me. I certainly didn't need Captain Flynn coming to my rescue after the role he played in that betrayal.

"James altered the will and made himself the heir of both the Allan name and North Star Line. When Father tried to claim he had paid for his share in the company over the past twenty-five years, the court asked for proof. You know what kind of businessman Father is."

"A piss poor one," Oscar said, rubbing at his chin.

"Exactly," I said. "The records Lord Allan kept were conveniently absent, so the court ruled that unless father could come up with one hundred thousand pounds to pay for his share, the company would go to James."

"Fuck," Oscar said, running his hand through his hair which was so much longer than last time I had seen him.

The last time I saw him was when I screamed at him and told him if he got on that ship, he was dead to me. I could still feel the rain pelting my skin as I watched him row into the inky darkness, the lantern's light fading into nothing behind the mist. A cavernous hole opened in my chest, never to be filled again.

"You want the Maravilla to pay the debt," Captain Flynn said.

I nodded, swallowing.

"Damn, Rosie, there are other ships to loot," Oscar said.

"Not any with a prize that will pay that sort of debt and pay enough to the crew to prevent them from mutineering for putting them in that sort of danger," Captain Flynn said.

"Shit," Oscar said.

I watched as he bit his finger while he considered options. It was so familiar that it sent a pang inside my chest. He was an idiot, and I hated him for leaving me, but I also missed him more than I could say. Even if I wouldn't admit it out loud.

"I do regret the position your family has been put in, Miss Bailey, but I cannot ask my crew to attempt a job of that risk. The benefit simply does not outweigh the risk, even with your promises, which I would point out you have no authority to promise. Even if we were to attempt this and come out unsuccessful, it would be for nothing. Your brother would have lost the influence needed to procure letter and pardons beneath the scandal," Captain Flynn said.

"Bash!" Oscar said, sitting forward.

My heart sunk far into my stomach. No wasn't an option I had prepared for. No wasn't something I could live with. I had made it this far.

"You will have the pardons whether you are successful or not," I said, tilting my chin up and meeting his gaze.

"How? If we don't get the money, then James controls North Star, and he would never advocate for clemency for piracy, and Oliver's influence will be eroded by scandal and poverty," Oscar said.

I swallowed hard.

I could feel Captain Flynn's eyes on me, seeing what I had left out.

"If you are going to ask me for my help, you might consider sharing all of the information," he said.

To be fair, I had intended to. It was the reason I had come today instead of letting Oscar come to me. I knew the ship had a mandatory policy of staying on Corpse Cove the first day and night of making port. It was to ensure nothing was stolen, prizes split properly, and to ensure there was no imminent danger of traveling to London.

I knew it was likely that the crew would be celebrating their return. All except its captain, who never left the ship the first day and night in port, if he could help it. So I had kept a close watch on The Sea Wraith's progress, and when I had heard she made port, I enacted my plan. All of that had been for naught because my brother was sitting beside me.

I met the captain's gaze. "I will tell you, but you will promise me that you will keep your *crew*," I said pointedly toward Oscar, "from doing anything dramatic."

"Oh, shit. Now I really need to know what it is," Oscar said, sitting forward.

I raised an eyebrow. "Captain?"

He crossed his arms. "My crew are not slaves, Miss Bailey. They have free will."

"Then send him away," I said.

"Absolutely not." Oscar shot up and stood next to the captain, both men staring me down. "You tell me what you are hiding right now, Rosamund Beatrice Bailey."

I groaned, rubbing my face in frustration.

"Not the middle name," I said.

"Beatrice," Captain Flynn said and I could just hear the smirk in his stupid voice.

"I will tell you, but you have to swear on Peaches' soul that you will not do anything about it," I said to Oscar.

Oscar narrowed his eyes, considering. It was a grave promise to make.

"It's really that bad?" Oscar asked.

"Who is Peaches?" Captain Flynn asked.

"Our cat," Oscar and I said as one.

Peaches was our beloved family cat. He was a gray tabby with the most beautiful purrs. He had taken to Oscar and me more than anyone else, and he was our pride and joy. He died when we were twelve and the mourning period had been the most pain either of us had ever felt. We prayed for Peaches' soul at every mass. After that, we had taken to making our most solemn promises on Peaches' soul's continued peace.

Oscar sighed. "Fine, I promise, but I know I'm going to regret it."

I held out my pinky finger to him, and he crossed his own with it. An unbreakable promise.

Once the deal was struck, I sat back in my chair and delivered the blow.

"I'll be able to restore the business and Oliver's reputation to get the pardons because James offered me a bargain that if I agree to marry him, he will give father back his share in the company," I mumbled quickly.

"I'll fucking kill him," Oscar said, marching to the door and slamming it behind him.

A few moments ticked by where I hid my face in my hands, cursing myself for not seeing that even our beloved cat could not prevent my brother from committing murder.

"Well, that went well," Captain Flynn said, kicking his foot off his desk. "Best go catch him before he gets himself hanged."

I stood up and shoved my shoulder into the captain.

"Thanks to you," I snarled.

I hated the sound of his laugh as I stalked out onto the ship.

Damn Pirates.

Chapter Eight
Smells Like Pirates in There

Trust is essential to any successful crew, privateer or not.

-An excerpt from The Mysterious Deep: A Comprehensive Understanding

"Oscar, get back here right now! You promised on Peaches!" I shouted.

The feen was crossing the deck with angry stomps toward the ladder. It was weird to see him in a relaxed shirt and pants, so different than the tight breeches and stuffed shirts of the aristocracy. I certainly felt out of place with my bulky skirts and long sleeves.

"I crossed my fingers!" he shouted back. "Billy, let's go. We are making for London."

Billy, who had found himself a nice barrel, had been munching on an apple; how, I could never be sure with the state of his teeth. At my brother's order, he tossed the apple into the sea and stood abruptly.

"Yes, sir," he said.

Sir? That was weird.

"Oscar Reginald Bailey, you are damning our cat to an eternity of hellfire!"

"Reginald," Captain Flynn snorted. "Your parents were terrible at picking middle names."

I shot a glare at him. "Well, we can't all have distinguished names like Sebastian Flynn, can we?"

He tilted his head. "It *is* rather good, isn't it?"

"I hope your middle name is something like Oswald," I said.

He smiled down at me, and I hated the way it made me feel.

It was inconvenient.

"No middle name. It would ruin the allure of a name like Sebastian Flynn."

"Yes, I'm sure your parents thought very hard about that."

I turned to my brother, who was swinging his body over the side of the ship. So dramatic. I ran to the side of the ship and watched him climb down the rigging.

"It isn't worth your life or Peaches' soul," I pleaded.

"I dun think cats have souls, Hellcat," Billy said as he swept past me and followed Oscar.

"No one asked you, Billy," I snapped.

"Be nice to Billy," Oscar called.

"I can take it, sir, like an oar to me gut," Billy said with a toothy smile up at me.

"Why is he calling you, sir?" I asked as I swung myself over the edge.

Just climbed up the damn ship and was already going back down. Not at all the plan.

"I'm quartermaster!" he said, nearing the bottom.

Quartermaster. My brother. Of The Sea Wraith. I didn't know much about pirates, but I knew that was a position of both power and honor. How my idiotic brother had been chosen for that after only a year was a mystery. Probably a lot of dead people in between.

I stepped one foot down onto the rope, and my heart sank. The distance below was...it was a lot. The going up part had been different. My stomach swirled, and I clutched the rigging in white knuckles.

"Problem, Miss Bailey?" Captain Flynn asked.

He was leaning his elbows on the edge of the ship, looking down at me with an amused expression that I resented.

"No," I snapped.

But as I turned to see where Oscar and Billy were, bile filled my mouth. The rigging was swaying with the effort of three bodies on it, and my stomach did not appreciate it. It would be a terrible way to die.

"Oscar!" I yelled as he landed two feet on the dock.

He didn't even bother to turn around as Billy hopped down next to him. How old was Billy anyway? He looked practically decrepit, but was as spry as a summer's day.

I lowered my foot once more, and a sharp breeze ran through, making my legs shake.

"You might save yourself the trouble of climbing down," Captain Flynn suggested.

I tilted my head up to see him, which was much preferable to looking down.

"I hate you."

His lip quirked up. "I believe you wish that were true."

"What the fuck, Inu?" my brother's voice rose high above the wind.

I made the critical mistake of turning my head too fast to see what he was yelling about and swallowed a mouthful of bile with the motion. Sour bitterness gripped me, but a small chuckle above me convinced me of the necessary next steps. I swallowed it down and my whole body shook with the wrongness of it.

"So damn stubborn," Captain Flynn said.

I ignored him and the assault on all of my senses as I slowly looked toward my brother. One slim figure stood at the end of the dock, blocking his path. They were exchanging a volley of words with Oscar, who was pointing a finger at them and then up to the top of the ship. From this far away, it was impossible to see whether it was anger or explanation.

A hand in my periphery caught my attention, and I looked up to see Captain Flynn holding his hand out to me. The deep callouses were the perfect blend of soft and rough against my skin.

Absolutely not. Better I take the tumble down this ladder than let those thoughts out.

I glanced below me and saw that Oscar was already climbing the rigging to reboard the ship. Whoever Inu was had my thanks. One for not making me go back down and two for making sure my brother wasn't hanged for murder and piracy. With that disaster avoided, I could tend to my next problem, which was not accepting the captain's help while also not falling on my ass a third time tonight.

One foot after another, Rose, people do it all the time. It isn't hard. His light laugh as I climbed back up was at odds with his murderous reputation: Captain Sebastian Flynn, the most accomplished pirate captain since Blackbeard. French, English, and Spanish ships had all fallen prey to The Sea Wraith. No nation was immune. Many captains had faced his sword and not lived to tell the tale. Not to mention that he was remarkably young, in his thirties, per the rumors. To have amassed such a reputation.

The truth was that very little was known about the captain. After all, some said he slew a sea monster upwards of a hundred feet by merely looking at it. Telepathy, some surmised. Another rumor said that the ghost of Blackbeard himself had found a young orphan boy and raised him to be his great successor.

Then, there were just those who thought Blackbeard had found the fabled fountain of youth and restarted his journey as a pirate. Either way, I ignored the infamous man and hoisted myself back onto the ship, exceedingly proud as I landed on firm feet.

"What a strong and independent woman. I assume you are quite proud of yourself," Captain Flynn said, arms crossed with the moonlight cruelly glinting off every muscle on him.

Stupid moon.

I took two very well-balanced steps toward him and tilted my head, pouring every ounce of arrogance of a person born to wealth.

"You assume much, Captain," I said.

His smile only grew as he leaned down, pressing his lips close to my ear.

"Who was it that said they would rather die than see my, what was it again, oh yes, two-timing pirate scheming scoundrel face, again? But you are on *my* ship, Rose, of your own volition."

His voice skated down my neck even as he threw my terrible insult said in a moment of passion back at me. It crawled down my spine, seeping into every pore and vessel. I had known he was as good as a siren with that raspy, deep voice the first time I met him, but part of me thought I would be immune to him now. The way my body filled with warmth and need said that was a dead man's hope.

Giving in was a choice, however, and I was nothing if not stubborn.

"Desperate times, and it's Miss Bailey to you," I said.

His eyes roamed over me, drinking me in like he wanted to memorize every little detail. No one had ever looked at me like that; it was exactly the problem with him. He was full of the things no one had ever done to me. Despite the anger I felt toward him, I could never bring myself to regret it.

"I missed you," he said, humor draining from his face, leaving a sincerity that I wondered how many saw.

"You lost the right to that the moment you stole my brother from me."

If we were being genuine, then I would confess as well because there was true pain laced between each carefully stolen word. The last year had been like walking through mud with only one foot. Oscar was my other leg, and without him, the world was simply wrong.

A long sigh lifted his chest. "He left of his own free will."

"You sold it to him!" I shouted.

"I answered his questions truthfully," he countered.

I took a step forward, shoving my hand into his hard chest. "You should have lied!"

He didn't flinch, didn't back away. It was like he was letting me have this satisfaction, which turned it to ash. The truth was that I wanted him to hurt like he had hurt me.

"He is happier in the life *he* chose," Flynn said gently as if that could soften the blow.

"But I'm not! I'm miserable!" I shoved him again, but this time, he caught my hand, holding it against his chest and gently stroking it.

I tried to pull away, but he held it there while taking his free hand and lifting my chin so that I was forced to face him. I felt them then—the salty, warm tears that had ripped from my eyes and claimed my cheeks.

His eyes were made for a life on the seas. Changing with his moods as swift as the weather to the ocean. Staring back at me were no longer the crystal blue waters of the Caribbean, but the murky gray of the murderous North Sea. Except it wasn't murder, but regret that painted them.

"I am more sorry than I could ever say for the role I played in your sorrow. I wish it had been different," he said.

I hated that I believed him. What did I know of the treacherous pirate Sebastian Flynn? Two nights did not a lifetime make. He had served his purpose up until the moment he had taken more than we had agreed upon. A bargain struck forever reduced to a sunken wreck. Maybe I should pay more heed to the rumors and less to the two nights spent in his bed. After all, men were known for their honeyed words when carnal pleasure was the prize.

"But it isn't different. My brother is branded as a traitor to the crown and lost to me," I said, stealing myself. "You feel sorry, Captain? Then take my bargain and save him. Save me."

His jaw twitched as he clenched it tight, fighting through the paths in his mind. He released my chin and hand at the same time, sending me adrift into the endless sea.

"If it were just my life at stake, I would without hesitation," he said.

I held his gaze, wiping at the offending tears so I could pretend they never existed. I knew he was sorry. The letter I had received from him and subsequently burned a month after he had taken my life with him across the sea said as much. Even the night they left me alone, I knew he was sorry, but sorry didn't fix a damn thing.

"Make it right, Captain," I said, as I heard my brother shuffle over the side of the ship.

His eyes flared, a tempest sea before he cracked his neck and reluctantly pulled his eyes from mine.

"You sent Inu? That was low for even you," Oscar said, barreling toward them.

Captain Flynn folded his arms against his chest.

"I was against the idea of seeing my quartermaster swing. She was in agreement," he said.

"I'm not goin' back ova this damn ship again ta'night, so nobody do nothin' about nothin' till morning," Billy said as he stomped down into the hull of the ship.

What a strange man and an even stranger pirate.

Movement near the ladder drew my attention to a woman wearing a black leather hat turned up at the side, creating the effect of hiding half her face. Her long, perfectly straight black hair settled down her back as she set her hand on her sword at her side, watching. She breathed as if she had been relaxing for hours with none of the quick breaths Oscar took from having just climbed three stories.

"Does she know what she is preventing me from doing?" Oscar said, whirling towards Inu. "Honor, you are preventing me from restoring honor to my house."

I thought I saw a hint of an eye roll on her angular face, but below the hat, it might have been a passing trick of the mind.

"I don't think she's buying it," Captain Flynn said.

Oscar growled and ran a hand over his face.

"Fine, if you won't let me kill him, then we sail for the Glass Sea," Oscar said.

"The Glass Sea is cursed," Inu said, her quiet voice accented strangely.

"Yes," Oscar hissed, pinching the bridge of his nose. "Why are you taking Bash's side without even knowing for what?"

I saw it finally. What I would have seen within a hair's breadth had it been a year ago. It was the way Oscar rubbed at his chest and refused to meet the woman's eyes. He wasn't mad. He was hurt. Betrayed.

Who was this woman to my brother, and why did that question feel like slicing my own heart open?

She said nothing, and Oscar accepted it. Another strange occurrence. Oscar was happier and funnier than me, but he was just as stubborn. He didn't let things go. Certainly not something that felt like betrayal, yet he let out a long breath and turned to face the captain.

Did I even know my own twin any longer? God, marrying James would have probably hurt less than this. Coming here was a mistake.

"You aren't going to let her marry him," Oscar said. "You know what he is."

My arms around my stomach, and the wall in my heart could not keep out the chill of those words. They were words that no one should have ever been able to say out loud. Oscar had promised, and he had broken it as easily as breathing.

I could feel Captain Flynn's eyes on me, coaxing me out of the shell I had retreated into, but it was better this way. Better to hide from what I knew he understood. The shame of it burned me from my toes to the tip of my hair, and all I wanted to do was go home. To whatever that meant for the six months until I succumbed to the inevitable.

It had been a beautiful dream. To think I could stand against such a wave. For what it was worth, I was glad that I tried. At least I would have that.

"Tonight has been..." Captain Flynn searched for the words, but they never came. "Let's all retire for the evening."

That was a nice thought, except I had nowhere to go, and I was fairly convinced old Billy was serious about not going back down the ship. At every turn this evening, I was reminded more and more of what a terrible plan this was. It had been born of desperation, and that never made for positive outcomes.

I watched as my brother turned to Inu and shared a silent conversation that ended with the slightest dip of her head. My brother exhaled, and the relief he exuded was further insult to injury. We used to share conversations like that. Oliver and Ruby would get frustrated and refuse to engage with us in any games because we always cheated. I knew my brother, and he knew me.

Now, we were strangers.

"You can stay in my cabin," he said, resigned like I was some sort of burden.

When I formulated this plan six months ago, I spent an embarrassing amount of time imagining what it would be like to reunite with Oscar. The most realistic version was when I yelled at him for leaving me for piracy, and he laughed and hugged me until my ribs ached. Then, we would carry on as we always had.

What a spoiled and indulgent fool I'd been.

"I think I'll sleep down in the hull, thank you all the same," I said.

"Excuse me?" Oscar said, mouth open.

I raised my eyebrow, daring him to make me say it again. When he stood there almost comically resembling a gasping fish, I turned on my heels and made for the hull.

"It smells like pirates in there, which is not a good smell, mind you. Not to mention Billy snores as loud as a leviathan," Oscar said.

I would say that I had worse odds, but in truth, I had known very little discomfort in my life, and we both knew it. Nonetheless, some matters were purely based on principle, and this was one.

I had nearly made it to the steps when Captain Flynn grabbed my arm. I turned to tell him exactly what was about to happen, but he beat me to it.

"Take my cabin. I'm headed ashore for the night anyway. You won't be disturbed," he said.

It was a better outcome than sleeping next to Billy after all his little tricks and lies. More than that, I recognized this for what it was. An apology. Whether it was for destroying my life to begin with, or because he was going to force me into a marriage with a man he knew the truth about, I couldn't say. And if I were being perfectly honest with myself, I didn't care.

I was too exhausted to care. Nodding once, he released my arm, his hand clenching and unclenching at his side as he walked me to his cabin. Oscar didn't say anything, and neither did the other two.

It was strange to have woken up this morning with such hope and possibility to now carry the heavy weight of defeat throughout my body. As heavy as if I had filled my pockets with stones.

Captain Flynn reached past me and opened the door to the cabin, saying nothing as I stepped through. As I passed, he pressed a small key into my hand.

What a horrible evening, I thought as I closed the door on him and locked it with the gifted key.

Chapter Nine
Three Stomps

While common belief is that pirates are savage and rule by strength. Most would be surprised to know that most ships operate under a cordial rule of law that resembles a democracy far more than the autocracy it is believed to be.

–An excerpt from The Mysterious Deep: A Comprehensive Understanding

The gentle sway of the ship around me, accompanied by the creek of wood and rolling waves, was something I thought I would like to memorize for the future prison of my life. Seagulls' distant calls would be a reminder that for one moment, one day, I was a free woman. I curled further into the thick white blankets, which were an odd choice for a pirate, and stretched my legs. I hadn't anticipated a bed on a ship could be quite so cozy, but with it right against two open windows, the sunlight hit just right.

This was the moment I would recall when I was forced to marry a man who would be better off rotting on the seafloor. I would even remember the smell of the plush pillows and fabric nestled around me. They smelt of him. Salt spray and cedar. A smell that had become a phantom to me over the last year much like a memory.

I sat up and looked out into the harbor. The town that was Corpse Cove was significantly more normal than I would have expected. Buildings were high with stepped roofs built close together, and signs dangled overhead. Men, women, and children were walking the streets as if it were simply Piccadilly Street in London—all of them simply living their lives.

It occurred to me then that Corpse Cove, much like Captain Sebastian Flynn, had carefully crafted their reputations. It was easy enough to guess at Corpse Cove's reasons. After all, it was a refuge for pirates who would be hanged the moment they stepped onto English soil. Captain Flynn was another story. I had yet to see any of the ruthlessness he was renowned for, which likely only showed how little I actually knew him. After all, two stolen nights didn't seem like a decent basis for knowing anyone.

The ship's creek was a gentle reminder that despite her sturdy appearance, the Sea Wraith was a piece of wood floating on an ocean that nurtured death more than life. I chuckled, thinking that Captain Flynn would likely take great offense to that, much like he had the flag. Which was, in fact, a terrible flag.

His cabin was fairly simple which didn't surprise me. He had told me once his life belonged to the sea and material belongings were attempts to hold onto a life that was on borrowed time. I confess, it was rather romantic at the time. That was before I knew exactly who he was and before he betrayed me.

The walls were painted a dark green that reminded me of deep forests. Gas lamps held on by golden fixtures clung to the walls between endless windows. A small hammock sat to one side of the room, where it gently swayed. I had been half tempted to sleep there, but the bed had been too alluring. Bookshelves sat on the opposite wall. I padded against the soft carpet inlaid with beautifully bright colors and patterns that swallowed each other until they melded together, and it became unclear where one ended, and one began. It spoke of a culture and a place unlike London in every way.

That was the first time I felt the stir in my blood, a restlessness in my feet. As I stared at the bookshelves, noting different languages, some not even using the alphabet as I knew it, and all the strange trinkets, I knew it would not be the last time I felt it. There was a sort of hunger that erupted with each foreign item.

A strange golden lamp. A wooden carving of a whale, or maybe it was a dolphin. A painting of a land of sand with giant triangular buildings. A small statue that was a mix of snake and feathers that were emerald green and golden.

Each had a story that I wanted to know.

A story I would never know.

The minute I walked out of this cabin, I would likely be sent on my way. A sincere apology and best wishes. I knew what I asked was dangerous, but I had thought the reward enough for temptation. To never have to worry about being hunted again. To be seen by the crown as an ally, free to continue a life without fear of death.

I also knew the things I would have to do to convince James to use his influence for this end. I meant it when I said I would procure the letter and pardons whether we were successful in retrieving the gold or not. Even when he returned my father's share of the company, Oliver would need James' help in restoring his credibility post-scandal. After a year engaged to him and a lifetime of knowing him, I knew James better than anyone except Oscar. He would agree, it just might cost me everything.

Letting my hand trace over each delicate piece once more, I made a point to memorize this image, too. As much as it stung to admit, much of my anger toward Oscar was jealousy. He had broken free and already seen a world I never would. If I left and never returned to London, I would be the reason my family fell into poverty. There were chains holding me, and I resented them with every fiber of my being.

Maybe it was that I hadn't seen them as chains before James gave me the ultimatum. The thought of running away to join a pirate crew with Oscar had never once occurred to me. As much as I complained about society, I enjoyed having everything I needed and wearing nice clothes. Truth be told, I didn't even hate the corsets.

Society was a fine place to be when you weren't forced into marriage, but this restlessness in my feet, that was new.

The best I could hope for was it would go away after each passing day in my new prison. Eventually, my body would recognize it was beaten, and then my soul would finally relinquish its ill-gotten hope. Hopefully, that process didn't take very long.

Grabbing the key from the table in the center of the room, I made for the door, but my reflection in an ornate standing mirror grabbed my attention. Same old me. The same dress I had left home in, the same boots, my hair still braided behind my back. Not one single thing about me had changed. My face was still plenty pale, and my eyebrows too bushy.

It was a marvel to me that I could still be me when there was this ache in my chest. The death rattle of my body begging me, *try*. Delusions of grandeur had never been my specialty like it had Oscars. A wild imagination and closely coveted dreams. Dreams I knew nothing about until it was too late.

With a frustrated breath, I went to the door and pressed the key into the lock. The sun greeted me, shining on my neck and face as if happy to welcome me to the day. Along with the breeze that gusted around me, I might have been able to convince myself it was whatever divine power was out there saying hello, you're where you're meant to be. But I wasn't.

"And then she stood up and waived her oar shoutin' 'I ain't a virgin, you prick!'" shouted an annoyingly familiar voice.

Sure enough, I looked to the left of the deck, and Billy was standing on a barrel holding an oar, surrounded by at least twenty pirates engrossed in his display. Horror washed off me as I realized exactly what he was doing.

He took the oar and pretended to slam it into his stomach. "And then she got me square in the belly, mates."

Apparently, that was rather funny as they all broke out into laughter and jeered that he should have tried for a kiss before getting hit.

I was going to die of mortification.

At least Oscar and Flynn weren't there to witness my humiliation.

"Good morning," said that deep, raspy voice.

The groan I released would have sent my mother and Ruby into stunned silence, followed by a well-intended lecture on propriety in private. However, I had no regrets then, and I certainly didn't on a pirate ship.

Twisting on my heels, I found the Captain of the Sea Wraith leaning over the railing on the next floor, smiling that devilish grin at me. The daylight loved him even more than the night. His tanned body a reminder of where he spent his days. Navy blue might have been his color, the way it accented his eyes, but contrasted with his black pants that were too tight to be practical on a ship.

"Are you enjoying the show?" I said with a false smile.

"And then, Davy Jones take me if I be lyin' to you, she fell right on her arse!" Billy shouted.

Raucous laughter followed.

Curse them all to wherever they came from.

Captain Flynn chuckled. "Billy is an excellent storyteller."

"More like a rat," I muttered.

"How did you sleep?" he asked, tone shifting.

I tossed up his key, which he caught with deft skill, and slid into his pocket before returning to his relaxed pose.

"None of your business," I said.

His grin slipped as he watched me.

"You are angry with me."

"What gave that away?" I asked.

Irritating pirates. Billy was now waving the oar around as some imitation of me attempting to fight the imaginary sea monster. Having had just about enough of everyone and everything, I marched right over to the pirate Shakespeare. The laughter died down as I approached, and some even parted for me, which gave me some satisfaction amidst the embarrassment weighing me down. Billy didn't notice anything had changed, still flailing about.

I placed my hands on my hips and, with great intent, kicked at the barrel he was standing on. It shook enough that Billy's bearded face turned pale, and he crouched down, dropping the oar in his haste to catch his balance. Everyone was silent as I bent down and picked up the oar.

"Aye, Hellcat, ya like my story?" Billy said, grinning.

I scrunched up my face with a mock smile and swiped the oar at the barrel, which toppled over, carrying Billy to the deck with a thump.

"You deserved that one, Billy," said one of the men.

At least someone agreed with me.

I turned my back, holding my oar to the side as laughter and cheers of 'Hellcat' broke out behind me. Warm satisfaction coated the places embarrassment had previously been, and as I walked the steps up to where Flynn stood, I didn't try to suppress my smile.

"Proud of yourself?" he asked.

I tucked the oar between my arms and leaned over the edge, resting my arms on the firm wood. Billy had managed to scramble back up with the help of his crew mates, who patted him on the back.

"Exceedingly," I answered. "How old is he anyway?"

"Old enough to have grandchildren, but young enough to keep up with the youngest of the crew," Flynn said.

"That's not really helpful," I said.

Flynn sighed and pushed off the ledge, meeting my eyes. "First lesson on pirating: you never ask questions about a fellow crewmate. Everyone is drawn to the sea for different reasons. Some come to her for adventure. Some come to escape. Some to forget. Some to remember. But a person's reasons are their own."

For some reason, the sincerity in his words made me feel small. Like I was shallow for having asked about Billy even though in London, it would have been a question eagerly whispered behind fans. That was if you didn't already know the answer. Everyone knew everything about each other. That was half the game.

"Why did you come to the sea?" I asked.

His lips curled up, and he shook his head. "You really are a hellcat."

I shrugged my shoulders. "Won't do me much good in my prison."

It was like I was adept at taking away his smiles, which should have brought me some joy after all he had done, but it didn't. Instead, that profound loneliness I felt last night set in once more, weighing my shoulders down.

He turned, resting his back against the railing, and raked his eyes over me, searching. I didn't know what he was looking for, only that he wouldn't find it.

"A prison would not suit you," he said quietly.

"Prisons don't much care if their inhabitants are well-suited or not," I answered.

Silence stretched between us and I counted the creases beside his eyes, three on the right, four on the left. They said that they came from laughing. Before meeting him, I wouldn't have guessed fierce pirate captains were in the habit of laughing. After all, they were murderers and thieves. That was before I met him.

Three loud stomps drew my attention away from him and to the deck where more people had gathered. Men and women with varying shades of skin color, hair of all types. I had never seen such different people gathered in one place. Not a spectacle, but an everyday occurrence. There was that pang in my stomach, the itching in my feet.

All gathered stomped their feet three times.

"You've been called back to the Wraith for a vote." My brother's voice.

I jerked my head down to see him standing a few feet in front of the crowd that gathered while Flynn and I had been talking. Oscar paced with his hands behind his back, his white shirt billowing with the breeze.

Three more stomps.

"A vote?" I whispered.

"We are a democracy, Miss Bailey. Does that surprise you?" he asked, once more resting his arms on the railing.

Yes. It turned out I knew very little about pirates. I had been led to believe the captain had the utmost authority. Yet, he wasn't even down there.

"I know you were all promised a respite from the sea, but an opportunity has been placed before us. You and I both know that there is no shame in what we are. That we are proud to call ourselves pirates and free," Oscar said.

Three more stomps that hit with the force of passion.

"Exactly. But, England doesn't see us that way. They call us murderers and thieves."

My cheeks colored as I remembered my own thoughts minutes ago.

"An opportunity has arisen to not have to watch our backs, to not hide in the shadows or live in fear of the noose."

A few stomped, but some did not, and I realized this was their way of showing their pleasure or displeasure at the words spoken instead of yelling. It was a strangely civilized notion. My heart skipped as Oscar's words sank into my mind, registering.

"They are voting," I whispered. "On me and the bargain I offered you."

Flynn kept his eyes on the proceedings.

"It would seem so." There was a note of displeasure in his voice.

"No prize such as this comes without a cost, my friends," Oscar said, going very still. "And I won't lie to you. The risk is great, but the reward... the reward would mean absolution and freedom to pursue our heart's desires."

A quiet snort from Flynn. I barely noticed, though, as I watched my brother take control of the crowd before him. A hundred men and women from all over the globe invested in every word he spoke. My brother had always been charismatic, able to talk his way through anything, but this was something else entirely. He was born for this.

"This is why I didn't tell him no when he asked to join my crew. He has a way with people that I have never seen. He listens to them, validates them, but also makes them think anything he sets his mind to. In one year, he earned the trust of every crew member who at first saw him as a spoiled rich runaway. He has saved our necks more than once."

I hated the pride that filled my chest because it was at direct odds with the bitterness I had nurtured for a year. Seeing my brother now, the way his steps were carefully timed with his words, the way he captivated them all, desperate for his next word. He was wasted in London society. Maybe loving someone didn't mean holding them by your side, but letting them be free to find their place. It was a sentiment I wasn't ready to accept, but it lingered all the same.

"We are the greatest crew to ever sail the seas. No one is more respected and feared than our Captain."

Thunderous stomps answered, but Captain Flynn made no movement as if he were made of stone.

"In every port from London to Tanguu, The Wraith is recognized for her reputation and that of her crew."

Chills filled me with the unison of stomps. These were pirates, but they were also proud. Defiantly so. It didn't matter that England saw them as criminals; they knew who and what they were. There must be its own type of freedom in surety like that.

"If any crew can do what I am about to put to vote, it is us. Where others have failed, let it be known that the crew of The Sea Wraith and her Captain are beyond the limits of mortals. As we are now, we are a household name, but my friends, we could be legends. We could be immortal."

Oscar let that sit with them for a moment, staring out into the crowd who watched with hungry eyes. He knew them all well and what each of them craved.

"What is the cost of freedom from the noose and immortality, my friends?" Oscar asked, every breath hanging on his words, "The Maravilla."

Whatever spell he had cast over them shattered to a thousand pieces. Some laughed, some booed, some cheered. Truly, it was such a sound that my ears ached with the force of it.

"It seems even he has his limits," Flynn said.

I knew I didn't imagine the hint of regret in his words, even if his face never gave any indication of how he was feeling. For the briefest of moments, I had felt hope. That my brother would come through for me with his charm and determination. That together, we might save our family and myself from the cage James offered me. Now that it was gone, I hated that hope. Hated that it ever existed. It was more painful to have believed for even a second, my fate would differ.

"Easy! Easy!" Oscar called. "I know it's insane."

"No ship has ever survived an attempt at the Maravilla. There are more wraiths there than anywhere else in the Glass Sea," someone shouted.

"And why is that?" another man said. "Because they are attracted to treasure, and the Maravilla has enough to make us free for the rest of our lives, and then some!"

"If we don't die first!" A woman with short brown hair said.

"The Glass Sea is cursed," Inu said to the side.

I was starting to wonder if that was her favorite thing to say.

"Listen!" Oscar pleaded.

"I'll take the noose over Sea Wraiths," a man with an eye patch said. "They say they drown you slowly, consuming your soul all along. Ain't nothing left of you when they are through."

A loud gong-like sound erupted behind everyone, stilling the words spilling from mouths. The crowd parted and Billy stood holding a golden disc and long stick.

"Did ya all ferget who talked the sea witches down from sinkin' us into Davy Jones Locker? Did ya ferget who got you, Lemmy, out of them cannibal's pot?"

The man with the eye patch turned to Oscar, a dip of his head. I struggled to understand what was happening. Sea Witches? Cannibals? What had my brother seen in the last year?

"And Inu, did you ferget who undid your chains?" Billy said.

Beneath her hat, it was hard to see how the words affected her, but I knew there was a story there I wanted to hear.

"Barry, who taught ya how to read?" Billy asked. "Ain't a person here who our quartermaster ain't helped. We chose him, so the least ya can do is hear him out."

It would seem that Billy was a good ally to have as the pirates quieted down. When the attention was firmly back on him, Oscar nodded.

"Joining this crew has been the single best decision of my life," he began.

The words were a dagger to the heart even as my mind tried to tell me I should be happy for him. I just couldn't rectify that his happiness was without me. Against all logic, my eyes began to burn. It was too much. This hope that came and went, destroying me each time. The reminder of what I had already lost and what I was set to lose.

I bit the inside of my lip and turned my gaze out to the sea, watching the waves gather only to break a few feet later. That was how this felt. Like just as I became whole, I was ripped apart.

"Being your brother is an honor I will wear with pride the rest of my days," he said.

It was worse than being ripped apart. I was being decimated. Shredded. I knew it was selfish, but I hated them and him. Being their brother was enough, but not me. I knew it was more than that, but damn if I cared at that moment.

This was a torture worse than any cage. I turned to walk away, but Flynn grabbed my arm.

"He is doing this for you," he said.

I sucked in a breath and willed my tears to recede, but they were as stubborn as me.

"I don't know why he bothers when his family is right there," I said.

Flynn turned to look at me. I didn't flinch or hide my pain. Let him see what his choices had wrought. I had trusted him, and he had taken everything.

"Your brother is going against a direct order which could easily get him executed by his crewmates or banished from the ship for you. He is willing to put his chosen brothers and sisters in direct peril where, make no mistake, many of them will die, *for you*. Maybe if you weren't so spoiled, you could see what he was risking. I may feel sorry for what you are facing, Miss Bailey, but I would never have even posed this death trap of a quest to my crew and I ordered your brother not to as well."

My loathing quickly turned into the warm, hot rush of shame. I hadn't realized. Hadn't seen. Knowing his words had the desired effect, Flynn went back to watching his crew and the proceedings he had forbidden. What did it mean that he hadn't stopped it the moment it had begun? If he truly thought it was a death trap, why allow Oscar to continue?

"I am not asking you to risk your life without reward. We, of all the crews who have sailed, will succeed in taking the Maravilla. When we do, we will not only be disgustingly wealthy, but also free. For at the end, we are being offered letters and pardons from the crown. No man or woman here will ever fear the noose again. So I ask you, not to do this for me, but for yourselves. What is the cost of your freedom?"

I had never thought a pirate ship would be quiet, but as Oscar's words faded, silence stretched over the Sea Wraith. It felt like an eternity, like this moment would never end. Even my breath came too loud. Flynn, next to me, was made of stone, holding his breath while his crew decided.

"Aye. I'll risk it," Billy said.

"Aye," another said, followed by another, making my heart stutter.

"Then I put it to a vote," Oscar said. "Nays."

The three thumps were loud. Loud enough that I would hear them all the days of my life.

"And the ayes," Oscar said.

The ship groaned beneath the weight of stomping feet. It felt like I was suspended in air, my stomach doing endless flips. It was hard to breathe.

Oscar turned, and I met his eyes. Silver lined them as he said, "The ayes have it."

We were going to the Glass Sea.

Chapter Ten
Kidnapped

–An old Sailor Proverb

Through the thunderous roar of pirates with a new hunt, Flynn grabbed my arm and dragged me down the stairs, ignoring my protests as we went. I was getting sick of this pull between hope and despair that had plagued me the last twenty-four hours. Just a moment ago, my heart swelled at the love my brother had shown me, at the possibility that my insane plan might actually happen.

Now I was being dragged by Flynn, who was probably going to announce that this plan was, in fact, not going to work, ayes or not. When I dug my heels into the last stair, he sighed and released me. My swell of victory was short-lived as he bent down and threw me over his shoulder. The brown of the deck and his black boots were all the company my eyes had. Absolutely not.

I had never been so manhandled in my life. I pounded my fists into his back, which did absolutely nothing. Not a damn thing.

"What is wrong with you? Put me down right this instant!" My voice was frantic and shrill.

I heard laughs that only added to the blood filling my cheeks. Next thing I knew, I was being hauled back into his cabin and into the seat across his desk where I had sat last night. I fought for breath to deliver curses I had heard my father's sailors use, but it was like the mortification took all ability to process straight out of my mind.

My mouth opened and shut like a fish out of water. I had never been so angry in my life. Fury, white hot, burned in my veins, desperate for release, but my mind could hardly comprehend what had happened.

"How dare—I cannot believe... what is wrong with you?" I sputtered out, making no sense at all.

I might have said nothing for all Flynn cared. Instead of being properly chastised, he sat across from me at his desk, tapping his fingers in an entirely irritating rhythm. His lips were pulled into a thin line while red crept up his neck, running toward his face. My anger wavered beneath the energy pouring from him. If he clenched his jaw any tighter he was liable to break it.

I opened my mouth to say—well, I really couldn't say what. Whatever came out was just what was going to come out, but the sound of the door opening released sounds of celebration into the tense cabin. It closed shortly after, but I didn't dare take my eyes off of Flynn who was reminding me of one of those creatures they called a lion that lived in the savannahs. A predator that could snap its prey's neck in a blink of an eye.

Strangely, it wasn't fear that paralyzed me, but instead a sense of wariness that lived in my extincts. Something ancient and primal guided my movements.

"Bash, I know you are mad, but—" Oscar began.

His words cut off as his hand rested on my shoulder, gently squeezing. Small veins on either side of Flynn's temple bulged, but he persisted with that same rhythmic tapping.

"Bash?" Oscar asked.

That same wariness that I was feeling emitted from the single word. This was no longer the smirking Flynn. This was the captain of The Sea Wraith, who had earned his reputation through blood and ruthlessness. It was the first time I had ever met him, and from the way my heart beat erratically in my chest, I knew I was afraid.

"I have never once regretted bringing you onto my ship." His voice was quiet, the kind of quiet that cut like a knife.

"Bash—" Oscar tried.

Captain Flynn raised his hand, taking in a short breath before returning to his tapping. "Do not speak, or I may forget why I shouldn't kill you right now."

Oscar, my smooth-talking brother who had gotten us out of every scrape and mishap with his pretty words, took the seat next to me without uttering a single syllable. That was when I knew we were in grave danger. I vowed not to breathe lest it set off the pirate before us.

The ticking of a clock, the creak of the ship, rhythmic tapping.

"You just called those people out there your family and then lied to their faces. Now *my* crew is preparing to take on an impossible job where many of them will die based on a lie," he said.

Oscar opened his mouth, and I reached for him, desperate for him not to speak. Captain Flynn raised his eyebrows, daring my brother to say a word. I was acutely aware of the pistol holstered at his side. Yes, it would take time to load and fire it, but the long sword at his other side was likely just as effective, if not more. I was under no pretense that any amount of history would sway the pirate captain before me.

"Do you think if you had mentioned that this job was offered by your sister, who is very unlikely to procure pardons, to save your erroneously wealthy family after your father failed to keep account of one hundred thousand shillings? Do you think the people out there would care very much for that plight to risk their lives? Do you think saving a rich girl from an unfavorable marriage would sway them? No, you don't, which is why you failed to mention it. You manipulated people who gave you their trust."

Tap. Tap. Pause. Tap. Pause. Tap. Tap. Tap.

The air was stifling. My vow to not breathe was quickly becoming a matter of life and death. I didn't dare look at Oscar, but Captain Flynn stared him down like a criminal on trial. Guilty of the most heinous crimes.

"Now, how long do you think before they start to ask who their benefactor is? Who is so desperate for gold that they would enlist The Sea Wraith to retrieve it? Exactly. The moment they find out those answers, you are as good as dead. They will turn on you and throw you to the bottom of the sea strapped to a cannon."

I had to breathe. My chest ached.

"And then they will turn on me. Because as far as they know, you and I worked together. You are an idiotic young bastard who thinks with his heart before his head," Captain Flynn said.

That was it. I was going to pass out.

Tap. Tap. Pause. Tap. Pause. Tap. Tap. Tap.

I gasped for air, drinking it in desperately. My lungs and chest burned with the effort. There was a buzzing in my mind as Oscar clapped his hand to my back several times, hard enough to make me cough.

"She holds her breath when she gets anxious sometimes," Oscar explained as if we were all casually discussing the weather.

"That's very impractical," Captain Flynn said slowly.

My vision blurred as I rubbed at my chest. Oscar making gentle circles over my back that reminded me of when we were younger and I couldn't sleep at night. When we were eight our parents decided we were too old to sleep together in the same bed. No matter how I tossed and turned, how I squeezed my eyes shut, sleep would not come. So I would sneak into his bed and he would rub my back where sleep would immediately find me.

Safe. I realized. That's how I felt then and despite the murderous captain before me, that same feeling swept over me. Oscar was here. We were together again. Maybe we weren't literally safe, but I felt it all the same.

"Are you all right?" Flynn asked, finally having ceased his tapping.

I raised my watering eyes to find him leaning over his desk, his focus entirely on me. All I could manage was to nod. I thought about asking him not to kill my brother and I, but words were hard.

"If you could refrain from holding your breath, that would be advisable. If it helps, I will not be killing your brother at the present moment. As far as I can see it, his life and mine, for that matter, are entirely dependent on you."

A very strange thing to say.

I pointed my finger at myself, still unsure about words.

The murderous Captain Flynn snorted and leaned back in his chair, entirely unbothered.

"Yes, you. We have two options. First and, let it be known it would be the wisest of actions would be for me to go out there and tell them the small details Oscar forgot to mention. They would be angry, but as no bodily harm has befallen them, they might just kick him off the crew. Now, Oscar here would be a pariah among the pirate community, unlikely to find his way onto any other crew. Likely, he would be forced to return to London and beg the favor of your family's influence for a pardon and protection due to that tattoo on his chest. Again, unlikely to happen. I hear your elder brother has been gaining influence, but given the scandal your family is facing, a pirate in the family would be a death blow to his career as a politician."

Oscar audibly swallowed.

Captain Flynn's eyes were locked on me, eyebrows raised.

Right, breathing. I took in a long, steadying breath.

"In this scenario, none of my crew dies, and I do not face a mutiny."

"What's option two?" I asked, voice cracking.

It was hot in here. Despite the windows being open, letting in the sea breeze, there felt like a distinct lack of air.

Flynn sighed and ran his hand over his face before setting it back on the desk.

"Option two is very stupid and only exists because I have a hard time forgetting when I owe someone a debt. I would be dead had Oscar not convinced a sea witch I was better off breathing."

He rubbed a hand over his neck as if remembering.

"I—" Oscar began.

Flynn held out his hand once more. "It would behoove you not to speak yet."

Sliding back in his chair, Oscar tapped the armrest with an irritated thump. Robbing Oscar of his voice was like a sea monster without teeth. Impractical and unsustainable. The fact that he heeded Flynn was enough to say he knew exactly what kind of situation he had landed in.

"As far as I can count, Billy and Inu are the only two outside of us who know who you are, Miss Bailey. Is that correct?"

Oscar nodded.

"Very well. Against all my judgment and self-preservation, I will not be going out there and telling them how you used them. Only because I believe there is a small margin of success in this job will we be moving forward. From here on out, you two do not know each other. You have never met. If any one of them finds out who you are, we are all dead. Which is why you will now go by Miss Smith, and you are now a hostage of The Sea Wraith."

Another strange thing to say. On the one hand, I was aware that I had woken up in the bed of a notorious pirate captain, but on the other hand, this all seemed rather like a dream. After all, I was the daughter of a respected aristocrat. My dress was fine fabric and the latest fashion. My shoes were. That was all correct.

I dragged my eyes over the space around me. It was smaller than the door behind the desk, which led to Flynn's sleeping chambers. In here, it was the desk and chairs at the center and windows. Lots of windows. They were open. It wasn't so unlike Bailey House.

A seagull squawked outside.

A dream, then.

"Excuse me, *she*," Oscar said, pointing at me as if I were the problem. "Is going back home where she belongs."

My stomach rolled very realistically, which was dampening my dream theory. On the one hand, the itching in my feet reminded me of a want I was not prepared to say out loud. On the other and very practical hand, I was in no way, shape, or form qualified to sail on a pirate ship. In fact, now that the issue had been raised, I was quite sure I hadn't made it this far in my planning. Six months of waiting for this all to set in motion and I had kind of skipped the sailing bit in my mind and gone straight to seeing James' face when I showed up with one hundred thousand shillings.

"She is the only way I can ensure the promises you made to the crew come through," Flynn said.

Clearly Oscar understood something I did not because he stood up and pointed an accusatory finger at Captain Flynn who was entirely unbothered. The deadly quiet of before replaced with the Flynn I was more familiar with. At least there was that.

"You are not kidnapping my sister!" Oscar said.

"I'm kidnapped?" I asked.

Both of them turned toward me, a question on their tense faces. It's just that they kept saying words, which was all rather confusing. In fact, I was fairly certain this was my plan, and I was the one in charge. Yes, my plan. I was in charge.

"I'm in charge," I blurted.

My cheeks colored with embarrassment at the words that spilled from my mouth. Flynn laughed, shaking his head which only made my embarrassment melt to anger. I was not a spectacle for his amusement.

"See, look at her. She's in no state to be a hostage. Listen, Bash, I know I fucked up, and I wish I was sorry, but I'm not. We may disagree, but neither of us wants to see her hurt. Let her go home, and she'll come through with the pardons. You know what she's like when she isn't freaking out. She will see it through." Oscar said.

Flynn ran a hand over his chin and then his bottom lip, thinking. My core pulsed as I watched the movement. It wasn't fair that a man should be so attractive. That had been my first thought when I had seen him a year ago outside of The Siren and The Kraken. Another night when I had been impulsive and suffered long-standing consequences. In fact, one might even say this very moment was one of those consequences.

"You have two choices, Oscar. Go out there and tell them how you used them and take her home or give the order to set sail with your sister on board," Flynn said.

There was a clock ticking somewhere nearby. It's tick, tick incessantly. Did I want to go home? I had left a letter for Oliver explaining the truth of where I went. For my parents, I left a note stating I was visiting Oscar in Paris. Would they assume I would be coming back? If I went home, what was to stop James from trying to force me to concede earlier? Now that I was thinking about it, once I returned, they would probably lock me up inside for having lost my mind.

Did I want to go home?

That itching in my foot started again. All those beautiful artifacts and strange writings in Flynn's room flashed before my mind. There were stories I wanted to hear. Things I wanted to see. As a hostage, I would be a victim instead of branded a pirate. I would be able to go back to society, my pretty dresses, and fine things without consequence. If they succeeded and our fortune was saved, I'd never have to marry. Even if they failed and I was forced to marry James, as a victim of merciless pirates, I'd be able to possibly lose my mind enough to seek an annulment.

A plan that would probably see me in the madhouse was not ideal. However, I was onto something. There was an idea somewhere in there. All I needed was time.

I stood up and met my brother's gaze.

"Give the order, quartermaster," I said.

His face drained of color, and for the briefest of seconds, I felt sorry for him. For using him. Then I remembered that he had left me.

Shaking his head and muttering to himself, he left me standing there. The moment I heard the door shut, I smiled.

"I'm in charge," I whispered with a wide smile.

Chapter Eleven
An Honorless Death

Kelpie embody the danger of the Mysterious Deep. While beautiful and allur-ing, the moment they believe their victim is theirs, they drop their illusion. All that lies beyond their facade can simply be summarized in one word-death.

–An excerpt from *The Mysterious Deep: A Comprehensive Understanding*

I was very much not in charge. In fact, as I stared out at the array of deadly pirates staring at me, I was sure my impulsivity would be the death of me. How many times had I heard my mother say, 'Slow down and think before you speak.' It was good advice that I very seldom took.

"This is Miss Smith, and while she may be a hostage, she is to be treated with the utmost respect. No one lays a hand on her, or they will answer to me personally," Captain Flynn said.

A well-respected hostage. I supposed I could do worse.

A reasonable woman would have felt intimidated, but it was hard to worry when the breeze was wrapping itself around my hair and body. The sounds of waves crashing against the ship were louder than any of the grumbles coming from pirates. And that sky. The most perfect light blue, decorated with fluffy white clouds of all shapes and sizes. It was hard to feel anything except wonder with all of that and the sun warming my skin.

"She is how we ensure our benefactor does not renege on their promise of pardons and letters, so I expect you to treat her as if she were The Maravilla's gold. Am I understood?"

A thunderous answer of stomps three times over was confirmation enough. Captain Flynn assured me that his crew knew better than to ask questions. I hoped that was true as I was, historically, a bad liar. Given that my brother's life was at risk, it was probably enough incentive to learn how to lie.

It was strange to think they would turn on him with how they all joked and smiled at him. Oscar was well respected, but I supposed his crime of lying to them for his benefit would undo all of that.

The crowd dispersed and went about their tasks. I never could have imagined how many jobs there were on a ship or working parts, but the crew of The Sea Wraith was well informed.

"Kelpie!" a look-out overhead shouted.

My heart stuttered in my chest. Kelpie. It was one thing to read about the creatures that lived in the Mysterious Sea and quite another to see them. Now that I was here, it wasn't an opportunity I was going to throw away. I ran to the side of the ship, falling against the railing hard enough to take the wind out of me, but it was worth it.

By god, it was worth it.

Magnificent creatures dipped and rose with the waves that hugged our vessel. At first glance, they were similar to the horses that pulled carriages across London streets. That illusion quickly dissipated with the sheen of their skin that was an iridescent blue and their manes that were rivulets of water that sparkled against the sun's light.

They were beautiful. Their neighs echoed the sound of land horses, but as if they were underwater, garbled but with a lyrical lilt. I counted them as fast as I could. Ten. Ten Kelpies kept pace with The Sea Wraith.

One closest to the ship met my eyes and I knew that whatever I had done to get to this moment was worth it. Its vibrant blue eyes blinked up at me. There was an undeniable intelligence in those eyes. I could read books all day about the creatures of the deep, but not one of them could capture what it felt like to see them with your own eyes.

My chest rose and fell in time with each dip she took into the waves, only to rise once more, her attention transfixed on me as much as mine was on her. She was beautiful, timeless. Against all logic and laws of science, she existed and thrived in these seas. Native to these waters, she had been here long before us and would be long after.

A shimmering rope hung around her long neck. I met her gaze and could have sworn she nodded. I knew enough to know that if a human were to take hold of that bridle, they would be able to control the Kelpie, but I didn't want to control her. Something so beautiful should never be caged. A neigh of silver bells said she agreed with me. Together. We could be together and free. Never behind bars for the amusement of men.

I reached out my hand, and she edged her rein closer. She wanted this as much as I did. The ship was much too high, but she was powerful. The water rose with her will, and she was just inches away from my hand, just a little further.

A force pulled me backward, severing the connection I had desperately sought out. I screamed in frustration, fighting to free myself from the arms around my waist.

Sound rushed into my ears all at once. The sound of people shouting. Thunderclaps against a perfectly blue sky.

"Fire!" Flynn commanded.

An explosion like I had never heard ricocheted against angry waters. A terrible sound like the crunching of bone amidst a shriek I would forever hear in my dreams.

"Load the silver!" Flynn yelled. "Aim starboard."

A force, heavy and insistent, rammed against the ship, sending me and my captor flying against the ship's edge. My head pounded into the wood as something cut into me, sending sharp pain across my ear.

"Fire!" he yelled again.

This time, the shriek was a roar, guttural and filled with malice. Despite the pain in my head, I shivered.

"What is that?" I whispered.

"That is the sound of the creature you tried to join, which would have led to a painful and watery grave for you." Her voice was sharp and quiet all at once.

Inu.

"If I let you go, are you going to try to die?" she asked.

"Port side fire!" Flynn shouted.

I shook my head and finally saw the chaos before me. Some carried large cannonballs that pulled at their arms. There were pirates with large harpoons with silver-tipped edges casting into the water.

"We need more speed, Mr. Murphy," Captain Flynn said.

He stood on the top deck, eyes flickering over every aspect of his ship, crew, and the ocean around him. As another force came from the side Inu and I were on, he didn't flinch, and the force did not affect him in the slightest.

"Fire!" he shouted.

The ship groaned with the explosion, and the eerie shriek of death answered. I couldn't explain why, but I needed to see.

"They're rocking us, Captain," someone yelled.

"Load all the cannons and wait for my mark. Harpooners fire at will," he answered.

I crawled to the side and hoisted myself off the ground, pain lancinating through my head.

My stomach heaved with the image that unfolded before me. Gone were the ethereal creatures I had first seen, and in their place were mangled horses made of rotted flesh. Their gums pulled back to show teeth that gnashed at the ship. Around them, foul-smelling gelatin coated the ocean.

To my left, a silver-tipped harpoon sank into the flesh of one of the kelpie. It reared back its head and shrieked, its thick hide slashed against the sea with a thunderous slap. Its cold, dead eyes met mine as it exploded into a brownish-black gel that clung to the sea.

I realized with a start that the gelatin was made of dead kelpie. Where there were many before, there were only four. With unnerving precision, they brought themselves into a head-to-tail formation and turned as one, charging at the ship. I had only a second to duck down as the force of their bodies careened into us.

"All cannons fire!" Flynn shouted.

It was a terrible sound. The smell of gunpowder and death thick in the air. The shrieks were full of an ancient rage. My ears rang with sharp pain, and when I couldn't take it any longer, I huddled against the ship and clasped my hands over my ears. It felt like an eternity until small hands pulled at mine.

The ringing was still there, but less. When I opened my eyes, Inu knelt before me, her delicate brow furrowed beneath her hat.

"It's over. They cling to that border of land; they won't follow any longer," she explained.

My eyes scanned the ship as people caught their breath and enjoyed their continued existence. I couldn't find words as Inu helped me to my feet.

"You English call the waters the Mysterious Sea, but my people, we call them," she said words that were strange and quick. "It means, endless death. Everything that lives in the water is incompatible with life. It seeks to see that nothing that dares to touch it lives to tell the tale."

Despite the pounding in my head, a chill ran over me at the way she radiated calm amidst the warning in her words. She was beautiful. Tilted brown eyes that saw more than they should. There was a hardness to her despite her small frame. Almost as if she were made of stone.

"Those that choose a life at sea are known as the honorless. There is no honor in chasing death, either greet it with dignity or deny its grasp." She met my eyes, and I was certain I had never been found more lacking. "That Kelpie was luring you with lies, and the moment you touched it, it would have been impossible to let go. It would have pulled you into those murky depths and devoured you. There is no honor in that."

No one had ever spoken to me in such a brisk way, and after everything that happened, my mind was lost to me. All I could do was nod once though the movement splintered my head in two.

"Are you alright? Shit, you are bleeding." Oscar's hands were immediately on either side of my face, tilting it this way and that.

Thankfully, he was free of any obvious injuries, in fact there was a color to his cheeks that made him appear more youthful.

"*Miss Smith* is fine," Inu said, grabbing my shoulders and directing me away from my brother. "I will bring her to Emille. You should see to the crew."

There was a warning in her voice. Inu knew who I was and she knew that Oscar's concern was more than a quartermaster concerned for a valuable hostage. The first test and we had both failed miserably. I ripped my eyes from him and focused on following where Inu led us.

"Miss Smith." Captain Flynn's voice cut through my haze like a thousand knives.

I winced as the sun caught my eyes and sent my head throbbing as I tried to look at him. His hands were gentle as he gently lifted my chin and smoothed my hair away from my face.

"I'm fine," I said.

He hummed an unconvincing sound, but released me. If it weren't for the pounding in my head, I would have to deal with the way his fingers burned where they touched me. A memory. A wish.

"Take her to Emille," he said.

"Yes, Captain," Inu answered, steering me away.

"You are going to get them both killed," she said under her breath.

My head swam, and my vision blurred.

What must have been swears in her native language burned across her tongue, but all I could recall was that sinking into the darkness wasn't as bad as I always thought it would be.

Chapter Twelve
A Truth For A Lie

Secrets are the greatest commodity.

—An excerpt from The Mysterious Deep: A Comprehensive Understanding

Hands threaded through my hair, rough and full of calluses. He was as hungry for me as I was for him. I had never been kissed like this. James had always been reserved, cautious with me, as if my honor were threadbare and likely to fracture with anything more than soft lips. I hadn't known it could be like this. Warmth and something magical coursed through my body, pooling at the apex of my thighs.

Maybe tomorrow I would regret this, but his mouth against mine, devouring me, said otherwise. No, I would covet this memory. When I went back to my broken and rigid life, I would replay these moments. My voice was hoarse and desperate as I pleaded for something I didn't even understand, but this man. This seafarer understood. His hand stretched low across my belly and further until I cried out.

"It's a mild concussion. She may have some confusion and memory loss, but that should be the worst of it," a voice with a strong French accent said.

That was strange. I knew this memory inside and out, and that was not at all what he had said. Warmth flooded me as I remembered.

'This is what you want? If I touch you like this, they will say you are ruined. Do you want me to ruin you?'

My voice was a breathy moan I didn't recognize. *'I've never wanted anything more.'*

"Why isn't she waking up? It's been a day and a half." It was his voice, but the words were wrong.

I could feel the memory sinking away like quicksand, eroding the feel of his hands on me, the way his breath had ghosted over my skin. As it faded, I was reminded of a closely guarded fear that had plagued me for the last year. That I would never feel this way again. That no one would ever elicit these reactions from my body. I would live my life knowing what could be while trapped in a prison of monotony.

"I understand she is important, Captain, but I assure you there is nothing more I can do. The wound is stitched up and already healing. No signs of infection. No signs of swelling in the brain. More likely, she is stubborn and will wake when she wakes."

"More like indeed," that raspy voice said. "Come back in an hour."

"Captain-"

"An hour, Emille," he ordered.

"Yes, Captain," Emille said.

His footsteps receded, and the sound of a closing door told me I was most likely alone with Flynn. Where though, had yet to be determined. I listened carefully, regretting the loss of my dream. The creaking of wood. The scratch of a pen.

I cracked one of my eyes open, and as blurry vision gave way to clarity, I realized I was in Flynn's cabin once more. It was dark outside the windows which were closed, blocking out the sound of the sea. Sitting at the desk at the center of the room, he stared at the paper as he crafted words onto paper.

As always, he was the most attractive man I had ever laid eyes on. I would never forget the first time I saw him leaning up against the wall of The Kraken and The Mermaid with his hood up like he was waiting for someone. I knew then that he was dangerous. It was in his relaxed posture that said he wasn't afraid of anything.

I never would have approached him, but fate demanded we meet that night. When a drunkard stumbled out of the inn and into me I forgot all my boldness in coming there. I had thought I had something to prove, that I would find it there, but when the smell of whiskey hit me, I knew I had made a mistake. I wasn't a heroine from a story; I was a sheltered, rich girl who had no business being at an inn known for debauchery.

The drunk man, however, felt like it was his lucky day that he ran into me. His hands were oily as he reached beneath my cloak and pulled me into his body. I could still remember the nausea that coated my stomach and crawled up my throat as the feel of his hands around my waist. Words failed to rescue me, not that he would have listened.

A scream had worked its way up through my throat, but when I opened my mouth, I was freed from my attacker. I stumbled back, clutching at my chest, only to see Flynn holding the man's wrist with one hand and his foot on his chest, pushing him down against the gravel. I was sure I would remember the words he spoke until the day I died.

'Lest you think it is acceptable to touch a woman without her consent again.'

The words were followed by a resounding snap as he twisted the drunkard's wrist. I had never enjoyed the sound of suffering more. It should have been enough for me to run home to my safe bed, but as the drunkard scurried away, cradling his arm, I felt something foreign tug at my soul. I still didn't know what it was, but I often wonder if it was borne of self-sabotage because when Flynn offered me his hand and a drink, I didn't say no. I just hadn't known who he was yet, but that was one of my great unanswered questions: would I have said yes if I had known?

A deep sigh blew from him as he set down his quill and ran a hand over his face before rubbing at his temples. The flickering light of the sconces around the room cast shadows over him, but there was no hiding the lines beneath his eyes. A string of guilt ran through me at occupying his bed again. Likely he hadn't had a decent sleep in days.

I knew I should say something. It wasn't fair to be watching him while he thought me asleep, but it felt like a crime to break this spell. It was a window into a man I was certain very few knew. I'd shared an intimacy I never shared with anyone, and yet I didn't know anything about him. I supposed that had been the goal at the time.

His eyes snapped up to where I lay cuddled beneath quilted blankets. For an instant, I closed my eyes as if that would save me from being caught before I realized that was ridiculous. I was a grown woman, and I certainly didn't put myself here.

Flynn leaned back in his chair and took a long breath.

"You're awake," he said.

"Apparently," I answered, unsure what I was supposed to do.

Why was this awkward? I had woken up twice in a far more compromising position with him, but somehow, this felt strained when that hadn't.

"How do you feel?" he asked.

The creek of the ship's movement was loud against the silence between us. Again, I was reminded of what a ridiculous plan this had all been. That I had been impulsive and rash. Had I known six months ago, when I sent that letter I would end up on his ship in his bed, I would have thought twice.

"Alive," I said.

That earned me a snort of laughter from him, which elicited a thrill that ran through my chest. I enjoyed that sound more than I should have. Slowly, I pushed up on my hands, trying to sit up, but my head swam with the movement, and I slid back down, groaning.

"Here, take this. Emille said it would help with the headache," he said, bringing a glass with clear liquid.

"The Frenchman? He's a medic?" I asked.

"I see you've been awake and failed to say so," he said.

Setting the glass on the table next to the bed, he ever so gently helped me sit up. While my head still danced with the movement, it wasn't as bad as the first attempt. When he was sure I wasn't going to fall over, he released me and handed me the glass.

"What is it?" I asked.

He bit the inside of his cheek, debating as he assessed me. His beard was a little longer than two days ago and now that he was closer there was exhaustion painted into the lines around his eyes. That was definitely guilt that burrowed inside of me.

"Emille was a doctor in Paris before coming to the Wraith. I learned not to question his methods, but I can tell you that I would take whatever he handed me without hesitation," he said.

"I can't imagine many doctors turn to piracy so it seems unwise of you not to question him," I said as I swirled the glass watching the murky white liquid.

"He is a good man," Flynn said, half to himself.

He squinted his eyes, and his jaw tightened as if he were remembering something painful. I knew better than to ask, but it was absurdly hard not to.

"You haven't slept," I said instead.

Another sigh fell from his lips as his eyes ran over me, assessing. I didn't flinch beneath his gaze. He had seen all of me anyway.

"Take the medicine, Rose," he said.

"I thought it was Miss Smith," I answered.

"Not in here." He pinched his eyebrows, lowering his voice. "Please take the medicine."

Ever since I was younger when someone would give me a direct order I would feel an uncanny need to do exactly the opposite. One governess said it was the devil in me though I doubted that. My mother just called it one of my quirks. That very same urge bubbled up, but it warred with the guilt I felt for his sleeplessness. Just this once perhaps.

I lifted the glass to my lips and winced at the peppermint that filled my mouth. Oh god, I hated peppermint. I winced as nausea ran through me. Absolutely not. I was not throwing up in front of him. I swallowed down the hateful liquid and thanked the powers that be when the glass was replaced with a new one filled with water. Tears pricked my eyes with the effort of not vomiting. The water did its best to wash away the peppermint, but it lingered all the same.

"That was horrendous," I breathed out, handing him the glass. "Maybe you shouldn't trust the French pirate doctor after all."

He chuckled as he walked away. Whatever tension had been abated returned tenfold. What were you supposed to say to someone who was meant to be a rebellious one night of exploration when you somehow, a year later, ended up on their pirate ship and in their bed? There was no etiquette protocol to guide me. No amount of head tilts and listening poses would cross the divide between us.

I wiped at my tear-stained cheeks, feeling like my entire body was too big and an inconvenience. What was I supposed to do with my hands? Did I stay under the covers, or was it weirder to get out of bed? Also, where would I go?

In fact, I had enough questions that I failed to realize I was not in the dress I came with. Instead, I was in a hideous white nightgown that had far too many frills than were practical. Oh, god, there were even frills around the neck. My cheeks bloomed with heat as it occurred to me that I had not dressed myself in this atrocity that smelled like it had laid dormant in a chest for a hundred years.

I lifted my eyes to find Flynn walking towards me with a plate.

"Who—" I tried for the words and came up short.

"Inu, though I have never heard so much complaint from her. She is usually exceptionally quiet. As for the origin of the... gown, I sent Billy to find you some suitable clothes before we sailed. In hindsight, he was probably a poor choice for that particular job," he said.

"This is payback for the oar," I said.

A huff of laughter. "No, Billy doesn't have a malicious bone in his body. I believe he felt it was a 'fine lady's dress,' and when the woman who sold it to him said it was from the queen's own wardrobe, he thought the ten shillings was quite the steal."

Despite my horror at being in a hundred-year-old gown, I laughed and appreciated when the swimming in my head abated. Maybe the good doctor wasn't such a failure after all.

I lifted my head to tell him exactly that, but his smile had fallen, and he was staring at me like I had three heads. I reached up to feel my face, sure that I had drooled, or, honestly, who knew.

"What?" I asked.

He shook his head as if waking from a daze. "Nothing, I just missed that sound."

My chest swelled with something foreign and unwelcome. My body remembering feelings better off dead and buried. It was hard to know what to say to that. Part of me wanted to tell him he couldn't say those things. That he lost the right the moment, he said yes to Oscar while I lay upstairs blissfully unaware of their treachery.

"I'm sorry," he said. "Emille said that you should eat when you woke up."

He held out a plate full of crackers and yellow cheese. I expected nausea, but instead my stomach grumbled with its opinion on the matter.

I wrinkled my nose. "I can't eat by myself."

His smile was more hesitant this time. "I remember."

As if it were nothing, he sat at the edge of the bed and placed the plate between us before picking up a cracker and taking a bite. It wasn't nothing, though. Ever since I could remember, I could never eat if someone else was in the room and not eating. I had absolutely no idea why, but my family never made me feel badly about it and neither had he when I confessed that first night. It had been one of the first things that cemented my reckless decision to be with him since it was so unlike James.

James, who had teased me and said that my family indulged my strangeness too often. That when we married, I would learn to get over my strange idioms. He would also follow up with how I was unlike any other woman, and he was lucky I chose him. Words that were meant to make me feel loved and special, but instead left me wondering why I couldn't be like those other women.

I might never forgive Flynn for what he had done, but I recognized a peace offering when I saw one. I reached for a piece of cheese and closed my eyes when it hit my tongue exploding in a richness of flavors. It was a dense and hard texture, but was unlike anything I had ever tasted. Rich yet tangy and bold with a nutty aftertaste.

"What is that?" I asked, covering my mouth.

His chuckle was hoarse. "It's from Italy. They call it Parmesan."

"I love it," I said, scooping up another piece.

"Sometimes it's unnerving how much you and your brother understand each other. When he first had it, he said you would lose your mind over it."

I had never heard something so bittersweet. I had never known grief like the way I grieved last year. That he was still alive and thinking of me made it feel strange and almost compromised. Like it wasn't valid.

Silence stretched between us as I tried to wrap my mind around the life my brother lived while I mourned him. Like anything that caused pain to lodge in my chest, I pushed it away. Discomfort was not something I handled well.

"A truth for a lie?" I asked.

I really enjoyed the way his lips curled up and the flash of his eyes that called it a fond memory. It quickly replaced the unease in me with a set of butterflies I had long since banished.

He held out his hand, "Ladies first."

I bit my lip to keep from smiling.

"I had never seen a mysterious creature before yesterday," I said, remembering the way the Kelpie met my eyes with intelligence.

Flynn nodded slowly as he took another bite of his cracker.

"The first time I saw a Kelpie, I thought they were the most beautiful creatures I had ever seen," he said.

This was the difficulty of the game that I had invented the first night we spent together.

We were both running from something and searching for relief which meant the deal was no one asked too many questions beginning with who we were. Except curiosity had always been one of my weaknesses, and Flynn was a dichotomy that fascinated me, which is how a truth for a lie came about.

One of us would say something, and if the other thought it was a truth, we would offer back a lie. There was no way to know what was true and what wasn't. A way to give small pieces of ourselves without the commitment.

It was hard to imagine him falling for the kelpie's tricks, which meant he saw the truth I confessed. That or there was a version of him that had once been naive. It was impossible to imagine this before he was Captain Flynn.

"Your turn," I said.

He hummed in answer, eyes searching the ceiling for his lie or truth. With his head tilted up, the beat of his heart was evident in his neck and the memory of my lips over that spot came back full force. It was a pulling deep inside me telling me I wanted more, but my body had never been good about knowing what I needed. *That had been a one-time thing* I reminded myself *he is your captor now.*

Exactly. I needed to remember that I wasn't on this ship as a guest, but a hostage. The thrum of my heart didn't seem to catch on, which only added credibility to my theory that my body was unreliable.

"I suspect the daughter of the mogul of shipping has very little knowledge of the mysterious deep and the creatures that lurk within her," he said, tilting his head.

Well, then. Waving my finger at him, I covered my mouth to hide the cracker I had just stuffed in there and said, "That's a question!"

The Captain of the Sea Wraith rolled his eyes and grabbed my waving finger, pulling it down between us. His touch sent a thrill through me that had no business existing. *Hostage.* His hand lingered on mine longer than it should, as if he were reminding himself the same thing.

Our eyes lingered on each other as I repeated the word in my head. *Hostage. Hostage. Hostage.*

He clicked his tongue and rubbed at his chest, the movement mesmerizing to my unstable mind.

"Fine. One question for two truths. That's the stipulation, correct?"

I nodded because words were hard.

"Very well. How much do you know of the mysterious deep?" he asked.

I swallowed down the rest of the cracker and prepared myself for the incoming judgment.

"Less than I probably should? I know a little bit. It just never fascinated me the way it did Oscar. My family has always been quick to tell me I am fickle and stubborn. If something doesn't interest me, it's like pulling my own teeth out to endure it. So, yes, my knowledge is limited, which is unfortunate considering you are holding me captive on a ship in the middle of the Atlantic Ocean."

He tilted his head, eyes roaming over me as if I were a puzzle.

"You are fascinating," he said.

"Ah, yes, just what every woman wants to hear," I rolled my eyes.

He chuckled. "What does interest you then?"

"Depends on the day. For a time, I was a very avid gardener. I grew a pathos that had vines two feet long. Then I woke up one day, and it no longer thrilled me. Then there was the piano. I was determined to be the most accomplished pianist. All I could think about was when I could next play. Then, as always happens, the notes didn't bring me joy like they used to. I've dabbled in crochet, pottery, reading, and most things a lady should be interested in. They all eventually lose their sparkle. It is the best feeling, though, when I find a new interest. It's like falling in love, consuming and intoxicating, but just like with love, it fades, and you can't remember why you ever loved it in the first place," I said.

Though I tried very hard not to think of James, the words were as good as a calling card for memories of him. At that moment, I realized I cared more about him than just an acquaintance. Lingering looks, long sighs, small touches. He was all I could think about and occupied all my waking thoughts, lost in daydreams of imagined futures. I could hardly eat or sleep because of the way my heart beat. I had been living for the hope of it all, and it was beautiful. Then it ended.

"I confess I am not an authority on the matter, but from what I know of love, it's not supposed to feel like that," he said gently.

I was well acquainted with the hurt and the sourness in my stomach that accompanied love. First James and then Oscar. Love brought pain. I may have been young and naive, but I knew enough of the world to know that was a universal truth.

The urge to tell him he knew nothing of love was strong, but my broken spirit felt like that was too much effort.

"You owe me four truths now," I said instead.

Silence stretched and I could practically feel the words he was holding onto, debating. Had I more energy, I would have begged him not to.

Finally, he lifted up four fingers and began ticking them off.

"I was deathly afraid of the dark as a child until I was twelve years old. I put an ungodly amount of sugar in my tea. I like cats better than dogs. Lastly, I am alarmingly good-looking."

The snort that ripped from me was involuntary but it lightened something in my chest all the same. I snatched up a piece of cheese and waved it in his face.

"That last one shouldn't count," I said, taking a bite.

He raised his eyebrows. "Why? Because it isn't true?"

"Your nose is slightly crooked," I said.

His laugh came from his chest and had that deep rasp that was so perfectly him. It sent a thrill through me, which was inconvenient at the very least. I spent the last year hating him for taking Oscar, but now here I was losing myself over a laugh. Once, when we were teenagers, I took Oliver's side over Oscar's, which was rare. However, Oscar had stolen the last macaroon that Oliver had been saving. When I spoke out in Oscar's defense, Oliver told me that I never did have the courage of my convictions.

Words casually thrown around over something as trivial as dessert had imprinted themselves on my very soul. They followed me everywhere I went no matter the efforts I went to banish them. I tried to devote myself and find something I believed in enough that I was concrete in that fervor, but always I swayed.

Just like right

now. An entire year devoted to hating this man, this pirate, and here I was, practically swooning.

"Ah, yes. There is a story for that, and all it costs is two truths," he said, winking at me like a cad.

"Too steep a bargain," I said.

He nodded his head. "Truth is our greatest commodity."

I didn't know if it was true, but it felt true. All at once it crashed over me like a wave, lost. I was lost in the middle of the sea. Adrift. All I could hope for was that I crashed upon an island or someone saved me. It was a sinking feeling that dragged my stomach down into its depths. I had felt something similar most of my life, but never like this. It felt an awful lot like hopelessness.

"Is it your head? This was too much. I'll go get Emille," Flynn said, standing abruptly.

I shook my head, but he was already gone on his quest. The prince off to find the broken maiden help. Except, he was a notorious pirate captain and I wasn't an innocent damsel in distress though the distress part was accurate enough.

I sank back against the pillows and closed my eyes, fighting back the stinging in my eyes. What a mess.

Chapter Thirteen
Eye on the Prize

Grindylow are creatures native to the water surrounding Great Britain first discovered in 1608 by Robert Hayes, who is credited as being the Father of Mysteriology. Though the creatures long plagued the shores near their habitats, lurking in the shadows and grabbing those who wandered too close to the water, their official name and most complete rendering was done in 1608.

–An excerpt from The Mysterious Deep: A Comprehensive Understanding

I was now morally and ethically opposed to Parisian doctors masquerading as pirates. Emille was an older man in his late fifties with a salt-and-pepper beard, dark skin, and a bald head. He was also alarmingly nice, reminding me of a kindly grandfather, except for the part where he kept making me drink horrible things every six hours.

"I am fully recovered, thank you. There is no need for your devil juice," I said.

"Miss Smith, you run the risk of confusion, dizziness, and even memory loss after a concussion like the one you suffered. This is to help avoid those consequences and not a punishment," he said with an infinite amount of patience.

"Feels like a punishment," I muttered. "So does this dress."

It was at least a hundred years old and with even more frills than the night dress, not to mention that it was an ungodly bright pink. As soon as I got out of this hostage situation, I was going to have a talk with old Billy. Either he had absolutely no taste in fashion, or these were punishment for hitting him in the stomach with an oar.

Maybe I was getting paranoid. However, given my distinct lack of interactions with pirates, it was hard to tell.

Four days at sea. One attack by a mysterious creature. One concussion. Given that we had a two-month journey ahead of us, that seemed like a poor start.

How was I going to survive two months at sea pretending to be a hostage who didn't have a brother as a quartermaster and a—whatever the Captain was? Especially with an ancient wardrobe. I could appreciate that no one on the ship had any appreciation for appropriate attire, however I did. Tonight was the Gardener Ball back home, and I was going to wear a beautiful deep green that reminded me of forests far from oceans.

Not for the first time, I wondered what my family would say about my absence. Likely the lie that I was off visiting Oscar in Paris while he pursued his love of the arts. A lie that would only hold out for so long. Hopefully, six months long.

"Miss Smith," Emille said while making uncomfortable eye contact. "Do I need to get the Captain again?"

Damn pirate doctor Frenchman. I snatched the vial and downed it while trying to suppress my gag reflex. Oh god, it was terrible. Why peppermint? It coated my throat like an ill-begotten frost. I quickly exchanged the glass for one filled with water, letting it wash away the vile liquid.

Emille patted me on the back gently.

"Well done, now it's time to get you some fresh air," he said.

"In this?" I asked, holding out the pink skirt that made my skin itch.

He shrugged, which I supposed meant yes.

I huffed out a long breath and stalked toward the door. So be it. The sun was an oppressive force, accosting me at the first opportunity. Raising my arm, I shielded my eyes as they adjusted slowly. Eventually, black spots gave way to functioning vision. The ship was filled with pirates doing things pirates did, which was still unclear because I hadn't the slight idea what that entailed.

"At least once around the deck," Emille said, behind me.

"Are all physicians bossy in France, or is it just the pirate ones?" I asked.

He laughed behind me. "Only the good ones."

I wrinkled my nose thinking I could argue that point, but it probably wasn't worth it. The waves of the sea crashed against us, threatening my unsteady feet. For the barest of moments, the Kelpie's gnashing, rotted teeth flashed before me, but I pushed it away, refusing to dwell.

I took a few steps forward, Emille coming to my side with an arm lightly pressed behind my back as if I were bound to fall at any time like some ancient grandmother. However, it was the other shadow to my right that followed with every step that concerned me.

As soon as my boot touched the deck, the shadow moved with me. I whirled around, which was far too fast for a recent concussion. My head swirled, making the blue sky, the ship, and the menacing figure before me mix in an unholy transformation. I waved away the good doctor who steadied me.

"Why are you following me?" I asked.

"You are the god's punishment for thinking myself wise enough to choose a destiny they did not design for me," Inu said, her eyes glaring at me beneath her hat.

She really was striking and unlike anyone I had ever seen. Her black hair was the color of ink that sometimes shone with blue against the sunlight. Her warm brown eyes reminded me of almonds, perfectly symmetrical, but it was her stare that was most captivating. A wisdom and ancientness that could not be tamed.

I didn't like it.

"As much as I would enjoy being responsible for all that, even I have limits. Why are you following me?"

A barely perceptible sigh. "I have already explained. To do so again would be a waste of my time."

"Captain asked that Inu watch over you to avoid any other injuries," Emille explained like a normal person.

"Ordered," Inu corrected.

"Which I think we can both appreciate is a compliment of the highest kind. Those pardons will mean a lot to the people on this crew. Especially our quartermaster, who I know you are fond of," Emille said with the same tone my father used to use when I was ungrateful.

Apparently, that tone was a well-placed weapon because just as it used to make me feel two feet tall, Inu pursed her lips and gestured for me to continue. While I knew that Inu was well aware of who I was, I didn't appreciate the idea of having a shadow.

"There is no world where I get a say in this, is there?" I asked, squinting my eyes.

"No," Inu and Emille answered as one.

"Excellent," I said, continuing on my mandatory stroll about the garden.

Pirates lined the side of the ship every few feet staring off into the sea which was not what I thought of when I thought of pirates. I supposed it was a nice view. Though it was mostly a lot of blue. Endless blue ocean beneath an endless blue sky. Blue, blue, blue. Green was a more preferable color.

As we made it toward the front of the ship, I heard distinct laughter. Just who I was looking for.

"That one neva seen it comin', aye?" Billy cajoled.

"Billy!" I growled, making my way to where he leaned over the edge of the ship.

He turned around, and his surprise faded to a bright grin showcasing his poor dental hygiene as he held a long pole in his hands. His eyes ran over my dress, and he leaned against the rail with undiluted self-satisfaction.

"Aye, Hellcat, that dress be lookin' good on ya," he said.

"Good? I've never seen so many ruffles in my life," I said, holding up my skirts as evidence.

"Aye, that's exactly what I said and why I paid the extra shillings. I said the Hellcat is a fancy lady, and she'll be needing fancy clothes."

"This is not—" I began.

"Billy, ya got one coming up," someone to the right shouted.

"Damn bastards. If you don't mind," he said.

Without another word, he turned, lowering his pole along the edge of the ship, and thrust. An indignant squeal that reminded me of trying to talk underwater came from the edge.

"Got 'em," Billy said.

My stomach sank, but my curiosity was greater than my self-preservation. Before Inu or Emille could stop me, I raced to the edge and saw a creature with long arms and legs with webbed digits lunging for the ship. It swam with precision, much like a frog crossing a pond, but when it reached the ship, its webbed hands latched onto the surface with glue-like slime.

My heart sank into my stomach as it turned up its green amphibian-like head and bared its teeth to me. Sharp, pointy little things that I knew would slide right through my bones if they had the chance.

"Aye, he likes ya, Hellcat," Billy laughed.

I couldn't imagine that there was a single thing to laugh about as it scaled the ship with determination. It might have only been two feet, but it was terrifying and unnatural.

"She looks like a lady, but she'll do you in, bugger, best take yer chances with the sea," Billy said.

One of the poles I had seen reached over the edge and smashed into the creature, eliciting the same unnatural squeal I had heard before. The creature raised its sickly green eyes to mine as it was flung into the waves before trying to make its way back.

"Reminds me of you. Neither of you know when to quit," Billy said with a wide smile.

Sure enough, the creature was making its way back, and I could have sworn its eyes were still on me even as the waves crashed against it. Like it had seen me, and it wouldn't rest until it had its fill.

James would have called me self-absorbed for the thought, reminding me I wasn't the only person in the world and that it only felt like that because I was spoiled. Of course, he would laugh and say that I was perfect nonetheless. I never saw those compliments for what they were until someone new came and it felt different when he said it. No jab at my character soothed with a nicety. The bitterest of teas served like they were gifts.

If I dwelled too long on it, I would consider that I would have to be guilty of the things he accused me of to not see it sooner.

"I would recommend not running to view every creature we come across, Miss Smith. Some of them are good jumpers," Emille said, gently pulling me back from the edge. "Inu, I am fairly sure your job description includes preventing such occurrences."

I turned to see Inu standing with a hand casually resting on the pistol at her side with her lips pressed into a thin line.

"She is like a child eager to walk when they cannot even crawl," Inu said.

I was sure I had never been so insulted in my life with her dry tone carrying the words so all nearby could hear. I felt the flush in my cheeks and hated the heat of embarrassment that coated my body.

Spoiled. Selfish. Immature.

"Nah, that's called courage," Billy's voice cut into James' voice, cutting my mind. "Hellcat has it in bucketfuls."

And just like that, James' voice dissipated into the back recesses of my mind. Castaway by a pirate with poor dental hygiene. It was improbable. It was a relief.

"What was that?" I asked.

"A grindylow, persistent creatures, though we are almost out of their territory," Emille said.

I knew of the small beings that had vice-like grips that dragged their prey into the watery depths. I scanned the deck and realized all the pirates I had passed before were similarly prying the grindylows off the ship. With a little more caution this time, I leaned over the edge and all down the line of the ship, grindylow swam for the ship and made to scale the side only to be pushed back into the sea by an iron rod.

"Why don't they give up?" I asked.

"It ain't in 'em," Billy said. "Shoulda nicknamed you afta them, but yer too pretty."

He laughed at his own joke, but it didn't irritate me like it did before.

"Why are you nice to me? I whacked you with an oar," I said.

"Aye, ya did, and I ain't likely to forget it," he said, with more laughter.

The pirate next to Billy laughed and shook their head. "I don't think the captain would appreciate you chasing after his pet."

My body stiffened beneath a mountain of lace frills. The echoing laughter of nearby pirates filled my ears, roaring their mocking's. Pet.

"You don't know half as much as ya think ya do, Amos Jones," Billy sneered.

"Oh, please, we all know you are the Captain's pet dog, too," the pirate said, turning to face me.

He wasn't like I had always imagined a pirate to be. In a loose white blouse, his blond hair was sun-kissed with steaks of gold, and his clean-shaven face boasted the bluest of eyes. If it weren't for the tattoo glinting over his chest, he might have belonged in London society. His smile held the same judgment and disdain I had seen a thousand times over as he looked me up and down.

"Why else would he give orders that no one is to touch her and then keep her locked up in his cabin? I thought this was an *equal* crew. Not even the captain took more than what we agreed upon in our articles. Doesn't seem fair to me."

I didn't know whether his disdain was for me or his Captain, but every word dripped with the sentiment. I felt a chill run over my body. Not once did I consider that being trapped on a ship with pirates would be... dangerous for me in that way. Whether it was because I knew that Flynn would never or because Oscar was here, it didn't matter. I should have considered it earlier.

Story of my life. Constantly unaware and running headfirst where I had no business being. Over the last year since I learned of James' infidelity, I'd begun to see all my faults in glaring color. Even the ones I was already well acquainted with were more insistent in their demand to be noticed. Somedays, I avoided the mirror because I couldn't see past my imperfections. My nose turned up slightly, which James used to tease me for, saying it was like a little button nose. At the time, I had thought it was endearing, but all I saw now was how childish it made me seem. The scattering of freckles only on the bridge of my nose. All I could see in my reflection was the lack of porcelain skin that likely would have kept him faithful.

I had never minded my impulsivity before. Now, I knew it had put me in a danger that was of my own making. Pirates, despite the few who were reasonable, were liars, cheats, and murderers. Thieving their way beneath the law, they were beholden to no one.

I took a step backward. "You will not touch me."

There was more strength behind the words than I would have thought me capable of. Maybe they were borne out of an exhaustion in my soul or from fear, either way I was glad they were mine.

I took another step back while on either side of me, Emille and Inu stepped forward, blocking me in. Emille had his hand firmly wrapped around the hilt of his sword at his side while Inu had taken her pistol out, holding it firmly between her hands.

"If you have a problem with the Captain's orders, take it up with the quartermaster," Emille said.

The blond man gave a bitter laugh and spit at Emille's feet. "Another one of his dogs."

The click of a pistol had my blood roaring with an unsteady rhythm. Billy lifted his pistol and pointed it right at the blond man's temple, who went unnaturally still, his arrogance melting away like ice beneath the summer sun.

"Sounds like you're on the wrong crew, friend. You see, here on the Wraith, we don't tolerate mutiny, which is an awful lot what you are sounding like," Billy said.

All his good-natured laughter was gone, and for the first time since meeting him, I saw him for what he was. A pirate. There was not a doubt in my mind that he would not pull that trigger if so provoked. In fact, many of the crew nearby had a hand on their pistols while their attention was all on the blond man.

"Easy, easy." A mirror image of the blond man spoke, coming to stand by his side.

"Get your brother in line, Charlie, or make your peace with him being grindylow food," Billy said.

Charlie held up his hands as he edged closer, his jaw tight, but a plastered smile speaking false confidence. The urge to backup and flee was a scattering of pricks down my legs, but it was hard to imagine I was safer than beside Emille and Inu, who had stepped in without a second thought. There was an emotion there, but I couldn't name it. It was hard to analyze my emotions when a gun was pointed at a man's temple.

"Aye, Billy, I hear you. It's Amos' first time on a crew. I'll get him in line."

When Billy didn't lower the pistol, Charlie edged in front of his brother a little closer, eyes locked with Billy.

"I swear it," he said.

Drops of sweat dripped down Amos' face despite the cool breeze rippling clothes and hair all around us. Some dark part of me, long suppressed beneath Sunday masses and Christian well-wishes, smirked at every moment he saw his life hang in the balance. I didn't know what that said about me, but my heart was beating too fast to question it.

Billy eyed Amos like a venomous snake. It occurred to me then that he had pronounced every word painfully clear since holding up his pistol.

"Billy, you know me; I've never caused a single problem on this crew and have given just as much to be here," Charlie said.

"It isn't you I've got a problem with," Billy said.

"I can—"

His words were cut off by a grindylow crawling over the side of the ship. I stared in horror as its beady eyes met mine and it lunged with malice in its eyes while his sharp teeth went right for Emille and Inu.

A burst of gunpowder rang in my ears, blocking out my scream. I clutched my ears, ducking, but when I opened my eyes, Inu and Emille had stepped apart, and the grindylow lay twitching in a pool of neon green blood. Its eyes were glassy but focused on me. I crawled backward, desperate to get away from the creature, as it made a gasping, nearly croaking sound.

"Is there a problem here?" Flynn's raspy voice was punctuated by a murderous edge.

Hands gently pulled me up, but the zapping and pulsing of my blood only knew that I didn't want to be touched. I squirmed and swatted my attacker away, my breath coming too fast.

"It's just me, Miss Smith, let me help you. You are safe." My brother's voice.

The voice that had lulled me back to sleep after nightmares and held my deepest secrets. Safe. It was hard to argue with that word when it came from him. From anyone else, it would have been a pretty lie.

Slowly, I nodded, and he helped me to my feet. Placing a hand around my shoulder, he pulled me into him. To anyone watching, it would seem like he was supporting me, but this close, I could feel the pump of his heart. He was scared.

"No, Captain, my brother just got carried away," Charlie said.

I turned my head to see Flynn standing with his smoking pistol at his side. He reached into his pocket and pulled out a small ball, sticking it between his teeth as he opened up his pistol and removed the ball from his mouth, meticulously placing it inside his gun. The sound of it clicking into place was loud against the sea's waves.

"Let me tell you what I see, Mr. Clark. Your brother must have gotten more than carried away to end up with Billy holding a pistol to his head, but more than that is the fact that his being *carried away* allowed a grindylow onto my ship and nearly cost me the hostage that is vital to this job's success. Do you see how that could be a problem for me?"

Billy's eyes and gun were still locked on Amos. Inu and Emille had stepped to the side where every member of the crew who wasn't currently warding off grindylows was watching the scene unfold. The sound of breath shuddering beneath water dragged my attention down to where the injured grindylow's chest rose and then went impossibly still. My skin crawled as I realized its eyes were locked on me despite my having stood up as if it had tracked me with its final breath.

I pressed closer into Oscar, who tightened his grip on my shoulder.

"Yes, Captain, it won't happen again," Charlie promised.

Flynn's eyes flicked to Amos as Billy lowered his pistol and stepped back.

"Is that so, Mr. Clark?" Flynn asked.

Amos' mouth opened and shut as if it were too dry to speak. Moments ago, that dark part of me might have enjoyed his struggle for words after what he suggested sharing me, but my entire body was alight with energy that was desperate to escape.

"Y-es, Ca-ptain," Amos stuttered.

Flynn ran his hand over his pistol, considering.

"Good," Flynn said, holstering his gun. "If there is even a whisper of trouble from you on my ship again, Mr. Clark, you will find yourself at the bottom of the sea. Do I make myself clear?"

"Yes, Captain," he said, swallowing.

"Then I suggest you get back to work. If another grindylow makes it onto this ship, you will be swabbing the deck for the remainder of the voyage," Flynn said.

"Thank you, Captain," Charlie said before leaning in and whispering something to his brother that looked like a sharp reprimand. As if nothing happened, everyone resumed their places, including Billy.

I watched as Amos whispered something back to his brother before returning to his station. As Amos turned, his eyes met mine, and it chilled my blood as much as the grindylow had. The urge to edge closer to my brother was loud in my mind, but I wasn't prepared to add to any remaining discourse about who I was.

"Inu, quartermaster, with me," Flynn said, turning on his heels.

Apparently that list included me as Oscar failed to remove his arm from my shoulder and ushered me along. He ignored the sharp eyes Inu cast on him. Careening my head back, I took in the dead grindylow once more, its lifeless eyes still on me no matter how I moved. Paranoia. Two pirates came and grabbed its arms and legs before heaving it into the sea for its brothers and sisters as a warning.

I doubted creatures of the deep heeded such warnings.

"You're all right," Oscar whispered.

It was the prettiest of lies. I was the epitome of unsafe. Aboard a pirate vessel in the middle of a sea full of creatures that longed to kill us. If the pirates like Amos didn't get me, then the sea would. It felt like a knowing deep in my bones. A fate long ago written by forces unknown.

James would have called me dramatic. Prone to fits of fancy. For once, I hoped he was right.

We passed beneath masts with white sails that bulged with the wind that pushed us along, further from land and ever closer to the Glass Sea. Ropes were seemingly everywhere, but I suspected each had its own purpose. I never really considered how much went into a ship of this size, but it was far more organized than I might have thought. Everyone had a job, and it took many hands to see it through.

We walked the entire length of the ship until we were at the opposite side, the stern, if I recalled correctly. Had I known I would be trapped on a ship for two months, I might have put more effort into learning about them. Probably not, though.

As it was with the front, pirates shoved persistent grindylow off the ship, but Flynn ignored them as he walked to a woman with long red hair beneath a wide-brimmed hat. Like she had been expecting him, she held out the spyglass she had been using to him. He took it and brought it to his eye, shoulders tense.

"Has it gotten any closer?" he asked.

"No, it's maintaining its distance so far. Strange behavior for a Cirein-cròin," the woman said.

"What's a Cirein-cròin?" I asked.

Some of the pirates nearby laughed, but Flynn turned, holding out the spyglass to me. I stepped away from Oscar, immediately missing the warmth of him, and past Inu who glared at me like she wished the grindylow would have finished me off. I ignored her, taking the spyglass just as I ignored the brush of his fingertips over my hand.

With surprisingly steady hands, I lifted the glass to my eyes and searched the endless blue sea. Nothing but white-tipped waves rose and fell.

"Over here," Flynn said into my ear as he adjusted the spyglass right and up.

There was no telling whether the shiver that ran through me was because of him or the blue-scaled creature dipping and rising with every wave. It was large. Too large to be rational, but here it was, existing. Its scales shimmered with each touch of sunlight. Its lithe body narrow like a snake. Giant fan-like fins lined its back, bluish-green as if it couldn't decide what it wanted to be.

"This is what most people would refer to as a sea serpent, but that's the same as calling every four-legged animal a horse." The woman spoke beside me. "They are each unique to the waters they inhabit, each with their own behavior, diet, even their very biology is different. This one is a Cirein-cròin. Usually, they are reclusive and stay in the sea near the Scottish border. Myths say it can shapeshift at will, but I have yet to hear of a case documented by more than just fishermen with big imaginations. In reality, little is known about them because they are reclusive, primarily hiding in underwater caves. What sightings there have been are short-lived because Cirein-cròin usually dive deep when ships draw near. Only once has there been an attack by one, but it was provoked. They hunted it, thinking it would make a good prize, but the Cirein-cròin broke apart the ship with one bite down the middle. That was ten years ago."

I lowered the spyglass and stared at the woman next to me, who stared out to the sea as if she could see the Cirein-cròin from here. Pale blue eyes and freckles every which way. She had round cheeks and her lips were permanently fixed in a smile that pulled up the right side. Like she knew something no one else did.

"Miss Smith, this is Cordelia Shaw, our very knowledgeable and irreplaceable myste-riologist," Flynn said.

There was an unmistakable lilt to the words that scraped against my skin wrong. A tone that I didn't quite appreciate.

"You can call me Dilly," she said.

I eyed the hand she held out to me before conceding that she hadn't wronged me and I had no reason to dislike her. Her smile was bright, like the insult of hesitation didn't exist.

"Then it will leave us alone?" I asked, remembering the giant creature following us.

She bit her lip and tilted her head, arguing in her own head.

"I honestly can't say. I've never heard of one coming this far out to sea. I've certainly never heard of one trailing a ship," she said.

"Which is why we are keeping a close eye on it," Flynn said. "But also why what happened earlier cannot be a recurring event. We can't afford to lose focus when threats lie close by. Inu, that grindylow should never have made it off the ledge of the ship."

Inu dipped her head, "My attention was on the immediate threat."

It wasn't an excuse, but an admission. Despite her determination to dislike me, she didn't relish the danger I had just been in.

Flynn and Inu exchanged a silent conversation that left me feeling out of place more than I already was. No one else noticed as Dilly went back to watching her Cirein-cròin, and Oscar watched Inu with an intensity, unlike my brother. Oscar never took anything seriously, but the way he watched her made my stomach sink. It reminded me an awful lot of the way Ruby looked at her husband and him at her. A love match.

"Dilly, I would appreciate it if you might spend some time briefing Miss Smith on what she might expect on our current course when there is time," Flynn said.

The use of the ridiculous name only irritated my skin more, a burning sensation that lingered too long.

"Of course, Captain," she answered with a bright smile in my direction.

Her easygoing manner was an insult to injury as far as my mind was concerned, even if it wasn't rational.

"Excellent," Flynn said.

I could feel his eyes on me, assessing, but I didn't give in to the urge to look at him. Instead, I followed Dilly's idea and searched the sea for distant sea monsters.

"Would you like to see it again? I can explain its arches and scales more. It's actually really interesting," Dilly said.

I nodded, because staring at monsters that could capsize an entire ship in one bite was less intimidating than addressing Flynn's attention. I raised the spyglass she offered to my eye and breathed a sigh of relief as the Cirein-cròin came into focus and Flynn's heavy boots retreated behind me.

Chapter Fourteen
See

Grindylows are known for long, spindly ligaments, webbed toes, and sickly green eyes that match their amphibian-like bodies. They also boast razor-sharp teeth that are able to cut through bone. They are able to emit a slimy green-like substance from their bodies that allows them to scale ships with ease. While they are not communal creatures, they tend to swarm and attack in droves. It is doubtful that this is a strategic maneuver, but more likely, they are drawn to life and attack of their own volition. Their territory extends about ten nautical miles out from the shore and lasts for about five more nautical miles. There have never been sightings outside of their known habitat. It is hypothesized they live amid the seaweed beds only the sand, but no confirmation of this has been made.

–An excerpt from The Mysterious Deep: A Comprehensive Understanding

The worst thing is being determined to dislike someone, and they slowly disarm you until you are forced to begrudgingly admit they might be all right. So it went with Dilly. Her enthusiasm and bright smile brought life to textbooks and long-winded journals. I had never been able to focus long enough on them to gain anything more than that the ocean was a scary place and only monster-hunting pirates, and bored aristocrats would ever traverse them.

Dilly's passion and patience painted an entire new picture and I was captivated by it. A world undiscovered with untold questions. So little was known about the creatures of the mysterious deep because those who encountered them had little interest in learning about them. I learned that Dilly's father was a pirate on another crew, and when he would come back to their home on Corpse Cove, he would regale a young Dilly with stories of the deep.

It was love at first story. She studied and learned all she could and found herself a place on a crew until she met Flynn, and he asked her to join the Wraith. I was beginning to wonder if that was what Flynn was good at. Not necessarily at being a pirate, but seeing the value in people. It had only taken a few hours with Oscar for him to see what his charisma and infectious smile were worth. It was a thought I tucked away for later.

"Which is why the Krakens are so feared. As far as we can tell, they only come up to feed, so every encounter is deadly. The question that I always have is what did they eat before ships were an option, most likely large whales like Humpbacks or Blue whales. Then again, there is another school of thought that the ships that meet a Kraken have just unluckily happened upon where one was resting. The oldest thought, was that they were sent by Davy Jones to collect a bounty from someone on board who bore a black dot. Superstition, though you'll find many sailors believe it still, so don't go painting a black dot on your hand unless you want to be thrown overboard." Dilly finished, somehow still with enough air in her lungs to speak.

I waved my hand and gave an awkward smile. "Pretty sure it's bad practice to throw the hostage overboard."

Dilly's round cheeks colored a deep crimson. Her lips pulled down into a frown before her mouth worked silently, trying to find the right words. It was painful to watch.

"It was a joke. It's fine," I said.

It did little to ease her as she finally choked out, "I'm sorry."

I shrugged my shoulders and placed my hands awkwardly behind me.

"It's fine," I repeated. "It hasn't been so bad, minus the almost getting drowned by a Kelpie, getting a concussion, being threatened by an angry pirate, and nearly jumped by a grindylow."

Her eyes brightened as she lifted her head. "I wanted to talk to you about that, actually. I was hoping if you were able you might tell me about your experience with the Kelpie. I heard you were very close to it. The grindylow, too, are opportunistic feeders; by all rights, they should have grabbed the nearest person, so to have bypassed others and lunged at you, that's highly unusual behavior."

What did one say to that? I wasn't sure if I was meant to be flattered or scared. Of course, Dilly didn't seem to notice as she lifted the spyglass to her eyes and checked for the Cirein-cròin. The sun had mostly set and was just a small blip against a pink and orange sky.

"We are losing the day," Dilly murmured.

An eerie shudder ran through me. "How do we track it at night?"

Dilly's lips pulled down into a frown. "We don't."

Excellent. A giant sea monster lurking in the darkness. I would sleep perfectly sound tonight.

"But it's been following us for two days, so more than likely, it won't attack," she said.

"Oh, perfect, I'm sure I won't have nightmares then," I said.

I regretted the sarcasm immediately, thinking I had offended her after she had been nothing but kind to me all day. I remembered how James used to tell me how uncouth it was for a woman of good breeding to attempt being witty only to achieve petulance.

Instead of judgment clouding her big eyes, she threw her head back and laughed, a sound that was chaotic and infectious, settling into my chest where James' words had long reigned.

The first moments of doubt were within the sound of Dilly's laughter. The first sprouting of something new begged the question, what had I ever seen in James when all he saw in me were my flaws and imperfections?

There was a desperation, like hunger, when someone important to you only criticizes and picks you apart. When they finally offer a compliment, it's like the first taste of water after a drought. Intoxicating and enough to sustain you until the next drought ends.

"Come on, might as well go get some food and enjoy ourselves in case the Cirein-cròin decides it wants to eat us," Dilly said, a wicked smile pulling at the corners of her mouth.

My stomach grumbled in answer, loudly conveying the fact that I hadn't eaten except for some forced cheese and crackers by Emille. Which is why when Dilly offered her arm, I didn't hesitate. Whether it was because of my stomach or the way she had single-handedly disarmed me in a matter of hours, I couldn't have said. I just knew that this was a decision that felt easy and not impulsive.

We made it a whole two steps before I remembered my shadow.

"She shouldn't be going below," Inu said.

Apparently, she took her new job seriously since she hadn't been more than four feet away all day. If it weren't for Dilly, I would have been annoyed. While I appreciated having someone to protect me from creatures like grindylows, who were no longer a threat per Dilly, and the lack of pirates warding them off, Inu was what I could only classify as bad company. Her mood was a constant state of irritation mixed with a healthy helping of disdain. Given how smooth her skin was, I doubt she had ever smiled.

What my brother saw in her was an absolute mystery as much as the Cirein-cròin behind us. If I ever managed two minutes alone with him, I might stomach the nausea enough to ask him.

"Is that the Captain's orders?" Dilly asked.

There was no sharpness to the words or insinuation. Like everything Dilly did, the question was genuine. She was an enigma. The daughter of a pirate raised on a lawless and vice-filled island, like Corpse Cove, with a heart of gold. I was raised in luxury and comfort and had never once looked at the world the way Dilly did.

"No, just common sense," Inu said.

As if that were a glowing recommendation, Dilly clapped her hands and beamed, threading her arm through mine and then Inu's on the other side.

"Perfect. Then the three of us have terrible food and rum in our future," Dilly said.

"Terrible food?" I asked.

The cheese and crackers I had last night had been wonderful, but as usual, I didn't stop to wonder what pirates ate while at sea.

"I hope you like salted pork," Dilly said.

If Inu were capable of it, I might have thought there was a sound similar to a groan that emitted from her stone barrier.

"Never had it," I answered.

"How delightful for you," Dilly laughed.

With her two prisoners in tow, Dilly dragged us down below where lanterns were already lit, dangling from the ceiling to illuminate an endless array of white hammocks, most occupied by a pirate eating a bowl with contents that were suspicious to say the least. Brownish-gray and dripping, my stomach did a flip that made me think maybe I wasn't hungry after all.

Turning to the right, Dilly led us to a small room carved into the edge of the ship, where none other than Billy stood in front of a pot of mystery meat that smelled of grease and salt.

"Hellcat! You're in for a real treat," he said, laughing to himself.

I stared in horror as Billy scooped two helpings into a bowl and handed it to me.

"Are you the cook?" I asked.

I took the bowl against my better judgment, which was questionable to begin with.

"Nah. Last cook took a trip down to Davy Jones' locker so I'm filling in till someone else takes the job." He grinned. "Want the job?"

I eyed the contents of the bowl and could have sworn something moved.

"I don't think I'm qualified," I said.

"Ah, that doesn't matter. I ain't either," he said, as he handed Inu and Dilly theirs.

"Thanks, Billy, smells amazing," Dilly raised the bowl to her nose and inhaled like it was roasted chicken with potato.

"Anything for you, Dilly Dally," Billy crooned.

Dilly Dally leaned forward and pressed a kiss to his sun-tanned cheek, leaving the old pirate beaming. I wondered then what it must be like to make everyone feel at ease and valued. As we followed Dilly down the line of hammocks, pirates old and young, scarred and sunburnt, smiled at her. Men and women who murdered and stole for a living were disarmed by a freckled redhead with a loud smile.

"You can take this one. Miguel is on crow's nest duty tonight, and that one is currently uninhabited," Dilly said.

"How do you do that?" I asked.

Dilly stuffed the mystery meat in her mouth and raised her head. "Do what?"

I eyed my dinner, sure I saw something move that time and held it a little further from my body. Inu apparently didn't have reservations either as she delicately ate her food, eyes lowered beneath the brim of her hat.

"You charm people without even trying," I said.

There was nothing calculated about how she interacted with others. No thoughts to remind her that a head tilt here would be perceived as interest, but blinking too much would act as a barrier, giving inattention. It was like she never thought about it at all. She just...was.

She shrugged, stuffing another mouthful. "Who said I don't?"

"See!" I said, pointing at her and looking to Inu to see if she saw it, too. She didn't. "That would be social suicide in London society, but not when you do it. It's somehow... I don't know. It's..." I struggled for the word.

"Organic," Inu said without raising her head from her dinner.

"That's it!" I shouted.

Heads turned and I was acutely aware that I was too loud. Too excited. Taking up too much space.

Except, instead of close headed whispers and discreet glances, the room full of pirates having seen us simply went back to eating, talking, or relaxing. There was no lingering judgment, no reproach from family, no cage.

For the first time since embarking on this scheme, I felt it. The first hint of a want I hadn't even realized existed. Freedom.

My chest filled with the weight of it, unusual and lighter than the load that had previously occupied it. The only problem was that I had never been good with change. I was a creature of habit, as my brother liked to tease me. The same breakfast every day, the same routine, the same books over and over. The novelty of freedom was overwhelming. The urge to flee back to the confines of my cage was how I imagined baby birds felt when they left the nest too soon. Panic forcing their wings into flight. The only options are to fly or fall to their deaths.

I could fly.

"My mum used to say that life was too short to be anything except what you are. I guess that's why she never tried to stop me from learning about the Mysterious Sea. She always encouraged my eccentricities."

There was a hint of sadness to the words. Despite their beauty and their magnitude, the undercurrent of grief was strong.

"I'm sorry for your loss," Inu said, raising her eyes below her hat.

Dilly dipped her head and took a long breath. "Me too. Everything I have achieved I owe to her. She died a year ago, and even with the money she stored away for me, it wasn't enough to keep going. I'm lucky the Captain found me and gave me this job. My other alternatives were... well, I'm just grateful."

"He seems to do that a lot," I grumbled.

Inu shot me a glare that made me feel like I was five years old and just caught sneaking a cookie from the kitchens. Part of me wanted to stick my tongue out at her and tell her I didn't give anything away, nor did I say anything untrue.

"My papa used to say the mark of a good Captain was someone who saw the worth in the people who sailed beneath them. He said the quickest way to end up dead was to sail for a man who treated people like they were expendable," Dilly said.

"That's good advice," Inu said quietly.

Dilly's smile brightened tenfold as she shoved another bite into her mouth.

"Thanks. He always had things like that. Maybe someday I'll write them all down."

"You're supposed to eat that," Inu said, eyes glancing down at my bowl.

"Mmhm. The problem is that I don't know what it is," I said.

"Oh!" Dilly said brightly. "That's the whole point! It means you have no preconceived bias, so you can enjoy the flavors for what they are and not what you *think* they should be."

"I don't think that's the point," Inu said.

"I still have considerable bias," I said.

"I know it's not what you are used to being in society and all that, but at least give it a chance."

I froze my stirring of the mystery meat and felt Inu's rigidness beside me. The worst thoughts crowding my mind and stealing all the peace I had found.

"Oh, sorry, I know that's all meant to be hush, hush, but it's all anyone can talk about. Who is Miss Smith? So far you are a cousin to the king, engaged to the prince, or a daughter of a wealthy businessman. There's even a bet going on for it."

Inu and I shared a glance, and for once, we were on the same page. This was dangerous territory. The last one a little too close to the truth. If they thought long enough about it, they might start asking the wrong questions.

A thousand things popped into my mind, but none of them seemed like they would make it better. So instead, I lifted up my spoon, closed my eyes, and shoved the concoction of meat and grease into my mouth.

My first instinct was to immediately spit it out, but years of etiquette refused to relinquish its hold. So I slowly chewed it, first came the salt which was surprisingly balanced and then a hint of garlic and lemon. The meat was tender and complimented the seasonings well.

Swallowing, I stared at Dilly, "This is actually good."

Dilly's laugh was sunshine and flowers.

"I know! Billy's actually a great cook. I know it isn't his job, but everyone keeps hoping we won't find a new replacement and he'll stay on."

"What a strange man," I hummed.

"Billy?" Dilly asked. "Nah, he's as uncomplicated as they come. A good man and a good pirate."

I let the assessment sink into my mind, settling itself to my own memories of the pirate cook. His easy laughter and fractured smiles. Despite only knowing him a short while, I was inclined to agree.

"He *did* tell everyone I wasn't a virgin," I said petulantly.

Dilly's lips curved up. "Yeah, but it also made you look like a force to be reckoned with. He was doing you a favor."

I hadn't considered that, and it still seemed like a stretch, but it wasn't worth an argument. Instead, I'd store it away for later when I could think clearer, given the amount of noise and stomping that had begun above us. Shouts and cheers erupted, followed by the sound of what could only be described as a body hitting the floor rang above.

"What is that?" I asked.

"All Fours," Dilly and Inu said at once with matching sighs.

"Excuse me?"

Dilly and Inu shared a long look punctuated by Inu giving the slightest shake of her head, which was promptly ignored by the former.

"It's a card game we play sometimes, but people get carried away with it and gamble up to the maximum bet allowed, and then that happens."

She pointed to the deck above as another body crashed, followed by muffled shouts.

"That's unruly," I said, wondering at the law and order on the ship.

Dilly snorted. "It's not that bad. Captain sets limits on how much can be bet and how much can be lost before they have to quit."

I hummed. I knew absolutely nothing about gambling except whispered judgment and condemnation at Sunday mass. It was a subject a lady should never busy herself with. The woman I was before I stepped foot on the Sea Wraith would have wondered in secret and kept her distance. With every nautical mile between the Wraith and England, I forgot a little more about who I was meant to be.

This was probably why I set down my bowl and made my way to the top deck, ignoring Inu's quiet protests and Dilly's words of caution. Someday, when this was all done and my family was free from James' vengeance, I would learn how to be who I was before, but I'd give in for now. I'd allow the itching in my feet to be relieved by the impulses that set my blood on fire.

Pirates gathered around a table at the center of the deck illuminated by a handful of lanterns placed strategically around it. The light of the moon showcasing their wide grins and expressive faces. Laughter and taunts lit the night and for the first time I saw them for what they were and not what I expected. Pirates replaced by people.

People finding joy in a game and being together. As one man boomed laughter and slapped the back of one of the four men sitting at the table, I realized what was so other-worldly about it all. How unreserved they all were. One holding a stack of cards pointed a finger at a woman who groaned and handed over a handful of shillings. There was no hidden meaning behind barbed words. No having to guess what they were thinking amidst smiles and well-wishes.

"Seas, you're quick," Dilly said, breathing fast.

"It's time you went back to the Captain's cabin," Inu said, decidedly unruffled.

I swung my head around and gave her my brightest grin. "No thanks."

Her sharp intake of air was the only sign that she was considering murdering me, but I ignored it as I marched myself over to a small hoard of pirates and the smell of liquor amidst sea salt air. Not one of them noticed as I approached, too engrossed in the cards laid out on the wooden table before them, with four people sitting in front of each set.

"I beg," said one woman with a distinct scar across her right eye.

"Aye," said the man who held the deck and passed her three cards face down.

The next person said, "I stand."

"Same," said the fourth.

"Place your bets," the dealer said.

Shillings made their way onto the table, glinting against stars that shone like beacons against the night sky. The clink of them shining in each of the four players like a promise. Oliver used to say that the point of gambling wasn't the winnings, but the elation and hope you felt before the play ended. That was why people kept coming back, why men ruined their lives all for that small high that they spent long nights longing for.

I always felt like Oliver had missed something vital in his assessment, that it wasn't just about the elation, but about how it could change someone's life. Watching the four pirates flip over their cards and take in their opponents made me think maybe I didn't know as much as I thought I did.

"Seas, I won!" the woman with the scar yelled, standing up and cheering.

"Aye, and you did the last three before that," said one of the men.

The words were inked with suspicion, which set off a chain reaction of eyes lifting to hers.

"He has a point, Val," the dealer said.

"And am I not allowed a winning streak now and then? I don't see you complaining when Barnacles does," she said, with her hand resting on the pistol at her side.

"That's because Barnacles is known for his luck," the dealer said.

"Surprising, since his name is Barnacles," I snorted.

Oh dear. All my long years of practicing restraint and thinking before I spoke were gone within a few days on a pirate ship. A stout man who had been sitting quietly with his losing hand stood up and raked his eyes over me slowly, assessing. Not in the way society men did when they were with their peers, but in a way that made me feel like he was counting my weaknesses one by one.

"And just what is wrong with my name?" he said.

Dilly heaved in a long breath behind me, but Inu moved forward, positioning herself in front of me. Unnecessary. I had always been a firm believer that if my mouth got me into trouble, I should have to fight my way out.

I stepped in front of her and caught the roll of her eyes. Hopefully, Oscar wouldn't be too disappointed that we weren't going to be friends. Though I imagined that wouldn't be surprising. Inu and I had exactly nothing in common. She was restraint and cool consideration while I was chaos and lucky if my own two feet carried me more than a few steps.

"It's an uncommon name for one. For two, I think four men ganging up on one woman wreaks of insecurity and incompetence. Three, if I were named Barnacles, I would not consider myself lucky." I finished with two feet firmly placed in my grave.

The woman, Val, narrowed her eyes. "I don't need your help, Princess."

I scoffed at the ungratefulness as well as the nickname.

"Oh, is that my name now? An eye for an eye, I see," I frowned.

Dilly leaned forward. "Some of the crew have taken to calling you that. You know, like a damsel in distress type thing."

"It's an insult," Inu clarified.

"Clearly," I said dryly.

The eyes of every pirate were locked on her, waiting for her to say the wrong thing so that the hands resting on their weapons would respond accordingly. I guessed their odds were about fifty-fifty.

"Can I play?" I asked.

Val snorted and shook her head, her long blond braid swinging over her shoulder. She collected her winnings while Barnacles sat back down as if she weren't worth his energy. Rude.

"No," Inu said.

The dealer eyed Inu while his mouth quirked up to the side. "What are you betting, *Princess*?"

I grinned and took a seat where one of the other men had vacated, sneaking off to lick his proverbial wounds. I leaned forward and met his eyes.

"I am very wealthy," I said, hoping it conveyed confidence.

His stare was blank. "We don't take I owe yous."

Hm. Clearly, I wasn't projecting how I thought I was.

I reached up around my neck and unclasped the small diamond star I always wore. A gift from my brothers when I turned sixteen. They were going to be very annoyed if I lost it.

"How much for this?" I asked, setting it down gently.

The dealer picked it up, and I fought not to shudder at the way his dirty fingers ran over the diamond. I was already having second thoughts, but as my mother had often lamented, when I got something into my head, I never knew when to quit.

"Twenty shillings," he said.

"Copper Hanson, that is worth at least fifty shillings, you cheat," Dilly said, hands on her hips and curls bouncing with indignation.

Copper rolled his eyes and set the necklace down before counting out exactly fifty shillings and sliding them toward me.

"Your funeral," he said.

"The Captain would not approve of this," Inu said.

"Such a shame he isn't here. You know my br—" I swallowed back the damning words. "I used to know someone who used to say it is better to ask forgiveness than permission."

The man to my right. "Sounds like Oscar."

Stupid. Stupid Rose.

I felt Inu's eyes on me, but refused to acknowledge her appropriate condemnation.

"How do I play?" I asked too quickly.

Val shook her head, "Just like a princess to bet a small fortune just because she can without knowing what she's betting on."

"I get the feeling you don't like me much," I said.

"Correct. You aren't worth the trouble you cause," she said.

"And just what sort of trouble is that?" I asked.

"For one, you've got the Bane on our—" she stopped abruptly as Inu came to stand at my side. "You aren't worth anything, as far as I can tell."

I narrowed my eyes at her and then up at Inu. The Iron Bane was a ship from my father's shipyard, one almost as notorious as the Wraith.

"What about the Bane?" I pushed.

"Aye, you going to play or not," Barnacles slammed his hand on the table. "Or are you all talk?"

Pirates had exactly zero manners and somehow it was refreshing. Like I could take a full breath because I wasn't holding it wondering what the people around me were hiding behind pretty words. I didn't have to pretend.

The moment I sank into the hard wooden chair and met all their eyes like the challenge it was I felt the chains loosen around my wrists. No need to tilt my head just so or blink three times. No need to coddle feelings and pretend that their self-worth was somehow more valuable than my dignity.

"Deal the cards," I ordered.

Copper gave a sharp laugh and dealt out the cards with a pep in his step that said he clearly underestimated me. They all did. Maybe it wasn't the card games of the aristocracy, but there was a reason my brothers had refused to play with me anymore. They didn't like losing, and I enjoyed winning.

I picked up my cards and eyed them as if they would begin spilling all their deepest secrets.

"Princess?" Copper asked with a wide grin that I did not appreciate.

"I beg," I said.

His chuckle was offensive as he handed over more cards.

"I stand."

"Stand."

"I beg," Val said.

"All right, princesses and gents, place your bet," Copper said.

"Watch it," Val snapped at him.

She was slightly terrifying with her long scar illuminated by the sway of golden lantern light and punctuated by the groans and creaks of the ship. She was more of a pirate than all of them combined. The reason I couldn't sleep at night when I was nine and convinced pirates would take over my father's ship on the high seas.

"You're more a gent than a princess, Val," Barnacles grunted.

Val rolled her eyes. "You are all idiots. I bet ten."

She pushed the shillings in, and I realized I didn't want to lose. Not for the money, but because it meant something. James' voice was loud in my head amongst the quiet of the night punctuated by the watchful stare of thousands of stars above. I wasn't clever enough. I always dove headfirst without thinking, chaotic and reckless. I needed him to save me from myself. A quiet voice of reason amidst my impulsivity.

"Princess, the bet is twenty," Copper said, leaning forward.

He reminded me of an apex predator knowing his prey was weakened and only had to wait them out. James probably would have agreed. That was always the way he looked at me till he had me. Once I was on his arm, a diamond ring around my finger, I was as good as a decoration. As inconsequential as the ring I wore.

"You can yield," Barnacles grinned, showing black teeth.

I could, but it would cost me more than I was willing to pay. I shoved all fifty shillings toward the center.

Impulsive. Reckless. Princess.

Val slammed her cards down. "Just like the rest."

The insult sank into my side leaving an ache. I was just like the rest of the aristocracy. Never placing value where it should be honored.

"Aye, I'll be a wealthy man myself tonight," Barnacles said, adding his money.

"Maybe this was a bad idea," Dilly began before Copper waved her away, calling interference.

The other man handed his cards to Copper, who eyed me like I was dinner. That was the thing about James and the rest of his species. They saw weakness and failed to see the rest of the picture. When the world was narrow it was easy to be on top.

"Flip 'em," Copper ordered.

Barnacles eagerly flipped his three cards and grinned up at me with triumph. I didn't take my eyes off him for even a moment as his mates clapped him on the back and cheered him on. I didn't want to miss the moment he realized he underestimated me. It was an arrow to James' voice inside my head, and it felt like a damn breath of fresh air.

Slowly, I flipped my cards and watched the realization hit him, each a blow to his chest. All went silent around us as they realized I had trumped every card. That was the thing about being impulsive, sometimes, every now and then, it worked out just fine.

I smiled sweetly, tilting my head, and blinked three times.

"Did I win?" I asked.

"Damn," Dilly said in a hushed whisper.

"What are you? A sea witch?" Barnacles said, disbelief raking over each word.

I gently pushed the coins to Copper, who stared with his mouth open.

"My necklace back, please."

He handed it back as if in a daze and I clasped it around my neck, sinking into the feeling of familiarity.

"Now, are we going to play again or not?" I said, stacking up the remaining of my winnings.

The silence was loud until Val slid her coins forward. "All right, princess, let's see how that luck fairs a second time."

Some of the resentment eased from her voice, and I thanked my lucky stars above. She wasn't an enemy I wanted, but mostly, I was sick of people underestimating me and seeing what they wanted. On land, I was what I was, but out here, on this open sea, I was my own woman, free to become what I wanted.

"Aye, who's in?" Copper asked.

Two new pirates took the place of the ones before, and I settled into my chair. It didn't matter if I won or lost now. I had made them see me.

They saw me.

Chapter Fifteen
Blackbeard

Though humanity has gone through leaps and bounds in their understanding of the Mysterious Deep in the last century alone, it would be foolish to believe we are aware of every creature that lives among it.

-An excerpt from *The Mysterious Deep: A Comprehensive Understanding*

The groans of the ship burrowed into my brain and splintered into my skull. Too loud. It was an affront to nature.

I moaned at the sway of the bed and batted away strands of hair stuck to my face.

"You might want the elixir on the nightstand," a deep voice said.

Much too loud. I also noted that I didn't appreciate the way my core tightened at the sound. Memories rushed back like incessant flies. I batted each of them away accordingly.

"I hate you," I declared, to him and to the flies.

"No, you don't, but I'm sure you wish you did," he said, I could practically hear the mouth tilt.

I rolled over, face first into the downy pillow, hoping it might smother the ache in my head.

"Fuck you," I mumbled.

Apparently, my insults were funny now. The tap of his boots on wood was the highest offense as each one punctuated a sharp stab to my brain.

"One night of drinking and gambling, and you speak like a pirate," he said, the clink of glass echoing. "Drink this, and you'll be mostly fine in ten minutes."

I pushed up on my arms, ignoring the wild strands of dark hair that went every which way in a mass mutiny. A sticky piece of drool clung to the corner of my lip, but I couldn't bring myself to care as I narrowed my eyes at the suspiciously pink drink held before me.

"It's going to taste bad, I know it."

"Does it matter if it does?" he asked.

Fair enough. I snatched it and drowned it in a matter of seconds, holding back the nausea as a citrus pine coated my throat and sank heavily into my stomach. It was somehow bitter and sweet all at once in a sickening mixture. I tossed it onto the nightstand and went back to my smothering pillow, counting to ten to try to keep down the nausea that threatened to make me see the elixir twice.

His footsteps retreated before the distinct sound of a chair scraping resounded throughout the room.

"Must you be so loud?" I asked.

"I believe this is called the consequences of your actions," he said.

"Too much rum," I agreed.

"Not even good rum," he said.

"Is there such a thing?"

"Sure."

I was saved from having to think about the cursed liquid by the slam of a door that ripped a groan from me as pain ricocheted through my head.

"You bet your necklace?" Oscar asked, though it was more of a yell.

"Not right now, Oscar," Flynn said.

I had never been more grateful, but it turned out Captain's orders weren't as foolproof as I had been led to believe.

"You got so drunk that Inu said you were reenacting the Battle of Bosworth Field with a knife," Oscar accused.

"It was very entertaining," Flynn said. "And historically accurate."

I groaned and shoved the pillow over my head. The ache that had been pounding against my skull already lessened. Emille's potion, most likely. He was a good doctor for a pirate. More concerning was that I didn't remember reenacting anything. After I won a few hands and then lost the rest of my money, I remembered drinking something Val had handed me. Rather than disappoint her after she begrudgingly called me Princess in a less menacing tone, I drank it.

"It was a pivotal battle that changed the course of English history and set the stage for Henry VIII," I said in my defense.

"Yes, we are all aware," Oscar said. "What is more concerning is why you think getting drunk on a ship where you are a hostage and going by an alias seemed like a great idea."

When he said it like that, I could see how it might have been a poor idea. I'll be damned if I conceded a single inch of ground, though.

"Go away, I'm dying," I ground out even though the nausea had abated.

I was quickly being abandoned by my body's hangover and left with only mortification for company.

"You are chaotic and reckless, Rose," he said, face close to the edge of the bed.

I regretfully lifted the pillow and found him kneeling before the bed, face ashen. He was worried. My brother, who basically betrayed his friends for me. Who risked mutiny for me.

"I had something to prove," I said quietly, feeling my stomach hollow out.

Oscar sighed and reached in to cover my hand with his.

"You are perfection, Rosie. If I could go back in time, I would make sure that asshole never came close enough to you to make you feel anything less than. You won't prove anything to him by being reckless out here. Prove it by showing up with the money and buying back our portion of the company," Oscar said.

I hated the way he understood so much without understanding the most important part. I wasn't proving something to James, but to myself. It wasn't worth the energy it took to explain.

"I don't think Inu likes me," I said.

Oscar laughed, making his eyes squint, thin lines appearing on either side.

"You are the opposite of her in every way, and she is... perplexed by you," he said.

"Do you love her?" I asked, wondering if I wasn't still a bit drunk to ask.

Oscar's smile faded, and he watched me for a second, considering.

"I do," he said.

I don't know why it hurt. Why it felt like losing him over again. All I wanted to do was to curl up into the blankets and forget this conversation ever happened. It'd been better to not know.

"It doesn't mean I love you any less, Rosie," he said.

"I'm not a child, Oscar. I don't need your soothing. However, I could use another day of sleep if you don't mind," I said, pushing the pillow over my head.

"We should leave her in Port Mallorca. Let the Iron Bane pick her up. She's a liability out here, even you can see that," Oscar said to Flynn.

Words tickled at the back of my memory. Someone had mentioned the Iron Bane last night. That they were on our tail. Understanding washed over me, and I sat up, aware I was still in last night's clothes.

"The Bane is following us," I said.

"Your Fiancé, presumably," Flynn said, scribbling words on parchment as if it were all inconsequential.

"And no one thought to tell me?" I shouted.

"We work on a need-to-know basis on this vessel," Flynn said, unconcerned.

"And you want to just hand me over to them?" I stared at my brother.

At least he had the decency to blush and lower his eyes.

"He's an asshole, and I plan on killing him at the earliest convenience, but it's safer than you going to the Glass Sea."

"And how do you know he won't strong-arm me into just marrying him before the deadline? Because he will, Oscar. He will see my scheme as an attempt to outsmart him, and he won't risk it happening again. He is possessive and doesn't like to lose. Are you actually serious right now?"

My heart was thudding erratically against my ribs like it was desperate to be freed from its prison. Desperate to end the torrential downpour flooding my body at the thought of James owning me. He had always been gentle with me, but I knew now that would never have lasted. He craved ownership. His tastes were... cruel.

"You may continue breathing, Rose," Flynn said. "We will not be conceding our hostage away to scorned lords anytime soon."

"Bash—" Oscar tried.

I rubbed at my chest, trying to convince myself he wasn't lying. That if I took the next breath, I wouldn't be handed over on a silver platter.

"Breathe, Rose," Flynn ordered, setting down his pen.

"Oh, god, Rosie," Oscar said, throwing up his arms and leaning over to pat my back before rubbing it. "Most defense mechanisms are created to preserve life."

"Please don't give me to him," I breathed out at once.

Oscar sighed, shoulders drooping. "You need to be more careful. No more gambling and getting drunk."

The chains snapped back into place one after another.

"I wouldn't have said anything that would have put us in danger," I said.

Oscar's face softened a fraction, lines smoothing out. "I know you wouldn't mean to, but rum, especially the rum on the Wraith, can make you say more than you ever wanted to."

It was useless. I may have been riddled with self-doubt and questioned myself constantly, but I knew that I would never put my brother's life at risk. Rum or not. The fact that he didn't know that carved another piece of my heart out. All that was left was a remnant of structural integrity that still let it beat.

"Okay," I said.

"Rosie—" Oscar tried.

"It's fine. I'm just tired."

"We have a lot to catch up on," Oscar said.

"Yeah," I whispered. "Maybe when I'm not hungover from cursed rum."

Oscar chuckled, and I was happy to hear the sound despite everything.

"It's not cursed, just strong as fuck, but okay. Get some rest." He leaned forward and pressed a kiss to my forehead and I wished it didn't feel tainted. By his leaving, by Inu, by his lack of faith in me.

I watched him leave, wrapping the blanket tight around my shoulders. Flynn didn't say anything as he continued scrawling words on parchment, the sound oddly comforting.

"Will the Bane catch up with us?" I asked.

Flynn set down the quill and leaned back in his chair.

"No. The Wraith is faster, and there's a Cirein-cròin between us," he said.

I let out a long breath that eased some of the muscles in my shoulders.

"Why follow then?" I asked.

"Because he is a man. Men see a free woman and are eager to be the one that caged her," he said.

The words were said without levity and not for the first time I wondered about the world that created Captain Sebastion Flynn.

"But not you?" I asked.

I knew the answer, but I needed to hear it. Flynn could have claimed some perverse ownership of me as far as London society was concerned, but he never did. He never made me feel like I was something to be put on a shelf. Another notch in his belt.

"I believe your newspapers refer to me as "demon" and "monster," those are probably more apt descriptors for me than just a man," he said.

"You scare them," I said, mouth feeling ungodly dry.

"Good," he answered, eyes locked on mine.

His eyes didn't wander down my body like so many would. Instead, his eyes focused on mine and sent a flush of heat down my body, making my toes clench. There was a hunger in them that I knew all too well. Two stolen nights, but it was at the end of our time that I first saw that glint. Maybe it was its own sort of claiming because it ran over me without consideration for my resolve.

Whatever curse had been brewing was snapped by a large gray ball of fur leaping onto the desk in front of Flynn. It padded over to his paper with fresh ink and circled three times before curling into an impossibly tight ball and rumbling.

"I'll have to redo that now," Flynn muttered.

I threw the blanket off and padded over to the purring creature until Flynn put out his hand to stop me. I glared at him for the audacity of denying me the right to pet all that fluff.

"That's Blackbeard, and he's mean as fuck." he said.

I relaxed and raised my eyebrows at him. "He doesn't look mean."

"Trust me, I spent all morning on that log. The only reason he's lying on it is because I'm afraid of him," he said.

I laughed, and it eased some of the tension of Oscar's visit.

"Are you scared of all cats?" I asked.

"No, just that one," he said, eyeing it like it might enact its vengeance at any second.

"It's just a cat, and it's purring, not to mention that adorable smooshed-up face."

I reached for it, but Flynn grabbed my hand tight in his. He raised those too-blue eyes to mine, and it was impossible to see the white swirls that reminded me of winds across the sea.

"I would appreciate it if, for just this once, you would take my word on this," he said.

God, I was a sinking ship pulled into the vortex that was him. Seeing I wasn't going to throw myself at the purring villain, Flynn released my hand, but his fingers caressed down it all the same, leaving me with a memory and hunger. It would be easy. Some part of me knew he wouldn't say no. It was in the way he watched me and the way he lingered too long near me.

It would be easy, but everything that came after would be hard. Better to have dealt with the past and leave it buried. Digging old graves never led to happier days, as my father used to say.

I stepped back and wrapped my arms around my waist because I didn't trust myself.

A knock on the door saved me.

Flynn didn't look away as he said, "Come in."

Why should anyone have a voice as deep as that? It wasn't fair.

Emille walked in, smiling when he saw me up, but when his eyes drifted to the purring cat on the desk, he jumped.

"Seas, how'd Blackbeard get in here?" he asked.

"I have given up trying to figure out his ability to appear at the most inconvenient of times." Flynn frowned.

"Why do you all keep a cat who you are afraid of on board?" I asked.

"I've tried to get rid of him many times," Flynn said.

"The notorious Captain Flynn can't dispatch one medium-sized cat?"

Flynn slowly stood from his chair, careful not to disturb the beast. "Laugh if you will, but there is something very wrong with that cat."

"And he catches the rats." Emille offered.

"Not to mention Billy would throw me into the sea for tossing the cat out." Flynn frowned.

"Billy likes demon cats?" I asked.

Flynn nodded, "He's the only person Blackbeard will tolerate."

"Interesting," I said. "Anyhow, I smell like rum, and my hair is libel to end with a bird nesting in it if I don't shower soon."

"I see you took the tonic," Emille said.

His lips drew into a wide smile as he edged closer, narrowing his eyes at my head. Self-consciously, I reached for it, trying to feel whatever he saw. He picked at something and made a loud humming noise.

"Is that—" he began, "A finch?"

Relief flooded me as I swatted away his hand, and his chest boomed with laughter that reminded me of my father. He would probably be worrying sick, thinking this was all his fault. I knew it would be hard on him, but I hoped in a few months, it'll all be worth it. Maybe we could all laugh about how I ran and joined a pirate crew on a mad campaign to retrieve sunken treasure. More like they would lock me up in my room and throw away the key.

"No birds, but you do smell." Emille wrinkled his nose.

"Rude," I said, twisting on my heels to gather clothes.

Luckily, Dilly had shared her clothes with me so I wouldn't be forced to traipse along with mountains of lace and frills anymore. I eyed the pants suspiciously. Dilly was leaner than I was and it felt like my entire life was rewritten once more. My sister, Ruby, had always been thin and dainty, complimented by everyone for her delicate frame. Then there was me. Taller and much thicker. People tried to soothe my feelings on the subject by saying how she was just built differently, like I was some sort of victim to genetics.

"I'll be going then," Emille said.

I was glad to be interrupted from my stare-off with Dilly's pants. If I had to go back to frills because these didn't fit, I was going to find another oar and take it out on Billy. That was a lie. It was hard to be mad at him when every time he saw me, he complimented my frills and told me how he paid extra, knowing it was worth it.

"Bye, Emille. Thanks for the tonic," I said.

I didn't wait for the door to close before taking my things and going into the adjacent washroom. It was one of the perks of staying in Flynn's quarters. I would hate to see what everyone else was subjugated to though I did wonder how often the men used it. The smell of them suggested the answer was rarely.

Damn pants and damn hair.

I squeezed my legs into the pants, but it was much like stuffing a sausage into its casing. I did a few squats and jumped up and down to try and stretch them out, but I was just as likely to break them. The shirt was slightly more forgiving, though it clung to my skin more than society would consider acceptable. By a long shot.

But it wasn't frills, and that counted for something. The real issue was my hair. Whatever I had done last night had more than tangled it. No soap or water would cleanse it from its demons. I slid the comb through only to get caught a third of the way in. I pulled and pulled, but it was no use. Stuck. The brush was stuck in my hair. I let out a frustrated scream.

I stared at my reflection and realized I looked crazed. Brush in my hair while the other half was frayed and going all directions.

An unwelcome knock at the door.

"Are you alright in there?" Flynn asked, a note of hesitation in his voice.

"No, I am not alright!" I shouted as I flung the door open.

Flynn took a step back and for a moment the corner of his lips pulled up as he took in the state of my hair, but as he drifted down to the rest of me his smile faded and he swallowed hard. Despite my hair, I felt self-satisfaction glide down my chest as he stuttered for words.

"Is the very bold and dangerous Captain Flynn at a loss for words?"

Flynn rubbed at his chest. "You have to know how you look in that."

I snorted despite the warmth flooding my cheeks. "Like a sausage?"

Flynn tilted his head, eyes darkening. "I have many things I'd like to say to that, but I will exercise restraint, except to say that you are always beautiful whether it's frills or—" he gestured to all of me. "This."

These were the moments when I wondered who Sebastian Flynn was. He was a pirate, but there were hints to him that said he was raised in a place that valued manners. Not quite society, but there was something I was missing.

"And this?" I said, pointing at the brush stuck to my head.

His lip quirked up, and he spun his finger around in a command.

I narrowed my eyes at him. "What are you going to do to it?"

"Rosamund, I would not dare to cut your hair, but if you, for once in your life, would simply listen, I will help you."

Desperate times. I turned and huffed out a long breath. Ever so gently, I felt his fingers tug on the strands of hairs locked into the brush. I expected it to hurt, but instead, he worked meticulously. It was strange standing there while a pirate captain fussed with my hair, and a demon cat slept peacefully on the nearby desk. Maybe if I could think of something to say, the silence wouldn't seem so loud.

"You are fidgeting," he said, voice low and heavy.

I looked down, finding that I had been digging at my nails. A nervous habit my mother had tried to beat out of me, theoretically speaking. Most of the time, I could control it, but sometimes, it didn't even occur to me it was happening till I was bleeding.

"I don't do well in silence," I said.

"Hm," he hummed. "I learned to do this for my mother. She had hair thicker and more unruly than yours. Curlier."

My fingers stilled in light of the words. I could hear the honesty in his words painted with a pang of longing, something lost. It was a truth. He had never offered up anything about his life before becoming a pirate and certainly not a family.

"I kind of thought you had just sprung up out of the ground as a pirate captain. It's hard to imagine you having a family," I whispered.

He made a sound low in his throat. "I suppose that's part of the image I sell."

Somewhere in the two nights we spent together, I knew there was a difference between who he said he was and who he was, but he wore the costume well enough that it was impossible to see where one ended, and the other began. More disconcerting was this pull deep in me that wanted to know. It was illegal and off-limits.

"I don't like Inu," I said.

Some of the tension broke as his chuckle eased the space between us. His warm breath coasting over my neck and sending shivers down my back.

"An obvious truth isn't much of a bargain, Princess," he said.

I groaned. "Not you, too."

The nickname stuck too well last night, and even though I was never partial to my alias, Miss Smith, it was at least more dignified than princess.

"I like it. It suits you," he said.

"Because I am so stuck up?"

"Because you aren't. They call you that because they only know where you come from, but if they only knew how brave and wild you are, they would call you princess as a sign of admiration," he said.

I felt the flush of my cheeks fall down to my toes. Even now, it was difficult not to hear an insult where it was obvious praise. When James had condemned my chaos as a sin, every time my mother corrected my posture, every time other women looked at me with judgment in their pursed lips and narrowed eyes, it all sank into my bloodstream, melding shame into the words.

Words failed me as I tried to recover. I tried to think of something self-deprecating to say that would spare me from his sincerity. If my insane plan worked, if I helped my father take back his portion of the company. If I succeeded in making my family wealthy once more and spent the rest of my life in blessed spinsterhood, would I ever stop feeling the sting of every insult laid upon me?

"How do you not care what people think of you?" I blurted.

To his credit, he didn't hesitate. "People think what I want them to think."

"But when they call you a murderer or monster, doesn't that bother you?"

"I am both those things, Rose."

I swallowed hard. It was hard to rectify the man who had held me long into the night and touched me gently and thoughtfully with the man he claimed to be. The man who patiently worked the knots from my hair with someone who struck fear into everyone else. It was a dichotomy I had yet to face.

"You didn't answer the question," I said, throat dry.

I felt the moment the brush broke free and blew out a sigh of relief. Already, an ache had begun to form where it had been tight against my scalp. I began to reach for it, but he was already running it through my hair again, untangling it as he went.

"It's hard to make sense of you. I don't think most bloodthirsty pirates also brush damsels in distress' hair," I said.

He was silent for long enough that I began to chastise myself for always saying the wrong thing. The creak of the ship and the purring cat were all mocking me for lack of tact.

"The moment you stepped onto my ship and demanded I agree to your scheme, you forfeited that image of me that you put on a pedestal. By the end of this farce, you will have to come to terms with what I am one way or another," he said.

I twisted around, and there was a hardness in his muscles that radiated tension. He hated the words he spoke, but they were genuine.

"What if I see who you are and think it's justified?" I asked.

His blue eyes flashed and my hand ached with the want to touch him. It felt like I was burning up from the inside with this desire that I fought back with every breath. I knew he had blood on his hands. I knew it, and I still wanted him.

The muscle in his jaw flickered and I could see the restraint was hurting him too. Maybe we were just lonely. It was probably in poor taste for a captain to seek comfort from his crew, and god knows no one had touched me in the last year. It was just the need to be touched.

"I should go," he said, stepping back.

"Why?" I asked, stepping forward.

He blew out a long breath and rubbed at his jaw. "You hate me, remember?"

"I remember wishing that I hated you."

He snorted and shook his head. "Maybe I have too much pride to be with a woman who wishes she hated me."

But the way he angled his body toward mine said he had just as much dignity as I had. He reached up with his free hand and ran his hand through my hair, ghosting over my skin. I closed my eyes and tilted my neck, sinking into that feeling. It felt good. Too good.

I felt him lean in close to me, breathing me in, and all of me reverberated with a tingling need that I could drown in. Anticipation chased every breath. His warmth seeped into my skin like it fit perfectly.

"You would hate me for this later," he promised, his hand wrapping around the back of my neck.

"It doesn't have to mean anything," I whispered, leaning further into him.

It was the wrong thing to say. He pulled away and put several feet between us, setting the brush down on his shelf of trinkets. I watched him crack his neck and grab his coat from the back of his chair. It was too fast, and the demon cat jumped up and swiped at him, an unearthly growling sound coming deep from inside him.

Flynn angled his body, narrowly missing the attack.

"Damn cat," he ground out.

There were words to be said if I could only find them. Maybe apologize? Unfortunately, my feet stayed glued to the wooden floor beneath me.

"We are making port in a few hours. You should stay on the ship," he said, making for the door.

That, at least, was enough to unfreeze me.

"You said you weren't going to hand over your hostage," I accused.

Tightening in my chest restricted the air from my lungs, and I knew it was happening again. The panic seeped into my bloodstream. James would not let me be free after this. He would find a way to manipulate me, twist my mind into thinking I didn't have a choice. I would end up Lady Allan and a trophy on his pedestal. A reminder that he didn't lose.

I wasn't prideful enough to think it was my good looks, or anything about me for that matter, that made him determined to chain me. It was that I had publicly humiliated him by breaking the engagement. He had fled to France amidst his father's anger and the eager gossip. They all speculated on what he had done that was so terrible. God, if they only knew.

"If I wanted to hand you over, I wouldn't have just told you to stay on the Wraith," Flynn said.

"Why are you making port then? The Bane will catch up," I said, rubbing at my chest to alleviate the pain.

Flynn sighed, nearly to the door, his back turned to me as if he couldn't stand to look at me. It was unfair. All we had ever been to each other was an escape. Nothing had changed since last year. To be punished now for calling it what it was felt like an excuse.

"Passage to the Glass Sea is granted by the Gharaq coven. Without them, you could search all your life and never find it. To find them, you need a lantern. There are three that I know of, and the closest happens to be in Port Mallorca."

"Is that the witch who Oscar talked out of killing you?" I asked.

My fingers and toes felt prickly, like there wasn't enough blood circulating in my body. I was spiraling. Next, I'd be holding my breath like an idiot. If there was a God and I managed to meet him, I would have several questions about why I was made like this.

Flynn rubbed at his neck just like he had the first time it was mentioned.

"Yes."

"And you are going to go back?" It was more a shout than a calm question.

Flynn didn't bother to look at me. "Stay on the ship, Rose."

He shut the door behind him hard enough that I flinched. The panic surrounded me despite my attempt to wrap my arm around myself. Why did I have to say something as stupid as "it doesn't have to mean anything?" Everything was fine. Was it a terrible idea? Sure, but it was fine. And for that matter, why did he have to react like I was slapping him? Wasn't that always our agreement? No ties. He was the one that stole my brother.

"God, men are so infuriating!" I shouted.

A cursory meow reminded me that I wasn't alone.

"I see how you got your name," I said, edging closer.

Sure enough, Blackbeard's chin was colored entirely black giving the illusion of a beard in his otherwise gray fur. His bright green eyes saw right through me as he sat straight at the end of the desk and he curled his tail around his body. Watching, waiting.

It was easy to see why Flynn called him a demon. This cat saw and understood everything.

I didn't back away from his stare. Instead, I raised my eyebrows.

"You shouldn't have missed. He deserved a good scratching," I sighed.

Blackbeard blinked twice and laid down once more into a small ball before his breathing took on an even rate, and the purring resumed.

Somehow, I felt like I had passed a test of some sort. Not with Flynn, but with the cat.

Chapter Sixteen
Deathy Puppy

Among the most well-known yet least understood creatures of the deep is the Cirein-cròin. They are reclusive, and sightings of these sea serpents were long considered to be tall tales made by drunken sailors. Some claim they saw it first as a silverfish, while others claim they are upwards of one hundred feet long. One thing remains true—if they wanted to, Cirein-cròin could make the seas inhabitable to humans.

–An excerpt from The Mysterious Deep: A Comprehensive Understanding

The closer we edged toward land, the more my stomach wrapped into knots that were determined to strangle me. Every seagull that swooped by was a reminder that the Port of Mallorca was an imminent inevitability. How long did it take to retrieve a magical lantern that gave a map to bloodthirsty witches?

The more I thought about it, the more I realized what an insane plan this had all been. What was even more insane was that Oscar and then Flynn agreed to it. Maybe none of us were responsible to make decisions. As I sat on a stray barrel and watched the crew prepare for docking, all I could see were lives lost.

I watched a red-haired man make several trips below deck, carrying up barrels upon barrels of who knew what. Sweat poured down his cheeks, but he always made sure to shoot me a friendly smile as he passed by. I could only imagine how my face appeared as I pictured him hanging from a noose and a warty witch cackling as it happened.

I hadn't known you needed a path opened to the Glass Sea. I thought it was just a place like any other. How much else did I not know, and how many would die for my ignorance?

"You are going to make yourself bleed," Inu said from beside me.

I'd mostly forgotten my babysitter was even there. It had been nice for a minute. I shot her a glare and ceased picking at my nails for only a moment.

Luckily, I was saved by Dilly huffing up the steps with a wide smile on her face and a looking glass firmly in her hand.

"How can you even breathe in those clothes?" Dilly asked.

"Carefully," I muttered.

"Best steer clear of the Captain. Word on the deck is that he's in a pissy mood," Dilly confessed.

She raised her looking glass to her eye and peered out past us, humming softly.

I could feel Inu's judgmental stare on me like it was my fault that Flynn was in a bad mood. She was giving me too much credit. He was pissy all on his own.

"Cirein-cròin still stalking us?" I asked.

"Yup," Dilly chirped.

"I can't keep calling it that; if it's going to follow us around, it needs a pet name," I said.

Dilly let out a squeak and jumped up, curls bouncing. "Like Lucky!"

I snorted. "That's a terrible sea monster name."

"Shi," Inu said quietly.

"Oh, that sounds nice." Dilly smiled. "What does it mean?"

Inu stared ahead, gone but present.

"Death," she translated.

I twisted to stare at her, open-mouthed. What on land or sea did my fun-loving, charismatic brother see in her? We would have made fun of her and reenacted her somber one-word deliveries back in London. Now, he presumably loved her. The best guess I had come up with was that the sea-salt air had addled his brain.

"Have you ever smiled in your life?" I asked.

One of her dark eyes popped out below her sun-brimmed hat. "No."

At least that made sense.

"What is puppy in Japanese, Inu?" Dilly asked, giving me a warning glance.

"Koinu," she replied.

"Well, that's lovely! Let's name it that," Dilly pleaded.

"Shi Koinu." I snorted.

"I think I prefer Cirein-cròin," Dilly pouted.

"Nope, Shi Koinu it is," I said, turning to Inu, "If I walk ten feet away where you can see me, are you going to follow me?"

She raised an eyebrow beneath her hat, and god, if I knew what that meant. Maybe I was an optimist because I went anyway. The sea air changed here. It felt thicker, more tangible. I was blissfully alone for only a minute, my body shielded by a stack of barrels set aside for trading in Mallorca, when I heard a voice that scraped down my skin like nails.

"Fucking asshole."

It was the twin, Amos, who had threatened me when the grindylows were attacking. It was a big enough ship that I hadn't run into him yet, but it had only been a matter of time. I peered around the corner and found Inu angled towards me. I hated that I was glad she was there. Hated that I felt like I needed her.

"If you didn't run your mouth, we wouldn't be hauling ass, now would we?" His brother, Charlie.

"Somebody's got to say it," Amos spat. "That bitch isn't worth the trouble. If he wasn't fucking her, then we wouldn't be chasing after ghosts."

"God, Amos, shut up," Charlie hissed.

"He ain't wrong," another voice said.

I recognized that one, too, but I couldn't place it. It was gruff, a deep sort of baritone.

"Didn't say he was, just that he should stop running his goddamn mouth before we find ourselves without a job or worse, at the bottom of the sea."

"Likely to end up there anyway, chasing after treasure and pardons," Amos said.

"Look," said Charlie with a frustrated breath, "I promised Ma I would look after you. If I didn't think it was possible, we would be getting off on Mallorca and finding a new ship. Big prizes come with high risk. It's the way of it out here. If we take this prize, we can give Ma whatever she wants and pay Pa's debts. Get him out of prison."

"He can rot there for all I care," Amos said.

"It ain't for him, it's for Ma," Charlie clarified.

"Everybody's got their reasons." The deep voice—Barnacles!

I knew I recognized the voice. It wasn't exactly surprising he was hanging out with those two, but I wondered how many more agreed with them. I had heard of mutinies, but never considered that my brother would be endangered from one. It was good they didn't know I was listening. Anything I could find out might help.

"My question is why he's in such a bad fucking mood today. Maybe his princess is getting boring. A rich English girl like that probably only knows how to fuck one way," Amos chuckled.

My cheeks burned. Maybe listening wasn't helpful after all. Shame and anger warred within me, both hot and unwelcome. I knew what they all thought of me by now, but after the other night, I hoped maybe it wasn't all they had thought of me. Why I cared, I would never know.

"Just shut up, Amos. I'm serious. I'm not hauling barrels up for you again. Watch your mouth and stay away from the Captain," Charlie said.

"Are you assholes done with your tea party, or are you going to keep hauling?" Val called.

I looked to my left, and her eyes flicked to mine and then to the brutes on the other side of the barrels.

"Aye, we are coming," Charlie said.

"Another bitch," Amos sneered.

"Watch it," Barnacles warned. "I happen to like her."

Amos muttered something as they walked away, but I could only imagine how crude it was. I watched Val and Barnacles share a look as the three men went back under before she made her way to me. In the light of day, Val was just as unnerving as she was underneath lantern light.

"If it isn't Richard III hiding in plain daylight," she said, lip quirked up at her own joke.

"I like to think I was impartial enough in my reenactment that I hid my bias," I said.

"Nah, you called Richard III a power-hungry bastard with something to prove," she said.

I hummed and crossed my arms. "That does sound like something I would say."

Val laughed and I wondered when we had become friends. Probably my reenactment.

"You should be careful, eavesdropping," she warned.

"Wrong place, wrong time," I answered, turning towards the sea.

The shape of land formed behind a wall of clouds out in the distance. We were close. The question was how close was the Bane?

"Still, it wouldn't have been good if they had found you. Stay clear of Amos. He has a short fuse and is looking for a fight," she said.

"You don't say." I spit out, half joking, half still feeling the sting of shame.

"Actually, you might want to lay low for a minute anyway," Val suggested, leaning into me. "Captain's on a rampage today, and enough people are blaming you."

"So I've heard," I sighed.

"A lot of the crew is newer. Impressionable. Those of us who have been around know it's being near Mallorca and the coven that's eating him up. He's always like this when we get close enough. Don't take it personally."

I opened my mouth to tell her that it was a little hard, but a small flock of cormorants swarmed over our heads. I hadn't even seen them coming. It was like they just appeared out of nowhere.

"Aloja," Val said, eyes tracking the movement.

"Excuse me?" I started, but my words fell off as I rounded the corner of my barrel sanctuary.

Three of the most beautiful women I'd ever seen stood on the deck in glittering gowns of the deepest emerald, magenta, and sapphire. Their golden blond hair shimmered underneath the sun, mesmerizing. Slowly, everyone put down their work and gathered a respectful distance away.

Dilly, above, took out her notes and began writing frantically, looking at the women and then back at her notes. A mysterious deep creature then, but not witches or sirens. These were different.

My breath caught as Flynn emerged from below, Oscar and Billy close behind him. His eyes flickered to me for a fraction, then to Val, then up to where Inu stood above, her hand on her hilt. When his gaze cut back to the three women, there was a forced gentleness to him that didn't exist. His smile too relaxed, his shoulders tugged down. Rehearsed.

It reminded me of when I would speak to suitors and calculate the best way not to be perceived as a threat. Which meant that these women were dangerous. The hum in the air turned to one of oppression. A stirring that made me want to shift my feet if only to move, but Val placed her hand on my shoulder, her grip hard.

Message received.

"Lucia, Caterina, Ramona," Flynn said, dipping his head.

"We were not expecting you, Captain. Ximena is pleased though we wonder for how long," The one in emerald sang, her voice as beautiful as an instrument.

"She does not like to be refused," The one in sapphire said.

"Last time, she wrecked three ships in her fury," The magenta one giggled.

"Even still, I would ask for safe passage into Mallorca. I have business there," Flynn answered, voice clipped, but somehow gentle.

I could hear the irritated undertones, but none of the women seemed to as they shared glances with each other, giggling. Finally, the one in emerald sobered and looked to Flynn.

"Passage is granted to the Wraith, but only if her Captain dines with Ximena underneath the moon," she said, her bright white teeth glimmering against her bronze skin.

Too much was happening that I didn't understand, but a rolling in my stomach said I didn't like it.

"Unfortunately, time is not a commodity I have in abundance. However, I have gathered tobacco, spices, gunpowder, and an assortment of jewels I picked out with your mistress in mind," he said.

The woman shared unspoken words before the magenta one stepped forward.

"Ximena has given her terms. Should the Wraith attempt to approach without intention of fulfilling the bargain, she will find herself on the bottom of the sea." Her smile was hunger incarnate, which was out of place against her beauty.

Flynn dipped his head. For the briefest second, his eyes flashed to mine, there and gone too quickly, but I understood. Stay hidden. Val stepped silently in front of me as I ducked behind her. Suddenly, I was feeling very grateful to have made a friend in her.

"I will honor the bargain."

The women clapped as one, beaming. "We welcome the Wraith to Mallorca."

Their voices echoed each other in stunning harmony before the air shimmered, and three ravens appeared where the women had been. One by one, they flew around Flynn and then back into the air towards the land mass before us.

"Make for port," Flynn bellowed.

He twisted on his heels and made to go below deck. I tracked his movements until his form disappeared. His words bounced endlessly in my mind, reminding me of when he said I would have to forfeit my image of him. If only I could decide what image I had crafted in the first place.

"Oy, Hellcat," Billy called as he made his way over.

Unfortunately, Inu was only a few steps away. Apparently, my ten feet of freedom was at an end.

"Hi, Billy," I grumbled.

Val chuckled and slapped me hard enough on the back that a cough ripped from my throat. That only made her laugh harder.

"Watch your back, Princess," she called behind her.

Billy's grin faded as he wagged a finger at me. "Now I know you ain't gonna listen, but you gotta stay on the ship. Mallorca may look nice, but you won't be finding friends on these shores."

"What does that even mean?" I asked, looking to Inu for help.

"It means stay in the Captain's cabin," Inu said.

"Aye. For all our sakes." Billy said, no hint of laughter on his lips.

For the first time I considered that there might be more danger here than just the Bane catching up. I just wished I didn't feel that itch in my feet that whispered a single word—*go.*

Chapter Seventeen
A Night Like This

Among the rarest creatures of the deep are the Aloja. Native only to Mallorca, they present themselves as beautiful women, but make no mistake—they may be beautiful, but they are born from the deep.

–An excerpt from *The Mysterious Deep: A Comprehensive Understanding*

"I've never seen an Aloja before, they were stunning. I mean, their hair, skin, dresses, even their teeth sparkled!" Dilly yelled, too close to my ear.

"So they are aquatic women who turn into birds?" I questioned, just to annoy her.

"Listen, Princess," she said, pointing a finger at me. "I could be ashore right now getting first-hand information, but I'm keeping you company like a good friend."

A brush of something akin to shame washed over me. The hull was empty tonight. Most everyone had gone ashore. I, Dilly, and Inu were lucky enough to have second-day mystery leftovers for dinner. A few of the pirates had stayed on board. I heard a couple superstitious whispers of Aloja women stealing souls, but Dilly classified that as ignorance.

"They are native to Mallorca and act as its guardian. Nothing comes in or leaves without their blessing. It's the reason Mallorca is so wealthy. It's good luck to be born there. I doubt there is a more prosperous coastal town."

"Why Mallorca?" I asked.

Dilly shrugged and scooped a mouthful of something I would spend my life trying to forget.

"No one knows. They don't answer questions about the mysterious deep. Even our Koinu knew to keep its distance," Dilly said.

"At least we can sleep without a sea monster lingering near," I mumbled.

"They are listening," Inu hissed as she scanned the ceiling.

Dilly frowned and set down her food. "It's a theory. There is certainly nothing that happens in Mallorca that they do not know about. How it works, no one is sure. Actually, I can't stand this."

Standing, she threw her arms around me, and I jumped at the sudden contact.

"I'm sorry, I will never forgive myself if I don't go," Dilly said.

I snorted and wrapped my free arm around her, patting her back gently.

"I'm impressed you made it this long, go," I begged.

She squealed and did a quick little dance with her feet, which might have been the most adorable thing I'd ever seen. Her spot was promptly taken by a gray ball of fur who tucked his paws beneath him and settled in a slightly crouched position.

"Oni," Inu murmured.

"He's not so bad," I said, patting Blackbeard's head gently.

Green eyes glared up at me, but he didn't kill me, which was a far cry from the way he treated everyone else. I don't know what Billy and I had that made Blackbeard tolerate us, but I wasn't questioning it.

"He is unnatural," Inu said.

"Are you afraid of a cat too?" I asked incredulously.

She ignored me, which I happily cataloged as a yes.

I stood up, wiped my greasy hands on my too-tight pants, and forced a smile. "Well, I suppose I'll be going to bed now."

Inu stood and set down her bowl.

Realization dawned on me, and I groaned.

"You are coming with me, aren't you."

Excellent. That wasn't inconvenient in the least. The thing was, the more someone told me not to do something, the more I wanted to do it. Even if I hadn't had an inkling to do it before, it would fester in my mind. Plus, there was that itch at the bottom of my foot that demanded to see the world before it was too late.

Every step to Flynn's cabin felt like one step closer to a prison cell. The lights of Mallorca were lit against a starlight night sky. It was beautiful. Music and laughter drifted off cobblestone streets and up into the bay. I want to be a part of it. I ached to live it.

"Have you ever been here before?" I asked.

"No," Inu said.

That was it, no explanation. Just a hard answer that left no room for conversation. She was insufferable.

"I'm trying to understand—" I swallowed, struggling for the words. "Oscar—"

"Are you ready to retire?" Inu said, turning away from the edge.

I sighed loudly. "Do you even want to know me?"

"I know what I need to know," Inu answered.

"Oscar—"

"You are a threat and a risk. You are reckless and impulsive. A flower may speak to the bee, but it still takes everything all the same," she lashed.

Lord, give me strength. "I'm the bee?"

Inu said nothing beneath her ridiculous hat. I was beginning to think that maybe there was no hope. I always imagined Oscar and I would marry and live near each other. Our children and spouses close. Now—now I didn't know anything at all.

There was no point in trying to speak to her. She was hopeless. I walked the rest of the way to my cell and shut the door without saying goodnight. She probably wouldn't have answered anyway.

The room was eerily quiet with not even creaking wood for comfort. The bay was placid. No wrinkles or wind to ebb and flow the top of the water. Magic from the Aloja. They controlled the bay and every drop of water that existed in it. I stared at the hammock that Flynn slept in and then to his bed that I had commandeered.

Blackbeard was purring loudly on top of the sheets while he padded his front paws into the mattress. Completely and utterly content with himself.

"How do you do that?" I asked him.

He merely continued on his merry journey with his padding. He certainly wasn't a normal cat and his ability to appear in random places would have been disconcerting if he wasn't friendly to me. A bubble of humor lodged in my chest at how Flynn would react to finding Blackbeard in his quarters once more.

That bubble popped quickly when I remembered where he was. Under the moon with a beautiful woman who may not have been entirely human, but that didn't matter. I had considered over and over why the Aloja's condition was that Flynn dine with their leader. None of it settled my restless stomach.

He knew them, and they him. There was a history there. My imagination conjured all manner of explanations, each worse than the one before. I shouldn't have cared. Instead, I imagined vivid scenarios that made me want to empty the contents of my stomach. A normal person would have shut it all out and distracted herself, but that had never been my way. Instead, I replayed scenarios that left me anxious and desperate. It was an unconscious punishment that I couldn't shake.

There was no scenario where I stayed on this ship. If I failed and didn't get the money, I would be relegated to a box only to be opened at James' discretion. If I succeeded, I would take my place in spinsterhood and settle amidst a cozy life with my family for company and a few cats. Never again would I be able to see a city protected by creatures of the deep, rich with wealth, and alight with joy and pleasure.

What would you do without me, Rose? I protect you from yourself.

James' voice echoed inside my mind. Maybe it was because he was close, but it felt more real than it ever did before.

I ground my teeth together and faced Blackbeard.

"Know a way out of this place that isn't the front door?" I asked.

He didn't even raise his eyes to me as he continued licking his front paws. Some excuse for a demon cat. Rude.

I walked to one of the windows and stuck my head out of it. Nowhere to go but down, and it was a long way down. The placid waters were deep enough to hold the ship, but I wasn't prepared to bet my life on it.

Damn.

Apparently, I wasn't cut out for pirate life because after one longing look at the city, I kicked off my boots and went to explore Flynn's shelf of trinkets. I wasn't escaping the ship tonight and part of me, the sheltered rich girl part, felt relief in that. To be able to predict the next few hours. The itching in my foot lessened against the feel of cool wood against it.

"Not so impulsive now," I mumbled to the phantom James that rang in my ear.

I reached out and picked up a shell. It was perfectly smooth with a brownish coating over porcelain white. It curled into itself with perfect ridges climbing up it. It wasn't like any shell that washed up on England's beaches. This shell had a story. Amongst foreign items and exciting tails was this small shell. I wondered what it meant to Flynn.

I set it down and ran my fingers over the edge of it once more.

Blackbeard let out a sharp hiss.

"I wasn't going to steal it—" I began, but quickly lost the words.

It turned out that Blackbeard wasn't worried about my morality, but was instead growling, his butt edged toward the sky with his fur standing straight up. His wrath was aimed at the goddess-like woman standing at the center of the room, her ethereal smile trained on me.

"Rosamund," she said.

My name on her lips was a dream. She was the most beautiful woman I had ever seen. Her long golden red hair was a color that didn't exist in the rest of the world. Her face perfectly angular and symmetrical. She wore a long, flowing dress that matched her hair. Perfect. She was perfection.

"Well, you aren't much to look at, are you?" she asked.

Strange that I was inclined to agree with her. Her voice was honey and cozy Sunday afternoons spent with my family.

"Are you a siren?" I asked, my voice hazy and distant.

A melodic laugh rang in the air. "No, I am much more than that."

She stepped towards me and ran a sharpened nail along my chin, urging me to tilt my head up. I complied. I got the feeling that I would do anything she asked of me.

A sharp pain on my bare foot jerked me from my daydream. Blackbeard backed away slowly, never taking his eyes off of the woman. His teeth marks left on my foot, but not enough to draw blood.

The woman laughed, but it didn't hold the same musical quality as before.

"Well, aren't you something?" she said to Blackbeard. "Sadly, I have business elsewhere tonight."

Ximena. The Aloja that the others spoke about. Now that I was released from whatever she had been doing to me, I saw her for what she was. Still beautiful, but dangerous.

"I did not mean to cause offense," I said, trying to think what Dilly would advise.

I should have listened to her more when she was going on and on about them.

"But offend you did," she said sweetly. "Away we go."

I didn't have time to suck in a breath before the wind whipped all around me. It surrounded me and choked me, a vortex on dry land. I was distantly aware of Blackbeard's growl, but it sounded far away. I grabbed at my chest, trying to gulp down air, but nothing came. My chest burned and ached; I couldn't even cry out.

Just as quick as it started, I was dropped. I drew in a breath, but water flooded my lungs as my body hit against the sandy ocean floor, hands digging into unsteady sand. She was drowning me. I pushed against the seafloor and tried to open my eyes, but the salt water burned them, making everything blurry. I finally broke the surface after a few seconds that had felt like an eternity.

I coughed and sucked in air all at once, which only burned my lungs. Heaving, I brought up the seawater that had choked me, all while trying to stay afloat.

"She's fine," Ximena hummed. "Come, child, the shore awaits."

I officially did not like her. It was nice that she thought I was fine, but I very much was not. Nonetheless, now that I had vomited up half the sea and my mystery dinner, I needed to make it to shore. I made to swim, but arms grabbed me.

Not again.

"I prefer not to do the spinny thing again," I said, voice hoarse.

I still couldn't see a thing, but would have greatly appreciated a towel to wipe my eyes.

"The less you say, the better."

Flynn. His voice was low in my ear, tension coating each word. When my feet grazed sandy floors, he lifted me against his chest. I took the opportunity to wipe my eyes against his somewhat still-dry shirt and blinked rapidly.

Slowly, my burning eyes gave way to vision, and I could see the tense line of his jaw. The veins in his neck pulsating.

"Ever the gentleman. I would hate to think you didn't believe me when I said she was fine," Ximena sang nearby.

Slowly, Flynn lowered me to the ground. My legs shook, but I fought for each moment I made it standing. She tried to kill me. A mysterious creature just tried to kill me.

"She's valuable," Flynn answered coldly.

"Yes, I am aware that is the sentiment," Ximena purred.

Slowly, hazy blurs gave way to clarity, and I found myself on a sandy beach illuminated by hundreds of lanterns. A small table sat a few feet away, a single candle at the center. Flynn lowered himself into one of the chairs and began tapping his fingers against the wooden table.

Tap. Tap. Tap.

Ximena stepped forward and sank down into a crouch in front of me. I swallowed hard, she wasn't beautiful anymore, she was terrifying. The way her eyes skated over all of me, calculating and weighing, I had the distinct sensation that she would enjoy killing me.

"Do you see those lights, over there, in the distance?" Ximena asked, pointing behind me.

I turned because everything inside me said that I didn't want to piss her off more than she already was. Out to sea, there was a ship, its form only distinguishable from the shadow the moon cast and its many lanterns.

My heart sank into my stomach.

"The Bane," I said.

"Quite so," Ximena quipped. "There is a charming man on it who claims you are his fiancé and that our mutual friend over there kidnapped you."

Of course, he would.

"I'm not kidnapped," I stated. "I walked onto the Wraith all on my own."

Her heart-shaped lips turned down into a pout. "I think that is true, which is good and bad for you. On the one hand, had you lied to me, well—it would not have went well for you. On the other..."

She hummed once more and stood, pacing back and forth while tapping her finger against her mouth as if thinking. I recognized it. It was how James acted when he thought he was being clever. It was the way he held himself when he told us that the will had been changed. A cat with a mouse.

"What to do with you?" she said, before twirling with her finger raised to the sky and her lips pulled back in a wide smile. "I know! We can invite your fiancé, and they can duel for you!"

She was more than dangerous. She was insane.

"Mena," Flynn said. "You do not need to make this into something it's not."

He sounded irritated, but there was an edge to his voice that coincided with the tap of his fingers.

"Sebastian." She frowned, tsking. "But it already is. Here I thought we would have a beautiful night together, but you were hiding another man's fiancée in your rooms. What do you suppose I am to make of that?"

"It was not meant as an insult. She is a means to an end," he said.

I hated how the words slid like a dagger across my heart. They reminded me how unworthy I was. How inadequate I was in every way that mattered. Not enough to keep James' attention and not enough to tempt the pirate captain. When had I started to give more meaning to those two nights than they were worth? And why did it hurt when I was the one who had just claimed it didn't have to mean anything? A means to an end.

I was a spoiled rich girl who was selfish and thought of myself far too highly. All those selfish pricks I insulted and judged at parties where they discussed their self-importance. Joke was on me that I wasn't that different after all.

"And she is the reason you ask me for la lanterna de camino? Why you seek the Gharaq coven?" Ximena asked, walking to him on feet that left no imprint on the sand.

It was like she glided on thin air. Her movements were soft and delicate when she was anything but. She stood behind him and wrapped her arms over his chest before letting a long red nail trail down his chin sensuously.

I stiffened as I watched him let her touch him. He remained as still as a statue, but the way she touched him was familiar. The way she said his name. How she demanded his attention and time. There was a history there. She rolled her head to rest on top of his and when she opened her eyes she gave me a wide smile with canines that were a little too bright against her red lips.

"She doesn't like it when I touch you," Ximena said.

This bitch. I ground my teeth, keeping from saying anything. This wasn't a game, and I wasn't interested in playing into her hand. However, I didn't for a second doubt that she would send me over to James if it amused her. If I got on that ship I would never get off of it a free woman. Whatever worth I had to Flynn would be null and void against attacking a North Star Line vessel. The crown would send out a fleet, and the Wraith would find herself unwelcome in every port in the world. I would lose everything.

"She's a spoiled rich girl whose idea of a scandal is touching hands outside of marriage. What do you expect?" Flynn said.

Asshole. Even if I saw the story he had laid out to get us out of this, he was still an asshole.

Ximena laughed and ran her palm down his throat, chest, and lower. I was going to throw up. I didn't want to watch this.

I pushed myself off from the sand and attempted to wipe the small desert from my soaked clothes.

"I *am* a spoiled rich girl, and Captain Flynn has agreed to help me remain that way as I happen to enjoy it. That man on the Bane is trying to see to it that I lose my independence and rely entirely on him. You seem like a strong—" I gestured to her, fighting for the words, "woman. Surely, you can understand my motivation. As for being in his cabin, his crew are a bunch of brutes, and I am not interested in having my reputation ruined by a baseless pirate."

A muscle in Flynn's jaw feathered, and I hope he enjoyed the insult since I was just a prudish spoiled rich girl.

Ximena let her other hand trail down his chest, but I forced myself not to look away. To not give up how much I cared even though I shouldn't have.

"Do you know what you ask of my Sebastian? How the Gharaq will greet him?" Ximena asked me before tilting her face low till her mouth was next to his ear. "It was a night much like this one, don't you remember, my love?"

"I remember," he said, his finger stilling its ceaseless tapping.

"And still, you don't forgive me?" she pouted. "We, women—"

She paused and winked over to me. "We are jealous creatures. Yet you won't forgive me for a simple act done out of desperation? It was you who drove me to it, but it is I you blame."

I hadn't the slightest idea what they were talking about, but Flynn was more tense than I had ever seen him and I realized what she was doing. She was baiting him. Preying on his weakness so that he would give away more than he intended to.

"I am told that Mallorca prospers thanks to you and the other Alojas. Maybe we can all help each other," I said.

Her fingers stilled over him and she stood, tilting her head like the hawk eyes the mouse. She raised her eyebrows in answer.

My hands itched to pull her hair which was an urge I was unfamiliar with. Instead, I attempted to pull my black hair to the side and began braiding it. Unconcerned, unbothered. I was unconcerned, unbothered. Not the mouse.

"If we succeed in our plan, not only will we have enough wealth to build an entire country from top to bottom, Flynn will have his reputation solidified. Untouchable. Even the English crown will concede that he is a force to be reckoned with. He will be able to bring wealth and prestige to Mallorca."

Flynn's eyes flashed to mine, and I could practically hear the lecture I was going to get if we made it out of this alive. If we made it out of this alive, I would gladly listen to it. The key was going to be the alive part because there was no doubt in my mind that Ximena would laugh while she watched the life drain from me.

"*If* you succeed," she said, walking toward me.

"Mena—" Flynn started, but she silenced him with a single hand.

There was command in every move she made. She was undoubtedly powerful. The seas around her port sang for her. They loved her and so did the people who lived here. She knew her worth. There was not an ounce of insecurity tied to her. I could only imagine what that felt like.

"And how will you see his throat remains intact when the hags of the Gharaq coven come for him?" she asked.

An excellent question. If we were talking about the same coven then it was possible. Oscar had somehow managed it which was half of why Flynn agreed to my plan in the first place. It would help if I knew why they hated him. Maybe I should have asked earlier.

I shrugged, tying off my braid and putting my hand on my waist.

"Everyone wants something. You want Mallorca to thrive, I want to be rich, Flynn wants notoriety, even a hag must have something she wants."

Her lips twisted as she sneered, her canines flashing. "You are a stupid girl who thinks she knows more than she does. The Gharaq only thirsts for blood. Revenge is all they care about."

My heart quickened under her glare. God, she could kill me in less than a second. My best guess was that ending Flynn was high up on the hag's revenge scheme, which wasn't really an option. Why couldn't I have been gifted my father and Oscar's charisma? This would be so much easier if I knew how to read people.

"She's right," Flynn said.

I couldn't hold back the sigh of relief that broke from me as she turned toward him. It was like my chest could finally rise and fall without her piercing green eyes on me. Seas, she was terrifying. If I lived through this I was going to be Dilly's favorite person.

"You would sacrifice yourself for this *child*?" Ximena screeched as she kicked up her leg, hitting me square in the chest.

All that air rushed from me, and I tried to take a breath, but her foot pushed me against the hard-packed sand. My body sunk into it as she dug her heel in. I grabbed at her foot, but it was fruitless. She wasn't a woman. She was something more.

"Of course not. She may be spoiled, but she's right that I want notoriety," Flynn said. "Do you remember when you first met me? You asked me what I wanted."

Ximena sighed, and her foot lessened the pressure on my chest. I greedily drank in the little bit of air that leaked in.

"You wanted the world to know your name," she said, her accent heavy over the words.

"Not one corner of the world will forget the name of the captain who finds the Maravilla and survives," he said, his voice edging closer.

I lifted my head to see him a foot away, holding his hand out to her. Her mouth settled into a light smile that made her look almost human. She took his hand as he pulled her into him. Releasing her foot from my chest. I gasped in air thinking how I was getting really sick of not being able to breathe.

"Imagine what I could do for you with a legacy like that." His deep voice was a caress that I recognized well. "Imagine how Mallorca would become the envy of every other city in the world when I make it my port of business."

"Si, love," she whispered, nuzzling into his neck.

For the briefest of seconds, his eyes flickered down to mine, and I tried to convey I was fine, but also damn ready to go.

"I'll handle the Gharaq. I've done it before and will again," he said.

It was the wrong thing to say because Ximena stiffened.

"I'm doing this for us, Mena. We will be untouchable," he said.

Her smile returned. Clever bastard. It was a good save.

She pulled away and eyed me like I was an insect on her favorite dress.

"And you need her to do it?" she asked.

"Unfortunately," he said. "Her family has influence and will provide the pardons that will officially make me untouchable."

She turned her lips into the most pathetic excuse for a pout.

"And that can't happen if I give her back to her worried fiancé?"

The words were spoken with a cruel smile in my direction.

"Unfortunately not. He is a hindrance to my plan," Flynn sighed.

She turned, wrapping her arms around Flynn and burying her face into his neck.

"Then I will delay him, my love. If you do not return to me, I will turn the seas into a *huracan*."

"Thank you, Mena. I will return," he answered.

His eyes settled on me, saying nothing and everything. Was I suppose to crawl away? Stab her? Could she even be killed? His intense stare was giving me nothing, but I very much wished I understood.

"Very well," she said.

The world swallowed me in another screaming vortex before I landed hard on my ass on Flynn's cabin floor with Blackbeard staring at me.

"What the actual fuck?" I said.
Blackbeard gave a small meow and walked away.
Touché.

Chapter Eighteen
Vengeful Promises

While many creatures of the deep are capable of speech and human-like behavior, such as the Aloja of Mallorca, sea witch covens, mermaids, and sirens, they will not speak on each other. Attempts to discuss creatures of the deep are always met with hostility.

-An excerpt from *The Mysterious Deep: A Comprehensive Understanding*

No matter how many times I washed, I still found sand in the most inconvenient of places. It was irritating, but at least I was alive. That counted for something. It had been at least two hours since I was plopped back into Flynn's cabin with no signs of him. Likely he had something more comfortable than a hammock to sleep on.

My stomach rolled as I flopped myself back into bed. Sleep would be a welcome friend so I could stop picturing them together. Stop seeing the way her hands caressed him. He wasn't mine. I wasn't his. I didn't care.

The detailed visions in my head said otherwise. Groaning, I pulled the covers over my head as a small thump landed on the bottom of my bed. I lowered the blanket and caught Blackbeard's eyes as he settled into the comfy little nest he made for himself.

"Why do I care so much?" I asked.

He let out a low huff and closed his eyes.

"You aren't very helpful," I muttered.

Close your eyes, Rose. Picture sheep hopping over fences. One, two, three. This wasn't so bad; I could do this. Four, five, six-

A knock on the door.

"No, thank you!" I called.

Seven, eight, nine—the door opened.

Delightful.

"Miss Smith?"

Emille. I would know that French accent anywhere.

"Present." I raised my hand from the bed.

"Dieu Merci." He breathed out.

In a few long strides, he was at my side, pulling off my covers.

"Excuse me very much," I said, sitting up.

He ignored me as he gently grabbed my face and tilted it this way and that.

"You were attacked and didn't say anything for two hours?" Inu asked, coming up behind him to glare at me.

Oh, I see. Now, it made sense. Glad Flynn could take a break from his love to send his physician to check in on me. How thoughtful.

"I didn't see the point in reliving my trauma with company. Seemed more like an alone activity," I said.

"Foolish," Inu muttered.

"Yes, I'm glad to be alive as well," I grumbled as Emille took out a well-used stethoscope and placed it over my heart. "You are a terrible bodyguard, by the way."

At least that made her quiet. Her long hair covered one of her eyes beneath her ridiculous hat. She was very small. It was annoying.

"Does anything hurt?" he asked.

Yes. My pride. There was probably a giant bruise on my butt. I doubted Emille could do much for it.

I shrugged.

"I need to see your chest," he said.

I stared at him open-mouthed. Words failed me. First of all, this man could have been my grandfather. Second, the audacity.

Emille sighed and rubbed the bridge of his nose as if I were the problem here.

"Your airway was constrained for a significant amount of time due to blunt trauma," he explained.

Oh. That made sense. I rubbed at it and winced at the pain that formed beneath. I hadn't even noticed. Too busy playing with my imagination.

"So nice of Flynn to spill all my secrets," I said.

"Miss Smith," he said gently.

I rolled my eyes, but if there was anyone I trusted on this ship, it was Emille. He had given me no reason not to, despite my early suspicion. I worked at the ties of my white gown and paused when I saw the shape imprinted into my skin in sickly bluish-green.

Inu hissed and stepped forward, her face paler than usual as she took in the large bruised footprint on my chest.

"Majo," she cursed.

"Agreed," I said, though I had no idea what the word meant.

"She didn't care for me much," I said, trying to keep panic from climbing further up my body.

I didn't want her imprint on me. I didn't want to remember a single thing from tonight.

Emille furrowed his brow and rubbed at his own chest.

"I'll make up a salve for it, but it will take a few weeks to clear. You have a lot of microscopic hemorrhages that will take time to heal. It will be very tender for a few days."

"Excellent," I said.

I began lacing up the gown much quicker than when I had undone it. I didn't want to see it. The idea of it hurt more than when I physically touched it.

"I can't stay," Emille said, his eyes drifting above, searching.

"Hm, all-knowing. That's fine. I need to sleep anyway," I said.

If I threw a foul gesture I saw Barnacles do, I wondered if Ximena would see it.

With a gentle pat on my shoulder, Emille left me. I rolled onto my side and watched as Inu took a seat at Flynn's desk.

"You are staying in here now, huh?" I asked.

Silence stretched for a minute with only the purring cat at my feet.

"I'm sorry," Inu said.

Oh. I was used to her being miserable all the time that I hadn't noticed the way her demeanor had changed. Her shoulders hung forward ever so slightly which was in stark contrast to her impeccable posture. Even her voice was softer.

"You can't be held liable for murderous, mysterious creatures who want to kill me," I said.

She said nothing, but her lips pressed into a thin line. Not only for consolation, then. It was fine, though, because I didn't know how much I had in me to make others feel better when my insides were as volatile as stormy seas. I felt like shit.

One, two, three, four, five... one sheep at a time.

Shouting ripped me from my nightmares, where a beautiful woman drowned me while laughing. As my soul left my body, I watched Flynn pull her against him and press his mouth against hers. Over and over.

"Secure the main sail!" Oscar's voice shouted.

Oscar. At least he was alive too. Glad he cared enough to check on his sister. A crack of my eye showed that Inu was gone, too. The telltale rock of the ship was a sensation I hadn't realized I missed.

We were moving. Thank God and the seas.

I sat up finding a set of black pants and a navy blouse. I held it up and smiled. This would fit a lot better. I would have to thank Dilly when I saw her even if it meant recounting my time with an Aloja.

Pulling on my boots, I stared at my reflection. The time spent at sea had darkened my skin and amplified the freckles across the bridge of my nose. I looked healthier on mysterious gruel than I ever had on fine dining. Even the sea-salt air had tightened my curls in a way I used to spend hours trying to achieve.

The sea agreed with me. It was a shame I didn't agree with it.

I ran a hand over my chest, wincing at the pain it elicited. Aloja or not, I couldn't see myself choosing a lifetime of this. For Oscar, the sea had called to him; it was a finding. I had never felt that. My star necklace sat high on my neck, the bottom of it barely missing the bruising below. No one would notice unless they knew. It might have been a shadow.

Even braiding my hair hurt with every movement of my arms. I wished I could remember what Inu had called her so I could say it again. Bitch would have to do for now.

Blackbeard was nowhere to be found. I was really beginning to get curious about where he went during the day. He was the strangest cat I had ever met, but he was growing on me all the same.

The bridge was busy with everyone going to and fro. Unfortunately, Mallorca was still visible in the distance, which meant we weren't far enough away for me to take a full breath. Every rustle of the wind felt like something was lurking behind me. Like at any moment, I would be snapped up in that vortex only to be plummeted to the bottom of the sea.

"Good morning, princess!" Val said, patting me on the back.

God, I wished she would stop doing that. I raised my hand to my chest as if that would take away the sharp ache that formed there. I opened my mouth to speak, but the words floated away on the tide as my eyes landed on Flynn. He wore all black today like he was in mourning, but all it did was make him even more devastating.

His eyes poured over me like a rainstorm. Clinical, assessing, but consuming. His eyes lingered too long over where my bruise was before his attention snapped away. I felt the loss of it in every cell of my body. I didn't want to care. I really didn't.

"Jameson, your Quartermaster gave you an order. If the mast isn't secured in the next three minutes, you are on pen duty for the next three months." Flynn's words were as sharp as a knife.

Several of the other pirates gave him a wide berth as he worked.

"Bailey!" he shouted.

Across the way, Oscar stood next to Inu, quietly exchanging words. As soon as his name was called, he strode across like he didn't have an ounce of fear for the pirate captain calling his name. It was more than most of the people on the ship could say. Oscar made it a foot across from him before his eyes flicked to mine.

For a moment, just one quick moment, he was my brother again. His face softened, and his lips turned down into the frown that I knew to mean, "I'm sorry." It was the same face he always gave me whenever we would get in trouble, but somehow, I got the brunt of the rebuttal.

"Maybe if you spent less time socializing, you wouldn't be risking us running aground by a poorly stripped front mast," Flynn snapped.

Oscar dragged his eyes from me and met his captain's cold fury.

"Yes, Captain, I'll do better," he said.

"I leave the deck to you, Bailey," he said.

Without another glance or word, he went below deck, probably to terrorize some other poor soul.

"You would be wise to hide while you can, princess." Val half laughed as she strode away.

Somehow, hiding didn't feel like it would get me far, considering I had been alone in a closed room last night before I had been nearly murdered. Either way, I wanted to see Mallorca fade into the distance. Once it was out of sight, I might be able to take a full breath.

Luckily, I knew right where Dilly would be. Sure enough, she sat on a barrel on the stern with her spyglass glued to her eye. At least there was some consistency onboard the Wraith.

"Is our Koinu following?" I asked.

A strangled gasp pulled from her as she nearly dropped her spyglass, barely catching it before it fell to the ground.

"That was mean!" she shouted.

I tried not to laugh at the petulant frown she wore that only made her somehow more adorable.

Murmuring an apology, I lowered my forearms to the edge of the ship and stared out at the dwindling form of mountains and hills that was Mallorca. What had seemed like a beautiful dream had quickly turned into a nightmare on her shores. I would die a happy woman if I never saw them again.

"Want to talk about it?" Dilly asked.

The nice thing about Dilly was that she didn't hover. She merely asked the question and resumed her stalking of our sea monster puppy. She was the last thing I expected to find on the Wraith, but I was grateful for her.

"I had a bad night, is all," I said. "How was yours?"

Her lips turned down. "Not great. I suppose that's what I get for abandoning you. The people that live there are very protective of the Aloja and won't say much other than singing their praises."

I fought back a snort. They probably had to say nice things on pain of death. Then again, there was no denying the wealth of Mallorca. Honestly, I didn't really care. Whether they ruled with a strong hand or made everyone feel the warm cuddles was irrelevant.

"How long do you think before we are out of their territory?" I asked.

Dilly wrinkled her nose. "My own ignorance is like a knife to the gut."

Despite my horrendous evening a laugh fell from my lips, but it was chased with pain that came with the movement. Alright, no laughing. I would just have to spend more time with Inu.

"When the mountains fade, we will be free of the Majo."

A rush of energy shot straight up through my toes and into my heart at Inu's unexpected presence. Clutching her heart, Dilly blew out a long breath.

"Why is everyone determined to scare me to death today?" she asked.

My own heart raced like there was a threat lurking beneath the deckboards. There probably was.

Inu gave no explanation for her behavior, but instead stood next to me staring out at the receding mountain line. Almost there.

It hurt to take a full breath, but even if it didn't, I couldn't. Not until I was sure there wasn't a chance I would be sucked up and drowned. Every minute felt like an hour. Even when Dilly pointed out a pod of dolphins following in our wake, I didn't take my eyes off those mountains. Beside me, Inu did the same.

For Dilly, those mountains were still a place of possibility and adventure, but we knew the truth. Those mountains were death.

"What a shame," Dilly muttered as the last of them faded into the sea.

My chest loosened until I deflated in on myself, shoulders dropping. My hands ached from how tight I had been clenching them, but it was over. I never had to go back there. Part of me ached to shout out obscenities on the off chance they could still hear, but even I wasn't that stupid.

"Miss Smith."

I stiffened. Every bone in my body recognized the command in that voice that was only slightly more raspy than normal. If I turned around, I would have to acknowledge him. Did I want to? No, not really. It would have been useful to have another year to process how I felt about last night in regard to him.

Had he pulled me from the water? Yes. Did he just sit there while his love tried to kill me? At least ninety percent. I could appreciate that he said a few words that might have aided my cause. That ten percent stung, though.

"I think he's talking to you," Dilly whispered as she sent a reassuring smile to Flynn.

Turns out I only needed about three minutes to process it. I was mad at him.

"I heard him," I said.

The pod of dolphins continued to chase the waves the Wraith made, clicking and diving without a care in the world. I used to know what that felt like. A year ago, before I learned of James' infidelity, that had been me. And I had been happy. I would have traded the entire last year of my life to have never lost that feeling.

"I will not ask again, Miss Smith," he said.

"You didn't ask the first time either," I grumbled.

"There is no order on a ship if there is no respect for her captain," Inu whispered next to me.

That seemed like more of a problem for the captain than for me. A pang of regret ripped through me, and it occurred to me for the first time since leaving that I was homesick. I missed Oliver and his banter. I missed my little sisters and how annoying they were when they wouldn't leave me alone. I missed Ruby's laugh. God, I even missed being lectured by my mother on proper etiquette. In all of the excitement, I had barely considered them.

Did they believe enough to tell the little ones that I was away visiting Oscar? Was my father angry at me? I should have stopped to consider that my mother might keel over the moment she read my letter. Selfish.

I was everything James had ever accused me of being. Even Flynn had been right last night when he called me a spoiled rich girl. Even now, when I was horrendously self-aware, all I could think about was if Oliver was working on attaining the pardons I had promised an entire crew of pirates.

"Miss—"

"All right, fine!"

I spun around to find several heads turned towards us, but more concerning was the hard set to Flynn's jaw and the way his eyes burned into me like he could will me into submission. He could never. I may have been a lot of things, but pliable I was not.

I stomped right past him and down the steps.

"Let's go, *Captain*," I called.

I ignored the open mouths and stares along the way to the cabin. I hope they enjoyed the show. They wanted me to be a princess? Here was a damn princess. Maybe I would be like Billy and put on a grand performance reenacting my near-death experience while their captain had a nice long sit on the beach.

It took everything in me not to slam the door in his face behind—well, it almost took everything. The door swung with lightning speed, but he was quicker. The smack of his hand against the wood ricocheted across the room and I hoped it hurt as bad as it sounded. I made it to the desk and turned to prop myself against it.

Flynn shut the door with haunting calmness before shaking out his right hand. Good. At least dreams still came true even out in the mysterious deep.

"Rosamund," he said.

God, I shivered. I hated myself. No one had ever said my name quite like that and I doubted they ever would. I probably should have been afraid. His tall frame was tight with tension, and hands clenched into fists at his side. There was no softness or humor in those pale eyes.

I would not be giving him the courtesy of my fear. Instead, I folded my arms over my chest and raised my eyebrows.

He lifted a hand and slowly lowered it like he'd thought better of it. Frustration rippled over his face as he opened his mouth to speak, but thought better of his words and closed it. I watched the struggle with smug satisfaction. Good.

"Your lover is a bitch," I said.

He let out a long, tense breath and rubbed at the bridge of his nose before his hand tracked down his face and over his beard.

"Rosamund," he tried again. "You cannot undermine me in front of my crew like that."

"If only I was sorry," I shot back.

Raising his finger he closed his eyes and took another breath like I was taking years off his life. He opened his eyes, and I stilled as they tracked down to where Ximena's foot was stamped on my chest. The urge to cover my hand over it was strong, but I clutched the desk behind me instead.

"I'm sorry," he said. "I'm sorry for what happened last night. I was arrogant enough to think I could protect you and didn't warn you about her."

The veracity in the words struck right over her imprint, tangling until my chest ached with more than a bruise.

"A warning would have been nice," I murmured.

The step he took was quickly compromised by the thoughts inside his head. A pit opened in my stomach as he clenched his jaw and nodded towards my chest.

"Emille says it's bad."

The words were heavy and hoarse, like he had to force them out. Like he wanted to run from it as much as I did, but I couldn't hide from it, and therefore, neither should he. I slowly undid the lacing of my blouse and watched as his face drained of all color.

My feet threatened to give out on me, but I could do this. I would do this. It meant something, even if I didn't know what.

My chest heaved while his didn't move like he was saving all his air for what came after.

"I'm sure she will enjoy knowing I'll think about her every time I see it for the next few weeks." I shrugged.

Why did I do that? Stand firm to make a statement and then make light of it like my entire body wasn't hurting after last night. Not just my body, but also something much more fragile. He had sat there and watched.

I don't know whether I appreciated the steps he took toward me or hated him even more for them. That he thought he should. That he could.

All I knew was that I didn't want to see what he saw in the outline of my chest. The lesser evil was staring at the imprint of Ximena's delicate foot and remembering what it felt like not to breathe. What it felt like to know I was dying and that my life had meant nothing in the end.

My eyes burned with the inconvenience of it all. Of being hurt, but mostly that I cared enough to cry. That was the worst part.

His finger beneath my chin, gently urged me to look at him, but I refused. I had given enough to him, he didn't deserve this too.

"Rosamund," he urged. "I swear on my mother's grave that I will find a way to kill her, and if it pleases you, then I will make sure you are there to watch it. I will make it as swift or as painful as you ask of me."

They were the only words that could have convinced me to raise my head to his. The only words that were stronger than the pain inside my chest. His eyes were born from a god of vengeance. I had watched this man lie to me and speak his truth in the same sentence. This was a truth as radiant and real as the sun shining above us.

"That's really violent," I whispered.

I didn't even achieve a hint of a smile on his stoic face. All right then.

"I thought you were a... thing," I confessed.

He inhaled sharply from his nose, but didn't pull away.

"She is a cancer I am forced to endure and my punishment, but she was never meant to be yours as well. For that, I am more sorry than words can say," he said.

I wanted to fall into the words and the emotions he held out to me with open hands, but I'd done that for a man once before, and I wouldn't make that mistake twice. I attempted to take a step back, but the desk blocked my escape. Fine.

I raised my eyes to him and let him see how angry I was. I held onto the anger and tried to push away the pain.

"How can you stand here and say that you want her dead when you just sat there and let her touch you?" I accused.

He sucked his cheeks in tight and licked his lips.

"Know this. In the Mysterious deep you are no longer the apex predator. You are the prey."

I let the words bubble beneath my skin, oozing and festering. No matter how much sense they made, I wasn't prepared to concede my anger. It felt like safety among barbed wires. It felt like hiding.

"You want me to forgive your actions last night on the basis that you were scared?"

He stepped forward, pinning me to the desk while he braced it beside me.

"I wasn't scared, Rosamund," he said, pinning me with his eyes. "I was terrified."

Oh. The sea air drifted off of him, and for just a second, I was back at The Siren and The Kraken, meeting him for the first time. A path without fear of consequences. An impulse that felt right for once. It would have been tainted if I had seen the road that would open because of it. Some things were just meant to live in memory, a single moment in time, preserved with profound bias and the possibility of what could have been.

"Do you realize how easily she could have killed you? I wouldn't have been able to stop her if she decided to, but know I would have followed you into the sea," he said.

God, all I wanted was to be mad at him. He couldn't even let me have that. Like ice faced with warm rain, I melted till all I had was the memory of anger.

"You should have told me about her," I whispered.

He closed his eyes for the barest of seconds, gathering himself.

"The Aloja are able to see and hear beyond what should exist. Had I given any hint that you meant more to me than a means to an end, she would have drowned you in minutes of arriving in her territory," he said.

"I mean something to you?" I asked.

Stupid, stupid Rose. That was not what I should have been focused on. Not the question that should have sprung from my lips like a frog catching a bug.

Flynn leaned forward, his thumb and finger dragging my gaze up to him. Our lips were a hair's breadth apart. I could practically taste him on the air we shared, and god, it shot a thrill through me that I thought I'd never feel again.

"You have never been nothing to me. Since the moment we met, you have been an obsession. I went to the other side of the world to try and forget the way you tasted. There isn't a day that goes by where I don't think about how you looked with your long hair spread over my bed, how you—"

I stopped breathing. It happened all on its own, but I was dying. Those words. They lit a fire inside me that was smothering all the air from my chest. I knew he had a wicked mouth, but hearing it now after last night, oh god.

He stepped back and released his spell over me. Regret settled where lust had been only moments before. As always, I had messed this up. I always said or did the wrong thing, but how could I even begin to know when I didn't know what I wanted. My body craved him, yes, but he also infuriated me. It was a conundrum, and I would need years of thoughtful recourse to tangle through the braids of small truths and hopeful lies.

"Breathe, Rose." he urged.

If my chest didn't ache inside and out, I would have told him not to tell me what to do, but instead, I ran my hand over it and winced as the pain rippled over me.

One. Two. Three.

Still, my chest thrummed with too much chaotic energy.

Breathe, breathe. In and out.

My chest loosened a fraction, and air came in.

My chest was pliable, able to hold all the air it needed.

Finally, air pulled into my desperate lungs, leaving me aching down to my bones.

"I'm sorry, I shouldn't have," he said.

I waved a hand, "It's fine."

It didn't soothe him, as he watched me with an intensity that said if I showed the smallest cracks, he would know.

"Really, I'm fine."

"Rosamund." he chastised.

Rolling my eyes, I took another life-sustaining breath.

"You say my name like it means something else. Regardless, you were an asshole for not warning me, and now is an excellent time to tell me anything else that might want to kill me along this merry trip."

He watched my breath like I would cease at any point which was fair, but I hated the concern in his eyes. I didn't want it, but at the same time, it felt like the only thing I had ever wanted.

"Ximena referenced another night like last night," he said.

Her name grinded against my bones. If I could wipe it from my memory, I would.

"Did she? I must not have caught it amongst almost dying a few times," I said.

He clenched his jaw even tighter, and I wondered if I was going to kill him. The tension in his shoulders made it look like he might keel over at any moment.

"Ten months ago, I made the mistake of becoming... involved with one of the crew. Only Oscar knew. Ximena still found out. She drowned her on the same beach she held you down on."

My chest ached with something new. Something sharper than physical blows. Ten months ago.

"Oh." I said.

My hands ached with the need to do something, anything. I pulled my braid over my shoulder and began fidgeting with the edge, but his words only moments ago crawled back into my mind. *There isn't a day that goes by where I don't think about how you looked with your long hair spread over my bed.*

Except apparently, there *had* been a day or two where he hadn't thought of it. Only a few months after stealing my twin and leaving me stranded, as if that were somehow romantic. Bile climbed up my throat, and I found I regretted asking for more information.

Chin up, Rose. Don't let them see you falter. My father's voice rang in my ears.

I willed my eyes to stop burning. We were nothing. No attachments. It never meant anything.

"That would have been more useful twenty-four hours ago," I said.

My voice was steady and strong. Better than I could have hoped for.

"I'm telling you because the Gharaq coven took her into their ranks, and they hold me personally responsible for her death. I barely survived the last interaction," he said.

"That's why you owe Oscar. He convinced them to let you go," I said.

Flynn ran his hand over his neck like he did anytime the coven was mentioned. For the first time, I wondered how close he had come to dying. More concerning was the relief that filled me at the fact that Oscar had been there to save him. It was a dichotomy I wasn't mentally prepared to analyze.

"He did, but the only way into the Glass Sea is with the tonic only they possess. The wraiths feed off emotion. It's as much a beacon to them as any lighthouse. To enter the Glass Sea without that tonic is a death sentence," he said.

"How does it work?" I asked.

He shook his head once and sat himself down on the unmade bed, exhaustion pulling the lids of his eyes down.

"It numbs you. If we knew more, maybe it could be recreated, but the Gharaq are the only option, and they know it," he said.

Well, that was inconvenient.

"Will they even give it to you at this point?" I asked.

It was quickly seeming like all of this had no purpose. That I had accumulated all this extra trauma for the fun of it all. I'd marry James and settle into a miserable life, but at least I'd have occasional panic attacks to remind me of my time at sea. Delightful.

"You were right that everyone has something they want. It's a simple matter of transaction," he said.

And just like that, I understood Ximena more than I had before and certainly more than I wanted to. Dread coiled around my heart like a snake preparing to strike its fatal blow.

"So what? You are just going to sacrifice yourself? That's not a plan!" I said, an octave too high.

He gave a bitter smile. "No, unfortunately, what you said about me was correct as well. I set out to create a name that meant something in every corner of the world. I will not be throwing all of that away for vengeful witches, no matter how deserving."

Relief cascaded over me, releasing its hold on my heart. The ignorant part of me, the spoiled rich girl part, never considered lives would be lost on an idea I had concocted. Maybe I could learn to cope with names I didn't know, but not him. Not Oscar.

A rock dropped into my stomach as I realized the list had grown. Dilly, Billy, Emille. God, even Inu.

I was a proper idiot.

He stood and I realized whatever this was, was about to end. I knew that distance in his eyes well enough. We were old friends by now, after all.

"We will light the lantern at sundown, and it will lead us to the Gharaq coven. Whether that takes one day or three, we will see. They are known for being elusive even with the help of the lantern. In the meantime, Emille will see to your injuries. If you are not in the cabin, then Inu should be no more than three feet from you, do you understand?"

"No." I snorted. "Also, can I have a new governess? I don't like mine," I said.

Apparently, I wasn't funny today, which seemed odd to me.

The door opened and Oscar's dark head of hair popped through before he quickly closed the door behind him.

I felt the smile lift my cheeks before I could think better of it. It was the same way he used to sneak us into the kitchen. I was willing to bet several shillings that he was just as bad at it now as he was then.

"Knocking is preferred," Flynn said, rubbing his eyes.

"Yeah, and not getting my sister killed is also preferred, so I guess we will both have to be sorry."

My brother's words were sharp without any of the usual softness that carried them. I had never heard him take that tone with another person, not even Oliver, when he framed him for breaking Mother's favorite vase.

This close, I could see the circles around his eyes that said he wasn't sleeping, decorated by crow's feet beside his eyes. He had the same appearance as when Peaches went missing one weekend. It turns out he had been having a grand time with the neighbor's Persian cat, which then gave birth a few months later to a litter of kittens with a tell-tale gray tail. Oscar hadn't slept the whole weekend and had spent most of it outside calling for our cat until Mother insisted he come inside lest the neighbors talk.

"I'm alive." I shrugged.

"Goddamnit, Rose," he said.

He quickly pulled me into a hug that hurt more than it helped, but I suspected that it was more for him anyway. I raised my hands and gently patted him on the back, biting back the urge to say "there, there" like Mother always did.

"I'm sorry, I should have realized that was a bad idea. I mean, I knew it was a bad idea, but I thought if we were smart about it. I'm a fucking idiot, and I'm sorry, Rosie. So sorry," he said in a rush.

"Only a quarter of that made sense, but also, I would really appreciate being told I might be vengefully murdered the next time *before* I get vortexed into the sea," I said.

Oscar pulled away and captured my face in my hands, squishing my cheeks together as he stared at me like I was a difficult child and he an exhausted parent.

"This isn't a joke. You could have died," he said.

"I'm aware," I said through tight cheeks.

He finally released me, and I rubbed at my face before a realization dawned on me.

"Oscar Reginald Bailey, you wanted to leave me on that cursed island and hand me over to the Bane?" I pointed a finger at his chest for emphasis.

At least he had the good sense to blush.

"The plan," he shot a glare behind him in the direction of the captain, "was to not give Ximena a reason to be suspicious."

It felt like that was a terrible plan, considering the last time they tried that. More so, an annoying part of me wanted to know the context of that particular accusation. However, I was not going to ask because some things were better left buried.

"Are you done yet?" Flynn asked, irritation combing the edges of his voice.

"Does it hurt?" Oscar asked, ignoring his captain.

Apparently whatever power struggle they shared in front of the crew didn't matter in here.

"It hurts worse than when Rebecca sacked me with her doll when I told her it looked like an elephant mated with a giraffe," I said.

His answering laugh was clipped, but it still eased the breath in my lungs.

"It *did* look like that," he said.

I didn't get any warning as he pulled me into him once more. I fought from letting out the squeak that climbed up my throat with the rush of pain against the bruise. It wasn't worth upsetting him.

"I have to go, but if you want to stay in my cabin you can. We will come up with a reason," Oscar said.

"Bailey," Flynn warned.

For some reason, unbeknownst to me, I preferred when they got along better than this, even though I had spent an entire year being mad about it. Time was strange.

"I'm fine, Oscar. Inu already hates me enough." I said.

His face fell, lack of sleep meeting disappointment in the way his shoulders fell forward.

"She doesn't hate you, Rosie." he said.

Nope, not doing this now, even if I started it.

A knock on the door saved me. I tracked Flynn's movement as he went to the door. I wished I hated the way he looked, that his tall and muscular form appalled me like the aristocratic men did. I definitely wished I didn't feel the pull of him like a thread that connected us.

Lust is different from affection, Rose.

If only I could separate the two, but I seemed incapable. Emille stepped through the creaking door, holding a small glass container. At least there was that.

"Bailey," Flynn ordered.

I opened my mouth and closed it fast enough that I might have swallowed a fly. I had almost answered him. Horror pooled low in me. Flynn met my gaze, and the color pulled from his face as he realized it, too. Had seen my error.

Luckily, no one else had noticed as Oscar stepped back, his face quickly hardening from my brother to the quartermaster of the Wraith, who was no one to me.

I wished it didn't feel like a stitch in my side, like I was losing something. More than ever, I knew why this ruse was important, but I hated every second of it.

"Twice a day," Emille said as he handed me the cool glass. "If you notice any fatigue, dizziness, or bruising anywhere else, let me know immediately."

I squared my hand to my forehead and saluted, "Got it."

Even Emille fell victim to the tension in the room and retreated out as quickly as he had come.

Flynn watched me a moment before he turned his back. "Three feet, Miss Smith."

The door shut firmly, leaving me with a sore chest, hurt feelings, and a vial of unknown salve.

All of that and still all my traitorous, lust-ridden head could come up with was, *There isn't a day that goes by where I don't think about how you looked with your long hair spread over my bed.*

Chapter Nineteen
There are Rules

It is unfathomable what lurks beneath the seas unbeknownst to men.

–A quote from the London Gazette

Dilly was there in moments, running her hands over it like it was another mysterious creature for her to learn.

She wrinkled her nose before pouting. "The fight was that bad, huh?"

Swatting her away, I self-consciously fiddled with it. It might have been a mistake. All right, it *had* been a mistake, but I couldn't get his words out of my head, and I was mad at him. It felt like a clever punishment until I was halfway through, and reality set in. By then, it was commit or sink.

"You should treat him with the respect he is owed," Inu said behind me.

I craned my head to fix her with a glare that I hoped she felt in her soul. "He's not my captain. I didn't sign up to be a part of this crew. I am a *hostage*, remember?"

"Yes, but a very well-kept and adored hostage." Dilly chirped.

At least Inu didn't have anything to add. She just stood stoic with her eyes hidden beneath her hat. Black hair trailing down to her waist. It was about time I made my peace that I would never understand her and Oscar. It was a mystery greater than even our Koinu.

"How's puppy today?" I asked.

Turning out to the sea, Dilly gave a long sigh. "Following closer since we left the Aloja's territory, but still not doing anything that makes me feel like he's a threat."

"Good Koinu!" I hollered out to it.

"Baka." Inu hissed. "Do not call out to shi."

A haunting bellow came from behind the ship, and all three of us stilled. Its call echoed through the endless sea and sky surrounding us.

"Did you hear that?" I whispered.

But Dilly was already rushing to the edge of the ship, spyglass to her eye. I watched her with dread and something else that gathered around me. Was it possible that Koinu answered? That was ridiculous.

"It's still following," she said. "Maybe it was a humpback; they tend to habitat here."

"Maybe," I said.

I opened my mouth to test the theory when commotion from the other side of the ship erupted.

"They are lighting the lantern," Inu said.

"Oh, I can't miss this!" Dilly shouted and took off without another glance.

"Well, off we go, governess," I said, holding out my arms.

She raised an eyebrow in question, but I just waved her away. The nice thing about Inu was that she was consistent. If I walked, she walked.

Nearly all the crew had gathered on the top deck, and I had to fight to squeeze my way in. At the bow of the ship, my brother and Flynn stood working over a dull black lantern. It certainly didn't look like it was worth almost dying for.

"Steady, Billy," Flynn shouted.

"Aye, Captain," Billy called from where he held the helm of the ship.

I stood paralyzed among the whispering conversations around us as Oscar held out a long knife to Flynn, who wrapped a thick brown rope around the lantern's ring several times. When he was satisfied with his knot he took the knife from Oscar and began working on the excess rope.

"Nice hair, Princess." Val appeared out of nowhere, slapping me on the back as per usual.

I choked out the cough she pushed from me. Maybe I regretted being friends with her, but whenever I saw the scar over her eye, I couldn't help but think better about her friend rather than her enemy.

"Shit," Oscar shouted.

Instinct took over, and I dashed my gaze to him, knowing that if something ever happened to him, I would know. It's how I managed the last year. If Oscar died, I would know. We came into this world together, and that meant something, but it wasn't Oscar who was hurt.

Crimson dripped from Flynn's hand onto the glass walls of the lantern and the ship's deck. Oscar quickly ripped a piece of cloth from his shirt and handed it to his Captain, whose eyes raised to mine for a fraction, the hardness there unreadable.

Good. I hope he felt thoroughly put out.

His eyes off of mine felt like freedom. It was beginning to occur to me that I was a hostage in more ways than one on the Wraith.

Val beside me laughed and slapped me on the back. God, I wished she'd stop doing that.

"Stop being a distraction, Princess." She laughed, making her way through the crowd.

I could feel Inu's disapproval beside me.

"I didn't do anything," I muttered.

"Oh, Princess, I think we all know what you did." Dilly chuckled.

My cheeks warmed against her words and the insinuation in them. I probably should have retreated into the safety of my bed at that point, having thoroughly mortified myself.

"I thought you were supposed to be my friend." I pouted.

Dilly's smile brightened against the nearly lost sun.

"I am, but also, I am just a girl who is fascinated by the tension between you two just as

much as everyone else," she said.

Just when I didn't think I could be any more mortified, I found myself wishing that the ship would open a giant hole and swallow me.

"There is no tension," I choked.

Dilly's laugh was melodious and offensive to my ears. It didn't matter if we both knew I was lying, there were rules. Protocols. You didn't just announce things like that. It was a delicate dance of pretending not to notice and watching from the shadows. For the first time since coming to the Wraith, I missed London society. There were rules.

"There are rules," I said, under my breath.

"Rules?" Dilly said, nuzzling closer to me. "Do tell."

"Please leave me alone," I said, sliding further from her.

"No one makes a sound until my mark," Flynn called.

All the whispers and side conversations died down and it was honestly a relief. At least Dilly wouldn't keep asking questions I didn't want the answer to.

My stomach sank to the sea floor as Flynn climbed over the bow of the ship. A very real, very loud part of me wanted to rush forward, but no one else was. No one else showed an ounce of concern that their captain was climbing up the long bowsprit that might as well have been a plank. As if there weren't a giant sea monster right behind us.

I opened my mouth, but Inu quickly covered it like she had been waiting for it. I glared at her and pulled her hand away. She merely lifted a finger to her lips.

Fine, we could all quietly watch Flynn fall off the Wraith into the sea and be crushed by his own ship. Delightful plan.

My feet filled with that itch, and I knew I wasn't going to last much longer. The silence with so many bodies gathered together while Flynn neared the edge of the bowsprit. He slowly and with more balance than I'd ever had a day in my life, lowered his body and began wrapping the cut rope around the end.

My chest ached with the telltale sign. I was absolutely going to pass out if this ended poorly.

Wrap after wrap, like his life depended on this lantern staying in place. The irony was that his life was probably safer without it. Unbidden images of what she must have looked like flooded me. Probably blond with a long and lean body. She must have been something for him to break his own rule and become involved with a crew member. Not to mention Ximena finding out. I hated the insecurity that ate at me like a biblical plague of locusts.

It shouldn't have mattered. Two nights one year ago without any strings attached shouldn't have left me feeling... Oh, I realized with a start that I knew this feeling. It was inky darkness that tarnished every moment before and after. Betrayal.

I would spend hours combing through the memories, trying to spot where I should have known sooner. When James had pulled me aside at a party and said everyone there was boring and we should retire early for the night. Why hadn't I seen then that he was being unfaithful? The times he would tell me he couldn't wait for me to be his wife and I would swoon with anticipation. I should have seen it coming. I should have known.

Even if Flynn and I agreed that it meant nothing, my stupid heart clearly didn't know how to do nothing.

I watched with growing horror as the sun sank beyond our sky and cloudy darkness set in. He wouldn't be able to see soon. This was a suicide mission.

I scanned the faces in front of me, but everyone was focused on the captain. All except one. Oscar met my eyes and mouthed a single word, "Breathe."

Inu let out a short hiss beside me, and Oscar turned back to Flynn. Stupid.

Luckily, everyone's eyes were focused ahead, but if anyone had seen they might start asking questions we didn't want asked. Inu beside me was like a vengeful rock waiting to bestow its wrath on unsuspecting souls.

Just as I began feeling the hazy dizziness of lack of oxygenation, Flynn struck a match and lit the lantern. It burned a ghostly blue that barely kept its light. Luckily, Flynn stood and made for the ship. I counted each step. One, two, three. My breathing eased with each increase in count. Seven, eight, nine.

I inhaled, feeling my lungs expand with life sustaining air. In the darkness, I could have sworn his eyes flickered to mine before he turned back around to face the lantern while he held on to a beam. Safe. He was safe and I knew how to breathe.

"East, Billy," Flynn called.

His steel voice cut through the night like a knife.

"Aye, Captain," Billy said, his thick accent hoarse like he had been holding his breath as well.

I heard the turn of the helm more than I saw it. Normally, the ship would be bright with lantern light, but tonight, there was only one light that mattered. Blue wisps continued, and I wondered what we were waiting for.

"South," rasped Flynn.

"Aye, Captain," Billy said.

The ship groaned as it turned and the waves crashed harder against the side, arguing the change in direction. The lantern light gave way and a sickly green smoke filled the glass.

"We have our heading," Flynn announced.

The ship erupted into cheers which died down as the green fire grew with strength. The light bounced off Flynn's face making him look like the god of the Underworld himself. I wished the shiver that ran through my body was made of fear.

"No lights except below deck," he said. "Barnacles, you are on first lantern watch."

"Aye, Captain," said a deep voice behind me.

I nearly jumped when he pushed through me and into the sea of bodies ahead at his captain's orders. I turned with a sinking feeling and found the twins standing a few feet behind me. The one who had threatened me, Amos, gave me a bright smile and raised his hand, wiggling his fingers. His brother quickly snatched his hand away and whispered furiously. I couldn't say I knew his type, but I did get the sense that he was a ticking bomb. Only contained for so long.

I took a step closer to Inu. For once I didn't hate her being there. For once.

"If the light dims or turns any other color, I hear about it immediately, am I understood?" Flynn said, command dripping off of him like the ichor of an immortal.

The answering chorus from his crew said enough. He was more than understood. He was respected and feared in equal measure. A balance that had to be carved out, no doubt. He was a dangerous man by any stretch of the imagination. So why wasn't I scared as he made his way through the crowd, coming straight for me?

Maybe fear was the reason my breath hitched. Maybe it was the reason my legs felt like grandmother's ancient gelatin dessert, desperate to remain vertical. More likely, it was fear that pulled me, too, like a gravitational force.

"Definitely fear," I whispered as he stood above me.

"Worried, Princess?" he asked, the corner of his lip tugging up.

Oh, I see. I may not have grown up around pirates and ruffians, but I had come of age in London society, and I was more than prepared for this.

I threaded my hands behind and smiled sweetly up at him.

"Not at all, Captain, though I suppose I did have some concerns about your distractibility. Do you often cut your hand while working?" I asked.

He sucked in a sharp breath through his nose, but I caught the pull of his cheek, the whisper of a dimple. It was there and gone in a single blink. Shame.

"There is a first time for everything," he said.

I tilted my head and nodded sagely. "Take care, Captain."

A twitch of the lips, but it was hidden as he dipped his head to breathe against my ear.

"I wonder what this version of you would look like—"

"Oh god," I shouted, earning a couple of stray glances.

"Take care, Miss Smith," he said, as he left me with heat burning up my thighs.

I choked out a cough as his words simmered in my blood and pulled at the strings of memory I carried like an oath despite my best intentions.

"So about those rules," Dilly began.

I took the opportunity to slap her arm and thoroughly enjoyed the yelp I got in return. It was more than deserved.

Rules were rules and all he did was break them. If the rules were changing, then I would need to adapt. The only problem with that is that I had never been good at it.

My sleep was a jumbled mess of memories mixed with things I was positive had never happened. It was just that it felt very real and very like a memory. His hands tangled in my hair, the pull sending a thrill through me that ebbed and weaved through each breath I took. His mouth hot over my neck, down my collarbone. The most wicked words coming from his mouth, given only to me.

I woke up with a start, drenched in sweat. The night was warm, but my blood was warmer. Throwing off the blankets, I sat up and found him peacefully lying in his hammock in yesterday's clothes, his chest rising and falling evenly enough that he had to be asleep. It was a luxury he had better appreciate.

My hands shook as I clutched the bed beneath me. That old ache had settled firmly between my thighs. I wanted to touch him, but more than that, I wanted to be touched. I craved that thrill that grew with every ministration. God, I wanted it more than I ever should. More than I could ever confess in any confessional. The priest would hear my words and order an exorcism.

There was something very wrong with me because that thought did nothing to curve the desire and need flooding my body. I was a terrible Catholic and maybe a terrible person. Flynn had ruined me just like he said he would.

If I touch you like this, they will say you are ruined. Do you want me to ruin you?

I ran my hand over my stomach, and then my breast. My nipple peaked in anticipation. It sent a shot of energy through me, and I nearly whimpered. I couldn't bring myself to regret it. Meeting Flynn and everything that came after. Sneaking out that second night, knowing I was going to meet him, was a thrill I might spend my whole life chasing. The moment I crested the corner and saw him leaning against the cobblestoned wall of The Siren and The Kraken, one leg kicked back with his arms folded over his chest.

He had been straight out of a storybook, but it was when he saw me that had been the dream. The side of his lip pulled up instantly before the other followed. He kicked himself off the wall and sounded just as surprised as me when he said, "You came back."

Despite the pounding of my heart I'd rolled my eyes and said, "Obviously," gesturing to my general being.

His laugh was looser and quicker than it had been the night before. It felt like trust when I hadn't done anything to earn it. For two nights, he made me his own, and I forgot about the man who had broken me. For the rarest of seconds, I thought that it would be all right. That the road had been broken and treacherous, but that it had led me to right where I was meant to be.

Foolish dreams meant only for moonlight because when the sun rose he was just a pirate and I was just a naive rich girl.

If I hadn't introduced Oscar to him. If I hadn't let him touch me. If I hadn't needed someone to touch me. If James hadn't—

No. I wouldn't think about him when my body burned like this. This was a part of me he would never have access to. Even if my scheme failed and I became his wife, this would always be only mine. He could touch me, and it would never be this. I controlled who could make me feel this way, and there was only one man I wanted to give it to, but I was mad at him.

I flung myself back on the damp sheets and blew out a frustrated breath. Rubbing my legs together, I bit my lips to keep the moan off my lips. I just needed to get it out of my system, and then I'd stop dreaming of him. I'd stop craving his hands over my body. Every callous edging me closer. The roughness of his beard as he trailed kisses over my neck and shoulder.

I needed this. I glanced towards the hammock and found him still breathing steadily, with only the glimmering flame of a lantern on his desk for guidance. It was fine. Just needed to get it out of my system. Needed to get *him* out of my system, but that was like trying to carve into stone. He was imprinted on me as long as I coveted his touch.

As long as I remembered in glaring color the way he had lowered his body over mine, kisses drawing alarmingly close to where my body pulsed with need. I should have run then and said an infinite number of Hail Marys, but instead, I threaded my hands through his hair and spread my legs wider. Needing what he was willing to give me.

And, oh, god, when his mouth found that need—there was nothing like it in all the world: fire and blinding desire. My hips moved of their own accord, but the pirate between my legs never wavered. His ocean-deep eyes lifted to mine, and I died a thousand deaths watching him watch me while his tongue ran over me, consuming me.

Pleasure ricocheted through me all too soon, and I lay panting on his bed, slowly trying to pull myself out of the memory. Flashes of it refused to leave me, and even as the aftershocks pulsed through me, I burned once more. God, this was insufferable.

I ripped my finger away from my center and held my hands over my eyes, trying to will my mind to cooperate. This wasn't normal. I wasn't normal.

Three consecutive blows to the cabin door sent my already careening heart into a fit that was liable to kill me.

I let loose a shrill screeching sound akin to a banshee from the spooky stories children passed by lantern light on dark nights.

Flynn, however, was apparently accustomed to this since he rose from his hammock and clicked his pistol that magically appeared in his hand. He had been too quick. My cheeks burned as I convinced myself that I hadn't been as quiet as I thought I was or that I misread his breaths for sleep. Mortification dripped slowly onto my skin, claiming the warmth that had been holding me hostage.

I hugged my knees to my chest as he walked by, sparing me exactly no attention. That was rude, but a good sign. He would have said something and wouldn't have wasted the opportunity to remind me how much I wanted him. This was fine; everything was fine. Shame my heart wasn't convinced as it tried to escape my chest.

Flynn opened the door and pointed his pistol at the unfortunate soul on the other side. "Christ, Bash," Oscar said.

I shuffled from the bed, not a single care that I was in a loose, thin white nightgown. I didn't appreciate a pistol being pointed at my brother, no matter my attire. I reached

Flynn, but he had already lowered the pistol. Relief flooded me, maybe it was my recent activities, but tension poured off of him in waves. His body rigid, and knuckles white.

Oscar's gaze ran over me and then back to Flynn with narrowed eyes. He held up one finger at the captain of the Wraith and opened his mouth.

"I wasn't," I tried, "We weren't—"

Oh, god, what were the words I needed?

"Speak," Flynn ordered.

"I beg your—" I began before I realized his stare was pinned on my brother.

Oh. Still rude, but at least it wasn't directed towards me. That would not have ended well for anyone.

"The lantern is red," Oscar said.

Flynn didn't breathe, standing stock still while he absorbed the words.

"Have Billy take the ship. Remind him of the conditions," Flynn said.

"What about Ro—Miss Smith?" Oscar asked, nodding towards me.

Nice to be included.

"She stays," he said and shut the door on Oscar.

"No, she does not." I rounded on him.

Oscar's chuckle through the door was oddly comforting and justifying.

Flynn disagreed as he grabbed his hat from his desk and lowered it onto his head. Silence unraveling all sense of justice Oscar had given me. Like this argument wasn't even worth having.

Fine, I could adapt. I left him and quickly pulled on my pants beneath my dress.

"Rosamund," he said, in that very annoying way of his. "It isn't sa—"

His words fell away and were replaced with an audible gulp as I lifted off my gown, my back to him, and replaced it with a fresh shirt. I didn't bother to fight the smile on my lips as smug satisfaction fell over me. It was one way to win an argument.

Now for the next part. I laced up my boots with lightning speed and didn't give him a chance to stop me as I bolted for the door. I hoped he was appropriately frustrated as I closed the door on him and made for the lantern where Billy and Oscar stood with Val, who had her arms crossed. Her scarred face lifted in a smile when her eyes landed on me.

"Princess," she called. "Are you going to dance with the witches?"

"No, she is not," Flynn said behind me, his boots thumping against the creaking wood like he would stomp through them.

Billy and Oscar shared a long stare that reeked of secrets. When they were in agreement of their quiet treason, Oscar nodded toward Val.

"Thanks for keeping watch, you can get some rest now," Oscar said.

Val's lips pulled up a fraction before she dipped her head to Flynn.

"Good luck, Captain," she said.

We all stood silent while she went below deck, knowing that Oscar had sent her away for a reason. The silence, with only the tilt of the ship and the waves crashing against her, reverberated against my clammy skin. Salt air mingled with the damp just enough to create a slight residue. Billy eyed Flynn, who stood with his arms crossed, staring at the lantern.

It was a ghastly red as if it had read about fire, but couldn't replicate it entirely. The red tendrils scraped at the top of the lantern, begging for release. An eerie shriek gathered in the starlit darkness, and I had to fight the urge to step closer to Flynn.

"Listen, Bash, Oscar and I have been talking," Billy said, rubbing at his scruff.

"Delightful," Flynn grumbled.

"The Hellcat should be going with you," Billy said.

"No," Flynn answered.

Oscar met my eyes and there was a conflict I knew well in them. He was choosing. I just wish he hadn't bit his inner lip because it meant he regretted his choice.

"I saved your neck once, but we both know it won't work twice. I'm shit sorry I put you in this spot, Bash, but she can make sure you make it back onto the Wraith," Oscar said.

Because if I hadn't shown up with this scheme, Oscar never would have had to tie Flynn's hands. Flynn would have been free to say no and never have to see the Gharaq coven again.

"I know what their matriarch covets more than my life. I don't need Miss Smith to board my own ship," he bit out.

I had never heard this visceral version of him. It was like he woke up and swallowed a mouthful of bees and blamed the world, blamed me.

"I'm going," I stated, glaring up at him. "And not to save you, though I have no idea why they think I could. I'm going because last time I got dragged in, and this time I would rather walk into it on my own two feet."

Flynn turned to me, and his eyes feasted on me like he was memorizing every imperfection. I hated that I didn't pull away, that I felt that heat bloom despite the muggy air beneath the center of his attention. It was just us and the sea song around us. If he touched me, I would burn.

"If I have to lock you in my cabin, I will," he said.

It would have been nice if I could say something like *'I'd like to see you try'* and have a small margin of probable success. As it was he was very tall and very strong. All I had going for me was determination and a restless spirit.

"She's coming with us, Bash. This one isn't your choice," Oscar said.

Flynn stared at me, willing me to concede.

He knew better.

The loss of his attention was like a blow to the stomach. I was sinking into muddy waters fast.

Get it together, Rose.

Even my angriest chastisement couldn't curb the pull of his orbit.

"This is a lot like mutiny," Flynn barked at Oscar and Billy.

"It's a lot like saving yer arse, lad.," Billy said. "I got the ship and before you ask, I remember the conditions. Sun up the Wraith leaves."

"Without us?" I blurted.

Oscar shook his head at me and mouthed, "Why?"

Fair. It was probably not the best question when I had just gotten my ticket to join their little getaway.

"The Gharaq determine who enters and leaves their domain. Linger too long, and their choice becomes easier," Flynn said.

"So be quick about it," Billy said, clapping Flynn on the back.

So quietly, I almost missed it when Billy squeezed my shoulder, "Watch his back."

Was that why I was going? Did I even want to watch his back? It probably wasn't worth letting a mysterious creature kill him.

Billy retreated below deck before Flynn lit a match and tossed it at the rope securing the lantern. It immediately caught in flames and all I could see was the very made of wood Wraith alight with a ship destroying fire.

"Why would you—"

My words were stolen from me as Flynn's hand clamped over my mouth and he pulled me against his chest as the flames crested up to the starry sky above.

"Do not speak unless she speaks to you, and then only say what you must. Do not lie to her. She will know," he said into my ear.

Oscar came to stand at my side and threaded his hand through mine, squeezing once, twice, three times, just like we used to do when we were scared.

Flynn slowly removed his hand from my mouth, but I stared at my brother, biting his lip. He regretted this. Was it regret for taking on my scheme or regret for bringing me?

The questions were swallowed by the rising flame that poured heat across my skin like a summer sun before it blew out leaving us in utter darkness except for the light from the stars. One by one they began to wink out and a gasp left me. It was like they were being plucked out of the sky by an invisible source. Before I had time to gasp, the last one went out and we were cast into a midnight thicker than the blood flowing through my veins.

A cackle that seeped into my bones drew out across the darkness.

I knew as well as I knew my own name.

The Gharaq were here.

Chapter Twenty
A Simple Yes Before the No

Through several costly expeditions since 1657, with upward of ten thousand lives claimed, it was discovered that the creatures of The Glass Sea were drawn to those who exhibited more fear and emotion than others. In 1665, Antonio Rossi, an Italian pirateer came across the Gharaq clan, a Great Western Sea witch clan. It is coincidentally the first documentation of their existence. The clan offered a serum that claimed when drank it would dull emotions so that the dead of the Glass Sea would not attack. In 1666, four months after the encounter with the Gharaq Clan, Antonio Rossi, and his crew completed the first exploration of the Glass Sea without casualties.

–An excerpt from The Mysterious Deep: A Comprehensive Understanding

As long as I lived I never wanted to hear that sound again. A second cackle joined, deeper than the first. Great, wishes didn't come true for errant daughters who ran away with pirates apparently. Stunningly, a third voice joined that had the grace of a seventy-year-old socialite widower.

The laughter from all of them grew, and it was immediately clear they had no interest in harmony. Instinctually, I took a step back, but Flynn's hand on my lower back steadied me. Even if I wanted to be locked in his cabin, at this point, it was probably too late.

Hard wood beneath my boots gave way to a mushy sludge that ended in a terrible crunch beneath my boots. I was saved by falling on my ass by Flynn's hands on either side of my waist, steadying me. His breath was loud and rough against me as his fingers gripped me tight.

What was it that made even the infamous Captain of the Wraith nervous?

The urge to ask what was happening bubbled up in my mouth before I could think about it, but just as I opened my mouth Flynn tapped two fingers on my side in reminder.

I shouldn't have gone to bed right after dinner. I should have waited up for him and demanded more answers. The problem with that was that I had never been good about asking the right questions. I was more of the "wing it and figure it out on the way type" which is how I so often ended up in less-than-ideal situations. Much like the one I currently find myself in.

The mud was now up to my ankles, but neither Flynn nor my brother were very concerned. Oscar's hand was tight around mine, and I might have bruises from Flynn's grip on my sides if we survived this. All right, maybe they were concerned after all. A chaotic energy balled in my chest, and I recognized it like an old friend. Hello, anxiety.

The salt in the air stung my nose mixed with something that smelt how I imagined decomposition might.

"Sebastian Flynn, Captain of the Sea Wraith, you dare to light the Tariq Fanus?" Said the first voice.

"Was our warning not clear?" Said the second against the first's fading echo.

"Do you court death like an eager suitor?" The third finished.

Flynn's fingers tapped on either side of me before he let go and stepped to my side. I immediately regretted losing his grounding presence. He was an asshole, but he was a reliable asshole.

"I have need of the tonic that only the Gharaq coven can bestow," Flynn said.

There was no hint of the trepidation he was feeling in his voice that was strong and commanding.

"And you are willing to die for it?" Cackled the first disembodied voice.

"A noose for passage?" The second laughed.

"His neck will crack so beautifully." The third said.

The sound of softly falling rocks scattered around us. I imagined we were at the center of a large basin, mud, and these horrible creatures were edging down the slope toward us. The faint drip of water echoed off the cavernous walls I pictured. Beneath the weight of total darkness, my imagination carved out images that were better left in the subconscious of my mind. Sulfur and rot mixed in my nose as I forced a breath in.

Death. It all felt and smelled like death.

I decided I was more terrified of the third. She didn't sound like she had much in the way of sanity. There was too much joy in the morbid words she spoke, too much hunger.

"I would prefer to avoid dying. Instead, I offer a trade to the Gharaq matriarch," Flynn said.

The strike of a match and then, one by one, blue lights flickered to life all around us. The single flames ebbed and flowed in their void of space unattached to anything. It was impossible and defied the laws of physics.

Their light quickly grew until my breath caught. The ground around me was dark sand filled with skeletons of all manner of creatures. Sea and land alike. A shriek ripped from me as I realized the crunch I felt beneath me was a human skull. I had cracked through its right orbit, shattering where its nose and mouth should have been.

I shook my foot out and made to step back, but Flynn caught me, and Oscar squeezed my hand in warning.

I wanted to go home. I was done with the sea, and I was done with mysterious creatures. I pulled at my brother's hand, but he turned his head to me and mouthed, 'breath.'

Unhelpful. I twisted to find Flynn raising a hand to his chest and tapping it once, twice.

The message settled over me like a blanket on a cold winter's night. The remnants of the memories attached to it still warm enough to provide comfort.

Just us. Not where we came from. Not our titles. Just us. Just this room. Not what came before and not what comes after. A moment in time. Infinite in its existence.

I swallowed and drank in the air, knowing it was rare.

"That one used to lure young girls like yourself down to the water with promises men know nothing of." The first voice said behind me into my ear.

I jumped with a scream that echoed all around us in this void of space and time.

"No need to be afraid, sweet one. The dead around you deserved their fate just as the Captain of the Wraith does." The second said, appearing before me.

Horror struck deep at my center and spread outward like spidering vines. Taking root and telling everything in me to run. I doubted I would get far.

She was older than any woman I'd ever seen. More wrinkles than skin evident on her body. Where there should have been hair, fine wisps moved as if she were underwater. Her eyes, though, were youthful and seeing. A turquoise that reminded me of pictures of tropical faraway lands where one could see the bottom of the sea through.

"A thief." The third said on the side where my brother had been only a moment ago.

I jerked my head around, but it was just me and three witches who hardly seemed friendly.

"Where did they go?" I demanded.

The first's hands gripped my shoulders and spun me toward her. She grinned at me with decaying teeth worse than Billy's. Her eyes were sunken in, and her nose was crooked three times over. She was less wrinkly than the first, but still older than logical. Her hair was a brassy mix of hair and seaweed that danced in an invisible sea.

"You cannot steal what is given," she said.

The second one spun me to face her. Her eyes scanned mine before she smiled with pointed teeth.

"It was not offered."

The third spun me toward her and caught me with two strong arms as I tripped over my own feet. When I met her eyes I saw she was beautiful. Not terrifying like the other two, but instead, her golden hair glowed against the dark void as it riveted. Her lips were a plump red, and her tanned skin shimmered as if the sun were perpetually warming it. She was more beautiful than Ximena could ever hope to be.

"More of a falling," she hissed, tilting her head.

Her eyes popped open and they were an impossible amethyst that glittered with what I had heard in her voice before I had ever seen her. Madness.

Just as quickly as they had appeared they were swallowed back into darkness. Replaced by Oscar who searched the darkness only for his eyes to find mine and relief settled over his face.

"Rosie!" he shouted, reaching for me.

Just as our hands grazed, a burning sensation took over my fingertips, and I bit back a scream and held my hand to my chest. My fingers were as red as fire, burning tingling coursing through them. I shook them out, trying to ebb the pain.

"It's fire, Rose. You can only see what they want you to see. Trust your instincts. Wounds made down here won't heal like normal on the surface," Oscar warned.

It sounded like advice that could have been given before we got here this far, but as I cradled my hand to my chest once more I decided I would avoid moving if at all possible.

"Lost and adrift." The first whispered in my ear.

"Ah! A finding!" Exclaimed the second.

"But not a claiming." The third breathed on the back of my neck.

I closed my eyes. I didn't want to see them, but I definitely didn't appreciate their lack of corporal forms.

"Open your eyes, Rose," Flynn said in front of me.

I shook my head and realized I was trembling. My breath was irregular and in danger of disappearing altogether. I had read about this feeling in countless stories, but until this moment, I had never known it. Not even when I thought Ximena was going to kill me could compare to the vines exploding throughout my body.

This was terror.

"An inevitability." The first said, her wrinkled hand cupping my cheek.

"A truth for a lie. I cut my hand because when I saw you on deck, I forgot where I was. I wanted to laugh at how damn stubborn you are, but I also wanted to tell you how beautiful you looked. That long or short hair, you are the most beautiful woman I have ever seen," he said.

My eyes shot open and he was standing a foot away from me, his eyes steady, unflinching on mine. My breath was rapid, and as the air began to turn to freezing, my breath appeared in wisps of smoke.

A lie for a lie.

"I did it because I wanted you to be mad," I chattered.

My arms around me could not keep out the cold and the way my air bounced off something in between us, I knew going to him wasn't an option. Fool me once. At least my fingers were less painful.

"Not necessarily an inevitability." The second said, appearing before Flynn.

He didn't flinch or move, but his lips had lost some of their color. His eyes stayed on mine, grounding me.

"A finding can be lost." The third said, her amethyst eyes appearing before me before disappearing.

"Eyes on me, Princess," Flynn said.

"Not lost if done with intent." The first whispered in my ear.

"I hate when you call me that," I said, through shivers.

So cold. It chipped away at any warmth I had ever known. Only what seemed like minutes ago, I had been in his cabin burning up. Now I knew what it meant to be in a world cold enough that dying felt like falling asleep.

"An abandoning then." The second said, peering up at Flynn.

"My hammock is more comfortable than my bed," Flynn said, his hands shook at his side, pale with the cold.

I snorted. Just like him to think I was lying about hating him, calling me the name his crew had given me as an insult.

Whatever humor we cultivated was lost as the third, beautiful witch appeared before me. She placed her long-nailed hands on either side of my face, and they were warm. I sighed with relief as I sank into the warmth she poured into me.

"Your anger is with me, not her," Flynn said through his own chattering teeth.

I wasn't mad now, though. I was warm. The beautiful sea witch brought her lips to mine and I drank in her impossible eyes.

"Cruel little witch," she sing sang.

I jolted back, remembering exactly who I was and why I was cold in the first place. This was a game for them.

"I'm not a witch," I said.

"Rosamund," Flynn called, but his tall form disappeared once more into a sickly green mist.

Instead I was left with three sea witches. One on my front with purple eyes and two ancient ones at my sides. They touched me as if I were an experiment in some laboratory.

"But you could be," One said.

"We were once adrift," Two said.

"Until the finding," Three said.

In eerie unison, they said, "Do you want to be found, little witch?"

It was all nonsense, but I felt a pull somewhere in my chest that was accompanied by that itching in my feet.

It was a wanting.

"All it takes is a yes," One said.

"But first, there may be no's," Two whispered as she tucked a strand of hair behind my ear.

"All it takes is a little swim," Three sang.

"But first, there is the sinking."

"Then the choice."

"And the answer."

They began to echo off each other faster than I could keep up. The pull in me replaced by nausea as they began to spin me once more with every word as if I were some child's toy.

"A simple yes."

"Deliverance."

"Servitude."

"Divinity."

"Cursed."

"Immortality."

I felt just as used as I had when I learned about James' infidelity. When I had spent days and nights combing through every lie and truth over the years I'd thought I'd loved him. Not thought. Loved. But could you love something that was never real?

"Yes." They hissed before whispering a single word. "Control."

I was dizzy enough that I thought I might lose consciousness. The swirls of colors began to meld into one, but then, just as they had begun, they disappeared and left me where I had begun.

In sinking sand surrounded by bones. Bones I was becoming convinced I would join.

I panted, trying to remember how to breathe. I knew the impulse as it settled in my chest. Hold my breath, wait for the storm to pass.

I crouched down as the cold began again. Just as my chest began to ache a woman appeared before me, crouching down in front of me. She looked like me, but not. Her dark hair was thinner as it floated in invisible water. Her cheeks were well-defined, and her body thin despite the muscles over her arms. She wore tattered cloth over her body which was the same as the witches. It ebbed and flowed as if pulled by an invisible current.

"Who gets the elixir?" The witches whispered around the woman and me.

"Who sees safe passage?"

"Who sees the endless abyss?"

The girl reached out and laid a warm hand on my cheek. Different than the witch had before. That had felt like ownership, whereas in these hazel eyes, I only saw understanding.

"Who, who, who?" they shouted.

Salt air bit at my nose, stinging, but the woman opened her mouth, and though no sound came out, I understood.

"We say."

"We say."

"We say."

I was forgiven. She was at peace. She was beautiful in a way I could never hope to be. Her skin kissed by the sun, and intoxicating intelligence in her eyes.

"You could say..."

"A simple yes."

"Before the no."

I wanted to bring her back with me. Save her from this fate.

She shook her head, a false smile pleading acceptance.

"It isn't so bad."

"The cold rushing down."

"Visions of regrets past."

"Panic."

"Soothing warmth."

Their crescendo of chaos grew around us, ringing in my ears. I searched my twin's eyes for answers, but they narrowed as she shook her head in warning.

"Darkness," they whispered, echoing on top of each other.

A single clap reverberated in the air and then it was all gone. The woman, the witches, the blue light, the sand, the bones. Even the air was still like the world was in stasis.

My breath hitched as I fought to blow out the air trapped in my lungs. It was aching. I was dying. I was dying in a void.

I clawed at my throat, desperate to find a way to breathe. No, no, no. I didn't want this. I wanted to live.

I wanted to fight with Flynn. To tell Oscar how he broke my heart when he left. To tell Oliver he was the reason I survived last year. To tell Ruby that I always wished I could be like her.

I wanted to live. To feel the touch of Flynn's hands on my skin even when I shouldn't.

I wanted to see the world, even the creatures that were determined to kill me. I wanted to taste new things and make mistakes.

I had been broken for a year, but I tasted life the last few weeks and I craved it more than I ever had before.

I wanted.

I wanted.

I wanted to see James' face when I took back my father's life's work and released these shackles from my wrists. I wanted to tell him that he had never made me feel an ounce of what a pirate captain had.

That he was a drop in the ocean compared to the world I experienced because of his treachery. The world was infinite, but he was nothing.

I wanted.

I wanted.

"Very well." The witches hissed. "Come back when you are ready, little witch."

The world shuddered and shook around me, and then I was back on the deck of the Sea Wraith, lanterns lit as usual with normal fire.

I gasped in air, my lungs screaming in defiance. My body shook and I just knew everything was wrong. It was a knowing. Fear clawed through me, feasting on every ounce of my flesh.

"Aye, Hellcat, yer ok. Yer back." Billy said, rubbing his hands over my shoulders from where he knelt in front of me.

I screamed and crawled backward, remembering the way the witches touched me. Remembering the woman trapped with them.

"I have to go back!" I screeched.

I crawled toward the lantern, but it was gone. No evidence it had ever existed.

"No, no, no," I sobbed.

She couldn't stay there. I needed to get to her.

"Hey, hey, hey," Oscar crooned, falling before me and scooping me up into a hug that threatened to strip the air from my lungs once more.

"I need to go back!" I cried, trying to free myself from him.

"Bash will be fine, it's okay," Oscar whispered.

Flynn. No, I wasn't worried about him. It was the girl. She needed me. I couldn't leave her.

"I have to go to her!" I pleaded.

My muscles felt weak. I was losing energy rapidly, but I just need to do this one last thing.

"Her?" Oscar asked, pulling away and smoothing back my hair.

Tears spilled down my cheeks, and my lip quivered as I met his eyes, willing him to understand and help me.

"I need to go to her. She can't stay there!" I sobbed.

"Bash," Billy breathed out a long sigh of relief.

I raised my eyes and found Flynn holding a large glass in his hand, his face pale and hollow. Bright red skin wrapped around his throat, the redness turning into a sickly blue-purple in some areas.

"I need to go get her," I whispered, begging whatever divine power that existed that he would understand me.

Flynn swallowed and winced. "She made her choice; it can't be undone no matter how much we wish it could."

No, that wasn't good enough. That wasn't true, couldn't be true. She had been trying to tell me something. There were words trapped beneath invisible water.

Flynn used his free hand to run it through his hair as he studied me. Pain and regret fought for control of his face. More emotion than I had seen from him since boarding his ship.

"You made it back," Billy said, his voice thick with disbelief.

"You were right," Flynn said, pulling my eyes to his. "She saved my life."

The words were haunted as he saw things that weren't there. Memories and ghosts fighting for control.

"It'll be dawn in less than an hour. Wake the crew and have them tend to their duties. We make for Tristan da Cunha immediately," Flynn murmured.

The ruthless captain was at the bottom of the sea among bone-filled sand.

"Come on," Oscar whispered to me, gently guiding me off the ground.

I didn't want to go. I had to get to her.

As he ushered me to the cabin, I knew the truth like it was tattooed on my skin.

There was no saving what was already dead.

Chapter Twenty-One
Carry, but Don't Bury

We understand there to be three truths regarding the Glass Sea. One—those that die within its waters are relegated to an eternity of mindless wandering and unquenchable hunger. Two—there is an impossible amount of treasure within the Glass Sea that has no reasonable explanation. Three—if a ship carrying treasure sinks on the other side of the world, it will inevitably end up in the Glass Sea.

–An excerpt from The Mysterious Deep: A Comprehensive Understanding

No amount of rays from the sun could warm the cold that embedded itself into my bones. Even when I raised my hand to the flames, it did nothing to alleviate the chill inside me. I was still at the bottom of the witch-infested ocean in more ways than I could count.

"It's time to change your dressing, Princess," Emille said from somewhere.

The ocean was angry today. Like it knew it had lost three prizes and felt it was owed retribution. Only the blue sky above disagreed with its wrath. The sky was a perfect blue scattered with the fluffiest of white clouds. The sun singing her happy song over the Wraith and her crew.

"She hasn't said more than a few words all day," Dilly said. "It was wrong of the Captain to take her to the Gharaq. There are only ten written accounts of surviving them and half of them were rendered mad after. She's a hostage, not a tool."

Her words were a gathering storm, anger growing with every brush of the wind around us.

"You can take it up with the Captain, but I wouldn't advise it anytime soon," Emille said.

"I chose it," I whispered, my mouth dry.

Flynn was a lot of things, but one thing he had never done was force me to do anything that wasn't all my choice. While Dilly's anger came from a good place, it wasn't necessary. I'd done this to myself.

The sun's rays were blotted out by bright red hair as she crouched before me. I blinked several times, adjusting to the change in light until her face came into focus. Her lips and brows were pulled down in a tragic sort of way. Dilly was meant to be smiling. I wondered if the woman at the bottom of the sea had been like her. Did she have more smiles than frowns before the claiming?

A simple yes, before the no.

Had it felt simple to her when she had consented to her phantom life? Every time I closed my eyes, I saw her. Gentleness and forgiveness that didn't belong amongst the Mysterious Deep. She was meant for the living. Not down there. Not the dead.

"Maybe if you talked about it, we could help you through it. Everyone's experience with them is different. Even though three of you went down, you all would have seen and heard different things. Still, talking to the Captain or Oscar might help." Dilly said, rubbing her hand over my arm.

The touch didn't register as it should have. Like something was wrong with the parts of me that I should be able to feel.

"I agree." Emille said. "Let me change your dressing and then we will figure out the rest."

A deep, airy moan behind us echoed throughout the air.

"Koinu," Inu said.

Dilly was up in an instant, no doubt a spyglass in her hand. I wished I could have brought myself to get off the ground and look. It occurred to me that even if the Koinu attacked, I probably wouldn't have moved.

Come back when you are ready, little witch.

Would I join them someday? Was that fate kinder than death?

"It hasn't changed course, but that sound—" Dilly began.

The Koinu cried out again.

"It's grieving." Inu finished.

Large hands tugged at me and I let them because the energy needed to fight was more than I remembered having. So cold. I was so cold.

Emille ushered me into the cabin, and I instantly regretted the loss of the sun. Without it, the chill inside of me grew until I was shaking. Emille and Inu exchanged words as he sat me at the desk. I was grateful for the blanket he draped over my shoulders, but it only kept the chill at a near distance, just as the sun had done.

"I left her there," I murmured.

"I don't pretend to know what you saw down there, but I know you well enough now to say that if you could have done something, you would have," Emille said.

I held out my hand to him, and he gently took it in his, unwrapping the white gauze around my fingers. Layers upon layers unraveled to reveal shredded skin that was too red and, in some places, too white. The tips of my fingers oozed through cracked skin.

A stinging ran through them and up my arm as he poured water over them that dripped into a porcelain bowl with blue flower edging around it. Blood mixed with the freshwater to create a whirlpool of pink.

A finding, but not a claiming.

"I knew what I wanted to do with my life by the time I was twelve years old. My father took me to a surgery where they were trying to operate on a beating heart. I watched while they cut the old man open and could see the pulsing of his heart. The way they used their hands to manipulate what only God should see was captivating. He died. The old man. But I knew that I wanted to be there when it was done successfully."

Emille gently dabbed at the tips of my fingers, drying them. I had never given much thought to how it would feel to die, but now my mind ran circles around it.

An abandoning.

"I dedicated my life to it. By the time I was thirty, I was one of the most celebrated doctors in Paris. I never lost my focus until I met Sophie. She was—intoxicating. Her love of life was contagious. I loved her more than I ever knew was possible. Within a year, we were married and welcomed our beautiful, perfect daughter into the world. Coralie."

Not so long ago, I remembered wondering what Emille's story was. I knew he was offering something precious, but it was hard to appreciate beauty when death had imprinted itself on my soul. Ximena's footprint had faded from my chest, but now there was something far darker stamped across it, death.

He pulled out a salve and gently globbed it onto the tips of my fingers. It only felt like another layer of cold on the chill. At least it wasn't painful.

"I should have paid more attention to them. I should have worked less. Yes, I saved lives, but I also missed her first steps, her first words, her first ball. Before I heard the ticking of the clock, she was grown. I think the two of you would have gotten along well, though the world might not have survived it. She had your tenacity and sharp mind. Sometimes-when I see you, I see what she should have been."

The words were forced, but given with such gentleness that even my chilled bones felt the call. I blinked slowly and reached out my good hand to lay over his where he was winding my new bandage. He paused and raised his eyes to mine where I saw silver glisten over darkened skin.

"I'm sorry for your loss," I said.

My voice sounded hoarse, like the sea had embedded itself into my lungs. Emille stared a moment before he cleared his throat and kept working on my hand.

"One night, when I told Sophie that I would be home before dinner, a lie that I always had an excuse for, a man brought his pregnant wife to me. She had been in labor for almost a full day, but the baby wouldn't come. The child was breached," he cleared his throat. "Legs first. The mother was already exhausted from the blood loss-—I hadn't performed many cesareans, but I knew if I didn't do something, both mother and baby would soon die."

He finished with my bandage and stepped back. I didn't want him to regret sharing this with me. Vulnerability was a luxury and I knew a gift when I saw one.

"You did your best," I said softly.

He nodded and ran his hand over his rough beard. His eyes glistened with tears for the past. For what he had failed to save. I understood now why he had shared with me the story, but it was easier to offer forgiveness to another than to forgive yourself. My father always said that we are hardest on ourselves because the truth was harder to hide from inside your own mind.

"Sometimes our best isn't enough, Miss Smith. I often wonder what would have happened if I had gone home on time like I said I would. It wouldn't have changed the fate of that poor woman and her child, but—"

He rubbed at his chest, and I knew there was more. My heart shattered all over, knowing that this kind man had endured more than anyone should have.

He nodded, steadying himself. "I spent entire days away from home researching cesarean techniques and reading articles on theories. I knew that if I was ever faced with it again, I wouldn't fail. The husband of the woman—I didn't—I couldn't have—he felt that I had stolen his world from him and was consumed by it. My beautiful Sophie and sweet Coralie. One night, when I was at the surgery, he came to my home and lit it on fire, and then when his vengeance didn't bring him peace, he succumbed to his demons. Five lives lost because of my failure."

I stood and wrapped my arms around him, wishing I could take the burdens away. He didn't deserve them. There were some truths that couldn't be refuted, and that Emille was a good man was one that I knew with my entire being. He had known loss and grief that would have left anyone else on the floor.

Slowly, he wrapped his arms around me and leaned into the comfort. We stood like that for a long time before he stepped back and ran a hand over my face, where it came back wet with tears I hadn't realized I'd cried.

"I'm sorry," I choked.

He nodded, and I wondered if there had ever been a sadder man.

"I lost my purpose for a long time. Merely floating from bar to bar until I had used up all the empathy in Paris. Soft apologies quickly turned to judgment. I found myself in underground fight arenas when the smash of my fist on another man was the most I could feel. It was that way for ten years. Until one night, a young and arrogant prick stepped into my ring. He was arrogant, but he was also clever. Used his speed and agility against my brute strength. He wore me out, and I was on my back before I realized what happened. He could have taken that last hit and did me in, but instead, he offered me his hand."

Emille's sorrow turned as he chuckled and crossed his arms over his chest.

"I should have known what trouble he would get me into right there. He said he was assembling a crew and was in need of a doctor. I told him I didn't do that anymore. He asked me if my wife and daughter would be proud of what I was doing with my life, and I decked him hard enough that he had a black eye for over a month. He didn't fight me back, though. He just drained his drink and said he would be staying at a local inn if I wanted to do something more with my life."

"Flynn," I said.

Emille smiled, remembering.

"I told you this to tell you what he told me. 'We can carry the dead without burying ourselves with them. Living is honoring them. Anything else is surrender.' I've carried those words right next to my mark for five years."

He pulled back the collar of his shirt, showcasing the black and white compass with kraken tentacles emerging from it that all pirates shared. Right below were the words he had spoken in perfectly scrawled French. I wiped away my tears and gave a long sniff as the reality of what Emille had shared washed over me. He lost everything and he was standing. I didn't even know the woman beneath the sea and for two days I became a ghost.

I never understood James more at that moment. All the times he had called me dramatic and told me I should enroll in theatre. When my panic would rise to the point that I held my breath, he would tell me to snap myself out of it. That I was making a choice. He was right.

"I didn't tell you that to make you feel guilty," Emille said, lifting my chin with his fingers. "Only to let you know that it's okay to grieve, but you can't keep yourself down as penance for living."

God, I was a blubbering mess. I didn't know why, but I rushed him and hugged him. It felt right when he wrapped his arms around me and laid a kiss to my head. I wished I could find the words to tell him that Sophie and Coralie were lucky to have him. The best I could do was hug him like they would have if they were there.

A soft knock on the door signaled the rest of the world still existed.

"Thank you, Emille," I whispered, pulling away.

His smile was soft and distant as he nodded. "Keep that dressing clean, and I'll change it again tonight. In my experience, wounds delivered by the Gharaq can last for a few months, but if you aren't as stubborn as my other patient, it should heal faster.

I nodded, but some of the peace he had given me eroded under the reminder of Flynn's neck. It was ghastly. A mass of dark purple, blue, and red with some areas open from where the noose had wrapped around his neck. I hadn't spoken to him since we returned to the world of the living and he was never in the cabin at the same time as me. Almost like he was avoiding me.

I hadn't found the energy to be offended by it yet.

Another knock, more insistent.

Emile gave me one last attempt at a smile before he turned to leave. I could only guess at how difficult the next day would be for him. It took a great deal of courage to drudge up the past. That he had done it for me was not lost on me.

"Quartermaster," Emille said.

"Hey, Emille," Oscar said. "Inu asked me—"

Emille shrugged his head to the side. "Take it easy on her."

"Of course," Oscar answered.

I wrapped my arms around myself, thankful for the salve that dulled the pain in my fingers. The warmth of Emille's kindness was momentarily shadowed by the way my heart stuttered in my chest at my twin's familiar face. Behind his new facial hair was the person who used to know me best in all the world. The one who would protect me at his own risk. Black hair and chocolate eyes now meant something different when I looked at them.

He shut the door behind him and for a moment stood there frozen in time. His eyes drifted over my face and to my bandaged hand. The wound that existed because I reached for him when I shouldn't have. A hard lesson to learn, but at least the wound would be around long enough that I might actually internalize it.

"Rosie," he said, regret and hurt in the endearment.

"Don't," I said.

Now that I had come out of whatever paralysis I had been in, I was beginning to feel too much. It was almost better the way it was before. Gently lowering myself into Flynn's chair, I crossed my legs and waved my good hand towards the door.

"You can go now. Tell them whatever you want them to believe, and leave me alone," I said.

Oscar's brow furrowed, making him look constipated. Once, I would have teased him about it.

"You are angry with me," he said.

I blew out a breath. "A right, Sherlock, you are."

"Rose, this was your plan. If you want it to succeed, you have to give a little. That's always been how you see the world, though. You think you can just demand something, and it'll appear without you lifting a finger, but that's not how it works out here. There aren't servants to go wait in line for the latest fashions or whatever your whim of the day is."

The words hit right where he knew they would. Spoiled rich girl upset at having to get her hands dirty. That was how he saw me. A year apart, and he didn't know me at all. I reached for Flynn's quill just to be able to touch something, to feel anything except this carving in my chest.

"I guess you have all the answers then," I said, biting back the tears that threatened to escape.

Oscar blew out a frustrated breath and ran his hand over his face like he always did when he was aggravated. Like I was some puzzle, he couldn't quite get right even though he knew he had a way of it. I was an open book, after all.

"I don't want to fight with you," he said.

"Then don't," I answered, tapping the quill on the oak desk.

Oscar stepped forward and placed his hands on the front of the desk, his mouth working silently. Great. I knew this phase of his frustration like the back of my hand. I braced myself for the impact of his next words.

"You are being a bitch," he said.

Despite knowing they were coming, they landed with precision against the last of my heart that would always beat for him. The part he had claimed when he decided to exist alongside me. The last year without him was better than this. I should have let him stay buried.

I leaned forward, my barbed wire I surrounded my heart with reforming with every pulse of my blood.

"If I am being a bitch then so be it. It's always been you and me, Oscar. When Oliver would try to earn points for tattling, who always had your back, whether it was a lie or not? When Ruby accused you of shagging her best friend, who gave you an alibi?" I said.

He slammed his hand against the desk. "We aren't kids anymore, Rose!"
I met his eyes with all the rage I'd suppressed for the last year.

"Obviously. Which makes sense why you felt the need to sacrifice me like I meant nothing to you! Like I was some pawn in your fucked up game."

Oscar stepped back like I had burned him. The beat of his blood pulsating on his neck with rapid passage. The knives landed right where I meant them to. An echo of where his had lodged into me. That was the thing about knowing someone inside and out. You knew just where to strike to land the most effective blow.

"That's not—" he tried.

Men like my father and Oscar, who had silver tongues but good hearts, were forced to wonder if they inspired people or were just master manipulators. When one of our ships had gone down in the North Atlantic from a Kraken, my father had spent several nights knee-deep in drink. He had convinced the captain of that ship that the route would be safe. He had done the calculations. No amount of soothing words from my mother would ever patch the guilty conscience he carried.

Many nights, Oscar and I had laid awake as I soothed his fears that he wasn't a narcissist, telling him actual narcissists didn't lay awake at night wondering if they were. Instead of believing me, he would recount all the conversations of that day and try to weed out where he had used his influence without dignity. I knew what kept him up at night, and I was angry enough to use it.

"He would have died without you. That would have killed you, Rose. I know you two are dancing around—"

"It was my choice to make, Oscar. Flynn had no intention of taking me with him, but you did. You planned it. You should have told me what to expect and left the choice to me," I said.

"You would have done it anyway!" Oscar shouted.

"Then why didn't you let me decide?" I screamed back.

Oscar slammed his fist on the desk and ground out a frustrated growl before pointing his finger at me.

"It's all about control with you. You would have walked nose in the air down to the bottom of the sea, but because it wasn't your idea, you are throwing a monumental hissy fit more than Roberta ever did when she was a damn toddler," he said.

"Choice matters, Oscar, or is that one of the things that is different out here?" I spat.

"He would have stopped you!" Oscar's face was red from keeping in the remainder of his temper, but some things couldn't be contained. "If he had known Billy and I planned to bring you, he would have locked you in here and thrown the damn key at the bottom of the ocean. If I had told you the plan, he would have seen it on your face, and he would have died. They would have held the noose around his neck just a few seconds more, and he would have been dead, and you would have died right alongside him. You will recover from the shit you saw down there, but you wouldn't have recovered from that. I was protecting you!"

I felt like a thousand pistol bullets had lodged into my chest. The pain mixed with shame, and I might as well have been adrift in the sea without a foothold. There were accusations and truths in his words that I wasn't ready to face. That I would never be ready to face, and he tossed them all on me like they were sandbags suffocating my lungs. I should have stayed in London. I should have accepted my fate and married a man who both hated and coveted me.

"I deserved to know what I would face down there. I am sick of being involved but not told anything. If you want to use me, at least have the decency to be honest with me," I said.

Oscar laughed, but it was sharp and bitter. "The two of you are so damn stubborn pretending like—"

"Who was she? The woman trapped down there—who is she?" I demanded.

Oscar sighed, some of the fight leaving him. "Flynn should be the one—"

"I'm asking you. I'm asking my brother." I urged.

He shook his head, but I knew I had won the moment he collapsed into one of the chairs across the desk. He ran his hand over his face, and I thought I saw a hint of gray on the side of his face. I hadn't noticed how much older he looked, but the way he slumped into his chair, he mimicked our deceased grandfather more than Oscar would have cared to know.

"Her name is Anne, and she isn't trapped. The Gharaq are beastly, but they don't force anyone into servitude. The women who join them are victims of drownings, and they are given the choice to take final rest or exist with them. They are fiercely protective of the women they take in. Anne was—"

Oh, God, I understood. It all clicked with a sickening squelch of blood. The way she had looked familiar, how she had forgiven me. I thought she was forgiving me for leaving her there, but I was so wrong.

"Ximena killed her," I whispered.

"Yeah," Oscar answered, looking anywhere but at me.

The dominos aligned and cascaded and I wasn't ready for the part where they ended. I was on treacherous ground. If I insisted on trudging forward I wouldn't be the same anymore. I wouldn't be able to pretend. There was a woman who had died and now lived amongst the darkest part of the sea who deserved more than my fear. I didn't choose her fate, but my hand was involved, intention or not.

"He said you saved him from his noose last time. How?" I asked despite the pleading inside my chest that chanted a single word, 'Stop.'

Oscar shook his head. "Don't make me tell you truths you aren't ready for, Rose."

Surrendering was for cowards, and I had been one long enough.

"It's my choice. Tell me." I demanded.

With a long sigh, Oscar leaned back in his chair. "Anne was angry. She knew they weren't... more, but to die for it—she was bitter. I told her the truth. I told her to look at me and see our similarities. That she looked like my twin sister."

I winced at the words. I was as complicit in her death as the rest of them.

"How did I save his life?" I asked, my words barely audible.

Not even my arms wrapped around my body could protect me from what I asked.

Oscar shook his head. "We all saw and heard different things, Rose."

"You were betting on me saving him. Tell me why," I demanded.

Some truths hurt worse than others.

"She needed to see you. To see the way he looks at you. Part of her didn't believe me the last time. The same argument wouldn't have worked twice. You gave her peace," Oscar said.

A treacherous tear ran down my face.

"I'm the reason she's dead," I said.

"You aren't, Rose. Neither is Flynn. Ximena's the reason she is dead. Anything else is misplaced blame," Oscar said, reaching out his hand across the desk in offering.

I couldn't bring myself to take it. It was a truce I didn't deserve.

"If I had never snuck out, if I hadn't—"

"I see what you are doing, Rose, I know how your brain works. Every choice we make has a series of consequences, both good and bad. Your choices also led to incredible and beautiful things," he said.

My laugh was bitter and sharp. "A woman died for them. I lost you. I've spent an entire year mourning you. I've carried around a broken heart for an entire year. Now that I am back with you, I don't even recognize you. Mother cries every Sunday brunch because she misses you, but she thinks you are in Paris, studying. Imagine what the truth would do to her? It would kill Father if he found out where you really were. Oliver blames himself and has dedicated the last year to learning pardons, but we both know it's my fault. That I had slept with a pirate captain who swept you away with promises of adventure. When I told Oliver he couldn't look at me for an entire month. How can you not say I was selfish and ruined lives for it?"

All the guilt I had been nurturing mixed with everything James had ever said about me, and I had never seen myself more clearly. My sins and selfish inclinations on brilliant display. Only cowards hid from the truth, so I supposed I could at least cross that word off my list. James broke my heart, so I ruined the lives of those I loved. At the end of the day, we are all dominoes waiting to fall and crash into each other.

Oscar stood and rounded the desk before kneeling in front of me, his fire gaze locked on me.

"Don't do that, Rose. Don't let him win. James is an ass, and I wish I had seen it sooner, but it's not my fault he is who he is. It's not your fault Anne died, it's Ximena's. It's not your fault I left. It was my choice. You don't get to take responsibility for the choices other people make," he said.

"You don't believe that," I said, sniffling pathetically.

"I do, Rose. I swear on Mother's life that I do. You want to know who I am now? I'll tell you. I'll tell you anything you want to know. If you want to know about Inu and me, I'll tell you. I kept my distance to protect you and to give you time. I didn't see how you would view it. I'm sorry. I love you. You are my other half, and it's been hell being away from you. I swear I have slept better in the past month than I have in over a year since you've been on the Wraith. It's me and you. Always has been," he said.

The tears fell freely now. Where his words had struck true, he now placed delicate bandages over them. Patching them up till I remembered why he was my person. Why no relationship I ever had would compare to the bond we shared.

"You are just saying stuff now." I choked.

His smile was a mirror to the father we shared. All that charm was too much power for one person to wield.

"I love you, Rosie. It's always going to be me and you, even if we're oceans apart," he said.

I wiped at the snot that was glamorously pouring from my nose and sniffed. Oscar laughed and I threw the quill at him which he caught effortlessly. My wounds had already scabbed over with his reassurance. If it was any other person I would have held out a lot longer, nurturing the salt in my wounds.

"Want to steal Flynn's best gin and get drunk?" I asked.

The stretch of my brother's smile was that of a Cheshire cat.

"What a novel idea, Rosamund Beatrice Bailey."

Chapter Twenty-Two
The Consequences of Gin

Long before humanity gained the ability to communicate between civilizations, all came up with their own explanation for the destructive power of the sea. For the ancient Greeks, it was Poseidon, the god of the seas. For the Romans, it was Jupiter, while the Norse worshipped Njord. No matter the culture or the timeline, one thing remains true- anger the gods, and the seas bear their wrath.

–An excerpt from *The Mysterious Deep: A Comprehensive Understanding*

My stomach ached as I sucked in a breath, trying to stop from laughing.

"God, it hurts!" I cried out.

"And then I convinced them that my wife was ailing and needed to leave lest she defecate on herself once more. I swear Bash considered taking off the kimono right then and there, but certain beheading was the lesser evil, so" he reached out to grab my arm as he doubled over laughing, "I swear to god he let out the loudest—"

The words were lost to his laughter on the wooden floor of Flynn's cabin, one empty and one nearly empty bottle between us. At some point, the sun had left the sky and we haphazardly lit the lanterns in the cabin that swung with the waves that were determined to rock the ship. If I wasn't so drunk, I just might have been seasick. However, the warmth in my body from the alcohol and good company was more than enough.

"He didn't!" I shouted, falling down on my back and holding my aching stomach.

Oscar fell back alongside me and slapped my arm. "He did! He did! I swear it on Peaches!"

Just when I thought I had caught my breath, it sent me into another fit of laughter. I snorted and tried to sit up enough to grab the not-empty bottle, but I missed and fell back with a loud thump.

"You're drunk!" Oscar pointed at me.

"Pish posh," I slurred, trying to sit up again.

The sea conveniently decided to toss us once more, and I rolled into Oscar, who caught me with a loud grunt while our empty bottle slid across the floor into the bookshelf.

"Boo, Ocean!" I chastised.

It was the funniest thing that had ever happened to us and we flew into another fit, my heart feeling lighter than it had in over a year.

The door opened, and a rain-soaked Flynn stepped in, dripping water all over the wooden floor. He took one look at us, the set of his jaw firm, and shut the door with one fell swoop.

"Oh, look, it's your dear wife Ami-San," I shouted.

Oscar roared and attempted to cover my mouth with his hand, shushing me, but I swatted him away.

"I do hope your stomach has improved." I giggled.

"She forced me to tell her. I'm innocent." Oscar laughed.

"You are both excessively drunk," Flynn announced. "With my best gin."

He looked so serious. Poor man. I mustered up my strength and sat up, helped by Oscar, who pushed at my back. Reaching for the still not empty bottle, I grabbed it and held it up to the captain of the Wraith.

"Some left," I said, my arm swinging with the sway of the ship.

Flynn sighed and took the bottle from me before grabbing the cork off his desk and shoving it in.

"Rude!" I chastised.

He didn't care much as he returned it to his liquor cabinet. That wasn't what I meant at all when I had generously offered him some.

"While you both have been indulging in my gin, there is a storm out there gathering in strength. A storm that would have warranted my quartermaster being of sound mind." Flynn said.

Oscar looked properly chastised, bringing down the energy in the room considerably. His laughter died on his lips as he pushed himself off the floor.

"Shit," he said. "Sorry, Bash, I didn't realize how bad it was out there. I'll go chug some water and sober up."

"It's fine. Billy is taking care of it. Take Inu and call it a night, though she might flay you alive first." Flynn said, righting the objects on his desk that had fallen victim to us or the waves.

"Shit," Oscar murmured again.

I hugged my knees to my chest as I watched my brother give me a bashful wave goodbye. Like children caught in wrongdoing instead of adults on a damn pirate ship. I disliked the captain even more than usual.

The door shut behind Oscar, and I immediately regretted the loss of him. Maybe Inu and I could trade for the night, and the two grumpy people could spend time together.

"You ruined my fun." I pouted.

Flynn turned to face me, surveying my disorderly shirt and gin-stained pants from an earlier debacle with the bottle.

"You could have picked any other night for this, and I would have let you drink yourself into a stupor. As it is, those are ship killer waves out there, and I would rather my quartermaster and hostage not go overboard because they are too drunk to stand up straight," he said, tight-lipped.

I saw it then. The tension in his shoulders and the way he clenched his fists at his side in between needlessly rearranging his desk.

"You're mad," I said.

He drew in a deep breath. "I'm not mad."

Liar. I pushed myself up off the ground rather gracefully, considering the way the room spun around me. It was the walking part that turned out to be tricky as I pointed and took a step towards him. However, the damn ocean tossed us to the side, and I fell backward. Flynn was there in an instant with his hand under my back, staying my fall.

God, he was pretty. It was in the way his blue eyes were darker around the edges, but in the middle, a light blue ring hugged his iris. It was easy to get lost in them, and I *really* wanted to get lost in them. I shivered as a shot of heat ran through me, making my gaze drop to his lips. They were perfectly shaped, and the way his facial hair lightly rested over them, flicks of red in the dark hair, reminded me of how it felt when he had laid kisses down my back ever so slowly.

"Rosamund," he said, his voice gravelly.

"Mm." I hummed in answer.

I just wanted to touch him. Before I could think better of it, I lifted my hand and ran it over his rough cheek. It felt rich under my palm. He felt right. It was too hard to be near him and not touch him. Not when I knew what it felt like to be consumed by him. Not when I knew how sensitive he was right behind his ear. My only regret was that I currently only had one hand.

My hand drifted up and stroked the spot. He closed his eyes and whispered a breath, leaning into my touch. I wanted him more than I had ever wanted anything in my life. It was a need that embedded itself into me. A need that I would obsess over until I satisfied it. Like a common alcoholic hoping that next drink would cure the need for more.

His eyes opened, and the resolution in them cooled my stoking flames.

"You're drunk," he said.

So I was, and apparently my punishment was to no longer touch or be touched by him. He set me upright and put several feet in between us. Half of me was now wet through from where he'd held me against him. Great, now I was wet and being denied the one thing I wanted.

"Me being drunk hasn't been a problem in the past," I said, hands on my hips.

"That was different," he said, grabbing something from his chest across the way.

"How?" I pressed.

He slammed the chest closed and turned to face me, rope in hand. I felt the heat rush up my cheeks as I pressed my thighs together. Goddamn hormones.

"Because you were consenting prior to getting drunk," he snapped.

"Since when do pirates have such rigid morals?" I asked, trying not to swallow too hard when he tossed the rope on the bed and stomped over to me.

"If you have to ask, then you haven't been paying attention, Miss Bailey," he said.

Oh no, he was not taking that tone with me.

I shoved a finger right into his chest, and he took a step back, which was wildly satisfying. Encouraged, I shot him with my most sober of glares.

"Oh, so it's Miss Bailey now? Not *Rosamund*," I did my best impression of his deep voice, "or Princess?"

His eyes swept over me, hungry. If I wanted him, then I knew he wanted me just as much. He just had more self-control than I had, which was by far the most annoying thing about him. I just had to break him down.

"Do you want me to call you princess?" he asked, his voice undoing me.

I stared up at him as he removed my finger, jabbing into him, and pulled me against his wet clothes. They soaked through me, but I hardly noticed against the heat that pulsated within me. He could burn me, and I'd say thank you very much.

"Sure," I whispered, leaning further into him.

He backed up, taking me with him. My feet following him like he was a siren and I, a helpless sailor. The ship tossed us, but he was made for the ocean's tantrums. I fell into him, and he lightly lifted me before turning and placing me gently on the bed.

I was on fire as he placed my hands behind my back and leaned to hover his mouth over my neck. It felt good, it felt right. There was no hint of regret here.

"You are the ruin of me, Princess," he whispered against my ear.

Heat flooded and pooled between my thighs. If he didn't actually touch me soon, I was going to die. Actually, I was a strong, independent woman. I lifted my hands to touch him and made it a whole five inches before something pulled them back.

He stepped away just as I looked at my wrist and found rope wrapped around each one, tied to the edges of the bed posts. Understanding dawned on me, and rage replaced all my fire.

"You fucking asshole," I said.

He walked to the door like I wasn't chained to his bed, unsatisfied.

"I meant what I said, Princess. However, I do need to make sure you don't fall and get concussed while I make sure we don't sink," he said.

"Absolutely not, get back here and—"

He shut the door, leaving me tied to a bed with my core still on fire, no matter how much I tried to pretend it wasn't.

"Can't even do it myself," I grumbled angrily as I twisted the rope so it wasn't pulling. Asshole pirate. Maybe he would get swept overboard, and the Koinu would eat him. A girl could dream.

Chapter Twenty-Three
Damn Rats

The idea of hunting creatures of the Mysterious Deep for sport, akin to hunting game by the British gentry, is problematic in many ways. For one, the creatures they target don't fight back because they are passive and gentle. More importantly, due to the sentience and intelligence of many creatures in the Deep, they may not tolerate it forever. Instead, there should be an abundance of caution and respect for all the inhabitants of the Deep.

-An excerpt from *The Mysterious Deep: A Comprehensive Understanding*

Being hungover was one thing. Being hungover in the middle of an ocean on angry seas was entirely another. I moaned into my pillow and fought back the nausea that was threatening to empty my stomach. I knew the sun had come up by the slightly less dark clouds outside the windows, but stormy waters didn't give way to much sunlight.

"Stupid ocean and stupid pirate," I grumbled into the pillow.

As mad as I had been last night, it had only taken a minute for me to adjust in my restraints to get comfy enough to fall asleep. It was entirely possible that if the ship had sunk, I wouldn't have noticed. The only reason I was awake now with a pounding headache was the nausea that forced me awake.

The sound of the door quietly opening signaled that my purgatory was near an end. I kept my face down in my pillow and stilled my breathing. Maybe Flynn would think I was dead and feel remorseful for his cruel manipulation last night. It would serve him right.

I waited till the heavy footsteps edged closer and held my breath. A large hand felt my neck before whispering, "Dieu Merci."

I groaned and lifted my head.

"I thought you were Flynn," I said.

Emille's slackened lips quivered before he let out a boisterous laugh.

"And you were hoping to traumatize him by being dead?" he asked through his laughter.

At least someone was having fun.

"Can you not be so loud? Also, did it work? Are you traumatized?" I asked.

He shook his head. "Very nearly, it was convincing for a moment."

"Shame it wasn't Flynn," I grumbled into my pillow.

I waited as Emille untied me before attempting to sit up, but the world spun violently, and I plopped back down onto my pillow.

"I've got your potion, as you like to call it," Emille said.

That was something worth braving nausea for. I sat up and grabbed the awful peppermint potion and downed it in one large gulp. Once, I may have doubted the efficacy of Emille's work, but I had witnessed its magic before and am a firm believer now.

"I need to do your dressing," he said.

I held out my bandaged hand in question as Emille knelt beside the bed. A violent hiss erupted from under my blankets, and Emille staggered backwards onto the floor. If I hadn't been fighting back nausea, I probably would have laughed. With my good hand, I pulled back the blankets to see beady green eyes glaring up at me.

"When did you get here?" I asked.

"That thing is a demon if I've ever seen one," Emille said, righting himself.

"Who? Blackbeard?" I asked as I patted the little beast on the head.

His answering purr was the angriest happy sound I had ever heard. Yet the moment Emille tried to return to the bedside, Blackbeard let out a fearsome growl.

"I have to clean it so it doesn't get infected," Emille said to the cat as he gestured to me.

Blackbeard gave another low growl before he crawled further into the blankets and spun three times, settling into his new nest.

"I think that was as much permission as you are going to get," I said.

Emille shuddered and inched forward before starting to work on my bandage.

"I don't know if I should be impressed by your ability to tame that beast or be scared of you for it," he said.

"Both?" I shrugged.

Emille worked quietly and efficiently. By the time he was done, his magic potion had already taken effect. I could fill my lungs without my jaw tightening and throat clenching.

"What's in that potion, anyway?" I asked.

The corner of Emille's mouth pulled up, and he clicked his tongue.

"There are many things in the Mysterious Deep that have yet to be researched. One benefit of being a pirate is that I get to be the first to test them," he said.

I frowned and wrinkled my nose. "You aren't going to tell me."

He winked and gathered his supplies. A low growl erupted from Blackbeard's nest in warning. Though how he thought anyone would be brave enough to go near him besides me and Billy was beyond me. The crew was more terrified of him than the actual sea monster tailing us.

"Is the ship and everyone all right?" I asked now that I could think without my head pounding.

"No casualties. A leak down in the hull, but it's contained. We will be able to make it to Tristan da Cunha."

"Where is that?" I asked, mentally scrubbing through my geography lessons.

"It's a very remote island between South America and Africa. It's difficult to find if you aren't looking for it, and it's not far from the Glass Sea. We will probably make port there for a few days."

I sat up, holding my bandaged hand to my chest, alarm pumping through me like a wailing siren.

"The Bane will catch up!" I said, much too loudly.

Emille tilted his head, considering me. The lines on his forehead wrinkled and smoothed as he debated something.

"It's very remote, and I believe we lost them in the rough seas last night. You can rest easily. No one knows about the Island besides our crew, and for many, that is where their families live. There is no one on this crew who would give up the location."

Immediately, the greasy-looking twin and Barnacles popped into my mind. Something told me they would sell anything if the price was right. At least I knew they had a mother they were trying to help. It gave me some feather of hope, but did nothing for the panic that gripped at my neck.

I was close. I had endured sea monsters, vengeful women, insane witches, and all that was left was the Maravilla treasure. The ridiculous and reckless plan I had concocted was nearly completed without a single life lost. If the Bane caught up and James found a way to convince Flynn to hand me over—

No, no, no. This was unacceptable. I could appreciate the need for some repairs, but *days*.

I grabbed my coat and threw it over me, not bothering to put it on properly.

"Princess," Emille called.

Nope. While I was exceedingly fond of the French doctor, I was not going to be convinced to stay inside while we coasted to a potential trap.

The moment I stepped out of the cabin, a light rain fell over me, the chill breeze making it feel more like ice. It was summer, but we were traveling to the Drake Passage where it would give to Antarctica. A land that was perpetually frozen and hostile to human life. How any animals survived there was a mystery as much as any creature in the deep.

In many ways, it made sense that the Glass Sea lay at the edge of her coast, after all, the dead were the only ones able to tolerate the cold.

A chill that had nothing to do with the wind or the rain ran through me. My plan was nearing the most dangerous part and celebrating any earlier felt like a bad omen.

"Oy, Hellcat," Billy called to me from the edge of the ship.

Working pirates securing rigging and shifting goods mostly ignored me, which was better than the judgmental and hateful scowls I had received previously. Progress.

Billy's stout form was rain-soaked, and his beard was significantly less fluffy than usual. There were rings under his eyes that said it had been a long night.

"You survived," I said, coming up to lean my back on the edge of the ship.

I scanned the deck, searching for the object of my ire.

"He's down having some breakfast with the crew," Billy said. "Also, I nearly died twice last night, and all I could think was if the Hellcat would mourn me."

I snorted and cupped his burly cheek, patting it twice.

"Aye, Billy, I'd miss you even though you are a horrid flirt," I said.

Billy wrinkled his nose and huffed a loud breath. "I ain't flirting with no one, but you. I'm a one-woman man."

The laugh that pulled from me felt wholesome despite the scoundrel coaxing it out. Despite my best intentions, Billy and his theatrics would be some of my fondest memories out on the Mysterious Deep. I realized with a pang that I would miss him.

"Why the long look? If this is about that French beauty I had a dalliance with, I swear it was just the once. My heart only beats for you," he said.

I rolled my eyes and kicked off the side of the gently rocking ship beneath gray skies. There was a thick mist around us that made me think of the horror stories Oliver used to tell Oscar and me before bed, just to see how long we gave in till we came banging on his door. Usually not long.

"I could be your granddaughter, you rake," I said, walking away.

"Aye, but yer not!" he hollered.

There was no reasoning with him, and I'd braved the windy chill for a purpose. I bounced up the steps onto the stern and found it remarkably empty of one redhead with a permanent ring around her eyes. I frowned and twisted.

"In the hull!" called Billy.

I waved a hand and made my way below deck. Before I made it two feet, a man carrying a barrel made his way upstairs, not seeing me at all. I quickly backed up to give him a wide berth. A normal human would have checked before barging up, but apparently, he was above that.

"You should watch where you are going," I said before instantly biting my tongue.

Just because they didn't all want to throw you overboard anymore wasn't reason to pick fights, Rose.

The moment he passed by me, I considered that maybe stitching my mouth shut might be a great plan of action if I survived the Glass Sea and the pirates in it.

Amos set the barrel down, and a thin sheen of sweat mixed with the light rain over his sun-tanned face. A face that lit up with a wide smile that made my stomach slick with dread when he saw me. He lifted up his shirt, showcasing pale skin over the hard lines of his stomach as he wiped at his face. Maybe I could sneak past without an issue if I was quick enough, but he kicked out a foot and blocked my path.

When he dropped his shirt, his quick breaths of exertion slowly gave way to easy breathing and he leaned against the opposite wall and fixed me with a smirk that probably made tavern wenches sigh loudly. If he had any sense at all, he would know it was wasted on me.

"If it isn't our hostage princess," he said.

"Yes, and I'll be going if you don't mind," I said, taking a step forward.

Confidence mattered with men like this. Men who thought they were god's gift and that there weren't consequences for their actions.

If this were London society, my captor would have been embarrassed at my polite dismissal. This was no aristocrat, though. He was a pirate and not a particularly endearing one. Amos swiftly moved to block my way and placed his hands on either side so I would have to duck under him, making it easy enough for him to grab me.

The rain wasn't very heavy, so if I screamed, there was a decent chance someone would hear, but I could also see the muscles carved into his arms and the thick rope of his neck. I'd probably make it a whole peep before he covered my mouth.

This was why chaperones were mandated in society, as well as being able to swear up and down that a lady's honor was safe. I snorted at the ridiculousness of it.

"Something funny, *Princess*?" Amos crooned.

Hm. Well then, I could work with this.

I tilted my nose up. "Only that you think you can intimidate me, but I would wager you couldn't even recite one line of Shakespeare. I've met dogs with more intelligence than you."

His face flashed where I hit my mark. It felt good to hit him where it hurt.

He leaned forward, his sickly breath running over my skin.

"Laugh all you want. Your time will come and I'll fucking enjoy watching it happen," he said.

I did not appreciate the way his threat settled in my stomach. He believed what he said, and that was worse than idle threats.

"I could tell your Captain and he'd toss you overboard," I said, steeling myself.

Amos's laugh was thick and lewd, making me feel dirty.

"I'm sure he would, Princess." He made a show of tapping his finger to his mouth. "Or is it, Miss Bailey?"

A chill that had nothing to do with the air bit into my very soul. I felt momentarily paralyzed by the sound of my name on his lips. How? Why?

"I don't know what you are talking about." I choked.

Years of society play, and I had walked right into his grimy hands. My response had been weak, childish.

"I'm pretty sure you do." He winked. "Seems like I'm keeping one of your secrets, so it only makes sense I give you one of mine."

"I'd rather not." I ground out.

Of all the things I had expected to happen today, including the possibility of the Wraith sinking or Koinu eating us, this certainly wasn't on my list.

"You can tell your lap dog of a captain that I know, but that would trigger the other people keeping your secret to tell. It's called a contingency plan."

I raised my eyebrow. "Is that a new word you recently acquired?"

My hands started shaking, so I slid them into my pockets and leaned against the wall. I would not give him an ounce of ammunition more than I already had. I was my father's daughter, and he had long since preached on the principle of 'the moment you believe you have lost your leverage, that's the moment your opponent wins'. I had leverage.

I stepped forward till my face was an inch away from his.

"Maybe you are right. Maybe I tell Flynn and you don't realize it until he slits your throat while you are jacking yourself off to some woman who doesn't even remember what you look like." I shrugged. "We miscalculate on who your allies are, and they say what they think they know. Flynn gets hung. Then what? You will still be dead, your body eaten by sharks or a sea serpent. Maybe even the Cirein-cròin will have a go at you. Either way, I'll still be here because my life has value, unlike yours. I *matter* in ways you can never imagine. So please do go on with your master plan."

His lips twisted into a snarl after going pale at the imagery I painted for him. He spit at my feet and let his arms fall down.

"You're a fucking bitch." he said.

"I certainly like to think so, but an alive bitch, unlike you. Maybe you should talk to your friends and reconsider what you know because this heart," I reached up and patted the rapid beating entity beneath my chest. "It's colder than ice. There's nothing you could say or do that would end with you getting out of this alive."

"I'll bet I could—" Amos began.

"Is there a problem here, Mr. Clark?" Flynn's rough voice cut through the panic I was fighting back.

Amos twisted his lips and cracked his neck, his eyes marking me like I was new land freshly discovered. Bile crept up my throat and burned me, but I would not give him the satisfaction. He didn't deserve it.

Twisting to face Flynn, Amos said, "Not at all, Captain. Just getting to know our hostage is all."

"Is that so?" I felt Flynn's stare on me even though the alley below was dark.

Amos twisted to face me and raised his eyebrows. A challenge.

I could do it. I could tell the truth and Flynn would deal with him before he had the chance to whisper a single plea, but Amos wasn't clever enough to lie. Barnacles and probably his brother knew the truth of who I was, maybe even others. If he died, they would say, Flynn and Oscar would swing, and I'd be sold at the highest price to the Bane behind us.

"It is. Amos here was just discussing how sonnet thirty-four is one of the most tragic that Shakespeare ever wrote," I said.

Amos's smirk reappeared. After all, the moment we all left this darkened area, he would have the upper hand again.

"Billy's probably growing impatient for that rigging, Clark. Best not keep him waiting." Flynn said.

A wink from Amos before he hoisted his barrel up once more and left me blissfully alone. I waited exactly ten seconds before I took my hands out of my pockets and watched them shake. Without the need to contain it, the tendrils of panic coursed through my bloodstream, touching every part of me.

I pressed my body against the wooden wall and gasped in a shaky breath. This was a disaster. We were monumentally fucked. Maybe we should all take one of the dinghies and take our chances marooned on some small island. It would be better than watching my brother and my-

"Come with me," Flynn said into my ear.

I nearly screamed at his sudden presence, but his hand on the small of my back reminded me that I was safe. For now, anyway. I nodded and let him guide me. When my hands wouldn't stop shaking, he took them in his own and dragged me along.

The galley was filled with exhausted pirates who held their heads over their food, quietly working through it still soaked through. It was obvious it had been a long night. I probably should have been grateful I slept through it.

None of them spared us a glance as Flynn pulled us into the hold, lit only by a single lantern. It was piled high with crates and barrels between poles that supported the weight of the ship. He didn't say anything as he dragged me further to the back until I couldn't see a single thing.

I had been so close. Nearly succeeding in a wild ploy. I was going to vomit.

"Tell me," Flynn whispered.

He released my hands now that we were at the back of the room, where we would surely hear someone else enter, but still remain hidden from view. I might have made a comment or two about how this probably wasn't his first time dragging a woman down here if my stomach didn't just somersault in the worst possible way.

I shook my head, swallowing down my fear. Flynn would know what to do. We would find a way out of it.

"He knows," I choked out.

"Knows what?" Flynn asked.

"What do you think?" I whisper shrieked with exasperation. "My favorite color? He knows my fucking name. He knows who I am and, by extension, that Oscar is my brother and that you knew, and now we have to go. We have to get away. He is dumb, but those are the worst because he shouldn't have gloated to me that he knew. It means he's unpredictable. We need to—"

"Rose," Flynn said.

Far too calm about all of this.

"Emille said we were going to Tristan da Cunha and that no one would dare give up its location and that it is remote, but he's wrong. That—that prick would sell it at the first chance at a shilling. You can't stay there. We have to go, we have to—"

"Rose," Flynn tried again.

Still too calm, still not understanding. I needed him to understand, or we were all dead.

"Bash, you aren't listening to me. We need to go now or else—"

His large hands cupped my face and silenced all coherent thoughts and words. It was like a match over a wick. Illuminating exactly how concealed we were and how very precarious our situation was.

"We aren't going to Tristan da Cunha," he said.

Well, that hadn't at all been what I expected. I anticipated him trying to tell me he would kill Amos and then I'd have to explain the logistics and convince him it was a good, but also terrible idea.

"What?" I asked.

He lowered his hands down my cheeks to rest on my neck. The warmth of his hands was a contraindication to his still-damp clothes.

"There are always five other plans in place. It's how you survive out here. I know Ximena, and she might want me to succeed in some ways, but it's all a game to her. She only held the Bane for a few hours. I am also acutely aware of who is on my crew and monitor their activity. Amos *is* a fool, which is good. It makes him predictable."

"You knew?" I asked.

"Suspected," Flynn answered. "I drove us into that storm to give us enough space from the Bane to change course without them noticing. When they get to Tristan da Cunha with the coordinates Amos gave them, they will find we are not there."

My nausea was long forgotten against the sheer amazement at the levels unfolding in front of me. The layers.

"You knew," I whispered.

"All we have to do is make it to port without them realizing our course changed, and then they will disappear. We lose crew members all the time to port cities. No one will suspect a thing," he said.

"But if he talks—" I said.

"He won't. Your fiancé offered them a considerable sum for your return. They won't take the chance on others and having to split it. Greed both motivates and isolates the small-minded," Flynn said.

I could breathe again. It was a reasonable plan. Again, I was informed far too late. It was getting more than annoying.

"You should have told me," I said.

Flynn's hand loosened on my neck, and I regretted it for only a second before he brought his thumb to my lower lip, sending familiar warmth down my spine.

"Loose lips sink ships," he said.

I let out a low breath, barely moving.

"I can keep a secret," I said.

He took a step toward me and edged me till my back was pressed against the wall. I was liquid in his hands. Drunk or not, my body knew him and craved him. I raised my hands on either side of his waist, challenging him. It was a violent game we played, and burns barely healed before the next match was lit.

"You are torture," he whispered against my ear.

I should have been mad at him for tricking me, but all I knew was this want. How much I wanted this clever, ruthless, complicated man to touch me. If I was torture, then he was my punishment.

The door creaked open, and we both stilled, mouths inches from each other. If I leaned forward an inch, I would taste him. His tongue over my—

"Nah, we need the sail repair kit. It's in the back," one pirate said.

Flynn stiffened.

Perfect. I could see where this was going.

Fuck me.

"What do we do?" I whispered.

A lantern swinging drew light ever closer. We were going to be seen. The shadows caught, and I could see Flynn's eyes on me, debating.

I groaned and threw my head back before I wrapped my good hand around his neck, the skin rough from recent insult, and gently pulled him down to me. There was only a hint of hesitation before he let me. His lips met mine, hungry.

My body burned as the flame drew closer. Flynn grabbed me and lifted me as I wrapped my legs around his waist. He buried his face into my neck just as the flame crested the corner. I sucked in a breath as Val came into view.

"Oh, shit!" she shouted, stumbling back.

"What is it?" the other pirate called.

I threaded my hand through Flynn's hair and shook my head slowly. Val's shock slowly gave way to a self-satisfied smirk.

"Nothing," she called. "Just some damn rats."

Rude.

Flynn huffed what was probably a laugh into my neck. Glad this was amusing to him. I was both on fire and mortified all at once.

Val reached over and grabbed a beige bag from on top of one of the barrels and gave me a toothy grin that screamed, "I knew it."

"You'd think that demon cat would take care of those," the other pirate said.

"You'd think," Val chuckled.

Neither Flynn nor I moved as the light faded. His breath was heavy over my shoulder. As soon as the door shut once more, we both let out relieved sighs, and I dropped my head into his shoulder.

"She isn't ever going to let this go," I said.

Flynn lifted his head and even though we were surrounded by impenetrable darkness, I could feel his eyes on me like a beacon over the rocks.

"Of all the people who could have walked in here, I'd say we were more than lucky," he said.

"Mm," I answered, precariously aware of how his body was pressed against mine and the way I would never be able to scrub the taste of him off me.

How I didn't want to.

Slowly, he lowered me, and I regretted the pressure of him.

"You should be good now. I'll follow a few minutes after in case there's anyone lingering outside," he said, voice gruff.

"Mmhm," I answered.

The walk back was punctuated by a regret that was more poignant than any I had known before. I lifted my fingers to my lips, still warm from the hint of his touch.

I had gone into that room scared to death, now I was just something else entirely.

Damn pirates.

Chapter Twenty-Four

Theories

There is no creature of the Deep more feared than the Kraken. No detailed sketchy or rendering of one exists and the reason for that is simple—to see a Kraken is to know death.

–An excerpt from *The Mysterious Deep: A Comprehensive Understanding*

"Every civilization, every culture has a story about the creature that lives in the sea. Yet no one stopped to think, 'what if they are all real?'" Dilly threw up her arms in exasperation.

"Maybe they were too afraid to ask." I shrugged from where I had perched at the stern of the ship while Dilly admired our Koinu.

When she didn't say anything, I braved the sun's rays to find her halfway off the ship with her spyglass glued to her face, entirely unaware that a stray wind would carry her the rest of the way overboard. I waited for her to notice and pull back, but the oblivious redhead pushed herself up even further, her toes no longer touching the floor. Jumping up, I wrapped my arms around her waist and pulled her back, ignoring the way my heart stuttered in my chest.

She gave a shout of protest before lowering her spyglass and staring at me, mouth agape.

"Why did you do that?" she asked.

Only Dilly. Only the sea monster-obsessed woman before me would be offended. I just saved her life from going overboard and therein the mouth of our beloved Koinu. At least the sun had finally cleared the gray clouds, and the seas had calmed beneath us. I had even felt brave enough to use one of the shirts with cut-off sleeves since everyone was saying this was one of the last few warm days we would have.

My mother would have fainted had she seen me in a navy blue sleeveless top that buttoned right at my cleavage, form-fitting black pants, and black boots. I had stared at my reflection in Flynn's floor-length mirror for a solid thirty minutes this morning. With my hair braided behind my head, I looked like a proper pirate, just missing the tattoo over my chest.

It felt strangely good. In so many ways, I was not the woman who had first boarded the Wraith. Clumsy still, yes. Likely to put my foot in my mouth, also yes. But I was bolder. More confident. The insecurities I had nurtured for over a year felt less loud inside my mind. More to the point, I was *happier*.

I had almost died at least twice, and yet I woke up each day with a sense of possibility. In London, I knew every step, every dance. I could anticipate my next response and the one thereafter. Everything out here was simply—unpredictable.

"Helloooooooo," Dilly said, waving a hand over my face. "Anyone home in there?"

I blinked several times before I realized she was speaking to me. Still scatter-brained as well it would seem.

"A better question is whether or not you consider Koinu eating you to be in the best interest of your research?" I said, pointing a finger at her.

She waved a freckled hand and glanced wistfully at the departing sea behind us.

"I don't think he'd eat me. It wouldn't be satisfying, not to mention he's a sweetheart. Look at him."

She shoved the spyglass into my hands and nodded encouragingly towards the sea. I highly doubted anyone in the history of the world had ever classified a sea monster as being a 'sweetheart.'

I squinted, my vision adjusting to the narrow glass that stretched across the vast ocean. Shimmering blue and green glinted against the sun's rays before dipping under the white of the wake the Wraith left behind. Half a heartbeat later, he emerged from the ocean, head first into the air and back under, his ginormous body following after with his scales reaching toward the heavens. For the first time, I could make out the narrow shape of his head that slowly enlarged till large scale-like fins jutted out from the back of his head, and two long tendrils flowed from the top. Those same fins appeared on the bottom of his belly instead of legs. He splayed them out to the side, reminding me of when my siblings and I would jump into the lake, arms wide. It felt like a lifetime before all of him made it below the surface.

"He's massive," I whispered.

"I know!" Dilly squeaked in excitement.

"One bite and we'd all be in the ocean," I said, watching him leap into the air before splashing onto his back, his large fan-like tail slapping down atop white waves.

The answering splash of water very nearly reached the Wraith with its force of impact.

"I know!" Dilly shrieked.

I lowered the spyglass and stared at her beaming smile and twinkling eyes with my mouth wide open in very real danger of catching flies.

"That should not fill you with wild joy, Cordelia Shaw!"

She didn't even have the decency to appear scolded. Instead, she did a cute little bounce-hop with her feet and let out a wild squeal.

"I doubt any other mysteriologist has ever had this much time to study a Cirein-cròin before. I've been able to document its eating patterns. Whales, dolphins, seals, and squid. I've seen him eat all those things. Not to mention that I can safely guess that Koinu is by far larger than any Blue Whale ever documented. Did you see how long it took for the rest of his body to follow his head? That's at least two hundred feet! Not to mention that his underbelly is smooth like a killer whale. Everyone always assumed they would be scaly like a serpent, similar to their top scales. It makes me wonder if maybe they have more in common genetically than we thought with cetaceans. I've been able to accurately draw out a very lifelike diagram that will impact future mysteriology for decades to come."

She was nigh on breathless as she held up the book to me, showcasing two pages of art. It was impossible not to love her. No one had ever had an ounce of the enthusiasm she held in her pinky in their entire bodies back in London. If the world were full of Cordelia Shaws, it would be a better place.

"Why is it following us?" I asked.

That sobered her enough to pull back her smile, and a blanket of guilt fell over me. It felt like a crime to dim her shine, even if the question sometimes kept me up at night. Dilly raised her finger to her lips and tapped it twice, squinting while she traversed the lines of thought in her brilliant mind.

"I *have* spent a lot of time thinking about it and I have a theory, but it's hardly scientific," she said, wrinkling her nose.

I waved a hand impatiently for her to continue.

She bit her lower lip before sighing dramatically. "Okay, but you can't freak out."

I raised a hand to my chest and blinked several times. "Moi? I am the epitome of calmness."

A melodic laugh loosened from her chest before she took a long breath.

"Okay. I was thinking about how strange it was that the grindylow, who is an opportunistic eater, didn't take a bite out of the first person they saw, but instead lunged for you. Then there was the Kelpie. I've taken detailed accounts from the Captain and Inu. By all accounts, that Kelpie could have easily grabbed you and taken you overboard before Inu got to you. It didn't, though. Almost like it was *waiting* for you. Then there is Blackbeard and how he seems very protective of you."

She stopped speaking and stared at me expectantly, like I was supposed to have garnered some kind of deep understanding. Dilly sighed and rubbed her hand over her forehead.

"I don't know, it's something about you. You are the only common denominator," she said.

Oh. Oh, I saw it now. Despite the accusation she laid at my feet, humor bubbled up within me and I burst out laughing. It was utterly ridiculous. Coincidence that had nothing to do with causation.

"Dilly, you are well aware that a mysterious creature very actively tried to kill me, right? And she could talk. If there was something in me that was appealing, she would have said."

Red curls bounced as she shook her head and pointed a finger at me. "I had considered that, but Ximena was an outlier. The sea witches, though, seemed to take more of an interest in you than Oscar. Not to mention, they very nearly killed the captain. Emille said five more seconds, and he would have been done for. I've written down all three of your accounts, and yours is wildly different. There was almost a... curiosity there, whereas with Oscar's they were primarily disinterested, and the captain's was vengeful."

Despite having recited in painful detail every word I could remember, I hadn't thought that Flynn would have done the same thing. I had a very real and consuming need to grab the book from her and read its contents. It was that itching in my foot, when I wanted something, that made me lean over and peer at the words carefully written onto the pages.

I barely made out the shape of my name on the top page before Dilly slammed the book shut and gave me her most scalding of looks that even my mother would have been impressed.

"Encounters with the Gharaq are highly personal. I have an ethical obligation to protect the knowledge gifted to me," she said, holding it to her chest.

I blew out a frustrated breath. Did she know that I had apparently saved Flynn? That we had a history? What if she knew about Oscar? With rising alarm, I reached for my heart that was beating wildly. I already felt guilty for lying to her. She still thought my name was Miss Princess Smith despite our friendship. If there was anyone I could trust on this ship, it would have been her, but I was still lying to her.

My vision filled with salt and pepper stars as I drowned in the worry and guilt that flooded me. I might have died there if Dilly hadn't pulled me towards her and cocooned me in the safety of her embrace. I didn't deserve her comfort.

"Hey, it's all right." She whispered into my ear. "I can only guess what you are worried I'll know, but I wouldn't ever tell. It's all for science. You are my friend. If it helps, the Gharaq mostly speak in nonsense that only they understand. I really don't know anything, even with all three accounts. I swear."

My breathing eased, and I shook my head.

"Aren't you mad that I have secrets?" I said.

Dilly laughed into my shoulder. "We all have secrets. I know who you are, and that's enough for me, but if they ever become too much of a burden, they would be safe with me. I promise."

The strangest thing happened. I believed her. A lifetime of honeyed words, and I had never believed anyone the way I believed an eccentric red-headed pirate. If they were just my secrets, I would have handed them all to her with a silver bow, but they weren't just mine.

"Thanks, Dilly," I said.

I took a shaky breath and pulled away.

"So what, I'm a siren for mysterious creatures?" I asked.

Scrunching up her nose, Dilly threw up her arms and shrugged her shoulders.

"It's a theory. Maybe it's something in your genetic code. Too bad you don't have family we can entice onto our ship to test the theory," she pouted.

The rush of guilt was well-deserved. If only she knew. If only I could tell her the truth. It felt like cutting her off at the knees to not give her more data. Unfortunately, that was a secret that needed protecting more than ever.

"Well, if you want to dangle me overboard and test the theory, just let me know," I smirked.

Dilly waved a hand. "No, thanks. The captain appreciates me, but not enough to survive that."

She was not holding back any punches today. My gut slammed with the words, and the way Val had been smirking at me, I was starting to wonder if I had any idea what was happening at all. Probably not.

"Yes, well, hostages are hard to come by these days," I said.

"Especially the pretty ones." Dilly chirped.

I batted my eyelashes and leaned my head towards her. "You think I'm pretty, Cordelia Shaw?"

She threw her hip into my side and laughed. "Something like that."

I narrowed my eyes at her and she exploded into laughter. That was the thing about Dilly, she had a way of making everything seem like it would be okay. If I had one wish, it would have been that nothing ever dulled that light inside her. It was rare and beautiful.

Even still, some wishes only ever remained wishes. Unfulfilled and lost to the sea.

Chapter Twenty-Five
To Live

Many superstitions exist among those who traverse the Mysterious Deep such as whistling onboard and changing a boat's name. However, the most infuriating by far is that women are bad luck on ships. Luckily, this level of stupidity only seems to affect shipping companies who have the misfortune of being born into a patriarchal society.

–An excerpt from The Mysterious Deep: A Comprehensive Understanding

As it so happened, Flynn's detour into the storm had made for higher casualties than they realized. The main sail was determined to tear despite all the godforsaken sail kits in the hull. Which meant we were going to make port much earlier than expected. My feet itched with the need to get off the ship. It had been over a month since I last put my feet on solid ground, and it was beginning to mess with my mind.

I loved the sea more than I ever thought I would, but the Wraith was only so big, and even Dilly was beginning to get on my nerves. At least I had the nights to myself. Ever since our time in the hold, he'd left me alone. Avoiding me like the damn plague. I didn't know where he was sleeping, but it wasn't in his bed or his hammock.

If this was a strategy to mitigate the hungry glances Amos and Barnacles were throwing at me, then it would have been nice for him to have said so. But by now, I knew that Flynn kept his reasons and his plans close to his chest. I just wish I didn't feel so irritated by that. That it bothered me at all was a symptom of something worse.

I leaned against the railing of the Wraith and watched the port of Santos come into view. A ramshackle array of buildings that bustled with goings and comings. Everything in me was desperate for freedom. If I were more coordinated and wasn't afraid Koinu would eat me, I would have jumped in and swum the rest of the way.

With the change of course, the sun had blissfully stayed with us, and my black sleeveless top was now more comfortable than traditional London clothes. How I would go back to a dress after this was beyond me. There had been no sight of the Bane since our storm, and even though it had been reckless, Flynn's plan had been worth the risk. It felt a little like breathing, knowing that James wasn't tailing me. Freedom even.

"You've probably never been to Brazil."

I jumped at the unexpected company before taking a step to the side as realization dawned. Blond hair, high cheekbones set with a distinct aura of evil, Amos stood next to me with a small smile on his lips.

"What do you want?" I snapped.

His smile faded and his eyes narrowed before his mouth fell open and he held up his hands.

"Oh, you've met my brother, I see," he said. "Wrong twin, happens all the time."

He held out his hand to me. "I'm Charlie."

When I did not take his hand he sighed and rolled up the sleeve of his shirt showing a port-wine stain that quite resembled the shape of England on his forearm.

"If you ever want to tell us a part, the birthmark always gives it away," he said.

"Why are you talking to me?" I asked, searching the deck for someone to hear when I inevitably screamed.

Luckily, the deck was filled with people going and coming, preparing to dock. Whatever this was, it wasn't a kidnapping.

Charlie sighed and leaned his arms on the railing, looking out to the city.

"You just looked kind of lonely, but if I'm being really honest, I'm procrastinating carrying up the barrels for trading. Talking to you seemed like a decent excuse," he shrugged.

"Your brother is an asshole," I said.

Did he know about Amos's plan to sell me, or was it just Barnacles who was in on it? Besides avoiding me, Flynn was also remaining tight-lipped on everything. While it may have been a strategy, it was also annoying. That Charlie felt he could talk to me at all was likely a direct result of Flynn obviously keeping his distance from me. I had seen the difference in the crew. Whereas they had been standoffish but polite, they now joked more freely. Apparently, I was no longer considered the captain's property.

Good. As it should be.

"Yeah, he is. Gets it from our dad, though he would never admit it," he said.

Silence stretched between us. This felt like a different kind of word dance than I was used to. How did one discreetly ask if someone was considering handing you over to your deranged ex-fiancé for a large sum of money? Maybe I should just ask if he knew my real name? If he said yes, I might be able to toss him over to Koinu.

Reaching into his pocket, he withdrew a small piece of chocolate. "Peace offering?"

"It's probably drugged," I said, wrinkling my nose.

In answer, he opened his mouth and plopped in the square with a wide smile.

"You don't trust easily," he said.

"Your brother is *really* an asshole," I said.

He nodded his head. "True, but I hope you won't lump me in with him too much."

There was something charismatic in the way he spoke. Maybe it was his American accent or the way he spoke out of the corner of his mouth. Only two minutes later, I felt like I could see the difference between them much clearer. It didn't mean I trusted him, though. It was rather convenient timing, right before we made port.

"You haven't said a word to me before this. Why now?" I asked.

Charlie gave a small smile, color coming to his cheeks that made him look more boyish than pirate.

"Back to work, Mr. Clark. I want the hull empty within an hour of docking." Flynn's voice called from across the deck.

I turned to see him with his beard freshly trimmed and eyes of steel cut toward the pirate standing next to me. He was the epitome of a pirate against the bright sun with his black loose shirt and tight black pants that hugged him like an old friend. It would have been considerably more ideal if he had been significantly less attractive.

Charlie clicked his tongue.

"Seems like I don't have a good reason after all." He tipped his straw hat to me, "Have a good day, Miss Smith. Brazil is known for its music and dance. Maybe we'll run into each other," he said.

Hm. Too charming. I watched his retreating back, thinking that even if the chocolate wasn't poisoned, it was still highly suspicious. Unfortunately, I might have been too trusting because something about him was endearing, or maybe it was just the glaring difference between him and his evil twin.

The feel of eyes on me were pricking at the back of my neck. I raised my eyes to see Flynn watching me, quiet stoicism eating right through me. A second later, he turned to yell something at the poor soul who happened to be close to him and stalked off towards the bow of the ship.

Bad mood. Excellent. I would be keeping my distance then.

"You are too trusting," Inu said, scaring my soul right out of my body.

I clasped my chest and let out a long breath that said at least I was still alive.

"Why on God's green earth do you always do that?" I shouted.

Inu raised a single eyebrow beneath her wide-brimmed hat as if that were answer enough.

"Also, I am not too trusting because it's been two months and I still don't trust you," I said.

She paused, contemplating. "Foolish."

I rolled my eyes. As much as I loved my brother, Inu and I were never going to be friends. It was impossible. We were far too different. For example, I knew how to smile, and she had never once done so in her life. I enjoyed laughing; she enjoyed glowering. I hadn't gotten much time with Oscar since our drunken mishap, but I doubted there was anything he could say that would convince me he didn't have some twisted trauma bond with the entity before me.

"Are you back to stalking me?" I asked.

It'd been glorious having a longer leash from her. With storm repairs, Inu had been forced away from me. All good things must come to an end, as they say.

She said nothing, which was all the answer I needed.

Lovely.

At least I would be off the ship in a minute. That counted for something. I turned my head to tell her that it could be our little secret if she stayed behind, but before a word could come out of my mouth, I ran into something hard, yet oddly squishy.

"If you wanted to touch me, Princess, you could have just asked."

My stomach soured as I turned and found Barnacles's stout form hovering over me. His sickly smile showcased black teeth on his too-thin lips. He was all brute with his thinning brown hair and grizzly beard, which was several inches too long.

"I can think of nothing I want less," I said, taking a step back and running into Inu.

God, there was no space on this damn ship.

"Oh, I think I could think of something you'd want less, *princess*."

The least he could do was be clever about threatening me. Maybe it was being sick of this damn boat or maybe it was irritation at the watch dog at my back, but I really didn't care that he knew who I was.

"Watch your mouth," Inu hissed.

I definitely did not need her help.

I took a step forward, thinking he would move, but he was a wall of stone, and this close, I could smell the rotting of his teeth.

"You *will* move," I said, proud my voice didn't waver.

He bent down and blew into my face. It was a miracle I didn't gag.

"Or what?" he smirked.

The distinct sound of metal sliding out ran through the air, and before I could turn to tell Inu that I could handle myself, silver glinted across Barnacle's throat.

"Do you have a death wish?" Flynn's gravelly voice said.

I swallowed slowly and leaned to the side to see Flynn standing behind Barnacles, his hand firmly around the hilt of his sword.

This had escalated quickly.

Not a single soul on the Wraith cared for the duties they had been given. Every single eye was trained on the dramatic scene I found myself a part of.

"I barely touched her." Barnacles spat.

At least he had deranged confidence going for him. Most men would have been simpering apologists by now, but he was committed.

"Barely is enough reason for you to end up at the bottom of the sea," Flynn said.

"Maybe we all should take a breather. It's been a minute since we've had a break from the sea. Let's get our work done, and we can get a drink and laugh about this later." Billy said in unbroken English.

I realized that was part of his tell.

He was worried.

I had to lean to the other side of Barnacles to see where Billy held up his hands in caution, eyes trained on Flynn.

"Yeah, Cap, a drink outta soothe it, don't ya think?" Barnacles said, eyes roaming over me like I was there for his delight.

"Bash," Oscar said, gently. "It isn't worth it."

His voice was low enough behind Flynn that I doubted anyone outside us heard him. I was tempted to lean back to see what Flynn was thinking, but any movement now meant the difference between life and death. While I would have been happy to see Barnacles's insides decorating the deck, I would wager a captain killing his crew was a death sentence of his own.

"The next person to touch our hostage will find themselves with a still heartbeat," Flynn yelled.

Barnacles hissed as Flynn withdrew his sword from his neck, small rivulets of blood trailing in its wake.

I might have enjoyed his wince of pain if it weren't for the way his chest rose and fell with his haunting chuckle. He took several steps back from me, but if I knew anything at all, I knew Barnacles wasn't sorry.

I'd wager Flynn knew the same as he sheathed his sword and strode away with clenched fists.

I wished I could have been the one to tell Barnacles that his time was borrowed, but even though the plan had always been to dispense of Amos and Barnacles when we made port, I wondered if that little show had been on purpose.

Even if it was normal for crew to leave at ports, Barnacles had just made sure there would be whispers when he didn't show up in the morning.

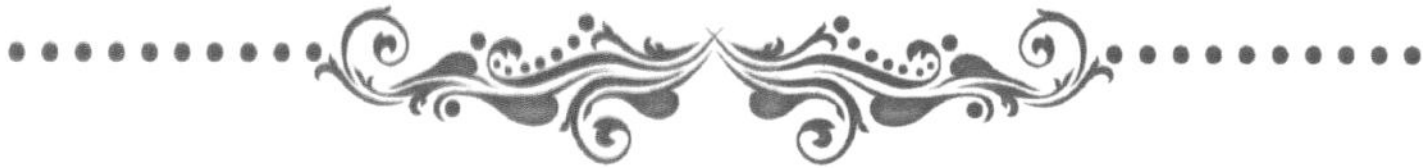

I felt her like a boil on my back as we slowly entered the port, edging closer to solid ground. My feet ached within my boots. Inu was twice as close since Barnacles had been a monumental asshole. Still, the port was there, just out of reach. I probably wouldn't even mind when I inevitably fell on my ass climbing down the ladder.

I bounced on my heels watching Oscar and Billy roll out the ladder. Oscar's eyes met mine for a brief second before he shook his head, laughing to himself. He said something to Billy, who cut his eyes towards me and gave me what would have been a toothy grin if he had most of them.

"Well, off with ya, Hellcat, fore' ya leave a hole in the ship from bouncing up and down." Billy laughed.

Several pirates nearby laughed as I bolted for the ladder. Good-bye Wraith. Hello, firm, layered, not bouncy ground. It turned out that climbing a ladder without a dress made for much quicker work. The moment my boots hit the wooden dock below, I spun and took in the beautiful sight before me.

It was a harbor much like London, but without the stacked smokehouses and gloomy weather. People of all shapes and colors went back and forth without paying me a single ounce of attention. White golden sand to my left was lazily being caressed by the sea's waves before being called back to her depths. I lit up from within imagining this is how it must feel to be a living firework.

I took off because I might die if I waited one more moment. I weaved through men and women who shouted to me in foreign languages, their reprimand apparent despite the language barrier. If only I cared. The smell of salt and the wind mixed with fresh catches of seafood that were hauled in with nets by women wearing colorful dresses of the brightest yellows and reds.

Running and attempting to take off my boots, I nearly fell face-first onto the rocky edge before sand met sea. Luckily, I remained mostly upright and by the time I reached the sand, my bare toes slid blissfully into its soft embrace.

I screamed with elation that came from the tips of my toes. Falling to my knees, I crawled towards the water, the sand gently grinding against my hands. Real. This was real and it wasn't wood and it wasn't moving. Thank the powers that be that my hand was mostly healed. Only a small area on my palm remained, but I could feel this and that's what mattered.

With another sound that had never once come from my body before, I threw the sand into the air and rolled onto my back, moving my arms and legs up and down fast and then slowly, just like my siblings and I used to do at first snowfall.

In all my life, when I was old and senile thinking my time on a pirate ship had been a dream, I would remember this. This moment. The feel of the sand between my toes and the breeze caressing my skin. The way the sun shined down on me was like it was just as happy to know me as I was to know it.

The women nearby exchanged a mix of Portuguese and native tongue before they broke out in laughter. I rolled onto my stomach and gave them my brightest smile. All three of them broke out into raucous laughter, which I considered our pact to be great friends.

"You look ridiculous."

I groaned before deciding I would not be letting a miserable woman ruin my great joy. Instead, I stuck my tongue out at the miserable sod before rolling like a log right into the ocean. The moment the water touched my skin, I felt myself come alive once more. Like I had been living in a coffin for two months and finally carved my way out. It was cold and fresh and real.

"Your hand!" Emille called, his accent stronger with frustration.

I might have forgotten about caution with my injured hand, which was now fully immersed beneath sea water. At least it didn't hurt anymore, even though some of the skin was slow to heal and regrow.

A cresting wave went over my head, and for a moment, it was just me and the sea, before I pushed myself up from the sandy floor and breathed in fresh air. A manic sort of giggle broke from me as I beheld Emille and Inu side by side on the beach with identical folded arms and unimpressed thinning lips.

"Sorry, Emille!" I called, waving my good hand.

The tall doctor's frustration melted away under his chronic good nature, and he gave a small chuckle.

"I hope it was worth it!" he called.

I stood up and spread out my arms. "This is the best day of my life!"

I fell back into the ocean and let her sweep me away. She carried me like I was her long-lost child, and she wanted me as much as I wanted her. My body was alive with the most divine sensations. I was alive, and life was meant for living.

By the time I dragged myself from the ocean, Inu had settled onto the beach with her wide hat covering her face. I could only imagine the grim scowl beneath. Had she ever known joy?

"Don't you want to swim?" I asked her.

"No," she shot back.

"Have you ever smiled before?" I asked.

"No," she retorted. "Emille says you are supposed to go get your bandages changed as soon as you are done... frolicking."

"Mm. Still more frolicking to be done, I think," I said, sliding on my boots.

"You are soaking wet," Inu observed.

"Indeed. I think I might be in need of a change of dress and some food!" I called as I made for the town up ahead.

A muttered curse behind me signaled my babysitter was firmly in tow. The docks weren't very different from London, but the buildings certainly were. Wooden walls and questionably stable shingles were a far cry from London's brick and mortar. Yet the dark colors and close quarters made everything feel warm and inviting.

There were endless stalls of goods to trade, and it was clear this port saw thousands of ships in its harbor each year. Coffee, tea, furs, exotic foods, endless clothes, and goods. The bustling of coming and going drowned out any chance at reasonable conversation, which was preferred in the current company.

A lovely coral blouse caught my eye and I instantly handed over the réis that a wrinkled old woman demanded. She gave me a toothy smile that stretched wide as she put her money into her skirt pocket. Meandering down the uneven ground of rock and sand, I breathed in the scents all around me. Spices and heat mixed with the promise of possibility. It was sea air, a cacophony of smells I had never experienced.

I had always been content with London and being able to predict the next moment, but there was no denying the beating in my heart that screamed, "live, live, live." A lifetime of self-doubt whittled away under that chant.

A fresh pair of black pants that were just the right fit later, and I was back to a semi-dry state. I stared at the blue sky above wooden beams and smiled. Maybe I could just stay here, and the Wraith could pick me up once they risked their lives to retrieve an impossible treasure. The idea became more appealing when I walked into a rather questionable establishment where a corner to the back was caved in with splintered wood and debris.

Tables of varying sizes were occupied by men and women with an array of weapons and scars that would have caused my mother to lose consciousness had she been present. I, on the other hand, was appropriately inspired. Ignoring the groan from behind me, I took a weathered stool at the bar and folded my hands over it expectantly.

With a distinct air of disapproval, Inu took the seat next to me, which was my own fault for picking a seat with a vacancy next to it. A dark-skinned man with a long black mustache curled up and raised an eyebrow at me as he came to stand before me.

"I'll take whatever you recommend," I said.

His eyebrow lowered, and he leaned against the bar, encroaching into my space, but I refused to back away and concede ground.

"English," he said, accent thick around the accusation.

"I suppose that's true, but mostly I just want a drink at this particular moment." I smiled sweetly.

"Can the English girl pay?" He smirked.

"Depends on if you can actually make drinks or if you simply interrogate patrons," I said.

His smirk fell, his cheeks puffed red, and I was acutely aware that I had let my mouth run away with me again. It would have been simple enough to pull out some réis and smile without showing teeth, maybe a tilt of the head for good measure, and a couple of blinks. Well, it might have been easier, but significantly less fun.

Just as I was prepared to concede that this establishment was not for me, the grizzly middle-aged man slapped his hand on the bar and burst out laughing. Unwanted attention drew our way, and Inu whispered something in my ear that was probably a curse, but against the loud conversations and roaring man before me, it was lost.

"Very well, English girl, I'll make you a drink and you tell me if it's any good," he said.

"I prefer a lack of poison if possible," I said, taking in a sharp breath.

He turned, shaking his shoulders, as he grabbed a glass lined with a mysterious brown coating that my father would have scoffed at. Even Oliver would have been offended. Pouring a clear liquid and tossing a spoonful of sugar, he finished with a squeeze of lime, which he plopped into the discolored glass and gently swirled it. With a great flourish of his arm, he placed it before me and stood with his arms folded.

"You are supposed to be getting your wound seen to." Inu reminded me.

"Which will be tolerated better with a—what is this again?" I asked.

The bartender's smirk fell back into place. "A caipirinha cocktail."

"Exactly," I said, lifting the glass into the air before taking a long sip.

It ran down my throat like a volcano erupting from within that was peppered with sweetness, even as it wreaked havoc everywhere it touched. I wrinkled my nose as the lime lingered a few seconds after the burning stopped and set the glass gently down.

I cleared my throat. "Lovely."

I was pretty sure my nose was dripping, but I would have rather died than admit it.

The bartender's lower lip quivered a fraction before his laughter encompassed every molecule of sound in a ten-mile vicinity. He placed a hand over his stomach and bent over laughing. For good measure, I lifted the glass to my lips and took another swallow, mourning the loss of my internal organs along the way.

"It's on the house, English girl," he said, still laughing, as he went to another customer on the opposite side.

Excellent.

It was hard not to feel like I had passed some sort of test. Whether it was the bartenders or my own, I couldn't have said. All I knew was that the drink tasted better with every sip, and it tasted a lot like I imagined freedom would.

Chapter Twenty-Six
The Princess and The Plague

It is an utterly strange and incomprehensible thing to get off a ship after months at sea and immediately run into the water.

-An excerpt from The Mysterious Deep: A Comprehensive Understanding

The thing about cages was that once they were opened, it was hard to close them a second time. Music accented with the bang of drums and a distinct lack of pianos and violins hummed in my blood. Fire flickered and warmed my skin against the cool starlight breeze. This was living.

"Better than your stuffy English parties, right?" Dilly hollered across from me, where she moved her body in alarmingly robust movements.

My gentle and only slightly inebriated movements were considerably more docile, however, my mother and sisters would all be horrified all the same. The beach was alive with locals and Wraith pirates alike. Some sitting on logs nursing their drinks while others had taken to dancing like Dilly and I. The best part was that no one cared what anyone else was doing.

"It feels like a different world," I called back.

Dilly reached for my arm and spun me in a wild, frantic circle that left my vision slow to catch up, but laughter followed all the same because this was everything I never knew I wanted.

"That's because it is!" Dilly sang.

"Lovely form, Miss Smith." My brother's voice came from behind me.

I turned to see him wearing a wide grin, his hands tucked behind him like a proper gentleman. He was handsome under the pale moonlight, the twinkle in his eyes an homage to the stars above. He was my charismatic, charming brother, whom I had spent a year being mad at.

"I have my faults, but being a poor dancer is not one of them," I said.

He furrowed his eyebrows, smile falling. "You have faults?"

It came from low in my stomach and erupted like a thousand volcanoes exploding at once. Laughter gripped me even as he held out his hand and bowed low. No thought of recourse, no would-haves or shouldnt's echoed in my ears. Only that this felt right. Taking his hand, he put his other on my waist and we moved past sashaying pirates, drunk and sober alike.

It was a waltz worthy of Buckingham Palace, but destined for shores lazily lapped by waves. My bare feet sank into the sand that caressed and pulled at me, begging me to lie down and become one with it. It might have been tempting if the wind that danced around us wasn't chipping away at my rough edges and old scars.

"A lovely evening, don't you think?" Oscar said, deepening his voice by several octaves.

"Quite, I especially enjoy the decor of drunk pirates," I answered.

"To be sure, the finest drunk pirates on any continent I'd wager," he said.

I snorted as he dipped me down until my shortened hair nearly brushed the sand. Just as quickly, he hurled me back up and resumed our wild dance. As we moved, I caught sight of Inu. She was sitting next to Dilly, who was chirping away quite contentedly while Inu sharpened her knife, her gaze locked on Oscar and me.

"My jailer seems particularly put out this evening," I said.

Even though the words were said with the lilt of a joke, they soured in my stomach all the same. She was like a cough that persisted in the worst way. I couldn't help thinking I would have enjoyed my time at sea far more if it weren't for her.

Oscar's smile fell as well.

"I wish you wouldn't be rude to her. She is only doing what Bash ordered her to do," he said.

I gritted my teeth against all the words I wanted to say, but shouldn't.

"I wish I understood what you saw in her. She isn't you. You should be with someone who laughs and smiles or knows how to make a joke. Someone who-"

"Maybe if you took a minute to understand her instead of judging her, you would understand," Oscar said, bringing our dance to a halt.

He refused to look at me, and the muscle at the edge of his jaw flicked in that tell-tale sign.

"You are mad at *me*?" I asked.

This was a twilight world that made absolutely no sense. Oscar was never mad at me. It was us against everyone else.

He forced his gaze to mine, and that was the moment I knew he wasn't just mad. This was something more—something that reeked of conviction.

"You are so stubborn, you think you know everything, and we should all bend to your will. Inu has been through more than you will ever understand, and the fact that she is still standing is an incredible feat worthy of the highest accolades. There is a reason they call you princess. You haven't known one day of hardship, but you think you can sit back on your throne and judge others."

His words tore right through me until my mouth was open and I was seeing bursts of stars throughout my vision. Never, not once, had my brother ever spoken to me like that. That he did now where others could hear in defense of a woman who had been rude and standoffish from the moment I met her grated along my bones.

I didn't even recognize him.

There weren't words for the way he cut me open. I stepped away from him once, then twice. Before I knew it, I was halfway down the beach. I wouldn't look back. Would not give him the satisfaction of knowing I cared an ounce about his reaction. He didn't deserve it.

The soft sand beneath my feet gave way to uneven stones lit by gas lamps and torches alike. Their flames seared my open wounds worse than the Gharaq's mysterious fire that had burned into my hand. Anything else would have been preferable compared to this.

I sank into the same bar I had been in earlier that morning and caught my breath against the splintered wood wall. The scent of alcohol and vomit mixing with rowdy laughter and too loud conversations. The space was now packed with primarily men who competed with each other on who could speak the loudest.

No one paid me any attention as if panting women running inside was an everyday occurrence. My chest burned and ached while I fought back nausea.

"Must you be so theatric, Rosamund?" James said inside my head.

The sound of his voice sent a rock into my stomach. How quickly he returned to my mind when I had only just shed the weight of him.

"You should return to the ship."

I wrenched my eyes open to find Inu leveling that unnatural stare over me. Mostly, I saw what she took from me. And for what? No amount of hardships could make her likable. If I was a princess, then she was a plague.

"I have never hit another person before, but I swear to the seas, to god, to any deity who has the misfortune of listening that I will if you don't leave me the fuck alone."

"You are lucky to have me. No one else would tolerate your outbursts and hysterics."

"Get out of my head!" I grabbed onto either side of my head and screamed.

The sting of tears punctuated my mental breakdown, which felt inevitable. Like I was always sailing towards it. A final destination marked with bold red lines in the shape of an x on a map.

"People are starting to watch. You need to come back to the ship," Inu whispered angrily.

It was the final straw.

I lifted my eyes to hers and saw every word she never said and every judgment she waged upon me. Cocking my fist back, I swung for her, but a firm grip around my arm prevented the satisfaction of hearing her nose crunch. My fist only one inch from her face, Inu didn't flinch or move in any way.

"That will be all, Inu," his deep voice rasped behind me.

Inu met his eyes for a long moment, having a silent conversation that I didn't care to know about. Finally, she stepped back and turned toward god knew where as long as it wasn't near me. Slowly, Flynn lowered my fist and moved to stand in front of me.

His cheeks were flushed, and his breath was uneven and fast. The ocean eyes that roamed over me were clinical and assessing—not judgment, but a simple knowing. He saw everything and cataloged it away. He was a captain who understood people—a feat more impressive than any battle won on English soil.

With aching slowness, he released one finger at a time from my arm, devising somehow that I was no longer a threat. That I wasn't worth the fight it took.

Before I could say "Henry VIII had six wives," my released fist swung right into his nose, a terrible crack sounded that I couldn't tell came from my body or his. The pain was instantaneous and well-deserved. I flexed my hand and jumped up and down, swinging it to try and shake out the pain, but it ricocheted up my arm with a vengeance.

"That hurts!" I shouted.

His chuckle was as deep as the sea at midnight. I stopped my ridiculous dancing and saw that he was cradling his nose in one hand while his shoulders shook with what shouldn't have been, but absolutely was laughter.

"Damn," his voice muffled, "I can't help but feel like I should have seen that coming."

"I'm sorry!" I yelled far too loudly.

Apparently, I was as good at regulating my volume as my emotions.

"As temperamental as a child in a grown woman's body."

I shook my head and, for a moment, was grateful for the pain in my hand even as it began to recede. It was at least louder than James's voice inside my mind.

Flynn's eyes ran over me, seeing too much.

"I'm sorry," I said, "Let me see it."

A long, steadying breath righted the stars that blurred in my vision. I was in control. I was more than my impulses, more than his voice inside my head.

"It's fine." Flynn waved me away with his free hand.

"It's not." I glared at him as if this were his fault. "I hit you like some wild beast. The least you can do is let me help."

I pulled at his hand, covering his nose, and with a long-suffering sigh, he lowered his hand, showcasing a deep red fountain of blood.

"Oh my god!" I shouted.

"It's fine," he repeated.

He returned his hand to its futile mission of collecting the free-flowing blood. It was entirely possible that such occurrences happened on a regular basis for the captain, which might have explained his utter lack of concern about bleeding out via his nasal passage. However, I was not used to it in the least.

I grabbed his arm and dragged him toward the crowded bar. Two men were silently drinking their drinks and staring forward like the ghosts they were chasing would appear at any second.

"Up, move!" I shouted at them as I wedged my way between them.

The gruff appearing men merely scoffed, but miraculously obeyed, taking their drinks to their next dreary vigil. I edged on to my seat and somewhat gently shoved Flynn towards the other.

He said something, but it was entirely muffled by his hand and the blood he had collected.

"What?" I shouted over the noise of the bar.

The bartender strode over and placed two glasses before us. He lifted his eyes and took in the sight of Flynn. With a long, suffering sigh and a sniff of his nose, he reached over and handed Flynn a dry towel, which he took with a grateful nod.

"I'll be charging you for that," he said.

"Of course," Flynn answered. "I would very much appreciate some gin as well."

"Make that two." I raised my hand hurriedly lest I lose my opportunity.

It was too big of a movement and too loud of a reaction, so as heat flooded my cheeks, I slowly lowered my hand, feeling the eyes of every person in the bar, whether they were looking or not.

"I said it was like old times," Flynn said, holding the towel to his nose and looking to the ceiling in an effort to stop the blood.

"You're supposed to lean forward," I said.

"What?" Flynn asked.

"You're supposed to lean forward!" I shouted.

"No, that can't be right," he said, lips turning down into a frown.

"I assure you that it is," I gritted out before reaching up and wrapping my hand around his thick neck in an effort to push his head down. He was like a trunk of a tree planted thousands of years ago with the way he didn't budge an inch.

"First you break my nose and now you boss me around," he groaned as he allowed me to push his head down.

"It's so you don't choke on your blood, you arse," I said.

The once white towel was now painted crimson halfway through. At least it had slowed a bit.

"I knew you cared," he said.

I scoffed, reaching for the glass of gin that had appeared and threw it back. It burned and ripped at my throat like it was trying to claw its way back out. Burning gave way to coughing, and I slapped at my chest, willing it to go down without murdering me first. It finally gave way, only to erode my lungs and stomach on its descent.

"That was awful." I gasped.

Flynn chuckled, setting the bloody towel on the bar top.

I turned to inform him that it was not in the least funny when he turned to me.

"Oh god!" I covered my mouth in an effort to hide my horror.

Flynn's lip curved up, showcasing a single dimple as he felt the outline of his nose.

"That bad, huh?" he said.

"It's—um—it's a..." I groaned and lay my head on the table.

"If someone was going to ruin my intractable and dashing good looks, I'm glad it was you," he said.

"Don't say stupid things like that, all I do is fuck things up," I said.

"Lord, what will London Society do with that mouth when you return?" he asked.

I turned my head so that my right cheek rested on the cool wood and eyed him and his horrendously crooked nose. Somehow, it had found a way to curve one way and then another, making it uncannily deformed.

"Well, either I am going back chained to a monster and paraded around like an exotic animal from another continent, or I am going back to be my own mistress and a cautionary tale about the dangers of independence for future generations. On the one hand, I will have to find a way to mask everything I am, but on the other, I like to think my foul language will be one of my charms."

"It would be a damn shame if you were anything other than yourself," Flynn said.

His pale eyes held mine and were far too sincere. Far too seeing. It might have made my heart stop if it wasn't for his nose.

"You look ridiculous." I chuckled.

His smile was just as crooked as his nose, and if I were being very honest with myself, I would have had to admit that he didn't look ridiculous at all. He looked like a painting that would become my favorite if I ever had enough money to buy it. Unfortunately, the price tag was far too expensive for this lifetime. Maybe the next.

His smile fell at what he saw on my face.

You are exhausting.

Clearing my throat, I sat up and dusted off my shirt.

"We should probably get you to Emille lest you lose your charm for the sake of a vengeful English woman," I said.

I placed my hands on the cool wood and began to push myself off it, but he reached over and gripped my forearm.

"Why do you let him win over and over?" he asked.

"Excuse me?" I could feel the blood drain from my face.

Forever seeing more than he should.

"If it would free you from him, I would find him and kill him, but somehow I think that wouldn't be the freedom you crave," he said.

When I said nothing and my eyes burned with likely the ascension of the gin, he went on.

"He isn't worth a single thought in that chaotic, beautiful mind of yours." He reached over and brushed a strand of hair from my face and gently tucked it behind my ear.

His touch felt warm and right. Like the coziest blanket on the coldest night. Easy to lose yourself in.

"I think he will always be there," I confessed.

"Do you want to forget for a moment?" he asked.

His thumb gently caressed my cheek, and I knew what he was offering. Maybe I was as weak as James always said I was, but in that moment, I didn't care.

"Yes," I whispered.

Chapter Twenty-Seven
How To Forget

Cats are often kept on ships to control the rodent population while at sea and are generally considered good luck by sailors. It is believed that if one were to throw a cat overboard it would bring remarkably bad luck, including ship-killer storms.

–An excerpt from The Mysterious Deep: A Comprehensive Understanding

Forgetting required three more gins, two self-deprecating jokes, and exactly one re-sounding crack of a notorious Captain's nose snapping back into place.

"Oh, god, I never want to do that again." My words were slurred, but I had never been more confident in the meaning of them.

Flynn ran his hand over his nose and hummed in appreciation.

"It could have been worse," he said.

I stared at him, mouth open and likely to catch a fly. However, my body buzzed with a comfortable layer of gin that had effectively silenced James and my own reservations. It was delightful.

We had only made it a few feet from the bar, which we had been essentially kicked out of. Apparently, Brazilians did not appreciate the subtle art of historical recollection of battles that changed the entire course of history. At least Flynn had appreciated it, though I was willing to wager my three gins to his six that he would have found even the recitation of the Magna Carta amusing.

He stepped forward, and I instinctively took a step back, but was pinned between a pirate and a lamp pole. God, he was beautiful to look at. If he weren't a pirate, he would have had a long line of English socialites throwing themselves at him. It probably wouldn't have mattered if he had only a small fortune. Looks like that were worth more than gold.

Actually, being a pirate might not even deter some of them. God knows it didn't deter me.

He gently took my chin between his thumb and forefinger and slowly closed my mouth.

"You are undressing me with your eyes," he murmured as he bent his head next to my ear. "It's very distracting."

A delightful shiver ran up my spine, and I could feel the remnants of its shock beginning a coil low in my stomach.

"I was promised a forgetting," I said.

What a stupid thing to say. Even drunk, I was beyond saving. All I had to do was murmur a few breathy sounds, and all would be well. However, I was me, and so that is, of course, not at all what I did. I braced for his retreat, but instead he placed a short yet lingering kiss to my neck before pulling away.

I was a puddle on the muddy ground.

"More of that," I whispered.

He made a sound low in his throat that I could only categorize as approval. Yet, he pulled away, which was not at all what we had agreed upon. The loss of his breath and the feel of his body near mine was a loss I would likely mourn the rest of my sad life.

"Not here," he said.

That was the only warning I received before he took my hand in his and dragged me along the uneven path. It was likely close to midnight, and the stars burned bright up ahead, but the drunken festivities had died down to some degree. Those still awake were much more interested in their drink or company to pay much heed to us. Which was more than ideal, given I was stumbling left and right. Luckily for me, Flynn was adept at keeping me upright.

The docks quickly swam into view, and I let out a crude laugh.

"You absolutely do not expect me to climb up onto that ship. We both know I can barely do it sober," I said.

He turned and flashed a crooked grin that was somehow devilishly charming and seductive all at once.

"Walls talk. If you want to forget, you better start climbing," he said.

I groaned. "Walls talk, my arse. You just want to torture me."

"You go first, that way if you fall, I *might* catch you," he said.

"Might?" I glared.

He shrugged. "Velocity and gravity do have a say in the matter, coupled by my level of inebriation factoring in against my reflexes."

Placing a hand on my waist and eyeing the long ladder up to the deck of the Wraith, I let out a long breath.

"I hate you," I said.

He winked at me. "Make it to the top alive and you can show me just how much."

Hardly helpful, all his words delivered with a smokey breathlessness did was turn my legs to liquid. However, I was pathetic and knew firsthand the tonic he was offering me. I wanted it enough to die for it.

His chuckle lit a flame within me as I passed him and began my ascent. It would seem that the promises at the top outweighed my clumsiness, and by the time I reached the top, I was giddy with success.

"I didn't die!" I shouted.

"Aye, Hellcat, I'd say you are fairly alive."

Alarm shot through me, eroding my victory down to ash and I jumped back and landed squarely on my arse hard enough that I felt it all the way up my back. Billy's laughter echoed over the lapping sea as distant thunder rolled in the distance.

"Look at that, you summoned a storm with that earthquake of a fall," Billy said between knee slaps.

Flynn elegantly and far too efficiently swung his leg over the edge until he was firmly on the Wraith. Rude.

"What did you do to her?" Flynn asked as he reached his hand out to me.

If I could have bottled up the smiles he was offering under the protection of moonlight, I would have no need of the Maravilla. I could sell those smiles and make a fortune that could never be swindled from me.

"I just agreed that she wasn't dead." Billy held up his hands above his head as if he knew what the word innocence meant.

"You ambushed me!" I accused him.

"Nah, I'm on watch. Been here for at least an hour," he said.

Unhelpful.

I pointed a finger at him, took two steps, and jammed it into his chest, twice for good measure.

"Listen here, you are trouble, and I know it. How'd you know I'd pick your boat the first night anyway? I could have easily taken one look at you and gone on to the next less shady-looking human."

Billy's smile grew by two inches, and he blew out a laugh that smelled of oranges.

"Captain said to be the first boat so I was the first boat. You'll have to take the how and why up with him," Billy said.

Narrowing my eyes, I twisted, ready to jam my finger into my next victim, but Flynn was already at the door of his cabin without two thoughts spared for me. Absolutely not.

I did not brave certain death just to be left behind. Billy's raucous laughter echoed in my ears as I made quick work of the freshly swabbed deck just as a light rain began to fall from the sky. Creaking wood and flickering flames were the only witnesses to our midnight tryst.

I threw open the door to see Flynn staring at a sturdy triangle shaped Blackbeard who sat on his desk. Accusations ran deep in those unearthly eyes lit only by the candle Flynn held.

"Of all the creatures of the Mysterious Deep, I am most scared of this one," he said.

I snorted and scooped Blackbeard up into my arms. He sank into my arm and began a deep purr that rivaled the thunder outside. His head rested over his front paws, and while his body was utterly relaxed, his eyes still tracked Flynn as he lit the lantern on his desk.

"He's just a snuggly bear. Nothing mysterious about him." I burrowed my face into his fluff, planting a kiss.

Flynn stared at me like I had lost my mind, or perhaps he was more shocked that Blackbeard hadn't scratched my face off.

He dared a step towards me until Blackbeard gave a low rumble that was not at all a purr, but a warning.

"I wish I understood you. I sometimes think that if I did, the Mysterious Deep would become an open book," he said.

Now, alone in his cabin, with only the thunder outside and the pattering of rain above us, his voice had taken on a breathiness I knew all too well.

I set Blackbeard down in one fluid motion, which earned me an indignant stare from him. I would apologize for it later and atone with many ear scratches, but right now, I had promises about to be fulfilled.

"Of all the people in the world, I would argue you know me better than I would like," I said.

My skin was warm with anticipation. His eyes drank me in like he was a man dying of thirst. If we were marooned on a tropical island, I would be all he would need to survive. It undid me in the best way. Stolen nights, forever locked away, quickly playing like a sonnet before me.

"I would argue that no one really knows you, not even you," he said, voice husky.

Only three feet separated us, but I was prepared to make him cross it. He was the one who put the distance there a year ago. It was his to atone for.

"See, that's exactly the thing someone who knows me would say." I rolled my eyes for emphasis.

I had expected him to put up more of a fight, but this want that burned in me wasn't only my burden. It lived in him too.

He vanquished the distance between us and placed his warm hand on my cheek as his fingertips glided over my neck. I leaned into the touch, desperate.

"When you figure out who you are, I hope I'm there to witness it," he murmured against my neck.

I breathed in a shaky breath. "I feel like I should be offended."

Though it was exceptionally hard to be offended when he was dragging his mouth and tongue down my neck, gently pushing aside my blouse to give him better access. My arms hung uselessly by my side as I fought to know what to do with them. It wasn't like it was our first time doing this. That had been different. Yes, still drunk, but the stakes were as low as they could get. He was a handsome rogue without a name, and I was someone else entirely.

He knew me now. I knew him.

"You shouldn't be," he murmured. "You are without a doubt the most fascinating and intoxicating woman I have ever known."

I dropped my head as he brushed against my collarbone, right where he knew it would affect me most. All the rules were changed. We weren't experimenting anymore. There was something to lose, and god, it hurt like hell the last time.

You are too much. You ruin everything you touch. When they see who you are, they will leave. Only I stay, and you would be lost without me. Who else would put up with you?

I let out a frustrated growl deep in my chest and took two quick steps back. It was hard to breathe. My useless arms, my too loud brain, my defective body. It all added up to something that wasn't worth whatever this was. I was cursed to remember, no matter how tempting the forgetting was.

"Tell me what is going on inside that beautiful mind?" Flynn asked gently.

He didn't make any move to come toward me, and I felt an awful lot like a spooked animal. It was in the way he kept his hands at his sides, unclenched, and non-threatening. How he masked his ragged breaths with subtle, long ones. I was the deer, but I would have been everything James ever said I was if I mistook him for anything other than the predator he was.

"It's loud," I whispered.

As if that could somehow explain the constant litany of self-deprecating thoughts that swam within the prison of my mind.

"Tell me one truth, one loud thought," he said.

I rolled my eyes, which earned me a raised eyebrow from him. It was a challenge, a calculated shot at my competitive nature.

I gritted my teeth and averted my eyes to stare at the trapped flame in the lantern. It swayed and edged toward the sides, never to be free; its only future was to live imprisoned and then extinguished. Forgotten.

"I am too much," I said.

I could hear him breathing despite the rain that now battered relentlessly against the Wraith. Distant thunder echoed the storm inside my mind. The words I had spoken so carelessly thrown out into the world to be used against me. This was cruel.

"If you asked me to choose a word that described how I felt about you, I would choose more," he said, voice gentle and deep.

That made sense. Ever since I was little, I was told I could have given more. If I had tried harder, I would have succeeded. Be quieter. Speak less. That he saw me the same, carved at some false sense of security I had been nurturing.

"The first time I saw you kick that drunkard when most women would have been cowering, I wanted more of you," he said.

My gaze jerked up to his, this primal need in me needing to see if he was mocking me, but steel eyes met mine and I felt the weight of each word. The lack of irony evident in the flash of lightning that illuminated us for just a moment.

"When you asked if I wanted a drink after I broke his wrist, which he deserved far worse, I wanted more."

He took a slow step forward, giving me the chance to flee.

I stood still.

"When you downed a beer in two gulps and I knew you were running from something, I was desperate for more," he said.

Another step.

One more and he would be there again, but it was hard to think over the way he painted our first meeting. Memories I had exhausted by replaying and analyzing.

"When you asked me if I wanted to spend the night with you, I thought I would be a fool not to say yes. That whatever you were running from, I'd be damn lucky if I was the idiot you chose and dammit, Rose, even after I had you, I wanted more. Even when I knew it was a mistake to come back the second night, I just thought of a single word. More."

The words washed over the holes in my heart and settled low in my stomach. His words could never heal me, but they were a salve I was happy to partake in. Which was why, when he didn't take that last step forward, I did.

I craned my neck to look up at him, and his face was relaxed, no feathering muscles, no clenched jaw. A rarity for the captain of the Wraith. A rarity that I had seen more than once. Maybe I was lucky after all.

Lifting my hand, I slowly ran my fingers over the progressively increasing beard that had begun as stubble. His eyes closed as he remained very still. Still afraid to startle me and make me run. Maybe that was the highest compliment that shone beneath his honeyed words. He wanted me enough to dance this delicate dance with me.

My hand drifted down his neck, and my fingers glided lower to pull at the strings of his shirt. His chest rose and fell with controlled breaths. He was the epitome of control, and while it was what I needed in that moment, I wanted him undone. I wanted to be the reason he said what he never intended to say, to do what he never thought he would. I wanted to be the reason why he couldn't calculate plans and intentions.

There was a time I thought I was that for James. Even though propriety had kept us from sleeping together, stolen moments in gardens where he would whisper the most sinful things in my ear replayed in my mind. It hadn't been enough to keep his attention, though. In the end, I was never going to be enough for him to remain loyal.

"Say it out loud," Flynn whispered.

I realized that my hands were trembling as I undid the rest. The way his eyes searched mine told me I wasn't hiding anything from him.

"That I'm not enough. That I could never be enough." I said, the damning words barely audible.

"I've spent a year trying to shake you. To fall asleep without you taunting me in my mind. You are more than enough, Rosamund Bailey. I've tried to forget you, knowing you would never forgive me, not to mention you are meant for ballrooms and comfort." He held up his hands, palms facing me. "I could never give you that, no matter how much I wanted to."

I took one of his hands in mine and traced the many calluses that decorated it. Evidence of his life at sea and just how different we were. My own hands were unmarred and delicate.

"Why did you become a pirate?" I asked.

I expected him to laugh and dance around the question like we always did, but his eyes met mine and despite the fact that we should have been too drunk to do this, his eyes were focused and clear. Maybe this was the real consequence of drinking. Too much trust. That was the riskiest behavior of them all.

"I did it to spite my father," he said.

My fingers stilled their exploration of his hand as I fought against the tide that we were creating. This was dangerous. Waves that playfully crashed, hiding a riptide beneath.

He waited for me. A quietness accented by the creak of the ship and the storm outside. Thunder and flashes of lightning illuminating our recklessness.

Maybe it was the liquor, maybe it was the insecurities I carried like they sustained me, or maybe I just wanted to. Either way, I resumed my gentle exploration of tracing the lines upon his hand, thinking how some said they held the secrets of our fates. When Flynn continued, I started to believe that might be true for the first time.

"My mother never had a fair shot. She was born to parents who died by the time she was twelve. Poorer than poor. She survived the only way she knew how." His words were hoarse as if they had been pulled from a dusty chest forever locked inside his throat. "When she was only nineteen, she met my father. He took a particular liking to her."

The words were like acid, and for a moment, I thought he might stop. That he would see how bad of an idea this was, and we would shatter like glass upon the floor. He didn't.

"He paid her mistress an excessive amount of money to ensure that my mother would be singular in her attentions," he said.

Understanding dawned on me, and I let out a small gasp.

"Your father was an aristocrat."

Flynn nodded.

"He was. Is." He cleared his throat. "When I was born, he paid for us to keep our room at the brothel, but still paid the mistress to keep my mother from working. We were surviving, nothing more. He has always been a possessive man, and even when he didn't want my mother anymore, he made it so no one else would have her either."

"That's terrible," I whispered.

"When I turned thirteen, he came to the brothel for the first time in over a decade. His only heir had died along with his wife. Apparently, he thought it was better to have a whore's son than no heir at all."

The pain in his voice was masked behind the way he clenched his jaw and stared at the delicate tracing of his hands. Like he was ashamed to meet my eyes. Like I could ever think less of him for where he came from.

I wanted to say the right thing like he always did. The way he would force me to say my fears aloud so that he could wrestle them. The words clogged in my throat, the right thing lost to my mind that was insufferably blank.

"At first I refused to go, but my mother was insistent. She convinced me that staying with her would be worse for her in the end. If I went and learned how to be a lord, I could come back for her and have influence. So I did."

"Your father was a lord." I stared open-mouthed at him.

The corner of his lip pulled up. "I like when I surprise you. Your eyes turn a lighter shade of green."

I swallowed hard, unsure how the praise fit in the revelations he was stacking like a house of cards. Fragile and easily toppled.

"I spent three years with him. Out in the English countryside and hidden from view. He wouldn't risk debuting me a moment before he deemed me ready. Whenever I would ask to see my mother he would strike me and tell me I was no longer the son of a whore. He poured a lifetime of etiquette down my throat in three years. At that point, he was satisfied with my progress and was going to introduce me as his heir. If anyone asked me about my heritage, I was to say I was his nephew from Germany." He snorted as if it were all rather hilarious.

I felt like I already knew the end to this story. It was in the way he couldn't look at me. In the way his shoulders were tight against his neck. This story didn't have a happy ending, when it wasn't a very happy story to begin with.

"Right before we were set to leave for my first season, I got word that my mother had taken ill. I asked to go to her, and he beat me hard enough that I couldn't remember anything till two days after. When I came around, I made up my mind. I waited till he was deep in his bottle and told him I was no son of his. That if he cared enough about his legacy to elevate a whore's son he could watch his legacy burn. I left that night and never looked back. A year later, I created Sebastian Flynn. I chose a name he would know so that every time Flynn did something that ended up in the papers, he would know that was his legacy. A notorious pirate for a son, and that he must live in fear of the day I finally remove the mask."

I took a step back from him just so I could see him properly. If only the sun was shining instead of flashes of lightning so I could see the truth of his words written on his face. In my wildest dreams I could never have known this was his story.

I could have said a million words, but instead I chose, "What is your real name?"

His lip quirked up, and I could see he was enjoying this. Probably because he was about to lay the first knife into his father's legacy. Anticipation was a precipice of anxiety, but I was happy to jump off with him.

"Edward Smith."

The world could have disintegrated around me and I would have been less surprised. Smith. Of course it was a common name, but there was only one Lord Smith in England and god help me he was as horrid as the father Flynn had described.

"Your father is Lord Sebastian Smith," I said.

The pieces fell together perfectly. Lord Smith regularly ogled me and spoke to me like I was an object more than a person—a man I had detested from the moment I met him. The previous Lord Smith had been even worse, though he had died shortly after my debut in society. I gasped, covering my mouth.

"Oh my god, Flynn was his father's name," I said.

Flynn's lips pulled up in a wide smile. "He wanted a legacy to leave, and I have done my best to oblige him."

"You could ruin him," I whispered.

"I intend to," Flynn said.

Suddenly I saw it. The plan. How he was desperate for his name to mean something. To make his mark on the world. It was all because he hated his father. All of it. I should have been grateful he shared this with me because for the first time since I got on this ship, I finally understood who and what he was.

"This is insane," I said.

He merely shrugged his shoulders like he didn't commit crimes and murder all to piss off a misogynistic old man.

Flynn's eyes darkened at what he saw in me as I was forced to rearrange everything I thought I knew. A shot of lightning illuminated the change in him. It was very nearly terrifying. A lethal predator with hunger in his eyes. God help me, the shiver that ran up my back was anything but fear.

He pressed his body against mine, holding me in place with one hand firmly on my lower back while he gripped my chin with his thumb and finger. He forced me to look at him, and I drank him in. All of him. The handsome features that, if I squinted hard enough, would reveal traces of a younger Lord Smith. The hard lines of his jaw were spent clenching it while formulating and enacting a plot that very few could have pulled off. He was insane and brilliant.

Most of all, he was dangerous.

"And now that you see me, Rosamund? Do you regret boarding my ship yet?" he said.

"No."

There should have been hesitation, but there was not even the idea of it. I felt many feelings that I carried like burdens, but regret had never been one I had associated with him.

His eyes softened for a brief instant that looked an awful lot like relief. There and gone behind the mask he had crafted with delicate intricacy.

"You should," he said, lightning flashing three times around us in warning. "I am a bastard son of English nobility. The disgrace of everything you love. If being a pirate wasn't condemnation enough. Or maybe you haven't considered that in ruining my father, I could ruin you too."

A delicious curling low in my stomach said I was not normal. The words he was saying. How roughly he held me in place. He was trying to scare me, and I was burning up with a need that might incinerate me.

"You already ruined me, remember?" I said, barely a whisper.

His nostrils flared with the deep breath he took, muscle flickering in his cheek. He was holding on by a thread, but Sebastian Flynn had control by the bucketful. Maybe everything I thought I knew was now in tatters on the floor, but one thing had not changed.

I wanted to be his undoing.

His mouth hovered just above mine, smelling of liquor and bare truths.

"Of all the darkness I inherited from my father, you should know the worst of it before you dance this dance," he said into my mouth.

He was intoxicating. However, I at least had some semblance of preservation because the fire cooled enough that I was able to process his words. What I now knew of Lord Smith was even worse than I could have ever imagined. The wariness that sank into me was born of knowing too much.

"And what is that?" I asked.

He lowered his mouth and nipped at my lower lip, evaporating my concerns and stoking that fire. I was clay in his hands, ready to be molded. He could have said he had horns, and I would probably hold onto them while-

I was going to hell.

"I am—" he paused, dipping his head to lay hot kisses down my neck, which I arched eagerly for him. "Unnaturally possessive. The moment you let me have you, you were mine, whether you realized it or not. The way I want you, Rosamund, is unnatural."

Oh god. My legs quivered with his words and kisses. His breath. His touch. He released my chin and ran his fingers down my chest, ownership in the way he gripped my waist hard enough to leave bruises.

"Yes," I panted.

His breath was loud and hungry. "Yes, what?"

The next words were my magnum opus.

"Yes, you can ruin me."

Chapter Twenty-Eight
To be Ruined

To surrender to another is the ultimate act of vulnerability.

–An excerpt from *The Mysterious Deep: A Comprehensive Understanding*

Ruination was a fever dream. A beautiful symphony of destruction that demanded my every sense. His mouth on mine was demanding and consuming. His tongue swept against mine, and I knew the rules of the game had changed. We were playing for keeps now. All our cards lay out on the table. Truths and lies disintegrated around us until there was only him and me.

The ship rocked with the gathering storm, but Flynn's grip on me was life-sustaining. In one fluid motion, he lifted me, and I eagerly wrapped my legs around him, desperate for friction already. It had been too long since he had last touched me like this. I needed him like I needed air to breathe.

"I'm going to die if you don't touch me," I panted.

That I hadn't meant to say that didn't matter, as he carried me over to his desk and set me down on it. Frantic hands pulled at each other's clothes. Thank god, my fingers were healed. This was not the romantic joining I had always imagined as a young and naive woman. This was more.

While I fumbled at his belt, Flynn made quick work of my blouse. Skilled fingers urging my hips up to rid us of my pants.

"Are you even drunk?" I asked as I finally managed his belt.

"More than I'd like," he said as he knelt before me.

Expectation and desire, more potent than any liquor, settled over me. The fire in his eyes was him without the mask. When he said he was possessive, I understood now.

I understood, and I wanted to drown in it.

"Why?" I gasped as he planted a kiss on the inside of my thigh.

He lifted his eyes to mine as his hands spread my thighs wider.

"Liquor makes for murky memories, and I want to remember this."

The way he held my gaze while he devoured me was wicked in every sense of the word. No amount of Hail Mary's and confessions could save me now. I would burn for all eternity, and all I could think was that with memories like this, I would be just fine.

Pleasure coursed through me in droves—no slow build or teasing to ease me into it. Starvation never made for leisure, and we had been hungry for far too long. He dragged his teeth over my center, and I let out a too-loud moan that not even the storm could drown out. If anyone was close enough, they would hear.

I should have been worried about what that would mean, but I was too lost to his mouth. The captain between my legs didn't seem to care either as he slid his finger into me and curled it.

Oh, seas, save me.

I fell back onto my elbows and threw my head back, eyes rolling. He was playing me like a damn instrument and I was singing beautifully for him.

"Please, don't stop," I begged.

It was there, waiting to crash over me. Release coiling tighter and tighter.

"You are so beautiful when you come," he said, in between long strokes of his tongue.

"Bash," I gasped.

His strokes slowed like he had suddenly discovered a sense of patience. Absolutely not. I sat up and threaded my hands through his dark hair. He murmured in approval in a vibration that sent fresh shocks through me. My hips bucked against him, and in answer, he added another finger to his ministrations.

"Do you want to come, Rosamund?" He licked me long and slow.

I whimpered and nodded my head. I was so close. Right on the precipice of that cliff. If he would only send me over, but he was toying with me. His fingers worked me slowly.

"Yes!"

He hummed softly, air blowing over my aching and throbbing center.

"Say you're mine," he ordered.

I would have said anything he asked of me, but it didn't make it any less true when the words left my lips.

"I'm yours."

His tongue stroked me slow then fast, teeth and tongue and fingers working in tandem. It was too much. I was dying. Oh god, the tension was excruciating. The coils burst violently, shooting through me like the lightning that struck around us.

"I'm yours, I'm yours, I'm yours."

My entire body shook with the violence of the release. My chest ached with the effort it took to breathe amidst the clenching inside me. My thighs held Flynn tight against me while I basked in the culmination of his efforts. I could feel him watching me, drinking me in. Something told me, drunk or not, this would not be a murky memory.

When the shocks subsided and the warm afterglow settled over me, I finally released him from my hold. He continued to kneel there all the same, his fingers drawing delicate circles over my thighs. This was more than the first time we were together.

I pushed myself up off the table, ignoring the books and papers that fell. Probably not important. His hair was deliciously ruffled, and his ocean eyes were as gray as the stormy sea.

It should have been enough. I should have been satiated, but this hunger inside of me was ravenous. I eased myself off the table while his hands gripped the outside of my thighs, steadying me.

How beautifully he waited for me. Like I could command him as surely as any power within the Mysterious Deep, and he would eagerly bend to my will. Eyes on mine, he held me as I lowered myself onto his lap, feeling how hard he was beneath me. How much he wanted me.

Not even I could pretend this was anything less than a need. Gently, he brushed a strand of hair from my face and tucked it behind my ear, his eyes roving over me, memorizing.

"You are so fucking beautiful," he said.

It thawed the ice that'd been growing in me for the last year. His face fit just right in my palms as I lowered my lips to his, showing him just what his words meant to me. How he saw me healed and remade me. We fit together just so.

When the kiss wasn't enough anymore, I gently pushed his chest in silent command. The captain obeyed. Dragging our kiss with him, he slowly lay on his back while I worked at the last ties of his pants. Desperation satiated just enough to make my coordination effective.

He was hard and thick in my hand, and I closed my eyes, savoring the sound of his groan as his head fell back. There were several days between us and the Glass Sea. There would be time to taste him and make him squirm, but I was greedy tonight.

I held him in place while I lowered myself onto him, still wet from the way he had consumed me. Flynn's hands gently gripped my hips, slowing my descent. A concern that wasn't necessary, and from the way his eyes sparked, a torture for him. Thunder boomed around us as the rain pelted harder into the ship. The full force of it meeting our shores.

I let my mouth curve up as I pressed down lower, taking all of him.

"Rose," he prayed, biting his lip.

The restraint was killing him. The need for release was as desperate as mine was.

I lifted my hips, sliding off of him and then back down, slow and sensual. His nails dug into my hips. It occurred to me that I might just be killing the Captain of the Wraith.

His restraint was going to be the death of him, so I said the words I knew would undo him. The weakness he had shown me, and like a monster, I wielded them at the first opportunity.

"I'm yours," I said.

His pupils constricted and blew beneath the lantern light and zigzagging lightning. He pushed himself up off the floor and threaded one hand into my hair while the other wrapped around my throat with gentle pressure. His eyes bore into me, a challenge.

"I'm yours," I repeated.

Lips crashed and hips bucked. He was more of a force than the storm outside could ever hope to be. My twisted captain hellbent on revenge.

Our bodies worked in tandem, pulling and driving, desperate to fall into one another. His hand around my neck grew in pressure as those coils folded once more, strengthening and gathering in my core.

The next words were instinct.

"You're mine," I said, breathless.

"Yes," he gritted through a moan.

"Mine," I said.

"Yours," he agreed.

My body released the pressure and was deeper and more than the last one. My body clenching and unclenching around him. I gasped in a breath as his fingers closed around my throat, his pleasure ricocheting through him. My head was dizzy, and I was drunk with more than just the drink we had.

In all the romantic books I had squirreled away and read, the heroine always remarks how once she had her love, she could die happy. Maybe stories didn't tell the whole truth, or maybe I was just as insane as Flynn, but all I could think was that if I died before I grew tired of it, then I would end up as a vengeful ghost as angry as any sea wraith.

Pirate ships were much better with company. I hadn't realized just how lonely it had been until I was lying with Flynn beneath the covers while the sea rocked us gently. The storm had finally abated, but the sea remembered. I didn't know which was better, my freshly washed hair smelling of sea salt and lavender or the feel of his relaxed breathing beneath my head. The rise and fall of his chest a silent testament to our afterglow.

It had been several minutes since either of us had spoken. Tomorrow we would set sail again, and with only a few days till we reached the Glass Sea, I was prepared to make the most of these moments. The only reason I even knew Flynn was awake was because he was tracing light circles onto my back and shoulder.

It was hard to wrap my mind around the fact that he was born from the same world I was, but if I looked close enough I could begin to see it. Though he was nothing like his father which was likely the point. To know just how terrible Lord Smith was made me want to put him six feet in the ground. That might not even be deep enough. God, Flynn by all rights was heir to one of the most prestigious estates in all of England.

Realization struck me, and I snorted. "I cannot believe you made fun of my middle name when you have a name like Edward Smith."

"Yes, but Sebastian Flynn is an excellent name. Very Pirate Captain-y," he said.

"Well, I didn't pick my middle name either. I feel like you are cheating."

I twisted my body so I could lay my chin on his chest and see his small smile. The one he only ever wore behind locked doors. I traced the outline of his rose compass tattoo and trailed the outline of the kraken tentacles that came out from under it. My hand wandered up to the rough skin over his neck that had healed as much as Emille said it would. The scarring would always be a reminder of the noose that was imprinted over his neck. I just wish it didn't feel like a premonition more than a painful past.

"And what would be your pirate name that would strike fear into the hearts of men?" he asked.

"Why? Is Rosamund Beatrice Bailey not terrifying?" I narrowed my eyes at him.

He chuckled, shaking my head gently. "Terrifying."

I enjoyed being able to use my own name again. Even if—

I sat up straight, sheets falling off of me in my hurry. Something lodged in my throat that choked my air.

Flynn's amusement melted in an instant as he sat up and let his hands ghost over me, looking for what had ailed me, but he wouldn't find it.

"The name you gave me when I came on the Wraith," I whispered.

Understanding dawned on him, and his furrowed brows relaxed as he traced his thumb over my jaw and lower lip, drawing a shiver from me. He smiled. There was no doubt that he took every enjoyment in knowing what he did to me.

"So I did," he said.

God, I could drown in the depths of his voice.

Morning light began to creep in through the windows. It appeared we would not be sleeping tonight. Maybe we could not sleep tomorrow night, too.

"That was rather devious of you," I accused.

The corner of his mouth pulled up, dimple on display just in time to melt all my resolve. He leaned in, placing slow and intoxicating kisses down my neck.

"Or do you prefer Flynn for a last name?" he said.

My eyes rolled back as he reached the space between my neck and shoulder, sending a jolt of energy through me.

"I think I prefer Bailey." I breathed out.

He chuckled into my neck.

I might have argued with him more, but I quite enjoyed where this was going. Slowly, he lowered me down and worked his way lower. His hand cupped my breast as he lowered his mouth to my peaked nipple.

I bit down on my lip, fighting back the moan that was gathering in my throat.

There was a sharp banging on the door to the cabin, and I wondered if maybe it wasn't too late to ask the Gharaq witches how to join them, so I could curse whoever had the audacity to interrupt us. Flynn appeared to have the same thought because he turned his attention to my other breast. Understanding we were ignoring them, I wrapped my legs around him, eager to keep him where he was.

More banging.

"Can you just kill them and then come back to bed?" I groaned as that coil began to grow.

Flynn laughed and nipped at the underside of my breast, earning a yelp from me.

"For you?" He winked. "Anything."

More banging.

"Dammit, Bash." Billy's voice growled.

Flynn stilled and eyed me, a debate forming in his mind.

"You said anything, remember?" I asked as I leaned forward to kiss him, reminding him of the stakes.

He met my kiss with eager attention, his tongue and teeth meeting mine with frenzied hunger. I would never get enough of this.

"It's not a fucking joke," Billy snarled.

Shouts followed his declaration, and we pulled apart, understanding. This wasn't just an annoying interference.

Flynn ran his hand over my cheek and down my neck.

"Stay here," he ordered as he exited the bed.

Honestly, he should have known better. I followed him and threw on last night's pants and blouse as he did the same thing.

"Rosamund," he warned when he saw my activity.

More banging.

I rolled my eyes. "Edward."

His eyes flashed, and in two long flashes, he had me wrapped in his arms and his lips crushed on mine. He kissed me like the world wasn't going to hell outside, which it most certainly was, given the increased banging and gathering shouts.

The door rattled violently.

"So help me if you're dead," Billy said.

When Flynn broke our kiss, he stared at me for a long moment, always memorizing. Just when I began to harbor the very small hope we were getting back in bed, he turned and made for the door. As soon as he unlocked it, his back was straight, and the hardness reset into his jaw. Captain Flynn once more.

"It's bad," Billy said.

"He's dead!" Someone yelled.

For the first time since the banging began, a sinking dread filled my stomach. Billy said something quietly to Flynn, who shot me one final warning glance before following after him.

As expected, I ignored him. The moment I stepped out onto the Wraith, the orange and yellow sunrise lit behind crew members gathered around the mast.

"Someone murdered him!" a voice shouted.

Who? My stomach sank as I recalled my last conversation with Oscar. How mad we had both been. All the stupid things we said.

Oscar.

I pushed my way through the crew, heart going still in my chest while I fought for air. God, please no. I couldn't live without him. It was one thing to know he was out in the world away from me, but not in it. That was a fate I couldn't face. I made it to the front and stopped dead in my tracks.

Vomit built in my throat.

There, strapped to the rigging holding up the main mast, stretched and tied for all to see was Barnacles. His eyes wide open, unseeing. His stomach was cut open, and his intestines spilled onto the ship's deck.

I couldn't even muster up relief at knowing it wasn't Oscar. I looked away, unable to stomach the gruesomeness of it, when my eyes caught Amos. With his arms crossed, he leaned against the ship. His lips turned up when he saw me and gave me a wink.

I leaned over and vomited a foot away from Barnacle's liver.

Chapter Twenty-Nine
A Touch of Mutiny

Despite the opinion of the general public, mutineers are uncommon at sea. Likely because no captain would risk their crew's wrath without an excellent reason.

-An excerpt from *The Mysterious Deep: A Comprehensive Understanding*

No amount of pacing could undo the unnatural swishing of my stomach. No matter how many times I emptied it, I could still smell the waste and the smell of Barnacles. Maybe worse was that I couldn't stop picturing Amos's smile. Like he enjoyed what happened. I had been relegated to Flynn's cabin while he threw out orders, and we set sail once more.

For once, I was fine with being quarantined. There was an eerie sort of air on deck. Whispers and shifting eyes. This wasn't an accident, and whoever did it had made sure it wouldn't be mistaken for one. Too many whispers of "who's next" followed me into the cabin.

The door opened, and that unsettling feeling in my stomach quickly shifted into my chest, making my heart leap. Anxiety. That's what this was. It was a terrible feeling.

Flynn entered with red staining his white shirt and hands. Even his cheeks held remnants of Barnacles, who now lay at the bottom of the sea, food for the Cirein-Cròin. His eyes ran over me, calculating, assessing. When he was satisfied I was in one piece he bit the inside of his cheek and removed his bloody shirt as he made for the washing room. I watched his retreating form and crossed my arms around my stomach as if that might ward off the worry festering throughout my body.

I didn't know much about pirates, but I knew enough to understand that what happened was bad.

The door opened once more, and my brother's lithe form entered, followed closely by Billy. Dark circles under Oscar's eyes said he hadn't slept either. Where there were usually crinkles beside Billy's eyes from far too much smiling, there was smooth skin. Worry was a virus infecting everyone it touched.

"It was Amos." I blurted.

Oscar raised a single eyebrow and placed his hands on his waist, throwing me his most condescending "you think so" smile. Just as it had since we were young, it enraged me. Someone had to say it instead of all of us thinking it.

"Aye, Hellcat, and he did a right job of it," Billy said.

He crashed more than lowered himself into the chair at Flynn's desk. At least in my pacing, I had the good sense to clean up the papers and books we displaced last night.

"Yet I distinctly remember giving you instructions last night to dispose of that problem. Now instead, I have a murder on my hands with a brewing mutiny," Flynn said.

His chest and face glistened with stray drops of water, and I would have spent considerable time appreciating the view if it weren't for my new perpetual nausea and lingering scent of intestines.

"Aye, ya did and he knew it well enough," Billy said. "The little shit made sure he didn't leave the ship and kept a big enough group around him that he was tucked safely away. After you two came back, Barnacles out there finally left the ship, so I tailed him, but he knew it and I lost 'em. Came back to find him decorating the deck."

Flynn tapped his fingers on his thigh, a sign that he was irritated and that his mind was working through the problems and creating possible scenarios. After a few moments, when the ship's movements were the only sign there was a world around us, he raised his eyes to Oscar, who was leaning with his arms crossed against the wall.

"And you?" he asked.

In that moment, I was very grateful not to be Oscar. His tone was the tip of a sword eager for blood. Anger simmered beneath the veins that stood out on his arms and all I could do was hope that Oscar chose his next answer very carefully.

Oscar stuck his tongue in his cheek, and his shoulders fell with defeat. When he raised his eyes, it was me he looked to, an apologetic smile hinting at his lips.

"Drunk and pissed." He held up his hands. "I know I fucked up. I was supposed to be on the ground watching the crew, but keeping up appearances with drinking turned into actual drinking, and then I let my feelings get the best of me."

For some unknown reason, a flush of guilt lit within me. I wish it didn't. It wasn't like I tried to fight with him.

"When I brought you on this ship, onto this crew, it was against my better judgment in some ways. Knowing your background was a deterrent, but you assured me you would work just as hard and that I wouldn't regret it." Flynn stalked toward my brother. "But here we are, and I am finding it hard not to regret it. I have a dead crew member, a plot to destabilize my authority, and a near mutiny on my hands. Not to mention, you went against my wishes in this entire farce. This entire situation is because you thought you knew best and now we are very close to being fucked."

By the time Flynn was done with his tirade, he stopped a foot away from my brother, fists clenched. Oscar's cheeks had gotten progressively more flushed with every word, and everything in me said this wasn't going to end well. Especially when he kicked himself off the wall and glared at Flynn.

Oscar flung a finger out at me without turning away from Flynn.

"Are you really going to pretend like you were going to let her marry that asshole? You are so full of shit if you think I'd believe that," he said.

I very much would have appreciated being left out of the conversation. In fact, it was doing nothing for the nervous energy cascading through me. I tapped my foot, needing to do something before I exploded, but that did nothing to help. There was at least an eighty percent chance this was going to come to blows. I only accounted for the possible twenty percent on the basis that I might pass out first and distract them.

I shot a pleading glance at Billy, but he caught my eye and winked before leaning forward and throwing a nut he found from god knew where into his mouth. As if this were another night at the theatre, he crossed his arms and leaned back, watching them.

"Of course not, I would have made him have an accident before we left Corpse Cove, but you tied my hands, and now we are dancing with death."

Oh. I barely processed the words. My chest was starting to ache, and my vision was blurring.

"Why the fuck didn't you say that?" Oscar spat.

"The less people know of plans, the less chance of failure, or do you not recall that particular lesson?" Flynn shot back.

I tried to suck down air, but my chest wasn't going.

"Maybe the two of you just need to find some common ground," Billy chimed in.

"Not helpful," Flynn snapped.

Oscar grumbled in agreement, but the rest was lost to me as black spots filled my vision. If I passed out, maybe I could just sleep through the whole mutiny thing, and when I woke up, it would all be sorted. It didn't sound so terrible.

"Well, the hellcat is about to go down, so someone ought to catch her," Billy said.

Down? No, I was mostly fine.

A wave of dizziness overcame the pain in my lungs, and I swayed. Oh, maybe I *was* going down. How observant of Billy.

I lost my balance, but before I could feel the cool wood beneath me, Flynn reached me and cradled me against his chest.

"Breathe, Rose," he commanded.

Bossy. Either way he should have known that I would have if I could. It wasn't an active choice.

"I won't kill your brother, and I can probably find a way out of this mess," he said gently.

"You just—" Oscar began. "Just kind of—like this."

He reached around and slapped my chest two hard times.

I gasped, pulling air into my lungs as if I'd just re-emerged from the sea's depths. Instead of salt air, I drank in the scent of gin and cedar. There were worse things, all things considered. Mostly, I was grateful to not have passed out.

If I ever found myself in a life or death situation I was probably fucked. However, the warmth of Flynn beneath me was a nice consolation prize for still being awake while we awaited possible mutiny. I let out a long breath and rested my head against his chest, letting the gentle thump of his heart soothe me.

"It was the twenty percent after all," I murmured.

Flynn bent his head down, eyes assessing me for damage.

"What?" he asked.

I liked how gentle his voice was with me compared to how he was a few minutes ago.

"Oh, nothing," I said.

Flynn carefully sat me down on the edge of the bed and ran a hand over my forehead and hair. No fevers. Just panic. I maybe should have said it aloud, but he probably already knew.

I glanced over at my brother's pacing and saw the redness in his cheeks that could only bespoke trouble. I knew that look. The cherry cheeks, pursed lips. He was fighting back saying something that he shouldn't. Probably something that would quickly erode my twenty percent and set me to panicking again.

"Maybe we should—" I began.

Oscar twisted on his heels and glared at Flynn. "And how did he get past you last night as well? You were supposed to have the bar covered."

"Poseidon, save us," Billy muttered, rubbing at his eyes.

Flynn stilled next to me, fist balling once more.

That was a very firm, no thank you, on all accounts for me, so I threaded my hand through his. Some of the tension released from his shoulders, but there was still murder sparking beneath his eyes.

"I know I told people you murdered my brother, but don't *actually* murder him. It's only funny if it's not true," I said.

Normally, Oscar would have found that amusing, but his chest rose and fell with agitation, and there was no distracting him from his lack of self-preservation. He held out his hand and gestured between Flynn and me.

"Are you really going to stand there and shit on me for not being where I was supposed to be when you were here—"

"Don't finish that sentence," Flynn warned.

Oscar shut his mouth, but the red that filled his cheeks was as loud as any siren.

"Best listen, boy," Billy said, no longer relaxed but leaning forward like he might have to intervene.

The lips pursed.

"God, don't do it, Oscar," I pleaded, tightening my grip on Flynn's hand like it could save us.

Oscar, now borderline purple, blew out a breath.

"While you were here fucking my sister." he finished.

I was inclined to think my brother had a death wish since he didn't immediately start running. Maybe it was a little bit of courage in the way he widened his stance when Flynn released my hand and in two wide strides landed a fist right to Oscar's face.

"You had that one coming," Billy said as he wrinkled his nose at the blood Oscar spat out.

"God, I think you knocked out my tooth." He spit into his hand, showing a small white kernel.

"You fucking did!" Oscar said.

In truth, I agreed with Billy. Oscar knew better, and like always, he stewed until he had the last word. However, he was my brother. Not just my brother, but my twin. My other half. Even if he was being a monumental asshole as of late.

I padded to the washroom and returned with a damp cloth and stepped between Flynn and Oscar. Shooting Flynn a glare for good measure.

"You said you weren't going to hit him," I chided.

"I said I wouldn't kill him," Flynn clarified, stepping back.

Oscar allowed me to wash the blood from his face and assess the damage. Luckily, it had been a back tooth that he wouldn't miss much. A small price to pay, all things considered.

"When are you going to learn to hold in the last word?" I asked.

His mouth quirked up. "Probably when you learn to breathe normal."

I rolled my eyes. Everything had felt strained between us, but this, the quiet banter and shared glances. This was who we were. Everything else was just noise. As I dabbed at the cut along his cheek he reached up and wrapped his hand around my wrist.

There was no humor or anger in his face as he met my gaze.

"I'm sorry, Rosie. Sorry I wasn't where I was supposed to be and I'm even sorrier for what I said on the beach. I shouldn't have—"

"No." I frowned. "You were right."

The words were bitter in my mouth, and I already regretted them.

His eyes narrowed. "Who are you and what have you done with my sister?"

I gently pushed him away, but my smile gave me away.

"I can't believe you just said that to Flynn. You knew he was going to punch you for it," I said.

Oscar took the rag from me and held it against his swollen upper lip.

"Yeah. I thought you were mad at him for killing me. When did that change?" he asked.

I shrugged and then frowned. "He's very attractive."

Flynn cleared his throat behind us.

Oscar nodded, considering. "True, I can't argue with that."

"It's the cheekbones," Billy said.

"Really? I always thought it was his thin, but solid build." Oscar mused.

"No, no, you have it all wrong. It's the cheekbones and those baby blues," Billy said.

"Are you all finished yet?" Flynn asked.

I turned to see him with his arms folded across his chest, but the tension he had been carrying was gone, and his shoulders were more relaxed.

"First of all, you are both wrong," I said, crossing the distance to Flynn, who arched an eyebrow at me. "It's the facial symmetry contrasted by the slightly crooked nose."

I lifted a finger to boop his nose, but he caught it and shot me a warning glance that was ruined by the twitch of his lips.

"It was more crooked last night thanks to you," he said.

"Please don't," Oscar groaned.

"At least I fixed it," I purred.

"Someone hit me again," Oscar whined.

"Don't tempt me," Flynn murmured, as he ran the back of his finger down my cheek.

"I see what you are doing, Rosamund," he said.

I blinked twice and tilted my head, "Me?"

His smile was reserved just for me.

I winked, "So now that everyone is more rational, how are we going to get out of this mutiny business?"

No one answered immediately, and I wondered if that was a poor sign.

Probably not.

Chapter Thirty
A Thousand Pieces

Many Mysteriologists debate whether the creatures of the deep have self-awareness and whether they are capable of communication. Though this may not be scientific and verifiable, this author is of the mind that there can be no debate. I challenge anyone to meet the gaze of a Cirein-cròin and try to make a case for lack of intelligence.

–An excerpt from The Mysterious Deep: A Comprehensive Understanding

The sun wasn't enough to keep out the frigid air, or maybe that was just the whispers and suspicion that graced the Wraith's deck. I crossed my arms over my chest and shivered, pulling the thick wool coat closer as if that could ward off the atmosphere. Another mournful song that pricked at my eyes came from behind us.

"I can't help, but feel like it's a warning," Dilly murmured.

Her brown coat had its fur-lined hood up over her red hair, but strands managed to escape all the same. Not that she would have noticed. Her spyglass had been glued to her eye for the last hour, and when it wasn't, she was scribbling in her notebook.

"I've read that not even sea monsters venture into the Glass Sea," I said.

The gray-gloom around us was unnatural given that the sun was still high in the sky, not hidden behind a single cloud. Even the Mysterious Deep had limits.

"None have been sighted, true, but our understanding of the deep is infantile in its nature. There is no way of knowing until we can collect more data." She frowned.

"Well, Koinu doesn't seem thrilled about our heading," I said.

Dilly didn't say anything, but instead placed the spyglass under her arm and began writing furiously in her journal. Her mind working faster than her pen.

I felt him before I saw him. Like warmth from a fire in the midst of a snowfall. The Captain of the Wraith was magnetic in every way. I would have known him from a sea of masks. Seeing him was rare, though. During the day, he was either making himself scarce or working alongside the crew to curb the chance of whispers and earn goodwill. It helped a little. With Oscar's ability to listen to the crew's fears, validate, but steer away from mutiny, and Billy's theatrical performances of hard-won scores for the Wraith, it was getting better. Less small groups with their heads together and less silence. The three of them were a good team.

I, on the other hand, was always in the way. The way the crew, except for a select few, avoided me was telling enough about how they thought Barnacles met his demise. Billy had bravely suggested Flynn make a show of tossing me out and having me stay in the hull with Dilly. Even if it was a good idea and Billy had taken a sound scolding for it, I was grateful for the nights spent in Flynn's arms.

"Miss Smith," he said as he lightly brushed my hand with his.

Dangerous. This game he was playing, that we were playing.

"Captain," I said.

Several crew members were watching us, and I took a subtle step away. Even if he didn't throw me out, he didn't have to give them fuel for their fire. The possessive captain who killed Barnacles for daring to touch his property. That was the story whispered on the Wraith. It was a shame they didn't know he was actually murdered by someone he considered an ally.

"Miss Shaw," Flynn said.

Seconds ticked by, but for Dilly, the world consisted only of the notebook she scrawled into like it was her lifeforce.

"Oh no, Koinu is charging the ship!" I said.

Nothing.

"It's a rare thing to have a passion so consuming," Flynn murmured.

I shrugged. "Mostly it's annoying."

I kicked out my leg, nudging her ankle. The physical contact was enough to bring her to the world of the living and she raised her head and did a small jump when she saw Flynn.

"Captain, when did you get here?" she gasped, tucking her book into her pocket.

I loved the small quirk of his lips that said he was amused. It was an effort in restraint that I refrained from reaching out and touching him. If only the sun could go down a little quicker. All my reasons and all my logic were eroded in a drunken decision to kiss him. I might have lamented my lack of willpower if I wasn't happy.

Because I was, that was the feeling that lodged in my chest—my days spent with Dilly and listening to her talk about her life's work and watching Billy regale the crew with heists and impossible odds while they ate dinner. Even Oscar had been around more despite his silver tongue whispering into the ears of the amenable crew members. Then there were my nights. Nights that I knew were numbered, but that I catalogued and hoarded like a dragon to gold.

"We are two days from the Glass Sea. Some of the crew have been, but a large portion are green. I wondered if you might tell them what to expect later this afternoon," he said.

Dilly's eyes widened. "Me?"

"You are the expert, are you not?" he said.

Dilly opened and closed her mouth several times, looking at me and then out to the sea for help that didn't come. When she had exhausted all her options, she bit her lip and huffed out a breath that materialized in the cold air around us.

"I don't do well with people," she confessed.

"It'll be better coming from you. Billy will just terrify them." He turned, eyes grazing over mine like a caress as he left us. "It's an order, Miss Shaw, not a request."

Dilly's shoulders fell, and she wrinkled her nose in distaste.

"Can't you convince him not to make me?" she asked.

"Me?" I asked, sounding much like her a minute ago.

Dilly rolled her eyes. "At this point, if you think either of you is hiding anything, you are more confused than a giant squid seeing the sun for the first time."

"Am I supposed to know what that means?" I asked.

I loved the way her eyes sparkled and the way her laugh cut into the gloom with expert precision. To know her was to love her.

"All I am saying is that I hope someday someone looks at me the way he looks at you. As long as I don't drool quite as much as you do." She winked.

I gently pushed her, and she laughed it off like there wasn't a mutiny brewing in the wind. If we were trading hopes, then I would have said that one day, I hoped to see the world the way she did—like it was in screaming color.

A mourning cry came from behind us as Koinu sang its tragic warning. We were probably foolish to ignore it.

Dilly had never looked more uncomfortable in her life. I was willing to bet my left hand on it. She shifted from foot to foot while alternating between crossing her arms and folding them behind her back. The crew of the Wraith had gathered on deck for her briefing. Everyone was wearing coats, and she was shivering despite them.

The closer we got to the Glass Sea, the rougher the seas became. More than once, I fought against nausea when the Wraith was tossed in a particularly brutal wave. From what Dilly had told me, it was only going to get worse.

"Hey there, Princess," Val said, sliding up next to me.

"Hi, Val," I grumbled.

I mentally prepared myself for the onslaught of rat jokes she loved. Of all the people who could have found us in that storage room, I was glad it was Val, but she did like to bring it up on a regular basis.

I opened my mouth to tell her to just get on with it, but Flynn's voice boomed over the icy wind.

"I've asked Miss Shaw to explain what you can expect on the Glass Sea. Our success and survival depend on full cooperation. I am sure I don't need to remind you that, should we succeed, you will all be wealthy people with clear names. However, one misstep and you will join the wraiths hoarding their treasure at the bottom of the sea. With that being said, I leave it to you, Miss Shaw."

I watched his retreating form as he went to stand by Oscar. My brother's cheek was healing nicely, but there were many whispers on how he had earned a fat lip and busted cheek. Most were true.

"Right, so," Dilly began, clearing her throat. "The Glass Sea is attached to Antarctica and just past the Drake Passage which we are nearly in. The passage can either be calm or be a ship killer depending on our luck, but the moment we enter the Glass Sea all of that will end. It's called that for its unnaturally still water that reflects everything perfectly. Even the wind doesn't touch its surface. At that point, we will all be taking a drop of elixir to numb our feelings. Wraiths feed on emotion, so they would swarm us in an instant without it."

"Feels like this might be a bad idea," I murmured.

Val snickered and shoved her shoulder into me far too hard. "Live a little, Princess. We will be in and out of there like two rats scurrying through the night."

I stared at her and shook my head. "That one didn't even make sense."

She shrugged. "I still enjoyed it."

"Once we arrive at the Maravilla wreck, we will send down several people to retrieve the treasure. By all accounts, wraiths need either emotion or physical disturbance to be awakened into a frenzy. However, it's theorized that they have what we call a hive mind. When one is alerted to a presence, they all are, and they swarm. If this happens—"

"We're dead," someone shouted, earning laughter from the crew.

Dilly's cheeks reddened. "More than likely."

"So if we don't touch them, we survive?" Val called out.

Shifting on her feet, Dilly frowned. "More or less, but there will be a lot of them. The Maravilla is arguably the largest hoard of wealth in the Glass Sea, meaning the wraiths are naturally drawn there. It will take finesse to avoid them."

"How long does the elixir last?" someone asked.

Dilly glanced at Flynn, who nodded his head.

"The more volatile your emotions, the faster you work through the elixir. There isn't a set time. We will be working on the assumption that we have twelve hours, which is the lower end of what's been documented. The Maravilla is approximately three hours into the Glass Sea, so that leaves about six hours to grab what we can," she said.

"What else is down there?"

I recognized the voice. I heard it in my dreams, attached to a cruel smile. Amos.

He stood at the front with his arms crossed.

"I don't know," Dilly confessed. "As far as I am aware, I will be the first Mysteriologist to cross the sea, so what is there is not documented well, and all theory. You should be prepared for anything."

"So we are basically gambling with our lives when we have the means to secure a prize without risking our lives," Amos said, turning to face the crew.

My stomach sank like an anchor to the sea floor. Val reached out and grabbed my arm, tucking me slightly behind her. Probably not a good sign.

"Amos," his brother said, pushing through the crowd. "What are you doing?"

He ignored his brother and instead turned and pointed a damning finger at me.

"She's worth a hefty prize if we ransom her, and no one has to gamble with wraiths."

Someone probably should have told him I wasn't worth more than a few pounds and that my family was balancing on the edge of ruin.

"Mr. Clark, I suggest you fall in line," Flynn warned, his words like the steel tip of a sword.

Amos clearly felt unburdened by self-preservation as he faced Flynn.

"Or what? Will I end up like Barnacles just for saying what we're all thinking? Why are we risking our necks when we could just trade your pet for a payout?" he spat.

Murmurs broke out among the crew, and it was becoming clear that others had wondered the same thing. I never wanted to give Amos more credit than he was due, but I couldn't help but marvel at his timing. He had stoked the flames of unease and then launched his attack at a moment of tension. When they would all be feeling vulnerable. It was a calculated maneuver I didn't think him capable of.

"Maybe instead of being a short-sighted, greedy fool, you might consider that the Maravilla isn't the only prize to be won here," Oscar said, stepping forward. "Sure, you could ransom Miss Smith and maybe get a few thousand shillings, but then we paint a target on the back of the Wraith. You think the British Navy will look the other way after we held her hostage and then ransomed her? No, they will make our lives hell, and we will be lucky to pull another prize."

"I figured you'd say as much given you—" Amos began.

"Or," Oscar raised his voice and began pacing slowly before the crew. "We do what we came here to do. Pull the biggest prize ever achieved by a single crew, secure our names among the history books, and return to the mainland as innocent men on paper. Never to be hunted again. Never to fear the noose again."

He stopped in front of Amos and met his gaze. I barely recognized my brother, who wore authority like a second skin. Who commanded everyone's attention merely because he willed it.

"You all face a choice. Take the easy way out, live in fear, risk something, and live like kings." he said.

The crew was quiet, considering. The flip of a coin teetering on the tip of a sword. Fate's weaving momentarily paused on a precipice.

"How many crews have you been on, Amos?" Val asked, shielding me from view.
His weasel-like face twisted with a sneer.

"That don't mean nothing," he said.

"I think those of us who have been here a few years might disagree with that," she said.

Several heads nodded and I decided I would thank my lucky stars everyday of my life that Val decided to like me.

"It don't change what I know," he said. "Her fiancé has been tailing us and willing to pay—" Charlie slid through the crowd and stepped in front of his brother, whispering furiously.

"I'd think very hard about the next words you say, son," Billy said, appearing from the left, hand on his pistol. "You are treading on a line that sounds an awful lot like mutiny."

Charlie placed his hands on Amos's shoulders, trying to get him under control, but I saw the same look I had seen countless times in potential suitors' eyes. It was the illusion of strength crumbling around them that turned to desperation. For my suitors, it often meant saying something they deemed hurtful, like alluding to a spinster aunt. For Amos—well, I knew what he would say if he opened his mouth.

I glanced at Flynn, who was watching with his arms crossed, but the tight set of his jaw said he knew what came next, too. Oscar was saying something to him, but neither could intervene without adding more coal to the flame. Hence why Billy stepped in, but his hands were nearly tied too.

How many times had I watched the world around me happen without being an active participant? How many times had I lamented that things always happened to me? Not today. Not when I was so damn close to achieving what I set out to do. I was not going back.

I ducked beneath Val's arm, ignoring her protest. Not today. James would not have me. I was going to save my family from ruin and watch as his face fell when he realized I had done it all on my own. All his deprecating comments summed up to a total of one hundred thousand shillings.

Amos shoved his brother off of him and opened his mouth to speak. For the second time in my life, I pulled my arm back and slammed my fist into a man's face. The pain was sharp and far worse than the last time. Probably because I meant it more this go around. I shouted and shook my hand as if that would shake away the pain.

"Shit," someone said.

Out of the corner of my eye, I saw Flynn stalking toward me.

 I was absolutely not done yet.

Amos was bent over, covering his eye.

"Fuck!" he shouted. "That bitch just hit me."

"Oof. Sounds painful," I said.

Just as Flynn reached for me, I gripped Amos's shoulders and kneed him right in the balls like I'd read about in a stolen book from my father's private stash. The cry that came from his mouth was a symphony to my ears. Even when Flynn wrapped his arms around my waist and lifted me off the ground, I was too proud of myself to be mad at his intervention.

"Fucking bitch," Amos said.

"Can't say you didn't have it coming," Billy laughed.

Laughter followed his words, and my smile was one of victory as I watched the crowd disperse as they recounted what had just happened with amusement.

"You really are a hellcat," Flynn said as we neared his cabin.

"My hand really hurts, but I feel amazing," I said, breathless.

He laughed, shoulders shaking.

"If I put you down, are you going to castrate him?" he asked.

I thought about it. "Best not to make promises."

"Thank you for your honesty," he said.

He shifted my weight like I was nothing, twisting me and throwing me over his shoulder. I released a loud yelp at the manhandling. It was largely ignored, even when he opened the door to the cabin and carefully set me down on his desk, ignoring the perfectly good bed or chair. I shook out my hand, which had only just healed, before I used it to punch two men within the span of a few days.

Flynn took it in his hands, running his thumb over the rough skin that had grown over the burns the Gharaq had given me. He wore a beautiful smile while he assessed the damage, working each finger to check for fractures.

"When you punch your next victim, tuck your thumb like this," he said, demonstrating with my hand.

"Are you sure you want to teach me that? You are probably my next victim," I said.

My body was alight with energy. It was a high I couldn't remember having felt before. I felt invincible, like I could go to the Glass Sea and retrieve the Maravilla entirely by myself.

"Probably," he mused.

Satisfied there weren't any breaks, he lifted his hand to cup my face. His eyes softened as he searched my eyes for something only he knew.

"You really are incredible, Rose," he said.

There was too much sincerity in the words. Meanings beneath meanings that neither of us had any business wielding. The truth beneath it all kept me up some nights. That he would eventually see who I really was. The faults transferred in perfect cursive. Today, though. Right in this moment, I liked being what he thought I was.

I spread my legs and caught him between them, pulling him close. His smile grew along with that glint in his eye that I had learned all too well. A glint that was all mine and like any wraith, I hoarded it like gold.

His hand drifted down to my neck where he wrapped it, firm, but not enough to cost me air. I felt the coil begin and that want that was reserved only for him.

"Entirely singular," he whispered, mouth ghosting over mine.

He was playing with me, but I wasn't the prey anymore. I knew how to undo him, and I had no intention of using my power wisely.

I nipped at his lower lip and said the damning words, "I'm yours."

He growled and pulled me into the kiss, our bodies fitting together like puzzle pieces. We fumbled with each other's coats that were much too warm now. Tongue and teeth battling for purchase. This was a hunger neither of us knew how to satiate.

He undid my coat before I was halfway through his. He eagerly reached in and ran his hands over my burning skin, my back, my stomach, my breasts like he was a man starved. I gasped out a breath when he ran his teeth and tongue down my neck.

"I need you," I pleaded.

I was burning on a pyre. If I didn't have him inside me within a few seconds, I was going to combust.

"You have me," he rasped, ripping my coat off me.

I was vaguely aware of the door opening, but it was impossible to see past Flynn or the feel of him on me.

"Oh, fuck," Oscar said.

"If you don't leave right now, I will violently murder you," I said.

Flynn chuckled into my neck, the hard length of him pressing against me, ready to give me what I needed.

The door slammed shut, and I didn't have time to think about how I was going to face him later. Flynn made quick work of my blouse and pants, but he wasn't moving fast enough. I reached down between my slick legs and pressed a finger to my aching center, and moaned when energy shot through me.

"Fuck, Rose, you are trying to kill me?" he asked.

I threw my head back and spread my legs a little wider for him so he wouldn't miss a second of my activity.

"If you get undressed sometime today, you can join," I said in between bated breaths.

He stilled, ceasing his work of unbuttoning his pants, blissfully shirtless. I circled my finger a little faster, and I knew I would be done soon. Release seconds away if I wanted it.

My activity was interrupted by him wrapping his hand back around my neck and forcing me to look at him. The roughness of it only heightened the explosion brewing within me. His eyes were on fire, and I was dying.

"Do you know what it was like to listen to you touch yourself and have to pretend to be sleeping?" he asked, his words harsh.

Of all the things I would have expected him to say, that hadn't been it. I stilled my finger and narrowed my eyes at him.

"You were awake," I said.

He tilted his head, marking me with his eyes. "Yes."

"But you ignored me after, like I was nothing," I said.

"Rosamund," he warned.

"Edward," I echoed.

His mouth devoured mine in an instant, and I was beginning to wonder if his true name was more of a weapon than telling him I was his. I would have to test out the theory. When he finally released my mouth, my lips were swollen and bruised in the best way.

"You were torture. The sounds you made, wondering what you were thinking of. I thought I would go mad with the need to touch you. To give you new memories to think of, but I didn't because you didn't want me to. But it almost killed me, Rose," he said.

"I was thinking about you, at the inn," I confessed.

"Tell me," he ordered, slowly stepping back and undoing his pants.

I reached back between my legs, but he shook his head.

"Tell. Me," he said, each word in its own order.

I gulped, hating that I was obeying. Well, I wouldn't make it easy on him. I braced my hands behind me, making sure to give a gentle curve to my stomach that hid nothing from him.

He rid himself of his pants, and my mouth watered with the need to take him one way or the other. His hand wrapped around his cock and I watched with rapt attention.

"Rosamund," he said.

I licked my lips. "I thought about when you asked me if I wanted you to ruin me. How you worked your way down my body."

He fisted himself once, then twice. A drop of pearly white was already beading at the top. This was a cruel game. My body ached for him, and he was right there, ready. I knew him, though; he was determined, which meant I had to break down his will.

"I thought about your mouth on me, devouring me, never looking away like I was a feast you waited your whole life for."

"Fuck," he said, fisting himself harder.

I leaned forward, knowing I was winning, but that didn't satiate the need in me in any way.

"I thought about your tongue against me, warm and perfect. How you watched me as I came against your mouth hard enough to see stars."

That was his undoing. He released his cock and lifted me off the table in one fell swoop. I clung to him and wrapped my arms around him while he pressed me against the wall of the cabin. He held me in place while he sank into me, and I screamed into his shoulder, the fullness like a drug.

"You're torture," he panted as he thrust into me.

I threaded my hands through his hair and pulled gently while his hand on my back held us tight together.

I loved being his torture. Of all the names people had called me, that was my favorite. No one would ever say my name the way he did. No one would ever make me feel the way he made me feel. My eyes stung with something I couldn't name. All I knew was I never wanted this to end. Never wanted to have to rely on memories again.

"I—" words were somewhere in my mind, bubbling to the surface.

His pace grew less angry and more controlled, like he was thinking what I was.

That our days were numbered.

I buried my face into his neck, wetness coming away. Probably sweat.

The coil inside me was tight with the promise of ecstasy, but this pressure inside my chest was something else. Something I didn't want.

"Please," I begged.

"Fucking incredible," he grunted. "You're perfect, Rose."

That was it. Words I could never believe crested over me, and I fell into that sweetness, contracting around him until he spilled into me. Following me over that edge like he would have followed me anywhere.

When my breathing eased, I lifted my head and his eyes narrowed as he looked over me. He cupped my cheeks and brushed a thumb beneath my eye coming away wet.

"Did I hurt you?" he asked, worry cresting in his eyes.

I shook my head. "No, you didn't."

I brought my lips to his and kissed him so he would know what I couldn't say. He answered with tender gentleness that cracked my glued-together heart into thousands of pieces. After surviving hateful words and trying to find who I was after it was broken, I had slowly put it back together. Yet here, in the pirate captain's arms, it was forever shattered. Never to be repaired again.

Chapter Thirty-One
The Man with Nothing

If humanity were to work with the Mysterious Deep and learn from her sto-ries, the implications would be far-reaching for medicine.

-An excerpt from The Mysterious Deep: A Comprehensive Understanding

In an interesting twist of fate, it appeared that when you were publicly wounded by a wealthy English woman, no one believed you anymore. Sure enough, with fractured pride, Amos had unmasked me as Rosamund Bailey, and despite my features that were similar to my brothers, no one paid him any heed.

It was wildly amusing.

Had someone had the decency to tell me earlier, I would have done it sooner.

"If you use that hand to roll in the sand, go swimming, or punch another person, I will be forced to consider amputation," Emille said as he finished bandaging it.

"It's pretty much better," I said, flexing it with only a minor pain.

He narrowed his eyes at me, and I sighed.

"Fine, I won't punch anyone."

For my reward, he handed me a vial full of pink cloudy liquid. I wrinkled my nose and stuffed it in my pocket.

"Does it have to taste so horrid?" I asked.

Emille chuckled and left me to go get dinner. While I appreciated not getting pregnant, I would have enjoyed it more if it hadn't tasted like ginger paste. At least Emille was subtle about it, but much like Dilly said the other morning, everyone knew. There wasn't a soul on this ship who was under any illusion that I wasn't sleeping with the captain after the way he had hauled me off yesterday and not emerged for several hours.

"All patched up?" Dilly asked.

She handed me a bowl of red mixed with possibly beans—no meat. Best not ask questions and certainly best not to look at it.

I scooped a spoonful in, waiting for the horror to commence, but it was a nice blend of garlic and onion mixed with tomato.

"This actually isn't bad," I said with a full mouth.

"That's because I made it," Dilly said, beaming as she shoved a bunch in her mouth.

"I didn't know you cooked," I said.

She winked. "I am nothing if not full of surprises."

"I wouldn't go that far," Oscar said as he and Inu took the bench opposite us.

The hull was filled to the brim tonight with the crew as the sea was currently in the process of throwing us around. How anyone was walking was a mystery to me. Even the lanterns threatened to go out when a particular vengeful wave happened by.

I briefly met my brother's eye, and he held up two hands in surrender before digging into his meal with profound enthusiasm. Apparently, that was our truce from last night when I threatened to murder him if he didn't leave. Sometimes I wondered what Oliver would have said if it were him instead of Oscar. While I loved our older brother, I suspected he would have notions of honor and chivalry to fight through.

Lord knew my sister Ruby would have likely had a fainting spell if she ever found out. Another wave made the ship groan in protest, and half of my bowl fell between Dilly and me. Frowning, I scooped it up with my spoon, but another toss made the food significantly less appetizing.

Emille returned with Billy in tow, taking seats at the table with us.

"Inu, you look a little green about the gills," Billy said, smirking.

I hadn't noticed before, but her normally pale skin was ghostly white.

"Are you all right?" I asked.

My answer was a glare that could have melted an iceberg. So much for a truce between us. We might both love Oscar, but some people were simply incompatible.

"The sea is unnatural," Inu murmured.

Oscar wrapped his arm around her and pressed a kiss to her forehead, which made me feel like I was witnessing something I shouldn't. He whispered something in her ear, and she nodded briefly.

"Actually, it's quite natural." Dilly chirped, holding up her spoon with authority. "It's because there are no major land masses near the pass, so the winds are magnified by lack of inhibition."

"Is that so?" Billy said with a wide grin. "I just thought Odin was pissed."

Emille laughed, and even Dilly smiled. It was odd that everyone was at ease after the last few days of uncertainty. My only regret was that I hadn't punched Amos Clark earlier. He was currently confined to the brig, which brought me immense delight. I only felt slightly bad that his brother was down there by fault of association.

"Here, Inu, you look like you could use this," Val said, taking the seat next to me.

She handed her a bottle of rum which Inu thanked her for quietly. Surprisingly, Inu drank like she had never been thirstier. Oscar chuckled, shaking his head before taking another spoonful.

"You seem to be handling it just fine, Princess," Val said, nudging me with her shoulder.

"I might be a pirate just yet," I said.

"I would place a wager on that," Flynn said, coming up behind us.

Val kicked me under the table and scooted further down the bench to make room for Flynn. She gave me a knowing smile while she chewed her food. Smug.

Her face was briefly obstructed while Flynn slid in next to me. When the next wave came, our bowls slid down the side of the table, but Emille and Val made quick work of catching them.

"Well, isn't this nice, a family meal before we go dance with the wraiths," Oscar smiled.

I glared at him thinking maybe he was a little too on the nose with that, but then again as I glanced at the faces surrounding us, I realized I would have trusted each of them with my secrets. My chest swelled with that emotion that was scarier than any wraith.

"I know the captain's been, but have any of you been to the Glass Sea before?" Dilly asked.

Billy raised his hand, and Val raised her spoon.

"It's how we paid for the Wraith, ain't it, Bash?" Billy said with a gleam of mischief in his eyes.

"Here we go," Flynn groaned.

Billy stood pointing his spoon at each of us in slow succession. "They said it couldn't be done. A small crew in a run-down ship? No chance they'd make it through the Glass Sea, but that was before the name Captain Sebastian Flynn meant something."

Flynn pinched the bridge of his nose. "Jesus Christ, Billy."

As if he had said nothing, Billy continued, now having garnered the attention of the entire hull.

"There were just six of us, all with their own reason for following a no name captain, but we all saw it before the rest of the world and I count my damn lucky stars I did." Billy met Flynn's eyes, emotion swelling behind them as Flynn nodded once to him. "So there we were, on a run-down ship. Vial in hand. Aye, we got lucky through the passage. She was as calm as a Sunday afternoon, but the moment we broke into the Glass, we all felt it. One or two thought about going back, but Bash wouldn't hear of it. We all took the elixir except for the captain."

Murmurs broke out, and it took me several moments to realize Billy wasn't jesting.

"A man with nothing has nothing to fear and everything to gain," Val murmured.

I stared up at Flynn, who took another bite of his food as if we weren't all staring at him.

"You didn't take the elixir?" Oscar asked, arm firmly around Inu, who looked half dead.

"It was a long time ago," Flynn said, waving a hand at Billy to continue.

While others saw him through the lens of bravery, my heart stuttered along with the truth. A truth that I knew only Billy and I truly understood. Flynn had no one and nothing when he set out to make his name. All he had was a hunger for vengeance. It must have been very lonely.

I reached under the table and wrapped my hand around his. He tilted his head towards mine in askance. I wanted to reach out and touch him, but I settled for a small smile that could never convey enough.

"We targeted the San José that had gone down a year before. Said to be a big enough trove to be something, but not enough to have all the wraiths of the Glass hoarding its treasure. She was deeper than we could manage multiple dives, so the captain volunteered to put a hook in her. I'll tell ya all right now, I ain't never been so scared as when I saw my first wraith. I went under to help set the line, and I shit you not, there was a wraith not two feet from us same as me to Oscar."

The galley was silent except for the protest of the ship. Everyone hanging on Billy's every word. He would have filled up any theatre worthy of Shakespeare if he had been only given the opportunity.

"I knew we were fucked. First toe in and we were joining the damned forever guarding treasure we could never have, but it looked past us with wide, dead eyes. Not seeing a damn thing. It let the current pull it along, and when it had passed, I swore I'd never take for granted another minute. If we survived this I would enjoy every damn minute left to me. Back on deck began the waiting. Captain wouldn't let anyone else go down with him, so the four of us waited. Waited. Too long under the water. Helmet or not, we knew he was lost."

"Speak for yourself," Val said, throwing back the bottle she reached over and stole from Inu.

"Just as we started talking about whether to turn back or send someone else down, Captain broke through. I swear I ain't never heard a sweeter sound than when he said, 'pull her in.' Our little ship earned her money that day, pulled the San José in with all that gold. When Bash purchased the Wraith, he gave us a choice. Take our share of the prize and go on, or join his crew. Well, all I can say is I ain't ever regretted that choice."

"Here, here," Val said, raising her bottle. "To Captain Flynn, the bravest fucker I've ever known."

Shouts of here, here followed and everyone downed what liquor there was to find except for Flynn and I. Appearances be damned, but I couldn't look away from him. Somehow, Billy's story didn't feel like it was coated in embellishments like normal. Every word meant something to him, and the emotion pulling at the muscle that feathered in Flynn's jaw said it was all true.

I rested my head on his shoulder and murmured, "Here, here."

Because the more I knew, the less I could pretend my chest didn't carry a terrible ache. Flynn squeezed my hand once in askance, and I raised my head, shaking it subtly. I was fine, this was fine. I raised my eyes to find Oscar watching us. There was no amusement or praise on his face, but instead his cheeks grew red and he cleared his throat.

He raised his glass to me with a small smile.

I remembered that day months ago when I'd seen him with Inu and knew that it was more than a passing tryst.

My heart sank into my chest as my eyes burned once more. I buried my face into my coat sleeve with a false cough.

For the first time since setting off on this insane plan, I wasn't worried about the Glass Sea. I was ready for the elixir if only it would do something about this ache.

Chapter
Thirty-Two
The Kraken and
The Wraith

The first evidence of a Kraken was discovered in 1610 when a Norwegian ship was found in such a state that one could no longer surmise it had ever been a mighty ship. The next sighting was in 1701 off the coast of Norway when a small fishing boat claimed they saw a massive beast rise from the deep with brightly colored tentacles that slammed into a shipping vessel of English origin. As with the case in 1610, there were no survivors, and the ship was beyond recognition.

–An excerpt from The Mysterious Deep: A Comprehensive Understanding

The night was pitch black without a single star or moon in sight. Worse, the lanterns couldn't keep their flame. I had never felt fear like this. It consumed me and constricted my throat. Even when I was sure Ximena was going to kill me, I never imagined there was a fear like this. It crawled inside my skin and infected every part of me. No amount of emptying my stomach was of consolation.

The Wraith lurched violently down, its bow going into the sea while her stern raised toward the sky. We were going to die. I'd read stories about the Drake Passage in my father's books. I'd read about ten-foot waves and ships threatening to buckle. The waves battering against us were easily fifteen feet. I stumbled headfirst onto the bed with the violence of the ship's pull. Pain lanced through me, but the fact that I was conscious was reassuring. Reaching up, my hand came away wet with what I could only assume was blood. Something clattered against the back of the room, and my heart sank right into the sea below.

"Dilly?" I cried.

The silence that followed was worse than any mysterious creature.

"I'm fine," she groaned.

Relief flooded me, but it was short-lived as the next crash came.

"Please come over here and tie yourself to the bed with me. I can't keep wondering if you died."

"I need to be by the window to document this. Nothing like it has ever been recorded. That last wave was at least twenty feet!" she exclaimed. "I wonder if Koinu is still following. I wish I could see outside of the lightning."

Panic and frustration roared in my ears. I was securely tied, triple-checked by Flynn, to the bed. I wished it was as scandalous as it sounded, but unfortunately, it was all practicality. His logic was that the safest place for me was in here, but if the massive window broke at the stern, I needed to be firmly attached to the wall in order not to roll into the sea.

It was sound logic. However, Dilly had raged at being locked away when there was "history to record." The compromise was that she would be tethered to the wall near the window, but not so close as to risk falling out. She had only conceded because it was an order, but prior to the lanterns going out, she had worn the sweetest scowl anyone had ever known.

The ship lurched back, and I fell back onto the bed, damp with probably whatever was leaking from my head.

"Oh my seas, did you see that?" Dilly gasped.

"No, I was a little busy being tossed around like a cricket ball," I said.

My muscles hurt, and I was pretty sure that was a headache coming on.

A ripping tore through the night, followed by a crash that hollowed out my insides. We were going to die.

We were absolutely going to die.

"That's impossible," Dilly said. "It's never been recorded."

I really didn't want to die here. There were revenge plots I still had to see through. My family needed saving. I had more questions. Significantly more living to do.

"I am not dying here," I whispered.

In answer, the Wraith groaned something like I imagined a giant might have done if he were breaking all his bones.

"My god, it is," Dilly shouted.

I hadn't seen Blackbeard since the night before but hoped he was cuddled somewhere safe. Something told me if we all died, he would be fine. Still, I worried.

"I'm going," Dilly announced.

"Excuse me," I choked.

A flash of lightning, and I caught sight of her undoing her knots.

"Have you absolutely lost your mind?" I asked.

Maybe I wasn't the only one with a head injury. Sure enough, she undid her rope, and as the ship drew up, she slid back while my rope held me tight as the Wraith fought to right herself. With a loud crash and the sea screaming her fury, we fell forward once more.

Dilly wasted no time running for the door.

"Dilly!"

She stopped before me and pulled me into a hug, planting a dry kiss on my cheek.

"We are probably going to die, but if I can die seeing a Kraken, then that is exactly how I am going to go," she said.

My eyes widened in the dark.

"Kraken?" I stuttered

She squeezed me tight and squealed with delight like the mad woman she was. As if the sea wasn't doing a good enough job of murdering us, she called a Kraken to help.

We were actually fucked.

Strangely, I actually understood Dilly's logic. Ropes and knots were for survival, but as the Wraith cracked and shifted, I knew the truth. We weren't making it out of this alive.

I wanted to say goodbye to my brother. To Flynn.

I grabbed the long knife Flynn had tucked into my boots in case of emergency and sawed at the thick rope. I was almost positive this hadn't been what he'd meant when he said emergency, but all was fair when death was imminent.

The moment I was free, the sea decided to toss us to the right. I landed with a thump into Flynn's shelf of treasures that were now scattered around the cabin. My back ached with the strain of pulling myself up.

I ignored my body's protests, finally making it to the door in time for another snap of wood, but at least a wave wasn't throwing us in an unnatural direction. The door was wedged in, but a few good tugs and it flew open, slamming me against the wall.

God, at least I wouldn't have to endure all these bruises much longer. Wind and rain pelted across my skin, accompanied by shouts coming from all directions. My hair whipped around with the magnitude of the wind, and I finally understood what it meant to see a ship killer.

The sea rose and fell around us in a chaotic symphony. More concerning was the bright purple tentacles that flashed with every hit of lightning. I moved my mouth in silent horror as I counted them, holding onto the cabin door for stability.

One. Two. Three. Four. Five. Six. Seven. Eight.

Eight tentacles with suction cups twice the length of my body, its underside coated in a teal that reminded me of stolen moonlight.

Dilly hadn't been hallucinating. That—that was a damn Kraken.

Any hope I had concealed about surviving this was quickly dashed. No one survived a Kraken. No one.

Purpose ran through me as bright as the lightning that flashed ahead. I ran. I ran with everything I had in me, managing only a few feet before the ship lurched and I lost my footing. Everything shifted, and before I knew any better, I was sliding feet first down the left side of the ship. Sliding further and further. I clawed at the floorboards for purchase, but they were too slick. What a stupid way to die, I thought as I neared the edge.

Just as I was sure I would feel the bite of the icy water, arms wrapped around my waist. I breathed out a solemn prayer that probably fell on deaf ears.

"What the fuck are you doing out here, Princess?" Val yelled.

The ship righted itself once more with significant protest, and Val pulled me upright. I was soaked through, but I didn't feel a bit of the cold. I believed that was called adrenaline.

"Where's Flynn?" I shouted over the storm.

She shook her head. "You're an idiot!"

"I really like you, too!" I shouted back.

A rough snort broke from her, but she must have been thinking the same thing I was. We were going to die anyway. She pointed toward the upper deck near the helm. I should have known. The captain goes down with the ship after all.

Well, at least he would have company.

I squeezed her hand once and took off as fast as I could, knowing I had seconds before the Wraith shifted once more. Broken planks splintered, leaving gaping holes in the bowels of the ship. A flash of light illuminated the tentacles that had firmly surrounded the Wraith. Which meant it was probably under us with its giant beak about to snap the hull in two.

Pushing out a breath of icy air, I climbed the steps as a wave tossed us to the right. By some divine intervention, it was less forceful and deposited me right at my captain's feet.

"Secure the main mast! She's slipping!" he ordered.

Save it to Sebastian Flynn to shout orders on a doomed ship. I crawled over and used his leg to pull myself up.

"What the—" he tried to shake me off, but a flash of lightning gave me away.

His red face from constant wind and hail twisted with horror.

"Rose!" he yelled, reaching down to help me up.

He wrapped me in his arms tight enough that I couldn't let in any air, but it seemed like a kinder way to die, so I held him back, breathing him in so I could memorize the feel of him in my last moments.

He released me and started working on the knot around his waist. Deft fingers undid his sailor's work, and before I realized what he was doing, he pulled me flush against him and tied it around both of us.

"Why are you out here?" he asked.

"If I am going to die, I want to be with you," I said.

He stilled, and when the next strike of lightning came, I was reminded how truly beautiful he was—like a work of art. I would have liked to commission a painting of him so that future generations would wonder who the impossibly beautiful man with ghosts in his eyes was. Oh, the stories they would create.

He cupped my face and his lips crashed against mine, hungry. I answered his call because I couldn't think of anything I would rather do with my last breaths than give them to him. This pirate who had found me broken and lost only to forge me into something stronger than before. Like iron forged with carbon makes steel, I was infinitely stronger with him at my side. It made sense that we would die at sea; the world wouldn't have survived us anyway.

"You aren't dying," he said when he finally broke our kiss.

"I think my parents would have adored you," I said with a grin.

Flynn growled and wrapped his hand behind my head and pulled me against his chest.

"This isn't a lie for a truth, Rosamund," he said.

"We're losing ground, Bash!" My brother's voice called over the wind.

Flynn made a sound of frustration and twisted me so my back was to his front as he tightened the rope around us. With white gripped hands, he turned the helm to take us alongside a massive wave.

The scene that unfolded before me was chaos incarnate. An image that would haunt me past my death. The sea was white and angry around us, and the tentacles waved, toying with its food. Bodies flew across the deck, falling into the sea without a sound.

With each lightning strike, I searched for Oscar, growing more frantic with every second.

"He's on the main mast securing the rigging," Flynn said into my ear.

Sure enough, the next shot of light showed my brother climbing higher up the mast while the sea roared around us. There was a rope secured about his waist, but a fall from that height was more than fatal.

"Oh god," I whispered.

"We aren't dying," Flynn repeated. "I haven't had nearly enough of you yet."

"I don't think you get a say in it," I said, eyes stinging with everything I was losing.

"The fuck I don't," he said, turning the wheel.

I stared in awe as he rode us alongside another wave. For just a second I thought he might do it. The way he brought us next to, but not into each wave. No one else could have kept us afloat this long. We were going to make it.

Lightning struck and hit the top of the main mast. The ship cried out with its fatal hit, and the top half of the mast snapped in half, Oscar falling several feet. I screamed his name, but he didn't hear. He fought to wrap his legs around the main rigging, but the control the mast allotted us was lost.

"I love you," I shouted, knowing this was the end.

A wave at least twenty feet was barreling straight toward us, and I knew the words I wanted to die with in my mouth.

"I have never regretted a moment of you. Even when I was angry enough at you to murder you, I didn't regret the time we shared. I have never felt more seen or more cared for than when I am in your arms. You made me happy in the best ways possible. I love you, Bash."

He released the helm, and it rotated violently, but he buried his head into my neck and wrapped his arms tight around me. It suited us. Two old people in bed together, taking our last breaths, was never our fate. We were too chaotic, too meant for the reckless.

"I would find you in any life. The afterlife will be no different," he promised.

My heart leapt as I braced myself for the wave to drown us, but moments gave way to seconds that gave way to hours and it never came.

The world went still around us and no sound broke the air. Death had been far more peaceful than I ever thought it would have been. It was tight arms and promises.

The sun shone down on my skin, warming everywhere it touched. If this was hell, then I had spent too long dreading it.

I cracked open an eye and sucked in a breath.

No waves, no tentacles. No bottom of the sea.

Instead, pink endless skies with a large sun at its center overlooked perfectly still water that reflected the sky above like a mirror.

"The Glass Sea," I whispered.

Flynn's grip on me loosened, and I drew in a breath.

"We made it," he said, his voice thick with disbelief.

I watched as the living slowly righted themselves and stared out at the endless sea. We had survived, but no one cheered. No one celebrated the impossible miracle of fresh air entering our lungs.

We were alive, but death was all around us. Waiting for an invitation.

Against all odds, the woman who should not have set foot on a ship was staring at what few had seen. Even fewer have seen and lived to tell the tale.

I was in the Glass Sea.

Chapter Thirty-Three
The Man with Everything

The elixir presented by the Gharaq Clan is without a doubt effective at masking emotions such as fear, but with that comes a certain inhibition. More importantly, one must wonder what the Gharaq clan have to gain from humans venturing into the Glass Sea.

–An excerpt from The Mysterious Deep: A Comprehensive Understanding

The elixir was thick like jelly paste with an earthy taste that tasted an awful lot like dirt. It coated my throat and sank into my stomach with a terrible thump. As disgusting as it was, I was grateful for the reminder that I was, very much so, alive. At least for a little longer.

"My tonics aren't so bad now, huh?" Emille asked.

I winced as his needle pierced my skin once more, stitching the gash in my head together. The pain was almost immediately numbed by the magic coursing through my blood. It was all still there. The pain, the anxiety, fear, adrenaline. It all existed beneath the elixir, but it was muted like it was being stomped on by a thick boot, pushed down till it was a distant thought.

"That's eerie," I murmured.

"It's dangerous," Emille countered. "Imagine what a person could do with their emotions suppressed. Guilt suddenly becomes less of a deterrent to commit a crime. Empathy no longer humanizes others."

I searched the abyss that now held my emotions and found that he was right. When I thought about what it would take to achieve my goals, the list I usually ran through was non-existent. I still cared, but it was more like a memory.

Surveying the Wraith, all I could see was a thousand reasons we should have been at the bottom of the sea. Holes littered the deck, a broken mast, and though the debris had been pushed to the side, several places in her hull were caved in.

"Oscar's leg got caught in some rigging and has some swelling and rope burns," Flynn said, coming up behind us.

"I'll make him my next stop," Emille said, eyeing the captain. "What about you?"

"I'm fine," he answered.

He came around to study Emille's progress, his eyes narrowing as he took in the wound.

"She needs a salve for infection," he ordered.

Emille straightened, pausing his barrage of sewing to raise a single eyebrow at his Captain.

"Have you taken on medical studies as well as pirateering?" he said, the glint in his eyes giving away his amusement.

Flynn paid him no heed as if he were as inconsequential as a fly.

A few people moved around the deck, but the passage had cost us greatly. Where we had started with eighty people aboard the Wraith, we had lost twenty-five souls to the unforgiving waters. That any of us survived at all was a miracle I couldn't account for.

"How's Dilly?" I asked.

Flynn's lips thinned. "Fine. She's lucky Billy caught her before she could be thrown overboard. A broken leg is a small price to pay."

I waited for the worry to settle into my chest, but it never did. Instead, it bobbed beneath the surface like a buoy riding the waves of the sea with ease. Dangerous indeed. I should have been drowning in anxiety, especially given that in my panic and surety of death, I had told Flynn I loved him. Words he hadn't echoed back. If I had full control of my emotions, I would have been squirming right now, but instead, I nodded to him, earning a warning from Emille to hold still.

"What about Val?" I asked.

"Unharmed," he answered.

His tongue pushed against his cheek in irritation while he watched Emille work.

The doctor sighed as he slid another stitch through my raw skin, making me wince.

"If it's all the same to you, I'd rather not have you breathing down my neck while I work," Emille said.

Bash made no indication of hearing him, his hands clenched into fists at his side.

"I'm fine, really," I said, awkwardly. "I am sure other people need you more than I do right now."

His eyes flashed. "I don't care about other people."

Emille chuckled and shook his head. "Do us all a favor and go take your elixir before you attract all the wraiths in the sea to us."

"An hour left till we arrive," Billy said, coming up from the hull.

When he saw me, he wrinkled his nose.

"That will make a right scar, Hellcat," he said.

I grinned at him, enjoying the pride in his voice. I liked the idea of having a reminder that this all had been real. When I was safe and comfortable in my London home with several cats for company and gray hair, I would always know I hadn't dreamt it.

"Is there something you needed, Billy?" Flynn snapped.

His bite was sharp and eager to draw blood; however, Billy just shook his head and gave a full belly laugh.

"You are going to burn through that elixir in an hour at this rate," he chuckled.

Understanding dawned on me.

"You already took it?" I asked.

Emille straightened and eyed his handiwork. "Does that meet your expectations, Captain?"

Bash merely reached out his hand to me, ignoring both men and their poorly hidden humor. I took it without hesitation. The elixir really was dangerous because I had absolutely no inhibitions about going to him. Not who was watching, not how he was acting, not a single thought for maybe this wasn't a good idea.

Gently, he pulled me into him and cupped my face, tracing his thumb an inch over my forehead.

"I should have known you wouldn't stay where I put you," he murmured.

"If it makes you feel better, that happened when I was where you left me," I said.

"It does not," he answered.

I rested my hands on his waist while he inspected the doctor's work. I doubted any set of stitches had ever been inspected so thoroughly. When he was satisfied, he lowered his eyes to my lips, his hand lowering to my neck. I leaned into his touch, pressing myself closer against him.

Still beneath the haze of emotions was the want that had always been his. I craved his touch and his smell like an opium addict. I doubted I would ever have enough of him.

"Are you sure you are all right?" I asked.

"No," he answered too quickly.

A faint sense of alarm pulsed within me, and I stepped back, inspecting him, but he quickly pulled me back into him and kissed me like we weren't underneath an unnatural pink sky and still water infested with murderous cursed sailors.

Worse, I didn't seem to mind either because I kissed him like he was life-sustaining. He might have been. I had no evidence to suggest otherwise. His lips were soft and pliable under mine, with those earthy undertones that spoke of magic. I could have gotten lost in him if it hadn't been for Billy clearing his throat.

Flynn's hand on my neck tightened, and he released a sound low in his throat that made me think the glass and debris in his cabin wasn't such an imposition after all, if only it would give us some privacy.

He broke the kiss with a frustrated sigh, though his hold on me was nearly hard enough to bruise, which I wasn't about to complain about.

"I am struggling," he grunted. "My inhibitions have been diminished, and control when it comes to you is... difficult. I feel... very protective of you."

I smirked as the ghost of humor caressed my chest.

"That was really painful to watch," I said.

At least some of the tension in his shoulders and on me was released with the joke. I had never seen him locked in a battle like he was now. The control he exerted everyday was diluted leaving things like duty, image, and reservation at the wayside.

"Why did you take it?" I asked.

The moment I asked it, I wished I could put the words back in my mouth right next to the "I love you" I screamed at him a few hours ago. Sometimes things were better not spoken aloud.

He closed his eyes, visibly wrestling with himself. For someone with dulled emotions, he was exhibiting more than he normally did, unless we were alone. Far more possessive than I had ever seen him. I was reminded about how he said he had inherited that trait from his father. For the first time I understood a fraction of what had been sleeping within him.

It sent a diluted thrill through me when any sane human would have seen the warning for what it was. After all, I had spent the last few months running from a man who wanted nothing more than to own me, but what Bash wanted was—it was more than that.

Worse, I was willing to let him have it.

"A man with nothing has nothing to fear and everything to gain, but a man who has everything knows only fear because he has everything to lose," he said, running his thumb over my cheek.

If I had full control of my emotions, I might have fainted right there for the surge of understanding that roared through me. Instead, I smirked.

"Because your unhinged revenge plot is nearly at its peak?" I asked.

His eyes flashed. "Rosamund."

It only encouraged me more. Some depraved part of me enjoyed seeing his struggle, knowing I was the root of it. That when he couldn't feel, he knew only desperation for me. The power was intoxicating. When I regained my emotions, I hoped I wouldn't lose sight of this moment. The self-doubt and past hurts wouldn't cloud the truth of what I meant to him.

I raised myself on my toes and placed a soft kiss on his lips, which he answered with hunger. His tongue swept across mine, and I melted into his arms.

Billy cleared his throat.

"I don't need a damn chaperone," Bash snarled.

"Aye, ya do," Billy answered, humor dripping from his mouth. "And you ain't going in the water unless you take a second dose."

Bash raised his head to scowl at his friend. "We need to conserve them."

"That's fine with me, but I ain't letting you go in the water like this. You're like a damn siren with your emotions," he said.

"The elixir doesn't completely work?" I asked.

Bash's jaw tightened, and he took a slow step away from me, the veins in his biceps straining. Almost like he was in pain.

"Nah, not for some. The more suppression, the more the elixir's inhibition allows for those emotions to rise up. A second dose oughta do it though if the Captain wasn't too damn stubborn."

"I'll be fine," Flynn said, "I just need a minute."

Billy stepped over with a small smile, understanding alight in his eyes. He lifted the small vial from his pocket and held it out to Bash in one hand, while placing his other on Bash's shoulder.

"You won't stop worrying for her, and she won't get hurt because you don't care what happens to her. It only dulls the feelings, it doesn't take them away," Billy said, gently. "But like I said, if you want to be the one to get in the water, you'll take what I'm giving you."

Bash cracked his neck and tore the vial from Billy, downing it in one gulp. Within moments, his grip on me softened a fraction. He wrenched his eyes open and searched me for something I might not ever understand. The breath he released was rife with tension, but when he blinked once more, there was clarity in his stormy eyes.

He reached to his side and withdrew his pistol and placed it gently in my palm, wrapping my fingers around it.

I stared at it in confusion, disliking the way the metal felt against my skin. Like it didn't belong there. It was a weapon of death and power that had absolutely no business in my hand.

"I need you to do this, Rose," he whispered in my ear.

I felt my emotions bubbling low, like simmering stew, but none rose to the surface. I understood all the same. If my learning how to use this gave him any peace of mind below the surface, I would do it. Though I prayed to the powers that were, I didn't need it.

He raised my arm with his and slid behind me, his hands guiding mine. I was shapeless in his hands, ready to be molded into anything he asked of me.

Only for him.

"Aim for where the mast is split in two," he said.

I stared at the main mast, where it hung loosely by only a few strained pieces of wood. Lifting my arm, I squinted.

"What if I hit it and it falls?" I asked, thinking about the already tattered sails that were propelling us forward by sheer willpower.

"It needs to come down. It's more of a liability as it is now," he said.

Well then.

I focused on the target several hundred feet in the air and closed my eyes just as I pulled the trigger. A lackluster fizzing sound released from the barrel of the gun. I squinted one eye open and stared at the pistol and then at the mast. Still carrying on as if I hadn't shot it.

"Pistols are more likely to misfire than to shoot," he said, pulling a small metal ball from his pocket and placing it inside the pistol.

Oh, I hadn't shot it.

"That seems... unhelpful," I said.

Bash lifted my arm and turned me so I could face out towards the edge of the ship.

"Aim just below the rail," he ordered. "And don't close your eyes this time, it makes for errors, and you can't afford those."

I did as he said and focused on the part where the wood was just a shade darker. Without second-guessing it, I pulled the trigger, and a sharp blast punctuated by sparks and smoke shot out before my eyes. With calmness that was all to do with the elixir and nothing to do with me, I stepped forward and ran my hand over the hole I had created, only a few centimeters from where I had intended.

Bash came up beside me and nodded once. He still radiated tension, but nothing like he had been before. Still, there was always that what if.

"Maybe you shouldn't go in," I whispered, raising my eyes to him so he understood.

There was no hesitation in his answer.

"I will not ask my crew to do something I am not willing to do," he said.

"But what if you are putting them at risk by doing it?" I questioned.

"I'm fine," he answered. "You lift here and reload it by sliding one of these in."

He demonstrated with calloused fingers that effortlessly worked the pistol into submission.

Unease whispered in my mind. Nothing I said would make him reconsider risking his life. Not even how he felt about me would make him forget his duty to his crew. It would seem some things surpassed even vengeance for Edward Smith.

"I asked Dilly how all the ships came to be in the Glass Sea. I mean, it's crazy to think they sailed out here on purpose. We are in the middle of nowhere. Not to mention, all that treasure-"

"What did she say?" he asked. "Aim for the floorboard ten feet away."

I did as he said, but forced myself to speak the fear I had tucked away. With my emotions quieter, I knew it was now or never. I aimed at the floorboard, careful to miss the five-foot gaping hole in between us and it. Too many holes littered the ship, some going all the way down into the bottom hull. Not to mention the several cannon-sized holes that were quickly patched during the storm because of how much water they were letting in.

"She said that there is a story in Norse mythology. What they call the World Serpent. Jörmungandr, they call it," I said.

"I've heard of it," he answered, leveling out my arm with his own.

"She said some people believe that the shipwrecks that happen are brought to the Glass Sea by it. That the wraiths are only guards, but it's the serpent who hoards the gold."

I pulled the trigger and waved my free hand, clearing the smoke that burned my nose. As it cleared, I knelt down to the new hole lodged into the ship, right where I intended it to be.

"I've been in this water. The only thing beneath it is gold and death," Bash said.

I stood and turned to face him, thankful my words were cool and steady.

"Maybe this is a mistake," I said.

He nodded slowly. "Maybe, but not because there's some mythical snake at the bottom of the sea."

I stepped forward and handed his pistol to him, but he shook his head and undid his holster. I watched as he pulled it off and wrapped it around my waist, tightening it until he forced the metal through to create a new hole and secured it. Gently, he pulled the pistol from me and slid it into the holster before placing a handful of bullets into my pocket that now felt too heavy.

"If they swarm, I don't think this will do me any good," I said.

"It'll be fine," he said, running his thumb over my cheek once more.

If he believed himself, maybe I would have too.

Chapter Thirty-Four
Of Elixirs and Love

Jörmungandr, or the world serpent, is a figure in Norse mythology who often signals the end of the world. Among sailors and Mysteriologists, a rumor has abounded that the creature lurks within the Glass Sea. The most likely reason for this is that the Glass Sea boasts an unparalleled finality and world-ending aura. Scientifically speaking, there is no evidence to suggest this creature or any other besides the known wraiths dwell beneath the still sea.

–An excerpt from The Mysterious Deep: A Comprehensive Understanding

The air should have been salty, the sky should have been blue, and the water should have rippled with the cool wind around us. Instead, a bitter sweetness coated my mouth, the sky was an unnatural pink, and the water showed my reflection more efficiently than any mirror ever had.

I looked older than my twenty-six years. As if the sun's rays and salt air had aged me another decade in the span of three months. My short hair sat above my shoulders, errant curls gathering beneath. My eyes were bright, alight in a way they hadn't been back in London. Like the things I had seen and done had been permanently etched into them.

"See any good fish down there?" My brother asked, sliding up next to me.

His left leg was bandaged from his calf to his thigh, and he gripped a long oak stick in his hand, which he used like a second leg.

"Bash said it was only some swelling and rope burns?" I asked, eyeing the way he held it limply.

Oscar shrugged. "I thought so too, but turns out my knee took the brunt of it and is broken."

"You aren't going in the water," I said.

A small current of relief drifted over me, and I wondered if Bash would forgive me if I accidentally broke his knee.

"He would still go even if you cut his leg off," Oscar said.

I turned to him, my mouth slightly agape.

"You know I hate when you do that," I said, though even I was impressed with his precision.

Oscar grinned, and he was just as I always remembered him. My twin and my best friend. I reached out and grabbed his hand, holding onto him as tightly as I could. Even all our disagreements couldn't undo the place he commanded in my heart. He had tucked himself there from the first beats of our hearts.

"Yeah, but you think loud even with magical elixirs," he said, staring out at the infinite and impossible sea. "I didn't know... how you felt about him. I knew how he felt, but you've never... I've never seen you look at someone the way you look at him."

I took a long breath. If we were confessing our sins then it might as well be under the influence.

"I thought the same thing when I saw you and Inu together. I know it's stupid, but I think that's why I dislike her so much, aside from her general self. I've always been your favorite person, but now there's her," I said, the words thick in my throat.

Oscar squeezed my hand once, twice, three times. Our signal that we were there, we understood when no one else did.

"You'll always be my favorite person, but Inu... she's my home," he said.

The way Oscar spoke, there was a calmness and sense of security I had never known. Even how I felt about Bash, how we felt about each other, it was chaos and stormy seas. A desperation and a claiming. In many ways, it was the antithesis to everything Oscar was saying, but what I knew more than anything was that I never knew myself better than when Bash looked at me. He was the key to my chains, and that was more than any sense of home I could ever hope for.

I guess in a lot of ways, love was whatever you needed it to be.

"I'm happy you found your home," I said.

Even if my feelings were suppressed, I knew it was the truth deep in my bones.

Oscar gave me a short smile, his eyes shifting to where Bash was helping hoist up new rigging.

"Rose," he said. "I love you and I love Bash. He's funny, smart, and entertaining when he's not brooding, but I wouldn't call him a good person."

A flash of irritation rose like smoke within me, snuffed out before it reached my heart. Here I was affirming his choices, and I was gearing up for a lecture.

"I know who he is," I said.

Oscar nodded, face soft and non-threatening, a technique I had seen him use a thousand times on our siblings when he had to be the voice of reason. Calculated to lessen the sting of his words.

"I know you do, but the way he feels about you—I just, I never want you to be someone who is owned. You have too much fire to let anyone control your flame," he finished with another squeeze of his hand.

Maybe my time at sea had matured me, or maybe it was the potion in my veins, but I let his words settle over me, considering them. I knew ownership. The way James hunted me and wanted to break me down until when I looked to the sky, I would only ever see him.

From the first minute I met Bash, it had never felt like that. He'd always given me the space to choose. I was his because I chose it. I was the one who placed the metal around my wrists and bound myself to him. More importantly, if the day ever came that I asked for the key, he would undo the lock himself even if it killed him.

Maybe all of it was wrong, but it was right for me. For us.

"If my flame ever dulled, he'd be the first to pour more coal into me," I said.

Oscar smiled, but it didn't reach his eyes; his reservations were too loud to be truly happy for me. I couldn't and wouldn't fault him for it.

"Have you both lost your minds?" Inu hissed behind us.

Always silent as the night, I hadn't heard her coming. Her long hair was tied in a red ribbon, her long sword at her side, but anxiety wafted off of her like the foulest stench. Her hands frantically worked together, gripping and shifting like she itched to use them for something else.

"Inu, are you—" Oscar started, letting go of my hand.

Her lips twisted, and her voice came out more as a whine than her usual quiet dominance.

"What if someone saw you two? Now that everyone knows about her and the captain, what will they think if they see the two of you holding hands? Have you both forgotten that the brig is filled with two men who know who she is? They see you two together, and suddenly everything Amos said makes more sense."

Oscar stepped forward and wrapped his arms around her, but she didn't relax in the slightest; her entire body was rigid like an arrow pulled back by the bow. She jerked out of his arms, and her body shuddered.

"Come with me. We will find Emille and get you a second dose. Everything is going to be fine," Oscar said gently.

She was scared.

When inhibitions were muted, the most repressed emotions floated to the surface. For Bash it had been his protective and possessive nature. For Inu, it was fear which meant she was scared all of the time.

I watched the way her eyes shifted wildly and was reminded of a doe running through the woods, desperate for safety. All at once, I understood her better than I ever had.

"It's all right," I said. "We made it here. Once we have the treasure, no one will care what Oscar said to get them here. He's not in danger anymore."

Inu jerked her head to me. "He's been in danger every second you've been aboard this ship. No amount of treasure will change that."

I disliked her for what she meant to my brother, but she disliked me for what I might cost him.

"Okay," I whispered gently. "We will be more careful."

Her shoulders dropped some of their weight, and Oscar took the opportunity to turn her away and throw his arm over her shoulder, guiding her to the hull. He looked back at me and mouthed, 'thank you'.

I smiled softly, but even without the full weight of my emotions, the world was heavier with the truth bared before me. Sometimes it was easier to hide.

A sharp whistle broke through my melancholy and straight into my heart. The ship's tattered sails were bunched together, and I wondered if they would ever let the wind carry them again or if we would all die here.

The large anchor was edged to the side, but not thrown overboard because we couldn't risk what it might touch. The Wraith slowed her speed until we came to a stop. No waves to rock us. With the sails wrapped, we barely drifted, making the anchor practically useless. Some of the crew gently lowered two dinghies into the water, their muscles straining with the effort of precision.

A gentle nudge against my leg drew my attention away, and Blackbeard weaved between my legs and gave a small meow. Leaning down, I scratched behind his ear, wondering if I should ask Emille if the cat needed an elixir too. In answer, he launched himself onto the railing behind me and stretched out his long, furry body and closed his eyes like napping was of the utmost importance.

Point taken.

Movement ahead caught my attention, and I stared in horror as Bash slid his jacket off and handed it to Billy, who watched him like a son going off to war. Emotion clouded his eyes even with the elixir. I wondered if Bash knew how much the old man loved him, and if he did, was the love of a chosen father enough to undo the wrongs of a bad one? As he kicked off his boots, I knew the answer. For Edward Smith, it could never be enough, but for Sebastian Flynn, it would always be.

When he was through, his eyes drifted to mine, and I wanted just one more. One more night with him. One more memory. One more laugh. One more kiss. One more touch of his hands. Just one more.

I had lied to Inu when I said I would be more careful. When it came to Bash, there were only reckless jumps into dark pits, and I would always jump. I crossed the distance to him and ignored the gathered crew who were also readying themselves for the Glass sea's embrace. He gripped my face in his calloused hands and kissed me like he knew it would be a memory I would revisit till my last days.

I gripped his waist and kissed him back in a way that dared him not to come back to me. After not nearly long enough, we broke apart and he searched my eyes before placing a kiss on the top of my forehead.

"Use that pistol at the slightest hint of trouble," he said.

"I will," I whispered.

"Stay close to Oscar," he ordered.

"I will," I said. "Unless you change your mind about letting me come with you, I am very

good at holding my breath."

"No," he said, not even smirking at my joke. "Please, just this once, do as I ask."

My humor melted away under the desperation in his voice. He was going into those cursed waters no matter what happened; the least I could do was send him with a clear mind.

"I swear it," I whispered. "I'll stay on the ship, I'll stay close to Oscar, and I won't hesitate to use the pistol."

He nodded slowly, the veins on the sides of his neck straining against the war inside his mind. Finally, he let me go, but not before placing one more kiss to the top of my forehead that melted me right there on the deck of the Sea Wraith.

I was forced to watch as he climbed down the side of the railing and into one of the dinghies. Inu going after him, her sword clutched in my brother's white-knuckle grip as he gave her a reassuring smile. She must have taken the second potion because her hands didn't shake, and she held herself in that deathly calm of hers.

One by one, thirty of our crew lowered themselves, leaving twenty-five people to man the Wraith if everything fell apart. The bare minimum required.

Bash held my gaze as he pushed their boat off the edge of the ship, but the moment he sank his oar into the still sea, he was lost to me. Eyes trained ahead and below. I prayed that wasn't the last time he would ever look at me.

Chapter Thirty-Five
The Deep Dark

Sebastian

Despite the lack of evidence accounting for life within the Glass Sea, there is no logical reason why so much wealth accumulates on its seabed.

-An excerpt from The Mysterious Deep: A Comprehensive Understanding

No amount of elixir could drown out the wrongness of what I was doing. Every swipe of my oar, I risked her. When everything else in my life had gone to shit, my instincts had always been right. Right now, everything in my body was screaming to go back to Rose. Not to rely on my lame quartermaster, a shoddy pistol, and Billy to protect her.

If I could go back in time, I would have thrown her off my ship that first night in Pirate's Cove. I would have drunk myself nearly dead to drown out the need to keep her with me and sailed away only after giving James Allan the death he deserved. Some mistakes couldn't be undone. The worst part is I knew what I was doing. People were like books; when you learned to read them, you could predict what they would do next.

It's how I knew Oscar would bring his case to the crew. If I had any sense in me, I would have stopped him, but I'd spent an entire year trying to shake her, and the minute she fell onto my ship, I knew I wouldn't be able to let her go twice.

The Devil knew I tried to be better than my father. To make peace with the fact that she could never be mine. It was why I'd taken Anne into my bed, ignoring the fact that I could only stomach it because she looked like Rose. In the end, it never quieted the demon in me, and she died for it.

The first time the Gharaq hunted me down to demand retribution for her death, I hadn't argued. She was within her rights to kill me; I only asked for more time. That when my work was done, I would walk into the sea and allow her to take her justice. It was a request they gleefully denied when they wrapped the noose around my neck. If Oscar wasn't there to plead insanity on my behalf, to explain it was love of his sister that drove me to act, I would be bones on the seafloor right now.

I knew when I sought them out a second time, I wasn't coming back from their depths. The least I could do was give Rose the chance to find the treasure and buy her way out of a marriage. I went knowing she would live her days rich as hell and independent, but she had saved my life more than Oscar ever did.

The moment Anne saw her, she understood what I could never say. She released me from her wrath, but the noose still burned around my neck.

I rubbed at the burns that would never quite fade. A good reminder of the cost of obsession. It was a sickness that infected everything I touched. If Rose had any sense of self-preservation, she would point that pistol straight at my heart and pull the trigger. Instead, she fed my sickness, not knowing she was building her own funeral pyre. I felt my lip pull. She knew exactly what she was doing, and she just didn't care.

That was what made her even more dangerous than me.

A low rumbling sound came from below, and I stilled my oar, motioning everyone behind me to do the same. I may have told Rose I didn't believe in Jörmungandr, but that was a lie. I'd seen enough of the Mysterious Deep to know something brought these ships into these cursed waters. Last time I was here, I hadn't seen any sign of a beast or serpent, but the San José was a much smaller prize. Not worthy of notice to a creature that hoarded wealth.

The Maravilla, though, that was worth noticing. If there were such a thing as the Jörmungandr, it would be watching our every move right now.

When the bittersweet air hit my lungs and no further grumblings came from the abyss, I resumed rowing, my crew following suit. I raised the compass in my hand and watched the red arrow shift a fraction to the left. There. I held up my hand and no one moved a mere muscle than they needed to. I didn't have to tell them what lurked below them.

It was the scratching along the back of their necks that told them they were among the dead. As much as the Underworld ruled by Hades had ever existed. Few lived to tell the tale of what endured here. Much like Odysseus had been forced to face his ghosts below, so would we. The only question was whether anyone would live to tell our story.

One would. Because if she didn't, I would claw my way out of death's embrace to bring her back to the living.

Maybe I was closer to Orpheus than Odysseus, but I damn sure wouldn't look back if it meant she lived. Even if it was a trick and she wasn't following behind, I would have burned the earth to ash until I was in the Underworld once more and tried again. I would have kept trying until I was dust.

I lifted myself, slowly, and lowered one foot into the water that pricked at my skin with its otherness. It's frigid water, uninviting. While I strained to lower myself evenly, Val sloshed herself over the other side, spraying water with the force of her descent. I shot her a glare, but she only grinned at me.

She thrived on these moments. It was why I had picked her all those years ago. She was running fast enough from her demons that only when her life was on the edge of a precipice did she truly feel alive. It's why she joined my crew instead of living a life of comfort with her earnings. Too much comfort made for loud thoughts. Neither of us was made for that life.

I hissed as the water came up my chest. The lack of blood seeping into the water was a good sign that we hadn't landed on a wraith, though they tended to be further down. The rest of my crew sat with even breaths. They should have been terrified, but that was why we risked our lives for the elixir. They had their orders. Wait till either Val or I could confirm our heading was correct. If no one came back in ten minutes, return to the ship, where Oscar would take command and decide from there. The right answer would be to leave, and I advised him of such, but I knew he wouldn't. Not when turning around meant selling Rose's freedom.

I would have made the same choice.

Val held up three fingers and slowly put them down one by one. I swallowed the last of my air and followed her beneath the glass. Just as unnatural as the sky and surface, there were no murky depths or shapeless forms in the Glass Sea. Her crystal waters didn't have to pretend to be deadly; she never hid from what she was. The Maravilla was twice as big as the tales said. Her three masts stood high, unbroken and still proud. If it weren't for the gaping hole in her side, there would have been no accounting for her presence on the seabed. However, the jagged edges said that the rumors were true. She was done in by a creature of the Mysterious Deep. All souls aboard were lost.

It was everything I ever imagined it would be, and it was about fifty feet below the surface, which meant half the people in those dinghies would be useless. Most of them could only manage twenty to thirty feet. More concerning was the number of wraiths.

It was more than even the most generous of estimates we threw around. If I were forced to put a number on them, I would have said anywhere from four hundred to five hundred. Easily twice what we'd prepared for. They floated aimlessly, their track the length of the Maravilla, while some walked the sea floor.

They had the shape of the bodies they inhabited in life, but nothing else about them was remotely human. Their eyes were black pits that saw nothing, their lips eroded past their gums, showcasing rotten and missing teeth and black gums. Their noses were in various stages of decay, while the oldest among them had large gaping holes in the center of their face.

Undead. Attracted to emotion and gold, but cursed to survive even as their bodies decayed beneath the pressure of the ocean. I often wondered if their minds were intact. If they relived their lives while their bodies carried on. It would be a cruelty worse than immortality. No, if there was any kindness left in the world, their minds perished along with their souls.

I pointed to the surface, and Val nodded, following me back up. When we broke through, her grin was nearly manic.

"There are more than we ever imagined," she said.

"Try saying it like it's not a good thing," I said.

She wrinkled her nose in answer. At least someone was having fun. Never mind that the likelihood of our survival had lessened considerably.

"Send anyone who can't make the dive of at least fifty feet back. Otherwise, wait for Val or me to return. If we aren't back in ten minutes, you have your orders."

Inu nodded and turned to ensure they were carried out. I had complete faith in her capability, which meant there was no reason to linger.

"Ready to dance with the dead?" Val asked.

In answer, I took a low and long breath, focusing on using my stomach to facilitate the entry of air. Letting it out, I began again. I'd spent countless nights practicing the technique. It was how I survived listening to Rose when she touched herself. I counted my breaths, focusing them past my lungs and into my abdomen. It had been an agony unlike anything I'd ever known. The restraint needed to even be in the same room as her was worthy of a knighting, but when I knew she was chasing her own pleasure, it nearly stopped my heart. Knowing she wanted me to touch her, but was too damn stubborn to admit it. I had patience in spades, but Rose took years off my life in the last three months. I suppose that was what made her so addictive.

Another short breath followed by another. When I'd taken in as much as I could and my muscles were as relaxed as they were physically capable of, I let myself drift down into the sea. Movement a few feet away said that Val followed. My focus was on the damned below us. Avoiding them would be difficult, but not impossible. Depending on where the treasure was located inside the Maravilla, we would need to go down only a few at a time. Sinking lower, my ears filled with a pop, but I pinched my nose and blew out, relieving the pressure.

About thirty feet deep, the proximity of wraiths became more frequent. In only a few strokes of my arm, I could reach out and touch one. I was grateful for my inability to smell below the surface. A wraith two feet away turned its body toward me. Black and green teeth looked out from his eroded mouth. He must have been at least half a century into his torment because half his nose was missing.

I forced myself to move slowly despite the instinct in me that told me to swim faster and put as much distance in between me and it. The only way to make a dive like this was to conserve as much air as possible which meant slow, controlled movements. Anything else would result in a loss of time at the bottom if I even made it there.

Forty feet down, and there were wraiths every couple of feet. All my attention was on marking their locations. They didn't swim like many once theorized, but rather glided on an invisible track, making their movements unpredictable. The most I could hope for was that if I fucked up and touched one, it would awaken only to Val and I's emotions and not those on the surface. Second best would be those in the dinghies who were affected. The last scenario I refused to consider. I reminded myself that the Wraith was a good enough distance away, and they had the elixir that muted their emotions. It needed to be enough.

The next ten feet felt like years. Billy had been right to insist I take the second elixir. Several wraiths I passed turned toward me like they sensed me, but not enough to activate whatever blood thirst controlled them. The first time I dove down into the Glass Sea, the wraiths hadn't even registered my presence, but then again I had nothing back then. Only a twisted idea of justice.

Now I had more than I ever wanted for myself. There had never been a part of my story that included loving another person. I'd loved my mother and that ended with my kneeling at a half assed grave in the cold, wet earth. It was a pain that leeched any capability of love from me.

When Rose said she loved me as we both prepared for our last breaths, she fractured something inside me I hadn't known was there. The desire to love. What I felt for her was incomparable. For the first time in my life, something mattered as much as my need to make my father pay for his crimes. It eroded the clean-cut path I'd spent years planning. I would have gladly gone to my grave if it meant she had everything she wanted from life. What I felt for her—it was toxic and infused with the sickness I'd inherited from my father. It was possession and dominance. It was ownership. What I felt for her—I wasn't capable of love.

My feet hit the sandy floor with precision so as not to displace more sand than I had to. Whether it would set off the wraiths, I didn't know, but it was a chance I wasn't willing to take. All I had to do was stretch out my arm, and I would learn what they were made from because, from the way their skin rippled, I was sure it wasn't flesh and blood any longer. Part of me felt a momentary regret at not allowing Dilly to come. However, she could barely dive ten feet, and her enthusiasm was bordering on reckless.

In short, she was a liability.

The least I could do was report to her in detail about everything I encountered. I slid the information I collected to the back of my mind. What mattered right now was that I didn't touch anything except gold and that I made it to the surface again. The hole that opened up to the hull was three times my height, the width at least twelve feet. I stepped inside, and it was blissfully empty of the dead, but alive with a fortune I doubt anyone had seen the like of.

I glided further in and ran my hand through the gold coins littering the broken hull. They were heavy and thick in my hands, drifting down to lie with their brethren when I released them. There was movement behind me and I instinctively reached for my pistol that was now being worn by Rose. Luckily, it was Val who entered the hull, her eyes widening as she took in everything.

Chests on chests, some open and some closed. Diamonds, sapphires, emeralds, and amethysts gleamed from their final resting place. Crowns and jewelry alike made up a twenty-foot expanse of space. We were down about three and a half hours for the potion, which meant we needed to account for four and a half to get out of the sea. That left roughly three hours I was willing to spend hauling it all up.

More than enough time to ensure not one person on my crew wanted for a single shilling the rest of their lives. More than enough to see Rose old in a home of her choosing with as many cats as she wanted. Hopefully, when I delivered her safely to London, she would take the demon cat with her.

I looked over at Val, and she already had several necklaces draped around her neck, and coins bulged from her pockets. She raised her eyebrows and gestured to the treasure in dire need of looting.

For the first time, I let myself believe what I hoped would be true.

Today would be the day I solidified the name Captain Sebastian Flynn into infamy.

Chapter Thirty-Six
Dead Man Walking

Rose

The moment you show you know you've lost is the moment your opponent wins.

-An excerpt from The Mysterious Deep: A Comprehensive Understanding

"And you know, it sounds crazy, and one could hypothesize that it was waiting to strike, but you know what makes the passage so dangerous is the lack of land masses to break down the waves, so I was thinking, what if it wasn't preparing to sink us, but actually was breaking up the waves. I mean, I told you it was a crazy theory, but first there was Koinu, then the Kelpies, then the Gryndelow, and yes, they very much wanted to eat us, but none of this has been documented before. We are literally recording history. All we have are theories, so maybe we need to consider the impossible. It's the only-"

I was going to die—not death by Wraith, but death by Dilly and her talking. For the last ten minutes, all I had given her were apathetic responses and murmured agreements. Nothing would deter her from her theories. It didn't matter how long I leaned upon the railing and stared out to the still sea; she never wavered in her convictions to burn a hole in my ears. Even Blackbeard gave up five minutes in and ran below deck.

I glanced over and fought a smile. She was more Oscar's twin in that moment than I was, foot bound and a stick in her hands, the ship supporting her weight with her back to it. Her freckles stood out on her tanned skin, while her wild curls bounced with every swing of her hand, which she used to drive her point home on occasion.

"What else could it mean? That has to be it, right?" she asked.

I nodded firmly. "I agree. It's the only solution."

Her smile could have tamed a damn grindylow. It was bright and enthusiastic and everything she was.

"My only concern is what they will say when I—"

I placed my hands on her shoulders and shook her gently.

"I love you. You are easily one of my favorite people in the world, but I am going to go insane if I don't hear myself think." I said.

Her smile faltered, and I hated myself. I should have just stayed and listened, but it had been two hours since Bash left, and I couldn't stare in the direction they had gone another second more.

"Okay," Dilly said, grabbing my hand as I made to step away. "He's coming back, you know. He always does."

My chest tightened.

"I know."

I wish I believed those words. Even with the elixir, I was finding it harder to take a full breath the longer they were gone.

I sidestepped several large chests filled with gold and jewels. As Inu and several others pulled up another chest via the rope system they had created, I couldn't help but feel the greedier we were, the more we risked. I had no idea the worth before us, but I knew every piece was one Bash and Val went back down for.

"When are they going to be done?" I asked, folding my arms over my stomach to ward off the chill in the air.

Inu turned, sweat on her brow as she pulled in sync with the other two on either side of her.

I might have imagined it or it was the elixir's affect, but her face softened a fraction. Very unlike her so probably delusion on my part.

"Another hour. Some of the wraiths are following us, so it's making it safer for them each time they go down. It's almost over," she said.

I stared open-mouthed at her, knowing she must have traded places with a wraith while she was out there because that was—that was almost kindness in her words.

"Aren't you supposed to be counseling us against dancing with death and issuing creepy warnings?" I asked.

The slightest, most imperceptible pull at the corner of her lips was the most unsettling thing I had ever witnessed. All I knew was that if I was going to spend more time with her, I would be risking life and limb for more of that elixir.

Not willing to risk unleashing her normal personality, I meandered down to the hull, its path lit by hanging lanterns that seemed wrong without their normal sway. No ship was meant to be this still. It only increased the hum of nerves that were gaining strength. My body has its own countdown for how much time till we linger past our welcome.

The hull was mostly abandoned. What was left of our crew were either hauling up treasure from the bottom of the sea or onto the ship. Which was probably why I found myself opening up the door of the brig and stepping through it. My emotions too stamped down to tell me it was a bad idea. Two iron cages sat at the end of the wooded hall, lit by small flames.

"I don't hear shouting from up above, and you look to be all in one piece, which means entertainment is lacking up top," Charlie said.

He sat on the floor, resting his head up against the bars that separated him from his brother, who was sound asleep. He had grown a decent scruff since being thrown in here. If I were being honest, I knew why I had come.

I stepped in front of his cage, a few feet back. He didn't bother moving towards me. Instead, he had his arms stretched out over his bent knees, flipping a chicken bone in his hands. Probably the most entertainment he had in days.

"Did you know what your brother was doing?" I asked.

Charlie flipped the bone and glanced at his brother whose only sign of life was the steady rise and fall of his chest. I had considered coming down here more times than I could count. There had been something in Charlie that I instinctively liked. Maybe it was because he was the antithesis to his brother or maybe it was poor judgment, either way I needed to know.

"No," he said after an eternity. "I should have though. He's always been impulsive. Part of me knew he wouldn't do well on a ship, but times are hard, and we needed the money. I thought if I watched out for him, I wouldn't end up in a brig. Joke's on me, I guess."

I bit my lip, debating. My urge to know more than the risk.

"He wanted to sell me to a man I hate," I said.

Charlie nodded slowly. "Yeah, he's always been only able to see one step ahead and not the whole map."

"Is he drugged?" I asked, eyeing the slumped-over feen.

Charlie chuckled and slowly stood, brushing dust off his day-old pants.

"Nah, the elixir just calmed him enough that he got his first sleep in a few days. He's been like that ever since we were kids. Would go days without sleep, but feel like he was the king of the world, only to crash like this for a week."

I didn't know what to say. The last thing I wanted to do was humanize someone who murdered in cold blood.

"He killed Barnacles," I whispered.

Charlie didn't say anything as he crossed the distance of the cell and wrapped his hands lightly around his cage. His eyes were soft and the small smile he wore was tired.

"Since it's just us here, I think we both know how important family is. Where is the line for what you would do for your family? You were willing to travel across the world and risk the lives of strangers all to save your family. Amos may be short-sighted and miss the mark half the time, but our mother is in a really bad situation. When he was given the chance, he thought one rich girl would live with a man she hates, but our mom will finally be free to be happy. Do you blame him?"

Not having full rein of my emotions was as dangerous as Emille had said it was, because even though I didn't want to, I understood. I had been willing to risk more than one life, and even if I hadn't realized the cost when I concocted my plan, I never tried to stop it once I knew. Those people who died in the passage died for my callousness. Yes, Bash and

Oscar were complicit, but maybe the line between right and wrong was written in some book. Instead, it was written by the one outside the cage.

"What is your mother's name?" I asked.

"Sarah Clark," he said.

"Where does she live?"

He met my gaze for several minutes, the sound of his brother's gentle snores the only thing between us.

"Norfolk, Virginia," he answered.

"Okay," I said. "When all this is done, I'll send her enough money that she can choose for herself."

His smile was haunted, sad almost.

"Because we won't be alive to give it to her, right?" he said.

I honestly didn't know. Maybe Bash had a plan for them, but right now, all we knew was we needed to get in and out of the Glass Sea.

"It's all right, sweetheart. We know too much. Liabilities, if you would," he said.

Regret, faint and just a whisper, coiled inside my stomach. It would hurt like hell when the elixir wore off.

"I'll talk to him," I promised.

Charlie gave me a reassuring smile and settled back into his spot against the door. Resuming his spinning and tossing of the bone. When he raised his eyes to mine, we both knew the truth.

He was a dead man walking.

"Flynn's a lot of things, but stupid isn't one of them," he said.

I fought for the words to say, but false placations weren't my specialty. They always seemed like their own kind of cruelty.

"I'm sor—" My words were stolen by the worst sounds I could have imagined.

Guns went off one after another, followed by shouting.

"Guess we are all on the same boat after all," Charlie said.

Chapter Thirty-Seven
To Bear Witness

Rose

One must consider that the gods and mythology of previous civilizations were rooted in truth. After all, to the people of Mallorca, the Aloja are goddesses. There is no doubt that sea witches are able to manipulate time and space in ways humanity cannot begin to fathom. Therefore, we must conclude that the gods of old could have existed.

—An excerpt from The Mysterious Deep: A Comprehensive Understanding

The blood roared in my ears as I ran upstairs, but it wasn't with shaking hands or a racing heart as it should have been. Beneath the surface, fear that was more like terror bubbled, but I was in control. What would it be like to die, but not feel the fear that should accompany it?

More shots fired, and I emerged to find a pink sky above, but all of our remaining crew leaning over the stern of the ship.

"Someone grab the harpoons!" Oscar shouted as he fired a shot over the edge.

"It ain't doing shit to them!" Billy yelled in between reloading.

"Because they are already dead," Inu answered.

They all spoke calmly despite the way they fired and reloaded without pausing to breathe. Someone ran by me and into the hull, but it was hard to make my feet move.

"Bash," I whispered.

"I've got one coming over!" Dilly shouted, hobbling back with one good leg while she gripped her pistol.

She fell after only a few paces and began crawling away, but everyone was too busy with their own fights, and the thing that climbed over the rail was worse than anything I could have imagined. Its mouth was long eroded, and even its teeth were mostly black, some hanging on by unnatural threads. Its black eyes were locked on Dilly, and somewhere my emotions screamed. Not Dilly.

With a steady hand and a steady heart, I took ten steps forward and aimed Bash's pistol at the creature's head. It fell backward with a squishing sound that reminded me of the last of the jelly being squeezed onto Mama's favorite cake.

As if it had been merely inconvenienced by the hole in its head, it began to push itself up on languid arms. A sickly green liquid oozed from where I had shot it. It had given Dilly enough time to reload, and she leveled out her pistol and shot right at the creature's stomach. It paused its approach for a second, and more green spilled from its abdomen. The smell of rotting eggs and a putrid salted sea air mixed to make my stomach roll.

I reloaded again and shot it in the right shoulder, by now it created a small puddle where it stepped, it's rippling skin sagging a little more.

"You can drain them," Dilly murmured when I reached her.

I wrapped my arms around her from behind and began pulling her back, but deflating body or not, the corpse was quicker. I should have been terrified.

"Oscar!" I yelled.

He turned and raised his pistol, but we were too far. Even if his shot was true, it wouldn't be enough. A thick chalky substance ran from its open mouth, landing two feet from Dilly's feet like it was drooling. Excited for its meal.

We had only made it a few feet at best, but the creature fell to its knees and began crawling towards Dilly, more of its drool landing in unnaturally large heaps that fizzed and bubbled where they landed.

"Rose!" Dilly yelled.

"I'm trying!" I panted.

God, she was heavy. It wasn't going to be enough. Even when Oscar's shot hit it, I knew he might have time to get to me, but not Dilly.

The thing hovered over Dilly, its mouth opening with an unhinged jaw that reminded me of a snake.

I let out a frustrated grunt, but just as I was sure I was about to lose my best friend, the creature stopped moving, and a giant spear rammed through its head. I should have had some sort of reaction, but I just stared as it careened backward and fought to combat the weight of the spear with the need to consume anything.

A heartbeat later, I watched as Charlie lifted the end of the spear, taking the creature with it, and slammed it into the plank till the spear was standing straight in the sky. The creature fought to gain purchase and right itself, but its deflating head was too firmly at the center of the weapon.

Charlie wiped his hands off and reached out a hand to Dilly and then me, giving me a broad smile that held more life than it had a minute ago.

"Guess you made the right choice letting me out," he said.

I nodded like that was the answer to everything.

"Yeah," I whispered.

"If we live through this, you're going right back in the brig, Clark!" Oscar yelled.

His declaration was short-lived, as he turned to fire another shot at a wraith that had breached the ship. The shot was a good one, and it flung the wraith back into the sea—a momentary lapse from the onslaught.

"You called me Rose," I whispered, my mind finally catching up.

Dilly smiled and shook off her pants that had small holes where the creature's drool had hit.

"I've known you since Brazil. You acted strangely after I mentioned it would be nice to have someone of your genetic makeup test my theory. Then that night on the beach, when you and Oscar went from laughing to fighting, I thought how you two reminded me of siblings," she said.

I stared at her. "And you didn't say anything?"

She shrugged and reloaded her pistol.

"Not my secret to tell, but I wouldn't have cared either way. I would have kept it for you the whole time," she said like it was nothing.

I wished I had my emotions because what swelled beneath the surface was something rare and beautiful.

I nearly knocked her over as I threw my arms around her and pressed a kiss to her cheek.

"The world would be better if there were more Cordelia Shaws," I said.

"Yes, but then you wouldn't appreciate me quite so much," she said. "Anyways, now that

you know I know, if we live through this, I would very much enjoy learning how you ended up here. I've been dying of curiosity."

I aimed my pistol at a breaching wraith and fired.

"If we survive this, I'll tell you anything you want to know," I said.

More harpoons were brought from below deck and were being handed out like an invitation to a ball. I took one and placed Bash's pistol back in the holster, hoping nothing got close enough to me that I would need it.

"Undo the sails!" Oscar ordered.

Even in the mist and haze of elixir, my blood ran cold. No. The answer was no.

I ran up to him and speared an approaching wraith, sending it over the edge, though its body weighed down my arms as I tried to pull the spear back.

"Don't you dare think about leaving him, Oscar Bailey," I said.

Oscar saw my struggle and gripped the pole and leveraged his weight against the ship's railing and pulled.

"I don't want to leave him any more than you do, but these are his orders, Rose. If we get overrun, we flee. Doesn't matter who is in the water," Oscar said, grunting as the spear finally gave way.

"It *does* matter who is in the water. I'm not leaving him behind," I said.

Oscar's eyes bore into mine, assessing, and I could see the practicality winning out before my eyes.

"What if it was Inu?" I asked.

"Then I would haunt him for all of his life as a vengeful spirit for risking himself for me," Inu said.

With a precision that was more akin to the wind than human, Inu slashed her sword across the middle of a wraith, and it slid apart in a slow, grotesque squelch. Boiling, slimy, green emerged from its corpse, emptied of black water and seaweed.

Emotions or not, the smell and contents were too much, and I leaned over and vomited right onto Oscar's boots. He stepped away and placed his hands on my shoulders, forcing my gaze, but I refused. Acid scorching my throat and fear rising despite the barrier, I wouldn't look at him.

"He asked me to make sure you got out safe. His life was always a necessary evil destined for the noose," he said.

I choked back emotion that shouldn't exist. "You sound as stupid as he does."

"That's because he told me to tell you if this happened," Oscar said. "He said to tell you that when you are content and sick of living with more white than gray hairs and at least nineteen cats, he will come find you for the next life and you'll try again."

My eyes stung with tears that had no business being there. I didn't want white or gray hairs if it meant Bash couldn't tease me about them. There weren't enough cats in the world that could soothe the loss of him. For as smart as Sebastian Flynn was, he was an idiot if he thought I was going to be soothed by romantic lamentations.

"Fuck that," I said.

I stalked toward where two sailors were climbing the rigging, pulled out Bash's pistol, and fired right between them, nearly hitting one's hand, which was undoing the tied rope. It was a fluke of a shot and not at all what I meant to hit, but it sent my point home more than I could have hoped.

"If either of you undo another centimeter of that rope, I'll shoot you right there," I yelled.

They shared a silent conversation weighing the what-ifs against my ability to not miss a second time. What they should have been considering was that at that moment, I didn't have a line. Not one single line I wasn't willing to cross to see Bash back on this ship.

"They are swarming for her; she burned up the elixir!" Billy called.

I chanced a glance at the stern of the ship and realized that if it weren't for Inu and her sword that moved like lightning, severing heads and limbs alike, I would have been dead several times over. They were coming faster than before, and it was my fault. However, one could have made the argument that it was Oscar's fault for abandoning Bash.

Billy speared two wraiths at one time and lifted his pistol to fire a shot to one's temple which only slowed it down. The two on the spear fought to pull themselves off. It was clear that the only permanent solution was Inu's sword. Several others realized it and before long everyone had a sword and was hacking at the wraiths, except for Dilly and Oscar who stayed back with their injuries, pistols were the only options they had.

The ship lurched beneath us, and my error came screaming into crystal clear view. I looked up, and one sail had unfurled. Fuck.

Loading the pistol, I aimed at the slower sailor and missed. My bullet went right through the sail, which opened two heartbeats later.

Oh god.

No.

I wasn't leaving him. That was the line that I wouldn't cross. Fear squeezed at my throat and clenched my heart till it was aching. I didn't want gray hairs, and I didn't want cats. I wanted my pirate captain.

"Emille, she needs more elixir," Oscar said in between shots.

The Doctor ripped his sword from a wraith's stomach and shook his head.

"None left."

"Then we need to put as much distance between us and the wraiths as possible. Dilly, take the helm!" Oscar ordered.

How quickly he replaced the man he called a friend. We were at a slow drift now, but soon the other sails would open, and I would miss my opportunity. At least if Oscar made it out, he could save our family, but for me, this was it. I left the Glass Sea with Bash or not at all.

I loaded my pistol and ran for the edge of the ship where the ladder leading to the dinghy was left forgotten. The Wraith could leave for all I cared, but I would take the dinghy and die trying.

"Rose! Don't you fucking dare! They will swarm you in an instant!" Oscar screamed.

I could feel too many eyes on me, calculating. It was now or never. I lifted my leg over the side, but the smell of decay and death flooded my nose as a wraith climbed up the ladder that was supposed to be my escape. Only a few feet from the top, I settled back onto the ship and held out my pistol. The moment the creature's head surfaced, I fired.

Smoke and the bite of gunpowder clouded my eyes as I realized it had misfired. It had misfired and the creature was falling overboard with the loudest grunt I had ever heard. That the undead were even capable of it was unsettling.

"Damn, Princess, you were really going to shoot us," Val said, swinging her leg over.

I stared at her, my mind not processing the image before me fast enough to make sense. Val stood and grabbed the wraith on the ground, but she was covered in the green and black seaweed that oozed slime over her skin. Like she was wearing the inside of a wraith.

"Are you just going to stand there or help me get him up. He needs to get to Emille." Val said.

The wraith needed Emille?

"Bash!" Oscar yelled.

The world rushed around me like it was fast-forwarding, whereas it had been in slow motion. I squinted my eyes and sure enough, the wraith I had nearly blown its head off was the man I was willing to die to save. My heart stuttered in my chest, and I fell to my knees, peeling off the decaying seaweed and wiping at the unnatural substance all over his face. His eyes rolled, but his hand clenched around my forearm, his grip iron-like, as if he put all his strength into that one gesture.

"Why the fuck are we still here?" he asked.

Emille crouched on the other side of him and counted to three. Val shouldering the other half of him. He let go of me with a cry of pain that broke my heart into a thousand pieces. I fought against the fear that held me to the deckboards, paralyzing me. He was alive. He was on the boat. We could leave.

Why couldn't I move then?

"What happened?" Emille asked.

"Matthias didn't see when one had come up behind him on our last dive. It ripped into his neck, and that was it. We barely made it out. They kept swarming the dinghy, but we realized if we covered ourselves in whatever was inside them, it threw them off enough that we could put some distance between us. We would have been fine, but Flynn tried to reach for Theo, and a wraith took a chunk out of his arm. I told him Theo had already been bitten, but he didn't listen."

I had never heard Val's speech, rushed and breathless. I recognized its cadence, and it filled my stomach with rocks. She was afraid.

"Someone take over for Dilly and take her and Flynn down below," Oscar ordered. "John, give us at least six more knots if you want to survive."

The deck was kept at bay by Inu and the rest of the crew wielding their swords, but the wraiths reminded me of ants, persistent and many. So be it.

I followed Val and Emille as they hauled Bash down to the hull. I felt my chest convulse when they laid him down on one of the dinner tables, and he cried out once more, his deep voice twisted with pain.

The world moved around me, and all I could do was witness it.

Witness as Emille bundled up Bash's sleeve to reveal a putrid, black wound on his hands that was moving up his arm as we bore witness. The sickly green that wrapped around his arm, turning black as it eroded everything beneath.

"It's spreading fast," Emille said, mouth open.

Dilly hobbled down the steps, and Emille raised his eyes to her, but there was defeat written into the words he spoke.

"What can be done for a bite?" Emille asked her.

Dilly shook her curls, tears falling down her freckled cheeks.

"I don't know," she whispered. "No one's ever survived it."

"Cut it off," Bash said through gritted teeth.

"Bash," Emille said.

"I'm dead if it spreads, so cut it off and see what happens. If it keeps spreading, put a bullet through my head. That's an order, Emille."

"Do it," Val said, gripping Bash's good hand in hers.

Emille's lips twisted like he was fighting back nausea, but he released the sword at his side and wiped off the black and green from it with his shirt, all the while clenching his jaw hard enough that the muscles in his cheeks twitched.

"What is happening?" I breathed.

There was commotion up on deck, but all I could see was Val handing Bash a stick she found from god knew where and him slamming it into his mouth while Emille ran his sword through the flame of a lantern.

"Rose, are you all right?" Dilly asked.

Absolutely not. They were really going to do this.

"Val, hold his legs down. Rose, I'm sorry to ask you, but I need you to help hold him." Emille said.

I nodded and moved like it was only a dream over to him. Bash reached up and ran a hand over my cheek that came away wet with tears I hadn't realized I shed. His eyes were strained, and his face was pale. He was in more pain than he was showing. Emille wrapped a belt around his elbow, and Flynn grunted as it tightened.

"I'm sorry," I whispered.

He nodded once and lay his head back on the table, closing his eyes.

"On my count," Emille said.

I lay my body over his chest, burying my face in his neck. His hand threaded through my hair as we waited for Emille.

"One, two, three," Emille said.

The sound of the sword meeting flesh was a sickening crunch, and something that, if I lived to be an old woman, I would hear in my nightmares. Bash's hand tightened in my hair, holding me against his chest as he screamed around the stick in his mouth. Tears flowed like they would never stop from my eyes. Three more hacks of the sword and the warm splatter of blood over my head, it was done.

Bash's grip on me went limp, and I lifted my head to see his head fall back and his eyes closed. For the briefest of seconds, I considered life without him now that I knew him. Life used to be enough with the love of my family and the comforts of wealth. Balls were entertaining, and I went to sleep each night knowing what tomorrow held. It now sounded like torture. That itching in my foot had subsided a few days in the ocean, and staring at Bash, I understood why.

This was where I belonged. I didn't long for anything because I was living it.

"He's alright, just passed out," Emille said. "Val, hand me the rum."

She did as he asked, and he poured it over the awful, mangled mess of blood and insides never meant to be seen that was Bash's left arm.

"It's still decaying," Dilly murmured.

My heart fell to the bottom of my stomach. I wouldn't let them put a bullet in his head. No matter what his request, he was going to live. Damn him for underestimating just how stubborn I could be.

I turned to Emille to say just that, but realized he was looking at Bash's severed arm lying on the floor where Dilly was crouched over it. The black and green mixed together until the entire arm became a deflated mass of decay.

"Emille!" Oscar screamed from above.

There was one time when we were eight that we were playing outside in the gardens. Oliver was proving that he was stronger than us because at twelve, he had developed far more muscles. He climbed a cherry blossom tree that had just gone into bloom, but his leg slipped. He fell to the earth with a thud, and when he sat up, there was blood and the distinct shape of a bone sticking out of his arm. Oscar had covered my eyes and screamed for our parents. Fear in every syllable.

That is what I heard in his cry for Emille. Eight years old, and sure death was imminent.

Emille grabbed his sword and ran. The worst of Bash's injury done for. Val followed close behind him, sword at the ready.

I met Dilly's eyes, and she nodded.

"I'll stay with him. Go."

There was something resigned about the way she said it. Like she had given it all to fate and was now meant to witness.

"I'm scared," I whispered.

"Me too," she answered.

As if that was enough, I pressed a kiss to Bash's forehead and ran up the stairs, pistol in hand. Maybe there was nothing left to do, but we could at least die trying. Maybe when we were all wraiths, we would forget who we had been and who we had loved.

When I made it to the deck, though, it wasn't pink skies that greeted me, but a perfect baby blue painted with the fluffiest, whitest clouds I had ever witnessed. The sun's rays caressed my skin like the warmest welcome. Rolling waves gently carried the Wraith along.

We made it.

The Glass Sea, its death, and its mysteries behind us. We survived. Lived the impossible.

"Aye, it'll be fine, I've had worse."

I jerked my gaze to the sound of Billy's labored words. Breaths coming in too fast.

"Once I had a piranha bite through my arse, that hurt worse than this," he said.

No.

I searched the deck and found countless bodies in various stages of decay and seaweed mixed with rot covering the ship, but what really mattered was my brother and Emille leaning over Billy's supine form.

I walked slowly and Inu, who stood with her hand on her sword sheathed at her side, shook her head slowly. A warning meant to be a kindness.

I bit my lip and, on shaking legs, peered over my brother's shoulder and saw what shouldn't have been. Billy's shirt had been lifted to show his rounded stomach, where blackish green had eaten through several inches and rotten organs had pulled outside his body. The smell was horrifying.

"Aye, that bad, huh, Hellcat?" he said with a chuckle.

"Billy, I'm—" I said.

"Nah, don't go saying things you don't mean just because I'm headed for the locker," he said.

"Billy, there's nothing I can do," Emille said, gently.

"Ain't gotta be no fancy doctor to know that," Billy said. "Give me a second with the Hellcat, and then you put a bullet in my head. If I turn into a wraith, I want Inu to slice me in half because she's better than all you combined with that thing."

Inu nodded like she was agreeing to Sunday dinner.

Emille squeezed Billy's hand and said words I was too scared to hear. Oscar leaned over Billy as he whispered in his ear, nodding and affirming him. When he was through, Oscar held out his hand to me, and I knelt next to them. Oscar pressed a kiss to my forehead and wiped at errant tears as he stood, leaving just Billy and me.

Wasn't it just yesterday I had hit him with an oar while he laughed himself silly? His eyes were glassy, and his breath was coming in uneven, labored gasps.

"This is going to hurt him," he said. "He'll pretend he's fine, but you and I both know the path he's set on. He'll walk twice as fast when he realizes I'm gone."

He coughed and black pulled at the corner of his lips, vomit rose at the back of my throat from the stench of it, but I held onto Billy's hand and waited for him to say what he needed to.

"Don't let him," he gasped. "Tell him I loved him more than a son. That giving him that bread was the best thing I ever did with my life."

I choked back the sob trapped in my chest, but nodded, trying to memorize the words.

"I can't save him from himself anymore, but you can," he said, each word more strained.

"I promise," I whispered.

Billy nodded and went into a coughing fit; this time, the black blood pooled in his mouth, and he choked. I tried to sit him up to get it out, but it wouldn't stop coming. Oh god, he was choking on his own blood.

"Billy," I tried.

The clear shot of a pistol rang out, and more blood spattered over my face, but Billy's head fell back with a gentle thump while his struggling stopped. His chest no longer fighting to lift and fall. Rot and gunpowder mixed in the salty air.

I raised my eyes and found Bash several feet away with the smoking pistol in his hand, blood dripping from his mangled arm, still with the belt tied around it. His eyes were glazed over, but he tossed the empty pistol to the floor and turned, walking away from the only father he had truly known.

We were alive, but the cost was higher than any of us had been willing to pay.

Chapter Thirty-Eight
A Vengeful God

Rose

In 1705, an ambitious Mysteriologist named Fredrick Schmidt theorized that certain creatures of the deep could be tamed. He sought to commune with the Nix, creatures similar to the mermaids found around the world. When the nix refused to answer his questions on the subject, he rejected Mysteriology and its principles. He is notable for creating a shipping line entirely devoted to hunting the creatures of the deep for the purpose of dissection. He is a disgrace to the pursuit of Mysteriology.

–An excerpt from The Mysterious Deep: A Comprehensive Understanding

There was something terribly tragic about a victory in the wake of loss. It tainted everything it touched, coating happiness with oil that dripped and ran over every surface. So it was for the Sea Wraith despite the wealth of treasure in her hull. Out of the eighty we started with, twenty-two survived.

Fifty-eight souls condemned to the sea. With only twenty people, given that Charlie and Amos were back in the brig, the wealth each of us had claimed was more than anyone could have imagined. We were individually wealthier than the Queen of England, though no one would have known between the state of our ship and the downturn of every eye.

I walked around the deck of the Wraith and thanked the powers that be that the passage was calm. As if it too knew we had given all we had to give and took mercy on us. One of our masts was snapped in half, two giant holes leaked on either side of our hull, patched up enough that we wouldn't sink, but we were racing the clock on how much the Wraith could take.

A few sailors meandered about their duties, but their hearts weren't in it. Exhaustion that couldn't be slept away, clinging to them. Even Dilly sat with her back to the bow of the ship, telescope in hand.

"No sight of Koinu yet?" I asked.

She shook her head.

"How's your leg?" I asked.

She shrugged. "Emille says it will take at least two months to heal. You know, sometimes I wonder if I wouldn't have gone out in the storm and broken it, that I have been more helpful and could have saved him."

"You would have been in the hull with Bash," I said.

She shrugged. "Maybe."

Silence ticked back, but we were both silently playing the what-if game. If I hadn't delayed our leaving, if I had been more helpful, if, if, if. No amount of time spent torturing ourselves brought Billy back, but still, we persisted.

"How's the captain?" she asked.

Unbearable. Angry. Heartbroken.

"As well as any of us," I said.

Dilly nodded slowly. "I love the sea. More than anything in the world, the sea is my home. I feel more myself on the water than I ever have on land, but all I want is to get as far from the ocean as I can."

It was a sentiment I wondered if Bash shared, only switching the ocean for me. It had only been a day, and I knew he needed time, but every time he looked at me, I saw what he wouldn't say. If I hadn't delayed them, Billy would still be alive. It didn't matter that Bash and Val would have been dead instead.

"I hope it doesn't always feel like this," I said, crossing my arms over my stomach.

"Me too." Dilly sighed. "I keep wondering what Billy would say if he were here. Probably something about no two scars healing the same way."

I smiled. "And then go into a twenty-minute performance about how he got the scar on his leg from a Kraken that he bested with one arm."

Dilly chuckled, and it felt like Billy was smiling somewhere.

"While drunk," she said.

"Oh, absolutely." I laughed.

The humor melted, and we were forced to consider that we would never hear another one of his stories.

"The world feels a little darker," she said.

"I think some people are like that. They take up so much space and joy that when they are gone, they leave a giant hole that can never be filled," I said.

She nodded and wiped at her tears.

"Where do we go from here?" she asked.

I shrugged, "We think 'what would Billy do' and then probably not do it. It's a fifty-fifty shot."

Her smile was as broken as we all were. "I think he would like that."

"Me too," I said.

Reaching over, I wrapped my arm around her and pulled her into me, pressing a kiss to her forehead. She gave a shaky breath and rested her head on my shoulder.

"I'm glad you're my friend," she said.

"And you mine," I answered.

We sat like that for a long time before her need to search for Koinu took over, and my need for him outweighed what I would see in his eyes. It didn't take long to find him at the stern of the ship, his Captain's coat swaying in the wind, left sleeve clipped up. With his sword and pistol at his sides and his hair being tossed by the wind, he was more a painting than I had ever seen. I squinted my eyes, memorizing.

One day, I would put paint to canvas and recreate this very image.

"Grief has the power to weigh down even the mightiest sword," Inu said, coming up behind me.

Of course, I hadn't heard her coming, but I didn't chastise her. I owed her too much. Not only was she the reason we all escaped, but she also saved Oscar's life when he was trying to protect me. We were both here because of her.

"I wish I could take it from him," I whispered.

"Our battles are our own, all we can do is bear witness," she said.

I turned my head to her and saw fresh scars over her neck and arms, but she was mostly unharmed. Her long black hair gently flowed in the wind. She was truly beautiful.

"Thank you, Inu," I said.

I don't think there was anything I could have said that would have surprised her more. Her eyes widened a fraction before she regained control.

"For saving us, for saving Oscar, and for loving my brother," I said.

Her shoulders rose and fell with what would have been a sigh from anyone else.

"None of that requires thanks," she said.

"But I give it all the same," I said. "And if you ever want to share your story with me, I would be honored."

Her jaw tightened, and she gave a slight bow of her head before twisting on her heels and walking away.

I took two steps forward.

"You've forgiven her for her crimes?" Bash asked without turning.

"How can you hear everything?" I asked, sliding in next to him, but careful not to touch him.

"A necessary skill," he answered.

I studied his face and the stubble that had already begun to grow despite his recent shave. His eyes were more gray than blue, mirroring the storm within him.

"How long before we break through the pass?" I asked.

"Not long," he answered.

That was his way, a few words, like he couldn't stomach more than that. Not to mention that he hadn't slept. In the night, I woke every few hours with nightmares that were all set in reality, but he refused to come to bed. A few times I found him writing at his desk, once staring out at the sea from the back window, and a third time he was nowhere to be seen. Oscar told me he needed time to process, but it felt more than that.

Maybe that was just my privilege and immaturity speaking. I knew it was selfish, but I just wanted him to look me in the eyes and tell me he still cared about me. That he didn't regret me.

"Bash," I whispered.

He gave a small hmm as he continued his stare out to sea. If constant vigilance could revive the dead, then Billy would have been laughing and telling us what a sad mop of pirates we were.

"Do you want me to move to the crew's bunks? I don't mind. I know you need space and time, and if in the end you can't forgive me, I can accept that. I don't regret giving you more time, and I'm sorry for that. I know what that cost, and even if the cost is how you feel about me, then I still don't regret it. I can't regret that you are alive. I won't. I—"

He turned to me and raised his right hand to wipe at tears that seemed to fall more lately than they ever had, like they were making up for the time when the elixir stifled them. His eyes bore into me, and I knew I was as selfish as James always said I was. I should have stood silently and borne witness like Inu said, but instead, I had said too much just to get him to see me.

"You think how I feel about you has changed?" he asked, it felt like anger simmering beneath the words.

Suddenly, I wasn't sure about anything other than I was a very silly woman who did very stupid things.

"I just—if I hadn't delayed us, Billy would be alive and you wouldn't be grieving, and you told Oscar to go the minute they swarmed, and I ignored your orders. Not to mention, this was all my idea in the first place. I was stupid and naive and didn't see the price, and I know I told you I love you, and that wasn't fair because, of course, you don't feel that way, and that's all right, but now things are awkward and—"

His eyes held invisible smoke, and his lips curled back in irritation. He was very much the Pirate Captain of the Sea Wraith. His hand tightened around my neck, and though I could never fear him, my heart stuttered in my chest with uncertainty.

"For the love of the seas, stop talking and breathe for one minute, Rose," he ordered.

I wanted to obey, but the impulses in me were much louder than my want. I opened my mouth, but he covered my mouth with his, and I fell into him because, god, I didn't think I would get this again. Even if this was goodbye, I wanted to remember it.

His tongue slid over mine, and it was desperation and claiming, the chaotic sea we had always been. His hand was tight around my neck, and I remembered how he used to place his other hand on the small of my back, pulling me into him. I wondered if he remembered, too, because he let out a frustrated groan against my lips.

That was okay, though, because I knew the steps to this dance. I pressed my body against his, and he deepened the kiss. It was intoxicating, and when he finally released my lips, I could feel the ghost of them still on mine.

"I didn't tell you I love you because I am incapable of something as pure as that. What I feel for you is singular to me. You are more essential to me than the air in my lungs. You think I am mad at you for staying? I am furious."

There it was. It felt just like I thought it would. Like a knife to the chest. I stepped back, unhappy with the answer I forced from him, but he pulled me back.

"Listen to me," he ordered. "I am furious that you risked your life for mine because there is a world out there for you without me, but there is nothing for me without you. What you did was impulsive and incredibly stupid, but not because of what it cost, but because of what it almost cost. If you had died—" he shuddered.

The tears came faster, and it blurred my vision. "I'm sorry."

He wrapped his arm around me and pressed a kiss on my forehead before setting his chin on top of my head.

"I don't know how to lose Billy, it's going to hurt for whatever days I have left, but I would be worse than dead if it had been you. So no, I am not allowing you to sleep anywhere other than my bed because I am a weak man. I doubt I would even let you go if you asked it of me. That's not love, Rose. If you had any sense at all, you would put as much distance between me and my ship as you could."

"Good thing I don't have any at all." I sniffled.

His chest moved with what might have been a ghost of a chuckle.

"I think maybe you're wrong about that not being love, though. I don't think love has a line, and that's not insanity. It just is," I said.

"The end of the pass is coming up, Captain," someone yelled.

With only twenty-two people alive on this ship, I should probably make an effort to learn their names.

Bash breathed me in, and even when he released me, his hand stayed on my back. I pressed my side into him, needing to feel that he was real. We watched the choppy waves settle ahead of us and give way to a lighter blue that gently rolled over each other like a silent symphony.

Oscar came to my other side and let loose a long breath.

"We really did it," he said, "I don't know if I really believed we would."

Bash grunted, and it sounded like agreement.

We were all so tired, but soon we could begin to heal.

"Ships up ahead, Captain!" The lookout in the crow's nest shouted.

I might not have thought anything of another ship or two on the sea, except both Bash and Oscar stiffened beside me.

"What?" I asked, looking between them.

They ignored me and engaged in a very annoying silent conversation over my head.

"We don't have enough to man the cannons. Even against one, the Wraith couldn't take it," Oscar said.

"Get Emille and bring up Amos and Charlie," Bash ordered.

Oscar spared a second to stare at me, his eyes flashing with unease.

"Go," Bash said.

He turned to me and cupped my face with his hand, "I should have prepared for this and I'm sorry that I didn't."

Before I could ask him what he meant, he wrapped his hand around mine and dragged me across the ship and into his cabin.

"Bash, what—"

He began pulling at the bed, and when his grip in his hand failed, he let out a frustrated cry that was tragic in its own right. I went and started pulling alongside him and when there was about a one foot gap between the bed and the wall he let go and went to the' other side, kneeling.

I stared as he lifted up a floorboard and looked up at me.

"Please don't argue, Rosamund, not this time. I need you to get in here and stay in here no matter what you hear."

My blood ran cold like ice.

"Bash," I swallowed hard.

"Those ships are the Royal Navy. I should have considered that they knew our route and would ambush us. This is the only way I can keep you safe, do you understand? Even if you hear gunshots and death, you stay here. Wait another hour after you hear nothing. If you come out and there is no one left, you fill your pockets with coin, get in one of the dinghies, and row northeast until you hit land, it'll be a place called Terra de Fuego. From there, you can buy passage back to London."

"I won't go without you," I said, standing firm.

He pulled me down to him, and I landed squarely in his lap. I twisted my body and wrapped my legs around him so we were face to face.

This fear was unnamed. Something terrible waited out there, and the not knowing was worse than any fear I knew. I ran my hands over his cheeks and through his hair. He leaned into my touch, closing his eyes.

"I don't want a life that isn't you," I said.

His hand gripped mine, holding it in place.

"I can't do what I need to do next if I'm worried about you. I'll come back for you, but I need you to do this for me," he pleaded.

I searched his eyes for the lie and found none. I kissed him like he was what gave me life, and the longer I loved him, the more it became true. My pirate captain, my vengeful god, my everything.

Slowly, he let me go, and I lowered myself into the pocket, which had barely enough space to fold my legs to my chest. He gave me a reassuring smile before closing the latch, and that's when I should have known that he was nothing if not a skilled liar.

Chapter Thirty-Nine
Infamy

Sebastian

The mark of a good captain is someone who sees the worth in the people who sail beneath them.

–An excerpt from *The Mysterious Deep: A Comprehensive Understanding*

In a lot of ways, it was better this way. Rose might never see it that way, but some day she would find herself safe and comfortable, and that's what mattered. It was cheating of a sort that I would only have to endure a few more weeks of replaying my bullet going into Billy's head. I deserved far worse than that.

He said to tell you that he loved you more than a son and that giving you bread was the best thing he did with his life.

Those words were shrapnel in my chest. The weakest parts of me were glad Billy wouldn't be here to see what came next. If there was an afterlife, I hoped Billy was drinking rum and telling stories instead of looking down here to see this. Strange that over a decade of planning, the end felt like it was coming too soon.

Billy would have told me that was my sign to change paths, as he had countless times over the years. I'd heard that more in the last few months than all the years before combined. Rose was everything he ever hoped for, and he'd been sure that I would change my mind. In the end, he knew me better than that when he told Rose I would walk twice as fast to the gallows. Though I think this exceeded even his expectations.

If he were here, as we watched two British Navy ships and the Bane approach, I would have told him that accepting that piece of bread was the best decision of my life. Sixteen years old and without family or a coin to my name, I'd been close to going back to my father and begging his forgiveness for leaving. Hunger eating at my stomach like insects on a vine. When a burly pirate offered a piece of bread, I hadn't second-guessed it.

Next thing I knew, he took me in and taught me everything he knew about being a pirate. Four years later, when I suggested we go to the Glass Sea and sail under our own flag, he had nodded once and said, "Aye, but it won't change your past."

He knew even then, but he never tried to talk me out of it or stand in my way. Instead, he would say, "Just you wait till you find the one thing worth more than dying."

If it was going to be anything or anyone, it would have been Rose, and maybe if there'd been a place in this world for us, she would have been. She loved her family and the life of privilege she lived. Even if her older brother secured the pardons, I would ruin her good name. She might have said she didn't care about what people thought, but she would have. When the other women turned their noses up at her at every ball. When the invites failed to come and the whispers were louder than the good wishes, she would have regretted the choices that led her there.

I didn't want to be her regret, and I refused to hold her back.

"You were right, they gave our charted course," Oscar said.

I didn't hear him coming, too busy watching the three ships begin their boxing course. One on each side and one at the head. The only question left was how to make them leave my crew alive.

I turned to see Amos and Charlie Clark with their hands secured behind their backs. A spark of recognition in Charlie's eyes while Amos frantically looked around, trying to catch up.

"I suppose I underestimated you, Charlie," I said.

"Sir?" Charlie asked.

He wouldn't risk a bullet to the head before his rescue arrived. I was almost eager for them to finish this just to see his face when he found out what British justice looked like.

"Was it The Essex Serpent or The Leaky Tavern that I found you in?" I asked.

I could hear him swallow before he answered. The ships were only a few minutes out now.

"The Serpent, sir," he said.

"You had counted the cards all night and won a small fortune by the time anyone started to get suspicious. You let them search you up and down because they never could have guessed the boy with an American accent had played them like violins," I said.

"But you did," he said.

I nodded, reminding myself that it wasn't betrayal if I was always going to end up here.

The ships were within shooting distance now. They could sink us in seconds if they wished. The English flags mocked my hard-won flag.

"I told you that a mind like that was a waste on gambling and whoring. I offered you a place on my crew as long as you never turned that brilliant mind against me. You said that'd be just fine, and a year later, when you asked me to allow your brother to join, I agreed."

"That's how I remember it, sir," he said.

I drew in a long breath feeling more numb than angry. I never thought I would know this feeling having only ever read about it. It laced my veins like the finest gin and lulled me into a sense of peace I'd only felt in her arms. I believed this was what they called acceptance.

"When did you decide to break your promise?" I asked.

The ships were alongside us now. He would feel safe enough, though it wasn't me he should have feared.

"Spain, sir. It was a lot of coin they offered and actual pardons, unlike the ones previously offered," he said.

Charlie grunted and Oscar spat, "Piece of shit."

I at least hoped it was a good hit to the gut.

I turned and took in what was left of my crew. Charlie doubled over, and Oscar's hands were in fists. Amos was grinning, staring at what he believed to be salvation. Emille's lips were thin, watching me closely. Dilly and Inu stood side by side watching the left ship throw hooks onto the Wraith and dropping planks to board her. Val's eyes burned into me, and I knew what she wanted. After all our time together, I hated to disappoint her, but like it or not, she would live. The others already had their weapons laid down, knowing we were out of options. Most of them were probably cursing my name. Their brothers and sisters dead at the bottom of the sea, and they faced the gallows instead of enjoying their hard-won treasures.

"Did Barnacles see it coming when you slit his stomach?" I asked.

Charlie at least had the decency to lower his eyes. "He didn't."

"I thought not," I said, walking past him and unholstering my pistol. "Time to see what you bought, Charlie."

When my friends saw me lay down my pistol and my sword, they did the same thing, though the fire in Val and Inu's eyes called me a coward all the same. I felt the corner of my mouth tug up. Of all the people I had recruited over the years, Inu was by far the most capable and the fiercest. Hopefully, she would get the chance to murder Oscar before the crown did.

"Lay down your weapons and prepare to be boarded!"

Billy would have made a comment about how he clearly didn't have eyes. It was another piece of shrapnel scratching against my heart. I reminded myself it was better this way.

Both sides of my ship were flooded on either side, two men in ridiculous wigs and too tall hats led the charge. How noble of them.

"My crew has already laid down their weapons," I said, hoping to draw their attention.

"Sebastian Flynn?" one asked.

"The very same," I said, holding out my arm.

Some of the effect was probably lost with only one arm. Shame. You spend your whole life imagining a single moment to have it end lackluster.

The man nodded to his crew, who flanked me like I was a sea serpent preparing to split them in half. I could feel the clove hitch tied into my poor excuse for an arm and the answering tie to my good one that pressed them together. The wound was incredibly fresh, and had I mentioned it, they would have been twice as rough, so I bit the inside of my tongue, drawing blood, to keep from grunting. It burned more than stung, but worse than that was that I could still feel my arm like it was still there, even though I knew it wasn't. That was a far more damaging pain.

"I'm prepared to discuss terms that you take what you came here for, but my crew and ship survive." I said.

"I see nothing you could offer that would entice me to keep pirates alive other than for the promise of the gallows like you have to look forward to," he said.

One by one, they swarmed my ship worse than any wraith. They forced my crew to their knees and tied their hands. Oscar let out a shout of pain when they forced him to his knees, his injury snapping with the sharp force. Fuck. They called us barbarians, but one glance would have proved otherwise. The most I could hope for was that Oscar would think about Inu and Rose and keep his head down. Unfortunately, he had the same reckless streak as his sister, though not quite as bad.

"Captain Edmonds, my fiancé."

I had imagined his face countless times. His thin frame and parted blond hair were as aristocratic as I had imagined. He was the illness, and before I was done, if the gods took any pity on me, I would be the one to kill me before the rope broke my neck.

"There is a woman on board your ship—" Edmond's said, surveying my crew like they were parasites.

"Ah, yes, I assume you are referring to Rosamund Bailey. Unfortunately, she did not survive the Glass Sea," I said.

Charlie raised his head and stared at me, but I met his gaze and hoped he understood our final conversation. That he remembered what I'd done for him and granted me this last shred of loyalty. When he lowered his head once more, I fought against the sigh of relief that threatened to give me away. Now all that was left was for Rose to stay hidden, and I could go to the gallows knowing she was safe.

"That can't be true. She was worth more alive than dead. A pirate wouldn't give up a treasure like that." James Allan spat, amber eyes half-crazed.

After all, he had spent months chasing his prize, and losing was something very few aristocrats knew how to do.

"Search the ship," Edmonds ordered.

"I was told that her family had fallen into poverty and that a ransom would fetch less than enough to warrant the hassle," I said.

"You piece of shit pirate, you knew damn well I would have paid for her which is why I've wondered for months why she was even on this damn ship."

Keep your head down, Oscar.

I shrugged. "I was promised pardons in return for enough money to buy out her family. Seemed like the best deal I was going to get."

Lord James Allan clearly had a short fuse as he turned the color of cherries.

"You had to know she couldn't offer that."

"On the contrary, she seemed rather capable. I imagine she could have done anything she set her mind to," I said.

The idiot sputtered and stared at me as he fought to rectify the woman he convinced himself Rose was, with who she actually was. A brilliant mind who could convince a notorious pirate captain to take her to the Glass Sea and back.

One of the soldiers left the hold, eyes wide and mouth open. Well, it was bound to happen. He whispered in Edmonds' ear, and I watched with considerable satisfaction as his rough countenance smoothed. He stared at me like he was seeing me for the first time.

"You actually did it? The Maravilla?" he said.

I grinned, feigning the pride that should have accompanied such a prize. "I earned my name, did I not?"

"My fiancée?" Lord Allan snapped at the soldier.

"No sign of her, Sir, we did a thorough sweep," he stuttered.

I watched with no small amount of satisfaction, even through the pain in my arm, as his mouth opened and closed, working.

That's right, you bastard, you came all this way for nothing. You will never have her.

With what could only be called a temper tantrum, Lord Allan stormed over to where Dilly knelt and lifted her up by the front of her shirt. My hand itched at my back, eager for my sword. The way I would have run him through slowly for having the audacity to touch her.

"Where is she?" he demanded.

Pride, warm and encompassing, filled my chest when Dilly met his eyes without an ounce of hesitation. "Bitten by a wraith. It infected her until she turned into one, and we were forced to shoot her."

"You're lying," he spat, throwing Dilly back to the floor.

It was rare I was wrong about a person, but Cordelia Shaw could never be one of them.

Lord Allan paced in front of my crew and all the pride was quickly displaced by an icy fear as he neared Oscar. Even with his head down, the parasite would know him.

"I can see why you chased her so thoroughly, Lord knows I mourned that mouth when she turned." The putrid words turned to bile in my mouth, but I swallowed them back down, reminding myself I would do what it took to keep them safe.

Allan lifted his head, and his chest rose and fell with the telltale sign of anger. The flush in his cheeks gave him away, though; he was more than angry. He was fighting the blow to his pride in witness of the British Navy and his hired crew.

"What did you just say about *my* fiancée?" he snarled.

I clicked my tongue, "Fairly certain she left you and was actively running from you. At least that's what she told me in between my co—"

Pain burst along my jaw, and blood splattered as he decked me in the face. It pulled in the back of my mouth while my jaw throbbed with the impact. I spit out as much as I could and made sure to give him my shittiest eating grin. Let Sebastian Flynn have this one.

"Shame you couldn't satisfy her because she made the most bea—"

Fuck, that hurt. For a pompous aristocrat, he was more than a decent shot. My gut rolled with his fist in it, and I fought back vomit. Still more to do. I grunted and righted myself.

Forgive me, Rose.

She might forgive my words, but never where they led.

"I'd punch like that too if my fiancée would rather fuck a—"

This time I fell to my knees and my face hit the hard wood of my ship. Pain exploded all around me, but it was better than the alternative.

I turned my face, breathing hard as I rested my head on the wood splattered with my own blood.

"You probably don't know the sound she made when—"

His boot hit my face, and my nose cracked, undoing all Rose's hard work to fix it. It was a damn shame. Black flecks filled my vision, and I realized I was almost out of time.

"Captain Edmonds!" I shouted.

"Shut up, you piece of—"

"Lord Allan, please control yourself. Do you not see he is baiting you?" Captain Edmonds said, stepping forward.

Smart man. Hopefully, he was smart enough to take what I was offering.

"Let my crew go safely, and I will give you the location of all the wealth and treasure I have accrued over the last ten years. I assure you, it is comparable to what is currently in my hull. Take my hull as well, but allow my crew to live and the location is yours."

I saw him weigh the options, was I honest, could I even be trusted? If I had more time I would have figured out his price, but time was a luxury I didn't have. I needed them off my ship.

When he didn't immediately bite, I knew who he was. He wanted a name as notorious as my own.

"I will also give you every pirate hideout I know, which you can imagine is most of them, given I've been doing this for ten years. Imagine. Captain Edmonds written into the history books as the man who eradicated piracy." I said, spitting out more blood.

I was laying it all on a little too thick, but desperate times and whatnot.

"They all deserve to die." Allan sneered.

The moment the captain's jaw tensed and released, I knew I had won.

"Sometimes we must sacrifice for the larger gain," he said. "How can I know your word is good?"

I let myself have a small sigh of relief. They would all live.

"Begin unloading the hull!" Edmonds ordered.

A small price to pay for them to live.

"My life is already forfeit. If I can ensure they live, I'll walk to the gallows freely and without regret," I said.

Edmonds clicked his tongue, "Rather noble for a notorious pirate captain, don't you think?"

I smiled, which was probably a horrifying image with blood staining my teeth. "The one thing pirates take more seriously than treasure, Captain, is brotherhood. You think us lawless, but our crew is our family, and I would gladly lay down my life for them."

It was the right thing to say. Edmonds nodded and gestured to his crew with two raised fingers.

"Take him to the brig. Ensure he has a window to see *his family* survives," Edmonds ordered.

Two men lifted me, and because I was a petty bastard, I leaned into the stewing Lord Allan and said, "She preferred death to your touch."

I realized my mistake too late. Every man had his limit. This aristocrat had spent months concocting a plan to coerce Rose to marry him, and she had outsmarted him at every turn. Now that there was no prize to earn, because he didn't truly care about ruining her family, he had nothing left. His amber eyes darkened, and I saw the moment he broke.

It wasn't his fist this time, but the pistol at his side he reached for. Fuck. If I died, nothing was there to keep my crew alive. Stupid bastard.

Captain Edmonds yelled for him to stop, but he was too far gone. I prepared for the blast, but what came next was far worse.

"James, stop!" Oscar's voice was full of command earned by his birth and his time at sea.

There was only one other voice that could have stopped him as thoroughly as Oscar did and I thanked every fucking star it wasn't hers. Though Oscar's was nearly as bad, and all because I couldn't set aside my own ego. Fuck.

Allan twisted, and I watched his mouth fall open as he took in Oscar standing beside his fellow pirates.

"That's—" shock gave way to something else, and he laughed. "This whole time, I couldn't figure out why she chose this ship, but I should have known you had something to do with it. You always were too attached. Unnatural."

"And you were always an asshole. I was thrilled the day she figured out she was too good for you," Oscar said, head raised high despite the way sweat poured down his face.

He was in pain, but he had forced himself upright and used his now broken leg to save my sorry life. If we lived long enough, I needed to tell him I'd been angry when I said I regretted bringing him on my crew.

I chanced a glance at Inu and saw silent tears dripping down her face. For that, I was more sorry than I could say. If I could go back in time, I would undo it, but life didn't work like that.

"You'll hang for this, Oscar," Allan said, nodding to himself like a madman.

"Oscar Bailey?" Captain Edmonds said, intelligent and ambitious.

"One and the same as it were," Oscar said with a smile.

"Why would you become a pirate?" he asked.

Oscar shrugged. "Boredom, I suppose."

Captain Edmonds furrowed his brow, too smart to believe him, even though it was a large portion of the truth.

"Very well, take them both and Lord Allan, control your temper if you wish to remain on board my ship," he said.

I actually liked him despite the red coat he wore. He would have made a capable pirate if his ambition had allowed it. I let myself be ushered past my crew, careful not to look to my cabin where she had, for once in her life, followed my request. I was grateful beyond words. The monster behind me didn't deserve to lay one finger on her.

"Captain Edwards, Sir," Charlie's voice called, and I closed my eyes, wishing he had been a little smarter.

Edwards turned, and I couldn't bring myself to watch.

"You might recall that it was my brother and I who gave you the schedule that led you to the Wraith. You promised us pardons and one thousand shillings each."

"Oh, Charlie, you stupid bastard," I whispered.

Smart enough to lay a plot thicker than stone, but too stupid to understand how people worked.

"And?" Edmonds asked.

The first string of doubt, "Well, sir, we did as we said we would."

Edmonds cleared his throat, and I heard the sound of shillings hitting the deck. The next few steps were heavy as I crossed the plank onto the navy ship.

"A man who betrays his own will betray his enemy. Enjoy your shillings, that is, if your *brothers* let you live."

I might have warned him, but some lessons had to be learned the hard way. Unfortunately, I had no doubts that Inu would be the one to end his life while Val ended his brother's. Some things were just written into stone.

"Who would have seen it ending like this?" Oscar said behind me, false humor in the words.

I couldn't find what I meant to say. The words were stuck in my lungs and choking me with every step. I'd been close to going to my death with a clear mind, but the man behind me was a casualty I wasn't willing to sacrifice.

My only consolation was that I knew people, and what I knew about one woman who was unparalleled with a sword was that she wouldn't let Oscar swing. One way or another, Oscar would live.

I, on the other hand, was finally seeing the fruition of a life's work. Soon, everyone would know the name Captain Sebastian Flynn and just what that meant.

A legacy worthy of infamy.

Chapter Forty
The Pirate and The Princess

Rose

The quickest way to end up dead is to sail for a man who treats people like they are expendable.

–An excerpt from The Mysterious Deep: A Comprehensive Understanding

My hands ached from banging them against the wood above my head.

"Fucking open!" I screamed.

I trusted him, and he locked me in here. What if everyone died or was captured, and I rotted away in this box? It'd been at least ten minutes since the gunshot reverberated in my ears. My mind kindly created image after image of where it landed. Frustrated tears ran down my cheeks. Claustrophobia wasn't an affliction I suffered from, but if I stayed in here any longer, I would never trust tight places again. I certainly would not trust pirates who placed me in them with pretty words.

"In here!" someone yelled.

I had never heard a more beautiful sound. Furniture scratched overhead, and I tried to slow the rate of my breathing. I didn't recognize the voice. What if I just gave away my position? As the panic coursed through my body, I realized I didn't care. I didn't care who opened this hatch as long as someone did.

A loud hiss came from atop my head.

Realization was ice cold over my neck.

I reached up and pushed at my prison, and it opened without hesitation. I peeked my head out, and green eyes stared back at me.

"You trapped me in there!" I shouted at my jailer.

In answer, he raised his right paw and began licking it.

Maybe he was a demon cat after all.

"Rose!" Dilly's voice came a moment before her arms pulled at me and lifted me from my coffin.

Blackbeard hissed and strutted away like it was all a large inconvenience.

"The gunshot—"

"Charlie and Amos. Val shot Amos and Inu—well, they are both dead," she said.

My chest eased with the knowledge that it wasn't someone I loved. Dilly wrapped her arms around me and squeezed until I once again couldn't breathe.

"We couldn't find you!" she panted.

That was the moment the world went black. My vision fading into a narrow tunnel.

"Bash knew where I was," I said slowly.

I hated the way she stiffened and pulled away.

No. Absolutely not.

I stood and jumped past her, making for the cabin door. As soon as it opened, Emille stood with his arms crossed and a frown on his usually smiling face.

No. I ran out onto the deck, past where Amos lay with a hole in his head and Charlie in a pool of his own blood, a thin slice through his stomach. His eyes stared up at the sky like it held the answers he searched for his whole life.

Dodging the holes in the ship's floor, I made it to the stern and stared at three retreating ships. Some sounds were louder than even bullets.

"They took Oscar," Inu said behind me.

No.

I didn't need to ask if they took Bash.

"And the Maravilla gold?" I asked.

"Gone," Val said, coming up beside me.

"So all we have is a broken ship and eighteen people," I said.

For the first time, I understood who Sebastian Flynn was without embellishment or rose-colored glasses. I knew it in the pit of my stomach, in the set of my bones. Only the beat of my heart reminded me there was ever anything else.

"Three of us know next to nothing about running a ship, so probably more like fifteen," Emille said.

"Koinu?" I asked.

"I heard him right before I found you," Dilly said.

If Billy were here, he would have said it could have been far worse odds than that. I was inclined to believe him.

"What did he promise in order to get them to leave you all alive?" I asked.

"Pirate hideaways and his gold," Val said.

"I assume you know where those are?" I asked.

"Sure do," Val said, and I could practically hear the smile in her voice.

Sadistic wench. Good thing I liked her.

"Then we have work to do," I said.

If I closed my eyes and listened closely, I could hear Billy's laugh.

The Bane and her escort faded into the baby blue sky, carrying my reason for existing in it.

"Where to?" Val asked.

I allowed one last tear to slide down my cheek.

"Terra de Fuego," I answered.

When I turned around, I surveyed what was left of the Wraith's crew. A mysteriologist, a doctor, a scarred pirate, and Inu. Thirteen other faces stood a few feet away, waiting.

Koinu's wail echoed the beat of my heart.

And exactly one sea monster.

I was sure more had been done with less.

"Well, what are you all waiting for? We have lives to ruin," I said, clapping my hands together.

Koinu rose from the sea next to us, and I could have sworn his purple eyes met mine before he dove back into the sea, his long body following in what felt like hours rather than seconds. Ocean water splashed over us.

Worse odds indeed.

End Book One
Of
The Vows of Vengeance Series

Acknowledgements

I would be be remiss if I didn't start every book acknowledgement with the two people who are responsible it's existence. V and Becca, the best thing I ever did was decide to be best friends with two strangers on the internet. Sometimes I think what if I didn't sign up for that writing circle or what if V didn't offer to beta read my first book? Then I get super anxious and tell myself not to ever think about it again. The truth is I love you both more than I have words for and we all know I have a lot of words.

To Jerry, thank you for your endless support. I am so grateful to have a partner who cheers me on whether that's selling my books to anyone and everyone or taking care of our children so I can write. Your faith in me means everything. I love you.

To my kids, Henry and Elliot, I am so proud of both of you. You shine in everything you do and your kindness and love of life are inspiring.

To my siblings- I don't know if any of you ever read these, but I am glad to have you all.

To Heather, thank you for being an amazing editor, but an even bigger thank you for being my friend. You've been there since day one and I will never stop being grateful you took a chance on me and my books.

To Kat and Tina, thank you for always being down to beta read for me. I think I would be lost without you.

To my ARC team. I couldn't ask for better readers. Your enthusiasm and hype keep me going.

Thank you to Fluffy the cat for inspiring Blackbeard. You are a strange looking cat and wildly misunderstood, but deep down you are the sweetest.

Lastly, thank you to *you* for picking up this book. Being an indie author means the walk can be daunting and lonely, but readers like you make the world go around for us. So thank you for being here and reading.

About the author

J.A. Good is the author of the hit novel The Swindler and The Swan: A Hades and Persephone meets The Swan Princess retelling. Stories have always been a safe place for her so she decided to create her own. When she isn't writing about sea monsters and romance, you can probably find her hanging out with her five cats, two kids, and husband.

Also by

www.ingramcontent.com/pod-product-compliance
Lightning Source LLC
Chambersburg PA
CBHW030536310726
48979CB00010B/1924/J